D1092743

CROSSCURRENTS

Santo Innis is developing a revolutionary engine to counter the effects of high-pressure steam. His backer is Richard Vaughan, heir to Frederick Tregarron, owner of the Gillyvean estate. His world is turned upside down by the unexpected arrival at Gillyvean of Melanie Tregarron, Frederick's illegitimate youngest daughter. Desperate to prove the viability of his invention, Santo persuades Richard to let him fit one at Gillyvean's brewhouse. But when Bronnen Jewell arrives to brew the harvest beer she's horrified, fearing her loss of income on which she depends. As the lives of these four become entwined all four face the future with fear and trepidation.

CROSSCURRENTS

Crosscurrents

by

Jane Jackson

Magna Large Print Books
Long Preston, North Yorkshire,
BD23 4ND, England.

British Library Cataloguing in Publication Data.

Jackson, Jane
    Crosscurrents.

    A catalogue record of this book is
    available from the British Library

    ISBN   978-0-7505-4123-7

First published in 2014 by Accent Press Ltd.

Copyright © 2014 Jane Jackson

Cover illustration by arrangement with Accent Press Ltd.

The right of Jane Jackson to be identified as the author of this work has been asserted by her in accordance with the Copyright, Designs and Patents Act, 1988

Published in Large Print 2015 by arrangement with
Accent Press Ltd.

All Rights reserved. No part of this publication may be reproduced, stored in a retrieval system, or transmitted in any form or by any means, electronic, mechanical, photocopying, recording or otherwise without the prior permission of the Copyright owner.

Magna Large Print is an imprint of Library Magna Books Ltd.

Printed and bound in Great Britain by
T.J. (International) Ltd., Cornwall, PL28 8RW

The story contained within this book is a work of fiction. Names and characters are the product of the author's imagination and any resemblance to actual persons, living or dead, is entirely coincidental.

To Mike as always, with love.

Acknowledgements:

With grateful thanks to David Heppenstall whose home-made model of an air engine gave me the idea for the book; to the Janets whose support and friendship mean so much; and to Hazel and her brilliant team at Accent – you are stars.

Chapter One

Santo Innis glanced up from his roast beef sandwich as the mail coach clattered past the window.
Moments later, passengers started coming into the
large, low-ceilinged room. They moved stiffly, flexing shoulders and backs stiff from the jolting ride.

Two couples, one young, the other of middle
age, crossed to booths along one wall formed by
high-backed settles on either side of oblong tables.
A maid followed, ready to take their order, for
breaks were short and food had to be eaten
quickly. Within fifteen minutes a fresh team would
be harnessed and the coach would leave again.

Washing down the sandwich with the last of his
ale, Santo saw a young woman hesitate in the
doorway, glance nervously over her shoulder,
then step inside the taproom.

Her dress of dark green plaid had full sleeves
tapering to a band at the wrist and a flat cape
collar with a small white ruff at the neck. Beneath
the brim of her straw bonnet he glimpsed chestnut hair and a heart-shaped face flushed with
distress. A long cloak of dark green serge was
bundled over one arm and she clutched a small
bag decorated with embroidery.

Her clothes proclaimed her as well-to-do. So
where was her travelling companion? Lurching in
behind her, a middle-aged man tried to grasp her
arm. She wrenched free.

Behind the counter, the landlord shook his head. The couples watched with open disapproval. The girl's blush deepened and though she tilted her chin – she didn't lack courage – Santo saw desperation in her grey eyes.

Hoping he had not misread the situation, for he had no wish to intrude on a family quarrel, Santo rose and went to her.

'Everything all right, miss?'

'No,' she whispered.

'Piss off,' the drunk slurred, thrusting his face up to Santo's. 'I saw her first.'

Gripping the man's forearm Santo beckoned the maid then turned to the trembling girl, speaking softly. 'Best if you sit down.'

As she obeyed, her mortified flush drained away leaving her face milk-white but for shadows like bruises under her eyes.

'Here, what–' the drunk began then winced as Santo tightened his grip. 'Let me go!'

'Hot chocolate for the lady,' Santo told the maid, then propelled the loudly protesting man into the passage and out of the open front door.

'Get off me!' The man wrenched free. 'You got no right–'

Santo's hand shot out and gripped the man's throat, choking off the complaint. 'The way I see it,' he said, tightening his fingers, 'you got a choice.' He waited until the now scarlet-faced man stopped struggling, then released him.

The man coughed, blinked and swayed. 'What choice?'

'You can sit topside for the rest of your journey. Or–'

'But I paid for inside.'

'Or,' Santo ignored the interruption, 'you can wait for the next coach.'

'You can't make me.'

Santo leaned forward. 'You want to bet on that?'

The man stumbled back, rubbing his throat. 'All right. No need to get violent. Look, you can't blame me for trying. She might be dressed nice, but come on.' He tried to nudge Santo and almost overbalanced. 'What decent girl would be on the coach by herself?'

That was exactly what Santo intended to find out. He gave the drunk a none-too-gentle push towards the yard. 'You'd better climb up, find yourself somewhere to sit.'

'This isn't right,' the drunk whined. 'I paid for inside.'

'Then be glad it isn't raining.'

'You just want her for yourself.'

As Santo swung round the man flinched. 'I'm going, I'm going.'

Santo returned to the taproom as the maid placed a pot of chocolate on the table. The girl glanced up, her expression wary and embarrassed.

Santo sat. 'He won't bother you again.'

'Thank you.'

'Sure you don't want something to eat?'

She looked away. 'I'm not hungry.'

He poured steaming chocolate into the cup and pushed it towards her. After a moment's hesitation she picked it up, steadying it with both hands, and sipped. He watched relief and gratitude soften her taut features.

'Come from London?'

Lowering the cup she nodded.

'That means you left yesterday morning.'

Rosy colour stained her pale cheeks. 'I have only a little money left. Buying food – it seemed unwise to leave myself with nothing.'

'It wasn't exactly wise to board the mail coach on your own.'

'I'd no choice!' She raised the cup again but not before he'd caught the glitter of tears in her eyes.

'You can't cry in here.' It emerged harsher than he'd intended. But he couldn't cope with her weeping. Yet nor could he have turned his back on her like the other passengers had. They must have seen what was happening, yet no one had tried to help her or warn the drunk off.

Aware of them watching, he looked round and caught surreptitious glances that quickly slid away as they saw his disgust.

Her chin came up. 'I have no intention of doing so!'

'That's all right then.'

She leaned towards him, her voice low and intense. 'Look, whatever you might think, I'm not entirely without sense. Before I got on the coach in London, I asked the guard if he would speak to an elderly couple who were also waiting to board and enquire if they would allow me to travel in their company.' She gulped down more chocolate.

'And they agreed?' he asked in surprise.

'Yes.' Though her tone was defiant her cheeks grew pink. 'I did have to stretch the truth a little. I told them I was bound for my father's house in Cornwall, which I am, only my aunt who should have been travelling with me had been taken ill in

16

the night. She could not travel, but I could not delay my journey. If I did not arrive as expected, my father would be dreadfully worried.'

'They believed you?'

She nodded. 'We introduced ourselves. Their name was Jefford and they were going to visit their son whose wife had just had a baby, their third grandchild, but all the more precious as the first two had died of diphtheria. They were very kind and everything was fine until the last stop when they got off and that horrible man got on. He had a silver flask and kept drinking from it. Then he tried to make conversation. I didn't answer. The other passengers just watched. None of them told him to leave me alone. It was as if they thought I deserved his attention. But I didn't. I don't.' Her mouth quivered and she raised the cup. It clattered against her teeth as she swallowed.

Turning away he signalled the maid. 'Will you wrap a slice of bread and butter, and a piece of cake or pie? And bring my reckoning.' As the maid hurried away, he studied the young woman. 'Where in Falmouth?'

She bent forward to refill her cup. 'Gillyvean.'

Santo stiffened. 'Mr Tregarron is your father?'

She looked up quickly, her expression eager yet shy. 'You know him?'

He nodded. 'I work for him. I'm an engineer at Perran Foundry. My name's Innis, Santo Innis.'

Setting the cup down she offered him her gloved hand. 'I'm Melanie Tregarron.'

A sharp blast on the guard's horn brought everyone to their feet. As Melanie picked up her cloak and handbag, the maid rushed across with a cloth-wrapped parcel. Santo motioned her to give it to Melanie then went to the bar to settle his account.

Boarding the coach, Melanie took the corner seat with Santo next to her and the husband of the young couple next to him. Opposite were the young man's wife and the middle-aged couple who, as soon as they had made themselves comfortable, closed their eyes.

As the coach rumbled out of the yard and onto the rutted and muddy road, Santo glanced at Melanie who held the parcel in her lap.

'You should eat something,' he whispered.

Her glance was startled. 'Not here.'

'When was your last meal?'

'Yesterday,' she admitted. 'But with the coach jolting and swaying so much I've had little appetite.'

Though he didn't believe her, he admired her pluck. 'You'll feel worse if you don't,' he warned. 'It's still another six hours to Falmouth. Besides, isn't it a bit late to be worrying about what people might think?' He raised his brows, regarding her calmly as she glared at him. Then she sighed.

'You're right.' Removing her gloves she unwrapped the cloth and picked up a triangle of bread and butter.

As she raised it to her mouth he was startled to see her nails were bitten, the skin around them raw and stippled with dried blood.

He wondered what anxiety or fear had driven her to gnaw at her fingers like that. Telling himself it was not his concern, he looked past her out of the window as she quietly ate every morsel, then folded the cloth neatly to contain the crumbs and dabbed her mouth with it.

'I'm obliged to you,' she glanced at him. 'I promise I'll pay you back.'

'No need for that. Do you mind if I ask what happened?' She could always tell him to mind his own business.

She was quiet for so long he thought she wasn't going to answer. Then she tilted her head towards his, speaking softly, for his ears alone. 'I was teaching at Oakland Park, a private seminary for young ladies. There was an incident – the father of one of the pupils–' Her breath hitched and she swallowed. 'The fault was his, but I had to leave. For the good of the school.' Her tone held as much hurt as bitterness.

'But to set out alone on a two-day journey–' Santo cut himself short.

Though she shrugged, her studied casualness did not entirely mask her hurt and dismay, first at the drunk's harassment, then at the other passengers' refusal to help. 'I had no choice.'

'Was there nowhere closer than Cornwall you could have gone?'

Anguish passed like a shadow across her face. She drew a breath, forced a smile. 'There was one person: my father's wife. I knew where she lived from something he mentioned in one of his letters. I took a cab, which I wouldn't have done had I known how much it would cost. But the driver helped me find the address. I hoped that in the circumstances she might–' she cleared her throat then, forcing a smile she shrugged.

Santo saw through her brave attempt at in-difference.

'She refused to receive me. Which she was perfectly entitled to do. I just thought–' she shook her head. 'The maid told me to wait in the porch. A little while later she returned, handed me money for the coach fare to Cornwall, and relayed a message from Mrs Tregarron. I should leave immediately and was never ever to go there again.'

He gave a brief nod. It wasn't his place to offer sympathy, or reveal the shock he felt. But he understood more now. As she carried Frederick Tregarron's name clearly he had acknowledged her. It was also clear that she wasn't a child of the marriage.

She smiled up at him. He saw the effort it cost her. 'Enough of my problems, I have no wish to bore you when you have shown me such kindness. Have you travelled far?'

'Only from Devonport. I went up on this morning's early mail to pick up parts for the steam boilers we make at Perran Foundry.'

'What sort of parts?'

'Safety valves, sight glasses, things like that. It's cheaper to buy from a company that specialises in boiler fittings than for Perran to make them.'

'Where are they?'

He pointed to the roof of the coach. 'Topside, in a canvas bag.' He smothered a yawn. 'Beg pardon. It's been a long day.'

'Why don't you close your eyes?' She gestured towards the sleeping couple opposite and murmured so only he could hear. 'You're not obliged to entertain me, Mr Innis. Nor would I think you rude. I'm used to solitude and can occupy myself.'

Opening her bag she took out a small pad of

paper and a soft pencil and began to make sketches of the couple opposite. The coach's sway and jolt over ruts and potholes seemed not to bother her as she worked on one sketch after another.

Pretending to look out of the window at the passing scenery, Santo's gaze was repeatedly drawn to the pad, mesmerised by the faces, soft and crumpled in sleep, she brought to life on the paper with a few swift sure strokes. He glanced at her, lost in her own world, and his curiosity increased.

He knew that most young ladies were supposed to be able to paint pretty watercolours, just as they were also supposed to learn the piano, and sing. But Melanie Tregarron's rough sketches put some of the pictures at Gillyvean to shame.

He closed his eyes. Yet despite a very early start and a long day, sleep eluded him. His relationship with Frederick Tregarron was already strained. Turning up at Gillyvean with this brave, vulnerable, foolhardy young woman wasn't going to improve it.

Chapter Two

After three more stops to change horses, it was just after nine when the coach clattered to a halt outside the Greenbank Hotel. The drunk had got off at Liskeard and reeled away. Melanie and Santo climbed out, followed by the two couples.

The driver and guard began unloading luggage from the roof.

In the western sky the last cream and gold tints of sunset faded as dusk crept in, blurring outlines and deepening shadows.

'You wait there a moment,' Santo told her.

'Where are you going?'

'The hotel keeps a dogcart. We need it to get you and your trunk to Gillyvean.'

Her eyes were tired, her face drawn. 'I'm putting you to a lot of trouble.'

'No, you aren't.' Contradicting his employer's daughter wasn't exactly polite. But this whole situation was unusual. 'Mr Tregarron would expect me to deliver you safe and sound.'

When they arrived, Santo jumped down, grabbed his canvas bag, then helped the boy unload Melanie's trunk. After paying him, Santo returned to the front door and rang the bell as clopping hoofs trotted away down the drive. He glanced at Melanie who was holding her handbag tightly, shoulders rigid, her face hidden by the brim of her bonnet.

The door opened.

'Evening, Ellen.'

'All right, Mr Innis?' Curiosity sharpened her gaze as she stepped back opening the door wider. 'Come in. If you just wait a minute I'll fetch Mr Vaughan.' She hurried down the hall and ran up the stairs.

Santo glanced at Melanie who wearily removed her bonnet.

Ellen reappeared. Behind her Santo saw Richard Vaughan, his employer's heir and man of business, buttoning his coat as he came down the wide crimson-carpeted staircase. Richard Vaughan's slim build was deceptive. Santo had seen him control a terrified horse and knew he possessed both a cool head and steely strength.

'Good evening, Innis.' Richard inclined his head then his gaze went briefly to Melanie. 'We will be more comfortable in here.' He gestured them into the drawing room. 'Thank you, Ellen.'

Santo guessed that within minutes the entire household would know of their arrival.

As the door closed behind the maid, Santo looked at Melanie. Despite her exhaustion and nerves, her spine was straight and her chin high. If there were rules for a situation like this he didn't know them.

'Miss Tregarron, this is Mr Vaughan, Mr Tregarron's man of business.' He turned to Richard. 'Miss Tregarron was on the same coach. When I learned she was bound for Gillyvean I offered to escort her.'

'She was alone?'

Knowing that single fact would, in Richard's eyes, cast doubt on anything she said, Santo had no choice but to nod.

Richard's gaze returned to Melanie, his expression unreadable. 'Have you any means of identifying yourself?' Though politely asked, Santo winced at the question and saw furious colour flood Melanie's face. But this was between them. She was in no danger and he had no right to intervene.

'I assure you I *am* Mr Tregarron's daughter. If you would kindly call him he will lay your doubts to rest.'

'Nothing would give me greater pleasure.' Richard's tone was as smooth as cream. 'Unfortunately Mr Tregarron is away from home, which he assuredly would not have been had he known you were coming.'

Melanie felt her legs buckle. She was so very tired. Drawing on the dregs of her depleted strength she faced him, proud and defiant. 'It seems I must reveal matters that are not your concern. I am Mr Tregarron's *natural* daughter.'

With shaking fingers she dug in her purse and found the last letter she had received from her father. Dated three months earlier it was worn and creased from many readings. So much had happened since she had received it. She offered it to him. 'You will see it is addressed to Miss Tregarron and begins *My dear Melanie.* No doubt you recognise my father's handwriting and Gillyvean's address at the top?'

While he read, her gaze darted round panelled walls painted soft green and hung with landscapes in gilded frames, to curtains of cream and gold damask caught back by tasselled ropes of gold silk.

'Miss Tregarron?'

She started, feeling foolish as he handed back the letter with a brief bow. 'Please sit down.' Crossing to the fireplace he tugged the bell-pull.

'I'll be off then,' Santo said. 'Goodnight, miss.'

'Thank you, Mr Innis,' Melanie looked up at him as she laid her cloak, bonnet and gloves beside her on a sofa upholstered in rose pink brocade. 'I am in your debt.'

He shook his head. 'Glad I was there. I wouldn't

24

stand by and leave a lady be treated bad. 'Tidn't right nor proper.'

She caught Richard's swift glance and raised eyebrow. The door opened, Ellen appeared, and the moment passed. But Melanie knew the reprieve was temporary. Richard Vaughan would want – demand – to know what had happened.

'A tray of tea if you please, Ellen.' As the maid left, Richard asked Santo, 'Shall Knuckey drive you home?'

Santo shook his head. 'Much obliged for the offer but after all those hours on the coach I'll be glad to stretch my legs. The bag is no great weight. I'll take the parts out to Perran tomorrow.' Then to Melanie's surprise the two men shook hands.

She caught herself. She should know better than to make assumptions based on appearance. Santo Innis might not be a gentleman but he had treated her with kindness and respect. *Which was more than could be said for Emily Barden's father.*

She watched Santo go, closing the door behind him.

Feeling very alone she folded her hands in her lap, her heart thumping. This wasn't the reception she had hoped for.

Richard Vaughan took a chair on the opposite side of the marble fireplace. She was grateful for that. At least he hadn't remained standing in a deliberate attempt to intimidate. Sitting back, he crossed one leg over the other.

'As Mr Tregarron's heir, I handle both his business and personal affairs. Therefore I was aware he had a natural daughter. However, I understood her to have returned to France to be with her

25

mother and stepfather.'

Overwhelmed by memories that had lost none of their power to hurt, Melanie kept her eyes lowered until she was sure she had herself under control. Then she met his gaze directly. 'I did go back to France, but for a few weeks only.' Long enough to have her hopes shattered. 'Then I returned to England.'

'Is there something you're not telling me, Miss Tregarron?'

'Mr Vaughan, I have only just met you. I accept that you are my father's heir and agent. You appear to have accepted that I am his daughter. However, I do not feel obliged to disclose personal matters that, with respect, are none of your business.' A lump formed in her throat and she swallowed it down. 'I apologise for any inconvenience my arrival has caused. Unfortunately circumstances did not allow me the luxury of sending advance notice.' As she stood up, so did he. 'I have no wish to keep you from whatever you were doing.'

'Please sit down, Miss Tregarron. Your arrival was a surprise. I cannot pretend otherwise. But nor can I allow you to retire without some refreshment. You've had a long journey.' As he spoke the door opened, the maid came in with a laden tray and set it on a side table near Melanie's chair.

'Ellen, will you ask Mrs Berryman to come up?'

With a quick glance at Melanie who, not knowing what else to do, had resumed her seat, the maid bobbed a curtsey. 'Right behind me she is, Mr Vaughan.'

'I never doubted it,' he murmured as she scuttled out, closing the door. He turned to

26

Melanie, indicating the tray. 'Please, help yourself.'

'Will you join me?' Good manners demanded she ask.

'No – yes. Thank you.'

She had expected him to refuse. So had he, judging by the surprise in his voice.

'How do you prefer it?'

'A dash of milk, no sugar.'

Melanie caught the inside of her lip between her teeth trying to steady her hand as she poured. Passing him a cup and saucer she managed not to spill any. She'd just added milk to her own when, after a brief knock, the door opened once more and a short plump woman in a black dress with a white shawl collar and frilled cuffs bustled in.

Leaving her tea on the table Melanie was about to stand, then remembered that in this house she was not an employee. She gripped her hands in her lap.

'Mrs Berryman, Miss Tregarron is disappointed to find her father away from home. I trust I may rely on you to make her comfortable.'

Even as she admired his skilful manner of introduction, Melanie braced herself, expecting disapproval as well as the inevitable scrutiny. But after a moment's surprise the housekeeper's sharp gaze softened. Melanie felt some of the tension lying like a heavy weight on her neck and shoulders slide off.

'Pleased to meet you, miss.'

'Good evening, Mrs Berryman.'

'Don't mind me saying, but you surely got your father's eyes.'

Recognising acknowledgement, and aware of

Richard Vaughan's brief glance as if checking the housekeeper's observation, Melanie felt her heart lift. 'How kind of you to say so.'

'I speak as I find, miss. Won't take but a few minutes to get your room ready. Come far have you?'

'From London, on the mail coach.'

'Dear life! No wonder you look so fagged. How about a nice hot bath while your bed's airing?'

The unexpected kindness made Melanie's eyes sting and her throat grew stiff. 'I—' she cleared her throat, 'I don't want to put you to any trouble. It's late—'

'Don't you worry 'bout that. The trunk all you brought, is it?' As Melanie nodded the housekeeper turned to Richard. 'Anything else, sir?'

'You appear to have thought of everything, Mrs Berryman.'

Melanie reached for her tea, blinking away tears of relief before they could fall.

'What I'm here for, isn't it?' With a nod to each of them the housekeeper bustled out. Melanie heard her voice receding as she called to Ellen.

Cupping the fragile bone china as she sipped, soothed by the warmth, Melanie watched Richard move about the spacious room. The carpet was Indian, the furniture a collection of old – presumably inherited pieces – and new. Such randomness should have jarred. Instead it felt comfortable. She became aware of Richard Vaughan's frowning gaze.

'May I ask when you expect my father home?'

'Tomorrow or possibly the day after, I regret I cannot be more specific.' He clasped his hands behind his back. 'Your father has a great many demands on his time and attention.'

So she would have to wait her turn. At least here she would be safe. She had so much to tell him. She hoped he would understand and not be angry. Quickly swallowing the last of her tea, Melanie replaced the cup and rose to her feet.

'My arrival interrupted you, for which I apologise. If you will excuse me I'd like to go to my room now.'

'Of course.' Though his expression did not alter, Melanie sensed his relief. Tugging the bell pull by the mantelpiece he inclined his head politely. 'Good night, Miss Tregarron.'

'Good night, Mr Vaughan.' She picked up her cloak, gloves, bag and bonnet, reaching the door as Ellen opened it.

'Miss Tregarron wishes to retire,' Richard said behind her.

Ellen bobbed a curtsey. 'This way, miss.'

Following the maid along the broad carpeted landing, Melanie fought down anxiety. Her father had never invited her to Gillyvean. She had come because she hadn't known what else to do. *Please don't let him mind.*

Chapter Three

Bronnen Jewell scooped a lump of butter from the pile on the perforated dish and tipped it onto a sycamore board.

Though the stone floor, thick lime-washed

walls, and small windows kept the dairy cool even in the hottest weather, her body burned with worry and frustration.

Picking up a pair of grooved wooden paddles she began to shape the butter into a block, her movements as tense as her thoughts.

She looked up as her mother entered the dairy carrying a large shallow dish. Left on the range overnight the cream had formed a thick yellow crust. When cold it would be skimmed off into dishes: one to keep, the other for Mrs Berryman, cook-housekeeper at Gillyvean.

Bronnen paused, resting the paddles on end. 'I'm not blind, Ma. It's plain as day that you're hurting.'

After a bitter winter had delayed planting because the ground was too cold, every farmer had worried as a wet spring continued into early summer. Then the rain had stopped and the clouds had parted allowing the sun to warm the soil.

Now the hay had been cut, turned, dried, and baled. Wheat, barley and oats were ripe and ready for harvest, and the cattle were feeding on lush green grass. Yet her father's temper, always unpredictable, had worsened. So too had his drinking.

Sarah set the dish down carefully. 'It was my fault. I said something that made him angry.'

'Stop it!' Bronnen rapped the paddles on the wooden board. 'You can't keep taking the blame for what he's doing.' Beneath her faded cotton dress and clean white apron, her shift clung to damp skin. She used the back of her hand to push aside a dark curl that had worked loose

30

from the coil high on her crown. 'I know he's my father and I'm supposed to respect him. But how can I? No decent man hits a woman.'

'He'd been drinking.'

'That's nothing new, and it's certainly no excuse,' Bronnen retorted furiously. 'No one forces him to drink. It's his choice.' Eyes stinging, she set down the paddles, picked up a wooden stamp carved with a gillyflower, and pressed it into the top surface of the butter.

Sarah came to her side, touched her arm. 'Please, bird. I know you mean well. Thing is, you're young. You don't–'

'Understand?' Still holding the wooden stamp Bronnen gazed at her mother. 'No, I don't. You brought me up to know right from wrong, good from bad. What Pa is doing is wicked. He shouldn't treat you this way. I'm not a child, Ma. If John hadn't drowned I might be married now.' *Would she? No. She might dream of escape, of being happy, of living without constant tension and the threat of violence. But how could she leave her mother?* 'One thing I do know, I would never *ever* permit any man to use me like Father uses you.'

Sarah reached up. Her fingers felt cool against Bronnen's hot cheek. 'So I would hope, bird,' she said softly. 'But life isn't always so simple. You see it in black and white, but–'

'I see bruises on your face and wrists. I see you wince when you bend or reach for something. I see Father stagger in drunk most nights.'

'He've got a lot on his mind–' Sarah began.

'Oh, please.' Bronnen's tone reflected her disgust and she saw her mother flinch. 'No, Ma, I didn't

31

mean – it's not you I'm angry with.' *But it was, a little, which made her feel guilty.* 'How can he afford to drink like this? Where's he getting the money?'

Fear flickered in her mother's eyes. Patting Bronnen's arm, she attempted a reassuring smile.

'Your father have been running this farm for Mr Tregarron since before you was born. Come the time for him to retire, Adam will take over. He'd never put that at risk. So you just stop your fretting. I'm all right.'

Though her mother hadn't answered the question, Bronnen knew better than to press her. But she was tired of lies and evasions, sick of pretending all was well when it so clearly wasn't. 'You're not. He's getting worse and you're paying.'

'Please, Bron. Leave it be.'

How much more was she supposed not to see, not to question? Hearing the drum of approaching hooves, Bronnen put down the butter stamp and crossed to the open door as the postman clattered into the yard. Drawing to a halt he rummaged in his bag.

'Letter for Missus Jewell.' He held it out.

'Ma?' Bronnen said over her shoulder.

Sarah wiped her hands down her apron. 'I don't know anyone who would write to me. Oh, Lord, do I have to pay for it?'

'No, missus,' the postman said. 'See that triangle with PD inside on the front? It means the sender already paid.'

Taking the folded sheet sealed with crimson wax, Bronnen passed it to her mother who retreated into the cool dairy.

'Would you like a glass of buttermilk?' she

32

asked the postman, whose red face was damp and shiny.

'Wouldn't say no. This here sunshine do make a lovely change after all that rain.' Removing his hat he dragged a kerchief from his pocket and mopped his forehead. 'But I tell you 'tis some hot riding in it.'

In the dairy Bronnen dipped a mug into the earthenware pitcher. 'Why don't you open it, Ma? You won't know who sent it until you do.' Though the postman called regularly at Gillyvean it was rare for him to come to the farm. Bronnen couldn't remember the last time her mother received a letter.

Draining the mug in four gulps the postman handed it back and wiped his mouth. 'Went down lovely that did. Much obliged. Right, better get on.' Settling his hat firmly, he gathered the reins and with a final nod rode out of the yard.

Back in the dairy the letter trembled in Sarah's hands. 'I wish he hadn't brought it.'

'It might be good news.' Bronnen scooped another lump of butter from the pile. Why did she keep hoping things might get better? The truth was they were getting worse.

Breaking the wax seal Sarah unfolded the sheet and began to read. One hand flew to her mouth. 'Oh my dear life.'

'What is it?'

'Dulcie's dead.'

'Who's Dulcie?'

'She–' Sarah swallowed. 'Her mother Mary is my cousin. Mary married Henwood Passmore. He's got a timber yard on Lemon Quay in Truro.

They had three girls. Dulcie was the middle one.'
She shook her head. 'I can't believe it. She wasn't
no more than forty.'

Bronnen glanced over her shoulder. 'What happened? Was it an accident?'

Sarah didn't answer, seemed not to hear.
Behind her fingers her lips quivered as she stared
into space.

Leaving the butter, Bronnen pulled a stool from
under the broad slate shelf. 'Here,' she said gently,
guiding her mother to it. 'Sit down a minute. Had
she been ill?'

Sarah caught her breath. 'What? I don't know.
It doesn't say.' She wiped away tears with a
corner of her apron. 'Poor little Dulcie.'

'Are you invited to the funeral?'

'That'll be long gone. She passed away three
weeks ago.'

'I wonder why they didn't tell you sooner. If
you had known, you could have–'

'No,' Sarah broke in. 'They wouldn't have
wanted me there.'

'Why ever not?' Bronnen was surprised. 'Surely
being family–'

'No, we was never what you'd call close, not
with them over Truro, and us out here.'

'Wouldn't you have liked to visit?' Her mother
rarely spoke of her family, and all she knew of her
father's background was that he had been born in
Penryn. He had never offered more and she had
learned not to ask.

'I got far too much to do here.' Refolding the
letter Sarah tucked it inside the bodice of her
dress and stood up. 'No need to tell your father.

He didn't know them that well.' Unrolling a length of cheesecloth she picked up the scissors. 'You're a dear girl, Bron. Mean the world to me you do. Don't ever forget that.'

Surprised, Bronnen glanced up from the new block of butter she was shaping. 'Goodness, Ma, where did that come from?'

'I just wanted you to know. Right, we'd better get on else the men will be in for their dinner before we're done.'

Chapter Four

Santo Innis strode along Market Street, avoiding busy women doing their morning shopping, and tradesmen's wagons that left yet more deep ruts in the muddy street.

But the sun's warmth on his back and a blue sky dotted with puffs of white cloud promised a spell of settled weather.

The scents of warm bread and freshly roasted coffee beans made his stomach growl. It was hours since his hasty breakfast.

He turned on to the brick-paved entrance to the Royal Hotel, passing beneath the broad archway that protected hotel patrons and passengers embarking on or alighting from the two mail coaches that left for London each day.

Bounding up the semi-circular stone steps, he pushed open the glass door into the hotel lobby and crossed to the reception desk. The proprietor, smart in black cut-away coat and stiff collar, was checking the hotel's booking ledger.

Two porters in shirtsleeves and green aprons carried a trunk bound with leather straps across the lobby and placed it with several portmanteaux. The fast mail left for London at seven a.m. But a slower stagecoach departed for Truro at ten-thirty.

'Good morning, sir.'

'Morning.' Santo removed his hat. 'I'm meeting Mr Vaughan. Has he arrived yet?'

'In the coffee lounge.' The manager indicated an open door.

Nodding his thanks, Santo crossed the patterned blue carpet. Behind the wide curving staircase, a passage led to the kitchen from which issued the faint clatter of cutlery, and the tantalising aroma of fried bacon.

Entering the coffee room overlooking the street, he saw his employer's heir and agent seated in one corner, reading. The table in front of him held a silver coffee service, two cups and saucers, several documents, and a folded newspaper.

Seeing Richard Vaughan's tailored blue coat, cream embroidered waistcoat, and pearl grey trousers reminded Santo that his own coat was five years old, slightly faded, and tight across shoulders bulked by the physical demands of heavy engineering.

Raking a hand through ebony curls in dire need of a barber, he shrugged inwardly. In the weeks since his return from Dartford he'd been working eighteen hours a day, at the end of which all he cared about was a meal, a bath, and sleep. But it'd been worth all the effort for he'd raised the money.

Ignoring glances of mingled speculation and disapproval from two well-dressed women in elegant hats seated by one of the windows, Santo made his way between empty chairs and tables.

Richard Vaughan put down the document he was reading.

'Sorry I'm late,' Santo said as they shook hands. 'I know how to make the displacer cylinder more efficient.' He spoke softly. 'An end cap made from three layers of copper sheet will hold the heat longer and that means more power for the same amount of fuel.' He poured hot coffee into his cup and added milk.

'How will you stop heat transferring from the hot to the cold end?'

'A gasket of hemp rope soaked in borax. I've tried it and it works a treat.'

Richard crossed one long leg over the other, interest clear in his keen gaze. 'I still find it hard to conceive of an engine powered solely by heated air.'

'That's the beauty of it.' Santo swallowed a mouthful of coffee. 'It's simple and it's safe. Which is more than you can say for high-pressure steam. Be a lot cheaper to run as well.'

'That should sit well with potential investors,' Richard said.

Santo turned the delicate cup between scarred and callused fingers. 'I've just paid Fox's the shipping fee for my marine engine. They'll contact Hall's and arrange for it to come down as deck cargo.' A wry grin twisted his mouth. 'All I need now is a bare hull.'

'I may be to help with that.'

Santo's head jerked up. 'Yes?'

'I'm negotiating with the Receiver to purchase Anstey's boatyard. I see no reason why the sale should not be concluded before your engine arrives.'

'Anstey's? There's a great workshop, a quay with a crane–'

'And a thirty-foot workboat hull.'

'Dear life! Be handsome that would.'

'In the meantime I fear I must add to your problems.' Richard crossed one leg over the other. 'Mr Tregarron is currently away from home a great deal.'

Santo nodded. 'The papers is full of this voting reform.'

'I am betraying no confidence if I say his interest lies elsewhere.' Richard's tone was dry.

'Ah.' So the squire had a new ladylove. No sooner had they married off the last of their three daughters than Mrs Tregarron had also left, apparently preferring the company of a widowed cousin in London to life in Cornwall with her husband.

With plenty of married women delighted to act as hostess for his dinners and supper parties, Frederick Tregarron relished his life as a country gentleman and made no secret of his enjoyment of all its opportunities.

'But surely–? I mean, what about–?' Santo shook his head. 'Beg pardon. None of my business.'

'If you are referring to Miss Tregarron, I wish it were not mine.' Richard brushed a speck from his immaculately pressed trousers. 'I find her … difficult.'

Since returning to Cornwall from his secondment to Hall's Engineering Works in Dartford, Santo had been relieved and delighted to find his employer's agent a man of open mind in engineering matters. This contrasted sharply to Frederick Tregarron whose views were influenced by peer pressure and profit potential.

Though frequent meetings had expanded professional respect into friendship, this crack in Richard Vaughan's habitual reserve surprised Santo. 'Angry, is she?'

'Why should she be angry?'

Santo shrugged. 'You're here and her father isn't.'

The crease between Richard's brows deepened. 'She informed me yesterday that I need feel no obligation to entertain her as she is perfectly content with her own company.'

Santo nodded. 'She said the same to me on the coach. I wouldn't call her prickly–'

'No?' Richard's tone was dust-dry. 'However, enough of that. Mr Tregarron wants you aboard the *Mercury* during the trials of the new high-pressure steam boiler.'

'Me?' Santo was startled. 'But Will McAndrew is Hall's chief engineer.'

'Indeed he is, and he will be aboard as well.'

'Why both of us? No disrespect, Mr Vaughan, but I don't feel right about that. Will is one of the best I've ever worked with. He was good as gold to me while I was at Hall's.'

'Mr Tregarron intends no slight. He holds Mr McAndrew in high regard. However, he has known you longer and trusts your judgement. Besides which,' Richard added, matching Santo's

39

ironic glance with his own, 'he hopes to convert you to the merits of high-pressure steam.'

'It will be a cold day in hell before that happens.' Santo's sigh was resigned. 'When?'

'Providing there are no more delays, the end of next week.'

With a nod, Santo started to rise. Richard put out a hand to stop him.

'One more thing: the water pump at Gillyvean brewhouse. At present it's hand-operated which makes it–'

'Slow and inefficient,' Santo said.

'Exactly. Could you replace it as soon as possible? Mrs Jewell and her daughter need to start brewing small beer ready for harvest. I apologise for giving you so little notice.'

'I've got a small hot-air engine that'd be perfect.' Richard regarded him thoughtfully.

'Come on,' Santo urged. 'What better chance to show its worth?' He waited.

'You're sure it's reliable?'

'I am and it is.'

'All right, when can you fit it?'

'I'll have it set up and working before the end of the week,' Santo promised.

The heavy wooden gates leading into Curnock's brewery yard stood wide open. Rain, sun, and the passage of time had faded both the yellow lettering and the dark green paint. To the right of the stone-flagged yard cellar-men were heaving barrels onto a heavy wagon built without sides to allow for easier loading.

Two grey draught horses with fringed hoofs the

size of dinner plates stood between the shafts of the dray, one waiting patiently, the other tossing its head and making the harness jingle.

Bronnen crossed the sloping yard, stepping over the shallow caunse that channelled rain-water and any spillages out onto the street. Steam drifted out of the louvred tower on top of the roof and the powerful aromas of hops and yeast overlay the smell of horse dung.

Since the age of eleven she had come here several times a year with her mother. Today she was alone. Her mother claimed she had baking to do. They both knew the real reason. Sarah would have found the long walk too painful. Though her bruises were fading, she didn't want to have to answer questions, lie about a fall that hadn't happened, or accept sympathy.

As she approached the brewery office Bronnen could hear George Curnock roaring like an angry bull. Her stomach knotted. She hated rows. Too often a raised voice became a raised fist. Pausing in the passageway she glanced towards the open door that led into the brewhouse.

From brewhouse and yard came familiar sounds she found soothing. A hammer clanged rhythmically against a driver as the cooper fitted an iron hoop onto a barrel. A pump rattled; pouring liquid splashed; the scrape of shovels told her the fireboxes beneath the two huge coppers were being stoked.

She stepped up to the office door. Raising her hand to knock, the argument raging inside made her hesitate.

'William Endean wouldn't give you a cold if he

could charge for it,' George bellowed. 'The only reason we're getting that discount is because he knows you buy on cost, not quality. The minute I opened that new sack I could smell it wasn't right.'

'You and your nose,' his brother Arthur scoffed.

'My nose has made this brewery the success it is!'

'You're too damn fussy. There's nothing wrong with the malt. It's all in your head. You'd be better off getting a good night's sleep in your own bed like any sensible person. Let your assistant watch the brew. That's what he's paid for.'

'Oh yes? What if something went wrong? Who'd get the blame? It wouldn't be Sam Jose, it would be me.'

'Listen,' Arthur snapped, clearly tired of the argument. 'Endean's malt costs half what your son charges. We can't afford to buy from Treeve, not while he's charging such ridiculous prices.'

'Then how am I supposed to produce top quality ales?'

'Who asked you to? Our ales meet all the necessary standards. Our customers are perfectly happy. If I didn't keep a tight rein on expenses your extravagance would put us out of business in a month.'

'It's not extravagant to demand decent wholesome malt. We should be bringing out new tastes.'

'Our customers wouldn't take kindly to changes.'

'How do you know?' George shouted. 'You won't give them the chance to find out. You think you're such a good businessman, Arthur. The truth is you're second-rate. And your way of thinking will sink this brewery.'

The door was wrenched open. Instinctively Bronnen stepped back as, crimson-faced and sweating, George glowered at her then stormed off down the passage. As he entered the brewhouse she heard him yelling for Sam Jose.

'I'm so sorry, Miss Jewell.' Arthur Curnock said. While the row had left his brother visibly upset, he seemed unmoved. 'Please come in. I hope you haven't been waiting long?'

'No.' She smiled politely.

Leaving the door open as convention demanded, he walked round behind his large desk, the surface almost invisible beneath several ledgers and scattered papers.

'Please,' he indicated a wheel-backed chair with a woven cane seat. 'Do sit down.'

Bronnen sat. She was familiar with the room from previous visits: the walnut desk placed at right-angles to a small-paned window overlooking the yard, a matching bureau set against the wall, the ornate gilt clock on the mantelpiece above the marble fireplace.

But she didn't recognise the armchair of polished wood upholstered in ox-blood leather. That was new. Arthur Curnock ran one hand appreciatively across the back before sitting down. So he would buy himself a new chair, yet refuse to pay for better quality malt.

Her thoughts jumped to Treeve Curnock. In the past when she had accompanied her mother to buy malt, she had remained silent, watching and learning. Though his manner was condescending his tone was polite. He valued the status of supplying malt to Gillyvean and would not risk a complaint to Mr Tregarron.

Twice since Christmas she'd had to go to the malthouse by herself. Though his welcome had been courteous, something in his eyes had made her uncomfortable. But she hadn't told her mother who had worries enough. It wouldn't be fair to add to them.

'So, Miss Jewell.' Arthur folded his hands over his mustard-yellow waistcoat. 'Am I right in thinking you have come to buy yeast to make small beer?'

'You are, Mr Curnock. Might you also have any spent grains for sale?' Her mother had told her to ask. The used malt was an excellent feed for the cattle and pigs.

'Unfortunately–' he broke off as the sound of anxious shouting was followed by footsteps pounding down the passage. As Bronnen looked round the door flew open and Sam Jose in shirtsleeves and a leather apron burst in.

'Beg pardon, Mr Curnock, Miss Jewell, but Mr George have fallen down the stairs.'

Sarah pulled a chair from under the kitchen table and lowered herself wearily onto it. Morley, Adam and the two labourers were busy about the farm. Bronnen had gone to Curnock's brewery for yeast. Apart from the ticking clock and the shifting embers in the range the house was silent.

She drew Mary Passmore's letter from her bodice, the only safe place she had been able to think of, and thought back to the day of Bronnen's birth.

Cradling the little pink body she had caught a tiny waving hand and kissed it, marvelling at the swirl of silky black hair as she smiled through her tears at the kitten-like cries. The surge of love that engulfed her was so powerful she had feared her heart would burst.

She drew a deep shaky breath. She must write a note of condolence to the Passmores. They would expect a response. Please God let that be the end of it. The truth had been buried so deep for so long she had almost forgotten. Now Mary's letter brought it all back. It was far too late to wish she had done things differently.

Rising stiffly from the table she used the iron hook to lift the cover from the firebox and dropped the letter onto the glowing coals. She could not pretend it hadn't come. Nor could she shake off a terrible sense of foreboding.

Chapter Five

Sarah looked into her daughter's eyes. 'I can't just sit home here, not when I'm needed.'

'Ma, you need rest and time to heal. That's more important than–'

'No, it isn't, Bron,' Sarah broke in, quiet but determined. 'I'm going tonight. 'Tis only three hours.'

Bronnen knew when argument was pointless. 'All right, but you can't walk down. It's too far.'

'I aren't daft.' Sarah's smile softened her retort.

45

'Adam can take me on the cart.'

'I don't mean to nag, Ma. It's just – I worry.'

'I know, bird. But I'm all right. Go on now. I'll see you dreckly.'

Knowing her mother was among friends and away from the farm, Bronnen would be able to concentrate on preparations for the brew.

She left the farm track and turned onto the carriage drive leading to Gillyvean house. On one side leafy beech trees edged the broad lawn, their shade welcome after the hot sun. On the other, honeysuckle and wild roses tumbled over the stone hedge, their sweet scent filling the air.

As she entered the brewhouse yard a man emerged from the open-fronted shelter that gave the pump and the person using it a measure of protection from the weather. Pausing, he wiped his hands on an oily rag.

In the sunlight his thick curly hair was raven black and glossy. Rolled-up shirtsleeves revealed sinewy forearms. A drab waistcoat was buttoned over broad shoulders and a deep chest. As he crouched to pick up a tool from a canvas bag, his corduroy breeches tightened across muscular thighs. Behind him a dark brown coat hung from a nail in the brewhouse wall.

He must be the engineer Mr Vaughan had promised to send. As he looked up, his eyes narrowing against the sun's glare, she saw strong features beneath straight black brows. A tug of awareness, *attraction*, took her by surprise.

He rose to his feet. 'Are you Miss Jewell?' He had a quiet husky voice. His accent was local but she did not recognise him.

Bronnen swallowed. 'Yes.'

'I'm Santo Innis. Mr Vaughan sent me to fix the water pump?'

'Yes.' The thought of moving towards him made her unaccountably nervous. Looking past him, she saw he had bolted the pump's long handle to a rod connected to a crank that turned the large metal wheel. This was linked by a leather pulley to the shaft of a much smaller wheel attached to an engine unlike any she had ever seen.

Dread propelled her across the yard. 'That's not a steam engine. What have you done?'

'No need to panic.'

'That's easy for you to say,' she threw at him. Then as her gaze met his, her heart skipped a beat. Confusion rolled over her like a breaking wave. Quickly looking away, she stared at the new additions.

'It's better than a steam engine,' he explained. 'It's simple to operate and–'

'Excuse me, but did Mr Vaughan know you were going to do this?'

'He did.'

Anger overrode Bronnen's nerves. 'Yet nobody thought to tell Mother and me? What if it doesn't work or – or it goes wrong? What if we lose the brew? I need this job, Mr Innis.'

His eyes flashed blue lightning and his mouth tightened. Heat rushed to her face as she braced herself for a stinging retort. But it didn't come. Instead his voice was patient.

'Do you think Mr Vaughan would have told me to fit the engine if he didn't believe it was reliable?'

'No,' she was forced to admit.

'Then instead of us standing here arguing, why don't I show you how it works? Where can I get a few sticks for the firebox?'

'There's paper, kindling, and logs in the store there.' She pointed. 'I always use wood for the copper fire. It burns hotter than coal and heats the water faster.' She was talking too much. Clamping her lips together, she turned away to unlock the brewhouse door.

Inside the small high-roofed building she dropped her basket on the wooden bench by the wall and pressed both palms to her hot cheeks. Then, pulling herself together, she went back outside.

He had laid a small fire on a shovel with a flat metal head and a wood handle. Curiosity overcame her anxiety and she took a step closer. Once the kindling and sticks were burning, he added some larger pieces of wood, slid the shovel into an iron box under the engine, and looked over his shoulder at her.

'This time next week you'll be wondering how you managed without it.'

'I wish I had your confidence. How does it work?'

'With heated air.'

As he straightened up, *close, too close*, she took a small step back. Their eyes met, held, broke away. Aware of the hot colour in her face, knowing he must surely see it, she tried to focus on the engine.

'No, I mean what makes it go?'

'I just told you. Hot air. See, when air in the cylinder gets hot it expands. That pushes the piston forward. The hot air passes to the cold end where it cools off and contracts, pulling the piston back again. Watch.' He lifted a wooden handle that raised a small wheel so it pressed against the sagging belt, tightening it.

Immediately the large flywheel began to turn. As it did, the crank moved the pump handle up and down.

Bronnen looked at him in astonishment. 'You can hardly hear it.'

He nodded.

'That's all you have to do?'

He grinned. 'That's all. You light the fire and give it a few minutes to heat the metal and the air inside. Then to pump up the water, all you need to do is lift the handle. That tightens the pulley so it grips. And this,' he jammed a stick under the handle to hold it up, 'will keep'n up tight while you get on with something else.'

As the engine ticked quietly Bronnen could hear the water splashing into the cistern in the brewhouse roof. She shook her head in amazement. 'That's awesome.'

'Better yet, it's safe.'

'What happens when the cistern is full? How do I stop the pump?'

He knocked the stick away with his foot. As the belt sagged, the big flywheel stopped turning and the pump handle stilled.

'That's all?'

'That's all. Like I told you, it's simple.' His gaze met hers briefly, before returning to the engine. She saw his throat work as he swallowed. 'If – if you need a lot of water it's best to keep the fire going. Then you just start and stop the pump whenever you want. When you've finished, you can simply let the fire die down or take out the shovel and damp the embers.'

Awed, Bronnen looked at him. 'How ever did you think it up?'

He pulled a wry face. 'I wish I had. The man who invented it was a Reverend Robert Stirling. He called it an air engine. His wasn't nothing like this. I been working on my own designs.' He shrugged.

'When I asked Mr Vaughan about a new pump–'

'You thought he'd be driven by steam?'

She nodded.

'I've got nothing against low-pressure steam. Mr Watt swears by it. But after engine manufacturers started using high-pressure steam boilers, two railway locomotives blew up and three American riverboats exploded. That's hundreds of people dead who shouldn't be. That's why I want–' he hesitated.

'What?' She realised she really wanted to know. 'What do you want?'

'To show there's another way, a safer way.' He rubbed his hands on the rag.

'To drive a ship? With one of these?'

Watching his jaw tighten she realised suddenly what he was up against.

'Ships will need two, side by side, and they'll be three times bigger 'n this.'

'But they'll work the same way?'

He nodded.

'Dear life, that's some bravish job.'

'Trouble is, people don't trust anything new.'

Bronnen felt the blush scald her cheeks.

'No,' he said quickly. 'I wasn't – I didn't mean you.'

'I could see what you were thinking.'

'I dearly hope not, Miss Jewell,' he murmured.

Her heart leapt like a fish and her breath caught in her throat. Though her gaze was on the engine she was acutely aware of him. 'With something so new and different people need a bit of time to get used to it.' She glanced at him. 'Do you know Mr Rowse, the foreman at Dene granite quarry up on the Longdowns Road?'

He shook his head. 'No. I've only been back in Cornwall a few weeks. Why?'

'With all the rain we've had this past eight months the quarries got awful trouble with flooding.'

'But getting him to try one of my engines–' Santo shook his head. 'You'd think people would be glad of something that made life easier.' The gleam in his eyes told her he was teasing.

'You got to be patient,' she returned. 'You built them so you know what they can do. P'rhaps if you asked him, Mr Rowse might come over and see this one working.'

His smile warmed her soul. 'I'm much obliged to you, Miss Jewell.'

'If it's as good as you say–'

'You'll find out for yourself, won't you?'

'Then give him a week he'll be wondering how he ever managed without it.'

Recognising his own words quoted back at him, he laughed, surprised by the pleasure he felt. As she disappeared into the brewhouse, he had to fight the urge to follow.

Her mass of dark hair was loosely coiled and pinned high at the crown without even a nod to fashion. He recalled the women in the hotel coffee room: their careful curls and ringlets framed by wide-brimmed hats trimmed with silk flowers, ostrich plumes, and large bows of ribbon colour-matched to their elegant clothes

Yet in her calico dress, faded from too many washes, Bronnen Jewell took his breath away. Escaped curls feathering her forehead and neck gave her a look of vulnerability. But despite her shyness he sensed strength, and she was certainly no fool.

He had no time for courting. The urge to know her better was too powerful to be ignored. *He had more work than hours in which to do it.* Somehow he would make time for her.

Chapter Six

Seated on the low stone balustrade surrounding the terrace, Melanie was sketching the distant view beyond the wooden fence that divided the lawn and shrubbery from the fields beyond. Though she much preferred portraiture, there was no one here she could draw.

Mrs Berryman and Ellen were far too busy to sit for her. So was Richard Vaughan. Not that she wanted to spend time in his company for, though unfailingly polite, his distant manner did not encourage conversation.

Knowing she was safe here, at least until her father returned, she allowed herself to relax a little. But, used to being busy, she had too much time to think.

What hurt most was the *injustice*. Despite being completely innocent and Miss Edwards accepting her account of the event, she had had to leave. Mrs Barden had insisted on it. As the Bardens were major contributors to school funds, Melanie knew Miss Edwards had no choice.

She must put it behind her and look forward. *But to what?*

Would her father come home today? Growing anxiety about his response to her uninvited presence pushed everything else aside.

The first morning, when Ellen had woken her with a cup of chocolate and a jug of hot water with which to wash, Melanie had asked about the household routine, anxious to cause minimal inconvenience.

The maid had needed little encouragement. Melanie heard all about Mr Tregarron's standing in the town and the dinners and supper parties he enjoyed hosting. Then Ellen had clicked her tongue as she confided that Mr Tregarron being so often away from home put a lot of extra work on Mr Vaughan.

The realisation that his aloofness might be the result of preoccupation with business matters and nothing whatever to do with her made Melanie felt foolish and embarrassed.

The French windows flew open and Ellen ran out onto the terrace.

'Oh, there you are, miss. Your pa is on his way up the drive.'

Melanie jumped to her feet, almost dropping her sketchpad and pencil tin as her heart tripped on a beat. 'Thank you, Ellen.'

She followed the maid back inside. But any hope of composing herself was lost when her father strode in through the front door, removing his top hat just as she hurried from the drawing room into the hall.

Above his florid face, framed by shirt points and a carelessly knotted black cravat, curling grey hair lay flattened and damp with sweat. His long-tail tan coat was unbuttoned revealing a patterned cream waistcoat. Mud and dust streaked his fawn breeches and topboots.

'What's this?' His first astonished words made Melanie's stomach clench painfully.

She dropped a quick curtsey and ran the tip of her tongue over paper-dry lips. 'Good afternoon, Father. I hope I find you well?'

'You do.' His sharp gaze narrowed. 'When did you get here?'

'Three days ago.'

'I see.'

'Mrs Berryman has been very kind.'

To her immense relief he nodded. 'So I should expect.' He addressed his valet who had just carried in two bags. 'A bath and fresh clothes, if you please, Hocking,' then turned back to Melanie. 'Come to my study at five. We'll talk then.'

After washing her face and hands, and tidying her hair, Melanie still had an hour to wait.

Unable to face sitting in her room she replaced her broad-brimmed straw hat then went downstairs and out into the garden.

Walking along the paved paths between beds of lavender and roses whose fragrance perfumed the warm air, she relived the moment of his arrival, recalling his expression and what it might signify.

Would he let her stay? Surely he must? But what if he refused? *How would she bear another rejection?*

At five o'clock exactly she stood outside his study door, her pulse loud in her ears. She squared her shoulders and drew in a deep breath before releasing it slowly.

Tapping the door with her knuckles she entered a comfortably shabby room with wood-panelled walls, heavy furniture, and a faint aroma of brandy and cigars.

Coming from behind his desk he indicated a leather armchair on one side of the hearth then seated himself opposite.

'Now, my dear.' Crossing dark-trousered legs he smiled at her, linking his fingers over his stomach. 'Tell me what happened. I believed you to be in France with your mother. How is she?'

'Very well, though her condition–'

'Condition?'

'She is expecting another child.'

'I see. And her husband?'

'Monsieur is also in good health,' Melanie answered, carefully expressionless.

'So why are you not still in France?'

'When my mother wrote inviting me to Paris, I thought–' *I thought she wanted to meet the daughter she had last seen as a four-year-old. I wanted to find out why she had abandoned me.*

Melanie cleared a painful tightness from her throat. 'I had many hopes for my visit.' So many hopes, so swiftly crushed. 'You know how important art is to me so I think you will understand my longing to see the paintings in the Louvre? Also, if it was possible, I wanted to visit the studios of some of the artists working in Paris.'

'What did you think of the Louvre? Magnificent, is it not?'

Melanie relived bitter disappointment as she shook her head. 'I did not see it. There was never time.'

'Why not?'

'My mother and her husband have a very busy social life.'

'Oh well, at least you made some new acquaintances.'

'No.' His startled expression had her torn between laughter and tears. 'I remained at their apartment looking after the children. They have four-year-old twin boys.' As Melanie had begun to wonder if her mother's friends knew of her existence, she realised her summons to Paris had sprung not from any resurgence of maternal affection but because her mother was at her wits' end.

'They are sweet boys but very boisterous. There have been numerous nursemaids but none stayed long. I think with more time I might have had some success. But when they told me about the voyage–'

'What voyage?'

'To Quebec.'

Frederick Tregarron frowned. 'Your mother never mentioned this when she wrote to me asking for your direction and my agreement to your visit.'

Within a week of arriving in Paris Melanie had seen her hopes of a joyful reunion with her mother for what they were: dreams with all the substance of mist. Her only value was as an unpaid nurse for the children. Her passion for art had been dismissed with the careless flick of a hand, of no interest to a woman who cared only for fashion and company.

'You did not wish to accompany them?'

'No,' Melanie said flatly.

'Don't be ridiculous,' her mother had cried. 'You must. I need you. Besides, what else would you do? You cannot stay here.'

Pretending a calm she did not feel, Melanie had said, 'I shall return to England as soon as possible.' *Please don't ask why.* What could she say? Of what could she accuse him? He had done nothing exceptional, said nothing untoward. He was handsome, wealthy, and her mother adored him. Yet the moment they were introduced and he bowed over her hand she had felt a shiver of unease.

But her mother did not ask. Instead, shouting accusations of selfishness and ingratitude, she had burst into noisy sobs and flung herself into her husband's arms.

As he patted his wife's back, Melanie saw the fractional lift of an eyebrow and the hint of a sardonic smile.

Her skin tightening at the memory, she looked

directly at her father.

'I could not remain in Paris. So I came back.'

His eyes narrowed. 'You returned to England alone?'

'I still had most of the money you had sent me. And before boarding the coaches or the ship I applied to an official to ask an older couple or a family if they would permit me to travel in their company.'

Reluctant admiration softened his frown. 'Well, that shows good sense and resourcefulness. Where did you go once you landed in England?'

'Back to Oakland Park.'

'To school?'

She smiled at his astonishment. 'Miss Edwards needed an art teacher and because she knew my character and my ability, she kindly gave me the position. I had my own room and was quite content.' She saw no reason to tell him how lonely she had been, just as she had put off writing to tell him of her return from France.

With a roof over her head, three meals a day, work she enjoyed, a small salary sufficient for her needs, and time to paint, her life could have been a lot worse. And then it was.

'Yet something must have happened or you would not be here.'

He listened without interrupting, the crease between his brows growing deeper as she told him about the incident that had forced her to leave, then Mrs Tregarron's response to her plea for help.

After the first halting sentences, she found it easier. By the time she had finished she felt as if she had put down a heavy burden. Yet one thing still needed to be said. 'I would be grateful if you did not share this with Mr Vaughan. He made it clear to me that as your heir and agent he is privy to all your business. However he has no right to know mine.'

Her father regarded her steadily. She waited, her heart drumming. His expression gave nothing away. With no idea what was happening behind that assessing gaze, dread slithered, cold and oily, along her veins.

Then he clapped his hands, making her start. 'Well,' he beamed, 'what a to-do. Still, you are here now, and here you must stay.'

She bent her head, her eyes filling as weeks of accumulated tension were released in a shuddering sigh.

'Thank you,' she whispered.

'There, there, no need for tears.' He paused. 'I shall host a dinner party to introduce you to the most influential people of my acquaintance. Richard can arrange it.'

'Is that necessary?' Melanie blurted.

'Certainly,' his brows lifted in surprise. 'If we are to establish you in town as a member of my family and ensure you receive due respect.'

That wasn't what she had meant. Why must he ask Richard to arrange it? Even as the thought occurred, so did the answer. She had been here only a few days. But that was long enough to learn that her father never troubled himself with matters he could delegate to someone else.

'You will need new evening gowns.' Rising, he returned to the chair behind his desk. 'Mrs Berryman will know the best dressmaker. You may order three to start with. Now, about a personal maid–'

'Please, Father–'

'Such formality,' he teased, his eyes twinkling. 'I know we have seen little of each other, but you are as much my child as my other daughters, so you may call me Papa.'

'Thank you, Papa.' Though it felt strange on her lips, his words warmed her. 'It's just – please don't think me ungrateful but I'm perfectly capable of dressing myself. As for my hair, I'm sure – if Mrs Berryman can spare her – Ellen and I will manage perfectly well.'

'How very undemanding of you.' Acutely sensitive, Melanie listened for criticism but heard only amusement and surprise. 'You're quite sure?'

'I am, truly.'

'Then it shall be as you wish.' He waved her away. 'Off you go, my dear. I'll see you at dinner.'

Having always been an outsider, Melanie was sensitive to the proper way of doing things. Mrs Berryman's good opinion would make a great difference to her life at Gillyvean. Asking her advice about Ellen proved a wise move.

'Dear life, miss! Be like a dog with two tails Ellen will. She've always wanted to be a lady's maid. But Mrs Tregarron had Miss Mabyn and she wouldn't give you the time of day, let alone teach Ellen anything.' Mrs Berryman leaned forward, lowering her voice. 'Truth is Miss Mabyn had Mrs Tregarron dressed to death and killed with fashion. You don't want that.'

'No, indeed.' Melanie had shuddered at the thought. 'But I don't want to cause you any incon–'

'Don't you worry about that,' Mrs Berryman flapped her hands. 'Ruth-Anne can help out when Ellen's with you. She been waiting to get out of the scullery and up over stairs. Ellen's cousin is a lady's maid with Mrs Harvey over to Mawnan. Mrs Harvey paid for her to have hairdressing lessons. She'll dearly love showing Ellen what she've learned. She got pictures too, out of they fashion magazines. You leave it with me, miss.'

The dressmaker was a plump middle-aged woman whose skills were evident in the cut and fit of her own magenta gown with its full sleeves, wide neck filled with fine gauze, a tiny ruff, and belt that defined her waist. Beneath her bonnet she wore a fine linen cap that covered her ears.

After politely asking Melanie to stand in the middle of her bedroom and turn slowly round, she had taken from her basket a length of tulle, several silk flowers, and one of the latest fashion magazines.

Showing Melanie several plates, she had expertly draped the tulle and pinned the flowers to demonstrate exactly how a neckline, sleeve or sash would look.

After daily fittings, Melanie escaped to the garden with her sketchpad, wanting to forget – if only for an hour – the knowledge that she would be the focus of attention: inspected and assessed. *These people were her father's friends.* She owed it to him to make a good impression.

Chapter Seven

Sitting at the kitchen table mending one of her brother's workshirts, Bronnen relived her conversation with Santo Innis. Apart from church, the soup kitchen, and half a day at the market selling eggs and butter, she rarely left the farm. Except when she went with her mother to brew at Gillyvean.

The closest she had come to having a beau was John Pascoe. She had met him at a church social. Mate aboard the packet, *Louisa May*, he had drowned off the coast of Valparaiso.

She had grieved for his parents losing their only son, and felt sad at a life cut short. But they had known each other only a few weeks and she had felt no deep attachment.

So why did her heart flutter and swoop each time she thought about Santo Innis?

The back door flew open, making her jump. Her father stumbled into the kitchen. Runnels of blood from a split lip had dried dark on his chin. Plum-coloured bruises and swelling distorted the left side of his face.

'Good God, Pa.' She jumped up, dropping the shirt on the table. 'Whatever happened?'

'None of your bleddy business,' Morley Jewell mumbled. He hung his hat on the wooden peg behind the door then winced as he started to take off his coat.

'Shall I help?' Bronnen started forward.

'Stop fussing. I can do it. Get me some brandy.'

Crossing to the range, she scooped up a small shovel of coal from the copper scuttle, hooked the cover aside and poured it into the firebox, then refilled the large black kettle from an earthenware pitcher and drew it over the flames.

Glancing over her shoulder she saw him hang his coat on the peg, his movements slow and painful. Still wearing his boots, he clumped to the wooden armchair at one side of the range and eased himself down.

'Gone deaf, have you?' He glared at her. Fresh blood welled from the re-opened split in his lip. 'Fetch the brandy like I told you.'

Taking a mug from the dresser, Bronnen crossed to the larder. Beneath the thick slate slab that kept butter, milk, and cold meat cool, a tub of cognac rested on a wooden shelf. Below it, on the stone floor, another larger keg held ale. She turned the spigot, forcing herself to wait until the mug was a third full before shutting it off. Her father was like a simmering pot with the lid jammed on. Spirits made him worse. But she dared not refuse.

He gulped down two huge mouthfuls, shuddering violently. Then, head bent, he unbuttoned his waistcoat with trembling fingers. His knuckles were bruised and grazed, his greying hair damp with sweat. Blood splattered the front of his collarless shirt.

Filling a basin with warm water, Bronnen set it on the kitchen table, pulled a towel from the brass rail in front of the range, and moved both within his reach. 'There's blood on your face. Do you want me to–?'

'No, I don't.' He waved her away. 'Bleddy horse shied,' he mumbled, keeping his head down. Fresh blood dripped onto his trousers. 'Threw me off the cart.'

He was lying. Those injuries hadn't come from a fall. He'd been in a fight, taken a beating.

'Where's she to then?'

Not *your mother* or *Sarah*. 'It's Ma's evening at the soup kitchen,' Bronnen reminded him. She closed her sewing basket and put it in the cupboard under the dresser. 'Has Adam gone down to collect her?'

'He got no time for that. There's a delivery to go out tonight.'

'I'll go then.'

'Please yourself,' he grunted.

Lifting her shawl from the peg alongside her father's coat, Bronnen slung it round her shoulders and hurried across the yard. It was early June, just after eight o'clock. In the paling sky the tops of purple and grey clouds were coloured apricot and edged with gold by the setting sun.

She saw her brother heave a hay bale onto the cart, then haul himself up to shove it into the remaining space. Jumping down, he raised the tail of the cart and bolted it in place then threw a large square of sail canvas over the bales.

At twenty-two Adam was two years older than her. He had inherited their mother's mousy hair and blue eyes, and their father's stocky build. Her own hair was dark and wavy, her eyes green with golden flecks, just like her gran's, her mother said.

'Don't ask me. I don't know where he've been,'

64

he said before she could speak. 'When we come out after tea he sent me down the bottom field to shift a tree blocking the stream. That's the third in a month. Ground's so soft with all the rain the roots won't hold. A puff of wind and down they come.' Fastening one corner of the canvas to a metal ring, he moved round the cart.

Bronnen ran her hand down the neck of the big horse whose eyelids drooped as, one hip cocked, he waited patiently. 'He said Prince shied, throwing him off the cart.'

Her brother didn't respond.

'I think he've been in a fight. He've certainly taken a beating.'

'Nothing to do with me, Bron. I don't want to know.' He finished tying down the canvas. 'I won't be back in time to fetch Ma.'

Bronnen nodded. 'Pa told me. Don't worry, I'll go.' She drew her shawl closer. The air cooled quickly once the sun went down.

Adam climbed onto the seat and picked up the reins. 'I usually meet her on the corner of Swanpool Street. If I drop you there, 'tis only a few steps to the soup kitchen.'

After waiting on the corner for several minutes with no sign of her mother, Bronnen crossed the road to Quay Hill. Slipping between the ragged people clustered outside the open double doors, Bronnen entered a crowded room that smelled of cooked vegetables, dirty clothes and unwashed bodies.

Unkempt men and women crowded both sides of a long table hunched over steaming bowls of stew, a spoon in one grimy hand, a hunk of barley

65

bread in the other. More queued along the wall waiting their turn.

At the far end, behind another long board resting on two stout trestles, women wearing white aprons over their plain dark dresses, simple white caps covering their hair, ladled out more soup and cut thick slices from large loaves.

As she made her way down the room towards a doorway at the end she could hear women's voices and the clatter of dishes. One of the women glanced up from serving.

'All right, Bron?'

'Mother here, is she?'

The woman glanced at her companions who were shaking their heads. 'Haven't seen her.'

'Tried next door, have you?' another suggested.

With a brief wave of thanks Bronnen made her way back outside and went next door to the clothing bank. As she raised her hand to knock the door opened, bringing her face to face with a plump rosy-faced woman wearing a beige cloak and straw bonnet, a large empty basket over her arm.

'Oh my lor',' she gasped. 'Made me jump you did.'

'Sorry.' Bronnen smiled in apology. 'I'm looking for Mrs Jewell? I'm her daughter.'

''Course you are. I seen you in the kitchen a few weeks back. I haven't been coming long so I'm still putting names to faces. I'm Mrs Rose. Esther. Everything all right, is it?'

Bronnen recognised the bright, eager gaze of a born gossip. 'Yes,' she lied. 'My brother normally comes for Ma. But he's been called away. So I've come instead.'

'Good thing too.' She turned the key.

'What are you doing?' Bronnen put out a hand to stop her.

'Locking up,' Esther said, clearly surprised by the question. 'Clothing bank is closed tonight. I just dropped off a basket of linen. I tell you what,' she went on, 'if I worked down there,' she jerked her head towards a gate made of iron bars between the two adjoining buildings. Behind it granite steps led down into shadow. 'I'd be afraid for my life walking home.' She shivered. 'Your ma must be some brave. I don't know how she and Mrs Fox and the others do it. I couldn't.'

Bronnen had no idea what Esther Rose was talking about. Her mother spent three hours each week helping in the soup kitchen, or at the clothing bank sorting and mending charitable donations of clothes and blankets, and assembling layettes for poor women who could not afford to provide for their own lying-in.

Esther stepped closer. 'Some of they young girls is no better 'n animals,' she confided. 'But when you got mother, father, and Lord knows how many children in two rooms, boys and girls all in the same bed, what can you expect? 'Tis all very well Reverend Carter calling 'em harlots, young in years but old in sin. Well, that don't help, do it? And why do he always blame the girls? What about the men who go looking for them? Anyhow, better get on. I said I'd take a turn dishing up and they'll be wondering where I'm to.' With a quick smile she turned and bustled away leaving Bronnen struggling to make sense of what she'd just heard.

By her own admission Esther was new and

didn't yet know everyone. Perhaps she had mistaken Sarah Jewell for someone else.

But if her mother wasn't in the soup kitchen and the clothing bank was locked...

Down there, Esther had said, indicating the iron-barred gate. After staring at it for a moment Bronnen lifted the latch and pushed. The hinges squealed loudly. Closing it behind her she walked carefully down stone steps that had been swept clear of debris.

Cholera had reached Liverpool, and with ships from that port calling regularly at Falmouth, the mayor and corporation had demanded all courts, alleys and opes be cleared of filth and rubbish and washed down daily. The town had never been so clean.

At the bottom of the steps a flickering lantern was fixed to the wall above a stout wooden door inset with a small barred grill. She knocked. Behind the grill a panel slid open. As it did so she heard a door inside slam, muffling a pain-filled scream. A child's voice rising in panic was soothed by motherly tones.

Hinges left un-greased to shriek a warning and a grill that protected those inside while callers were peered at. What was this place?

'Yes?' The woman's tone was cool.

'I'm Sarah Jewell's daughter,' Bronnen said quickly. 'I've come–'

'You bide there a minute.' The grill slid shut.

Bronnen waited. A few moments later she heard the scrape of a bolt then the door opened.

'Bronnen, isn't it? I'm Mrs Fox. Come in.'

Stepping inside, Bronnen found herself in a

short hallway with a closed door to her left, a flight of stairs to her right, and another closed door at the end. The metallic smell of blood hung heavy in the air.

Quickly shutting the door, Mrs Fox pushed the bolt across. Of medium height and lean build, she wore a brown dress with the cuffs turned back and a linen apron streaked with crimson.

'I've come to walk my mother home.'

'Doesn't your brother usually collect her?'

'Yes. But–' Bronnen thought of her father slumped bruised and bloody in the chair, and her brother delivering hay at night. That was no one else's business. 'He's been called away and Father's busy. So I came instead. I thought she–' No need to tell Mrs Fox she hadn't known this place existed; that she had believed her mother to be at the soup kitchen; *that her mother had lied to her*. 'I was afraid I might have missed her. Then I met Mrs Rose.'

Mrs Fox shook her head, and with a weary sigh tucked an escaped strand of hair into her cap. 'Esther Rose has a good heart but I wish she'd learn to guard her tongue. Anyway, you're here, and your mother will have company for the walk home. I never allow any of our helpers to leave here alone. The fathers of these girls don't like us interfering. Only last week two of our ladies were threatened. You need not be anxious, my dear,' she added quickly seeing alarm on Bronnen's face. 'It is unpleasant to be sure, but no violence has been offered. At least they have more sense than that.'

Each revelation was a fresh shock and Bronnen struggled not to let it show.

Mrs Fox lowered her voice. 'Before she joins us I should tell you I am concerned about your mother. She is a remarkable woman. But the situations we have to deal with can be very harrowing. Such demands drain even the strongest. Though we will miss her very much I believe she needs a rest. This last week in particular she has not looked at all well.'

'I'm helping her as much as I can at home and in the dairy. But I can't be there *and* up at Gillyvean. Father will be hiring extra help for harvest soon, and if the beer isn't ready–' She stopped, choking on the lump in her throat.

'My dear,' Mrs Fox's hand on her arm was gentle. 'I intended no criticism of you or your mother.' A wry smile tilted the corners of her mouth. 'I have come to know her well and admire her greatly. However, I am well aware that once she has made her mind up she can be difficult to move.'

'I didn't know she – about this–'

'No doubt she wished to shield you.' Mrs Fox was brisk. 'What we deal with is not for innocent ears.'

In the brief silence Bronnen heard other sounds: a muffled thud, a soothing voice, the clatter of jug and basin, water splashing, a child sobbing with weary desolation that made her eyes sting. A sudden sharp cry stopped her breath.

'It hurts! It hurts!'

Deeply unsettled, Bronnen wished her mother would come. She was desperate to escape the pain and despair that thickened the air like fog.

Upstairs a door opened and closed. Bronnen

heard quick footsteps along the landing.

'I expect this is her now,' Mrs Fox said.

Hurrying down the stairs, her face drawn with exhaustion, Sarah Jewell's gaze darted between her daughter and Mrs Fox.

'How did you know to come here?'

Bronnen glimpsed a fear she didn't understand. 'Mrs Rose told me. I thought I'd missed you.'

'You got no business here,' Sarah muttered, refusing to meet Bronnen's eye as she tied the strings of her bonnet with fingers that trembled. 'Adam always meet me on the corner.'

'He couldn't tonight, Ma.' *Please don't ask. Not here, not now.*

'Sarah,' Mrs Fox said, 'I admire your wish to protect Bronnen from the dark side of life. But she is no longer a child.' She turned her head. 'What is your age, my dear?'

'I'm twenty,' Bronnen replied, feeling heat climb her throat. Four of the girls with whom she had attended Dame School were married and two were proud mothers of baby sons. She did not even have a beau. Suddenly, vividly, she recalled Santo Innis emerging from the pump shelter, his black hair rumpled and gleaming in the sunlight, and his smile as he teased her.

'She's a young woman, Sarah.' Glancing at Bronnen, Mrs Fox smiled. 'One on whose discretion I am sure we may rely?'

Wrenching her thoughts back to surroundings she could not wait to leave, Bronnen nodded. Mrs Fox turned back to her mother.

'Sarah, before you go there's something I must say. You cannot doubt how much I, or indeed the

71

entire committee, appreciate your hard work and your kindness to these unfortunate girls. However, that said, I don't want to see you here for at least a month. No,' her raised hand forestalled any argument. 'We want you back, Sarah. But only after you've had a proper rest. I need you well and strong.'

Out on the street, Bronnen drew her mother's arm through hers and they started walking.

'All right,' Sarah said wearily. 'Why did you come down?'

'Father's hurt. He's got a split lip and his face is bruised and swollen.' Her mother's grip tightened and when she spoke her voice had a slight tremor.

'Did he say what happened?'

'He *said* that Prince shied and he was thrown from the cart. But it looked to me like he'd been in a fight.'

'You didn't say that to him?'

''Course I didn't. I got more sense than that. Adam dropped me at the corner. He had a load of hay to deliver. Though I can't think why he've got to take it out this time of night. Anyway, I waited for a while but when you didn't come I thought I'd better ask. I was afraid I might have missed you.'

'We was busy tonight. I didn't mean to shout on you. It's just – it gave me a start when Mrs Fox come in to tell me you was downstairs.'

As they passed Church Steps and the King's Head hotel the roar of male voices raised in song issued from the open door and windows. The smells of tobacco smoke, wet sawdust, beer, and roasting meat mingled with those of old fish, seaweed, and mud carried on the breeze that funnelled up narrow alleys from the foreshore.

It was nearly ten o'clock and daylight had faded to dusk. The only people on the street now were men entering or leaving the inns and ale houses, alone or in the company of gaudily-dressed street women with painted faces and bird's-nest hair.

'Why, Ma? Why do you go down there?'

'Someone got to do something for they poor girls.'

'But why you?'

'Because it's wicked, but no one – not the church, not the law – got the power or the will to stop it.' Her voice broke. 'Dear God, they're just children.'

'You're making yourself ill. 'Tisn't just me worrying. Mrs Fox–'

'I'm all right.' Beside her Sarah took a deep breath and straightened shoulders rounded by strain and fatigue. 'Been a long day is all.' She patted Bronnen's arm.

'These girls,' *that you have never spoken of,* 'are they grateful for what you do?' That at least would make her mother's efforts and exhaustion worthwhile.

'Course they aren't,' Sarah said tiredly. 'They're wary, sly, and would steal your purse soon as look at you. We can't do much anyhow. We clean them up, bandage cuts, put arnica on bruises, give them something to eat and maybe a dress that near enough fits. But don't matter how bad they been hurt, we can't keep them. We'd be had for kidnap. Even if we could, most wouldn't stay. They're too afraid. So tomorrow night they'll be back on the street again.'

'Then why do it, Ma?'

'Because – because they girls got no choice. Nor do I. Leave it now, Bron.'

While others had known where her mother was and what she was doing, she had been excluded, kept in the dark. Though she tried not to mind, it hurt. But with her mother looking and sounding so desperately tired, it would be unkind to press. Time enough in the days ahead to find out more.

Chapter Eight

The afternoon of the dinner party, Melanie bathed in scented water while Ellen washed her hair. After it was towelled, combed through, and left loose to finish drying, Ellen trimmed her ragged cuticles and rubbed rose-cream into the sore skin.

Two hours later, wearing one of her new gowns, her hair gleaming like a polished chestnut in a plaited coronet with two ringlets in front of each ear, Melanie took a final look in the long glass.

Cream lace edged the wide neckline of her gown of emerald satin. Puffed sleeves ended at the elbow, and more lace frilled the lower third of a full skirt that emphasised her neat waist. Silk stockings and emerald satin slippers completed her ensemble.

'Oh, miss, look beautiful, you do.' Ellen beamed. 'Got a little locket or necklace, have you?'

Melanie shook her head. 'No jewellery.'

'Up to you, miss. But it would finish–'

'No, Ellen, I meant I don't own any jewellery.' Melanie studied her reflection. When the other girls had received pearls or cameos or lockets as birthday gifts from their parents, Melanie reminded herself of her father's generosity in sending her to Oakland Park, and agreeing to Miss Edwards's request for additional art tuition. Gifts far more important than a necklace.

'Oh.' Ellen's shock was evident but she recovered quickly. 'I'm some sorry, miss. I didn't mean no offence.'

'I know you didn't, so think no more of it. You're right though. My throat does look rather bare.'

Crossing to the chest of drawers, Ellen opened the top one and held up a length of emerald ribbon. 'We never used it for your hair.' After tying it in a neat bow at the side of Melanie's throat she stood back. 'There. Not too tight, is it?'

'No, I can still breathe. As long as I can swallow I shall be fine.' Panic crossed the maid's face. Swivelling round, Melanie smiled up at her. 'I'm sorry, Ellen. I'm nervous. That was my poor attempt at a joke.'

'You sure it's all right, miss?'

'It's perfect. Perhaps I will start a new fashion.' Rising from the stool Melanie picked up her sketchpad and pencil tin from the bed. Bringing them down with her had been her father's suggestion.

'You have an unusual talent, Melanie. What better way to display it, and to flatter our guests, than by drawing them?'

Surprised and thrilled, she had thanked him. 'Should anyone want a proper portrait, Papa, may I accept a commission?'

'You may. For where one leads the rest will follow. We will soon have you established.' Smiling broadly he rubbed his hands together. 'Indeed we will.' There was an odd note in his voice. Then he had waved her away. 'Off you go. I want you looking your best tonight.'

While Ellen had done her hair, Melanie's thoughts had sparked like a burning log: reunion with her mother, devastating disappointment, her flight back to England, expulsion from Oakland Park, the exhausting coach ride to Cornwall. She straightened her spine. All that was in the past. Tonight held the key to her future. She must please and impress. *She had nowhere else to go.*

As she descended the stairs, bracing herself for the ordeal ahead, she heard voices. Her heart lurched in panic. Surely she wasn't late? Pausing in the hall to draw a deep breath she entered the drawing room.

Seeing her father and Richard by themselves, her immediate reaction was relief. Only then did she become aware of tension in the air. Richard moved away to one of the tall windows. Immaculate in white tie and tailcoat he looked even more forbidding than usual.

'I beg your pardon, have I interrupted?'

'Not at all,' her father said easily. 'We were merely passing the time.' He came towards her. 'Green? Not what I would have chosen.' As Melanie's heart contracted, he beamed. 'Which only goes to show how little I know of such things. It is perfect with your colouring.' Relieved, for she had chosen it over an ice blue that might have been more suitable for her age but made her creamy skin sallow, Melanie returned his smile.

Tregarron glanced back at his heir silhouetted against the window, his face in shadow. 'Do you not think so, Richard?'

'Really, Papa.' Embarrassment burned her skin. She would not have thought her father so clumsy. 'You put Mr Vaughan in an impossible position. He can hardly disagree.'

'I do have a mind of my own, Miss Tregarron.' Richard did not move. 'However, I cannot fault your father's observation.'

Hardly fulsome, it was still preferable to insincere flattery. Ever since her arrival Richard Vaughan had kept her at arm's length. At first she had wondered if he was simply shy. Yet shyness seemed unlikely for a man in his mid-thirties, especially one responsible for her father's business and personal affairs.

Perhaps he had simply taken a dislike to her, though she had no idea why he should. He did not know her. Nor, apparently, did he wish to. Fortunately she had no need of his approval. Let him think what he would.

A bustle in the hall indicated the arrival of the guests. The three ladies wore gowns similar in style to hers. But theirs had necklines completely off-the shoulder and enormous puffed sleeves edged with frills, lace, and bows of ribbon. Aware that every detail of her appearance would be noted and discussed, she had deliberately combined modest styling with an unusual colour.

As introductions were made, and Melanie responded to greetings, she pretended not to notice that she was being inspected like an exhibit at one of the country shows her father occasionally mentioned in his letters.

Mrs Martin was regal in gold taffeta with a triple-strand necklace of green stones. Her hair, an unlikely shade of auburn, was dressed in a double-looped topknot with fat roll curls on either side of her face from a centre parting to her ears.

Thanks to Ellen, Melanie knew the style was the height of fashion. But something softer and less rigid would have been more flattering to Mrs Martin's sharp features.

'So, Miss Tregarron, is Cornwall to your liking?'

'Very much, ma'am. The air is so clear and the light has a special quality.'

'Indeed?' Mrs Martin's brows rose.

'I suppose you would notice such things, being an artist,' Mrs Behenna said, her hair covered by a turban of burgundy silk embellished with egret feathers that matched her gown. Though her skin resembled crumpled tissue paper, her cheeks were pink and her eyes twinkled.

'You are kind to say so, ma'am. But the truth is I noticed because the air here is so much cleaner than in London.' As her father drew her on, she caught Mrs Behenna's whisper, 'Laura not here tonight?' realising just in time the question was not directed at her, nor was she supposed to have heard.

'That's all finished,' Mrs Dudley hissed back. 'She started getting above herself, making Arthur look a fool. Frederick wouldn't stand for that. He's always gone his own way but at least he was discreet.'

78

Her mouth set in a frozen smile, Melanie did not dare look at her father. But he seemed oblivious. Either he hadn't heard, or he simply didn't care.

'Dudley, allow me to present my daughter.'

'Miss Tregarron.'

'Mr Dudley is a business colleague, my dear. He and I have a financial interest in Perran Foundry.'

'How do you do, Mr Dudley.' As Melanie offered her hand, she glimpsed Richard Vaughan across the room, watching her. But as their eyes met he turned away.

Presented to Mr Behenna, a local banker, she was asked yet again what she thought of Cornwall. Answering politely, she was grateful to hear dinner announced.

Though it was not yet dusk, candles had been lit in the dining room and cast flattering light over crisp white napery, silver cutlery and gleaming glassware. In the centre of the oval table, bowls of cream and yellow roses perfumed the air with delicate fragrance.

Mingled anticipation and dread had stolen Melanie's appetite. But she knew if she didn't eat she would feel even worse. Besides, as her father had arranged this evening for her benefit she owed it to him to play her part.

Mrs Berryman had excelled herself. Green pea soup, salmon with parsley butter, and lamb cutlets with cucumbers were followed by braised ham with broad beans, and chicken in a béchamel sauce with baby carrots, peas, and new potatoes. Offered a choice of wines, Melanie sipped a little of the dry white burgundy, then asked Knuckey, who doubled as Mr Vaughan's valet, for water.

Seated between Mr Dudley and Mr Behenna, she turned first to the banker and remarked on the beauty of the harbour. That led on to the welcome change in the weather. Learning that he had daughters, she asked about their interests.

Mr Behenna needed little prompting, and Melanie was touched and a little envious of his pride in his daughters' singing and needlework.

'Hark at me rattling on,' he said suddenly. 'I fear I am boring you.'

'Not at all, Mr Behenna. It is a joy to hear a father talk of his daughters with such warmth and pride.'

'You are a good listener, Miss Tregarron. But I am keeping you from your dinner.'

As they continued their meal, Melanie recalled the girls at Oakland Park Seminary. They had loved to talk – about themselves, their families, people they liked and those they didn't, their hopes of making a good marriage.

When she asked if they had other hopes or ambitions they reacted with astonishment. What else was there? Marrying well was the ultimate goal. Not only did it unite families and enlarge one's social circle, it reinforced one's standing in society. Though of course it was different for her.

The careless cruelty of that remark opened Melanie's eyes to cold hard truth. She was intelligent, well-educated, a graceful dancer, and a talented artist. But none of it was sufficient to erase the stigma of being the child of unmarried parents.

Hating the injustice, for the situation was not of her making, she also hated being powerless against such ingrained prejudice. Then she realised she had a choice. She could continue accepting the whims that meant inclusion one day and rejection the next. Or she could step away.

So she stopped joining the girls at leisure hour gatherings. She gave up trying to belong. Instead she devoted her free time to refining her painting technique.

Sometimes the loneliness was overwhelming. But after a little weep she dried her eyes, reminded herself unreliable company wasn't worth the sacrifice of self-respect, and resumed her painting or went for a walk in the gardens.

At first the effort of appearing serene and confident was exhausting. But it became easier with practice. Before long she realised that separation had given her a fresh perspective and new insight.

She noticed the girls all had different reasons for talking. Some needed to impress. Some wanted to find out what others thought before voicing an opinion. Those from the wealthiest families set themselves up as arbiters of taste and expected everyone else to defer to them.

Then, to her surprise, girls who as a group excluded her began individually to seek her out, claiming to want a portrait painted as a birthday gift for a relative or godparent. She was happy to oblige. But what they really wanted was a confidante, someone they could trust. Melanie appreciated the irony.

She refused to offer an opinion or give advice; aware the person asking was either seeking approval for a decision already made or someone to blame if it all went wrong. She did not mind listening, but declined to be used. If asked 'what

81

do you think?' she simply returned the question.

When the sitter, having argued herself into or out of a course of action, rose to leave offering profuse thanks and seeking reassurance that what had been said would remain private between the two of them, Melanie replied that having been so focused on the portrait she had little memory of the conversation.

Suddenly she was jerked out of her reverie by the powerful sensation of being watched. No, not merely watched, *studied*.

She glanced round the table and saw Richard Vaughan turn away to speak to Mrs Behenna who laughed then murmured a reply.

Catching her eye her father smiled. In that tiny nod she read approval. Warmed, she turned her attention to the businessman on her other side.

Chapter Nine

Mr Dudley was harder work, for he had three sons but no daughters and she knew nothing of foundries. Yet apart from a slight pomposity he was pleasant enough.

The second course was removed, and cherry tarts, strawberry cream, cheesecakes, and ices were set down the centre of the table. After the servants had left the room the volume of conversation and laughter increased.

Relieved that the evening was going well, and released for a moment from the need to make conversation, Melanie found her gaze drawn to Mrs Dudley whose bosom resembled vanilla blancmange erupting from her purple and magenta shot-silk bodice. Draped downward from a centre parting then looped up and crowned with a knot of patently false curls, her hairstyle gave her face a moon-like appearance. But deep creases at the outer corners of her eyes showed she smiled often. She was smiling now as she listened to Richard Vaughan.

Clearly he was capable of being pleasant. Just not to her. She turned away. His behaviour and the reasons for it were his business. She would not concern herself with them.

Eventually the meal ended. Leaving the men to their port, Melanie led the ladies to the drawing room, preparing herself for what lay ahead.

Mrs Dudley and Mrs Behenna settled themselves on a pretty gilt and brocade sofa. Mrs Martin went to an armchair near the marble fireplace and waved Melanie to one opposite.

'Well, Miss Tregarron,' she folded her hands. 'How do you like Falmouth?'

'I have seen little of the town as yet.' Only she knew how tightly she was gripping her left thumb with her right hand. 'But I love to watch the river. There is always so much happening.'

'Is it very different from where you were before?' Mrs Dudley asked.

'Indeed it is, ma'am. London has many advantages, but I find I like Cornwall better.'

'So what brought you here?' Mrs Martin pressed.

Tempted to say *the mail coach* Melanie resisted.

83

She had expected this. The sudden appearance in their host's house of a young woman – a *daughter* – few knew existed was bound to arouse curiosity.

There had been no opportunity to ask her father how she should respond to the inevitable questions. Nor, faced with his aloofness, had she been willing to betray her uncertainty to Richard Vaughan. So yet again she was on her own.

The truth would be best – though not all of it. There were certain things she was under no obligation to tell, nor these people to know.

'After completing my education I went to France to visit relatives then returned to the seminary for a short time to teach art. The post was a temporary one and when it ended my father welcomed me here to Gillyvean.'

'You *taught* art?' Mrs Dudley's face was alight with interest. 'Well, I never! Good at it, are you?'

Gratefully, Melanie reached for her pad and flipped it open. 'Perhaps you should be the judge of that, Mrs Dudley.' She chose a soft pencil from the tin then took a chair opposite. 'May I?'

'You're going to draw me?' Mrs Dudley pressed a hand to her pillowy bosom.

'Just a sketch.' The pencil flew in quick sure strokes across the thick paper. After a few moments Melanie turned the pad. 'There.'

'Goodness gracious!' Mrs Dudley gasped.

Mrs Behenna leaned forward for a better view. 'That's you to the life, Frances. I can't believe it. Just a few lines and a bit of shading and she's caught you perfectly.' She beamed at Melanie. 'You have a gift all right, Miss Tregarron, no doubt of that.'

'May I see?' Mrs Martin's tone was more demand than request.

Turning the pad, Melanie watched a frown deepen the crease between Mrs Martin's brows. She braced herself.

'I'm astonished.'

How was she supposed to reply to that? Mrs Martin didn't give her a chance.

'Is this all you do, Miss Tregarron? Pencil sketches, I mean?'

'No, ma'am. Though I always begin with a pre-liminary drawing, maybe several, the portrait is completed in either pastels or oil paint depending on–'

'Are you accepting commissions?'

'Yes, ma'am,' Melanie said, managing to hide her shock.

'Would I be the first?'

'The first since my arrival here.' She decided not to say how many she had completed. Mrs Martin might consider that boastful and change her mind.

The thin mouth pursed. 'You may call on me the day after tomorrow and we will discuss a convenient time for sittings.'

The drawing room door opened and the men rejoined them. Mrs Dudley beckoned her husband to look at the sketch. Melanie accepted his congratulations with a modest smile, but inside she was bubbling with pleasure and relief.

As the sketch was passed to Mr Behenna, Richard, moving between the sofa and the window, glanced at it. He looked up, caught Melanie's gaze and without any change of expression briefly tilted his head.

It was acknowledgement of a sort, though of what? Her talent? Her handling of a difficult situation? But as he hadn't been present he couldn't know she had only made the sketch in order to escape further interrogation.

Handing the pad back, Mr Behenna motioned Richard aside for a few private words.

'I have to say, Miss Tregarron, I'm impressed.'

She wrenched her attention back to Mr Dudley, 'You are very kind.'

'Not a bit of it. I'd be obliged if you would consider a proper portrait.'

'John!' Mrs Dudley's pleasure lit up her face.

'I should be delighted.'

'After mine is finished,' Mrs Martin announced firmly.

'Of course, ma'am.' That Mrs Martin should be her first sitter was a surprise. Now it appeared she had a second.

Her father caught her eye and winked, beaming broadly. For his sake she was glad the evening had gone well. A few moments later, Hitchens brought in trays of tea and coffee.

Filling cups and passing them round she was acutely aware of Richard Vaughan. As he stalked the edges of the room, attentive to the other guests she sensed him watching her. Yet whenever she looked up his gaze was always elsewhere. It was unsettling.

After the guests had departed in a flurry of farewells and a reminder from Mrs Martin, Melanie picked up her sketchpad and tin. 'Goodnight, Mr Vaughan.' He would find no fault with her manners.

'Goodnight, Miss Tregarron.' His bow was brief and formal.

'Goodnight, Papa.'

'A word before you retire, my dear. No, Richard.' Tregarron stopped him. 'Don't go. This concerns you as well.'

Catching Richard's glance, Melanie glimpsed surprise. He had no idea of what her father wanted either. That came as a relief. For despite her father's generosity and Mrs Berryman's kindness she still felt very much an outsider, a guest rather than family.

But it was early days. Having no experience of family life she needed to learn what was, and wasn't, expected. It would have helped had she been able to spend longer with her father. But as everyone kept reminding her, he was a busy man with many demands on his time.

She watched him pour a small measure of brandy into a cut crystal glass. Turning to face them he swirled the spirit and inhaled the vapours before raising the glass in salute.

'Well done, my dear.' He swallowed a mouthful. 'It was a most satisfactory evening.' Draining the glass he set it on the silver tray. 'I'm going away in the morning.'

He had only just come back. She had hoped he might want to spend time with her. He was her father yet they were virtual strangers.

Seeing Richard's jaw tighten, Melanie guessed this was what they had been talking about when she entered the drawing room at the start of the evening.

Though Richard's remoteness made him impossible to know and hard to like, she felt a moment's sympathy. Her father's frequent absences must make management of his affairs difficult.

'Before you ask, Melanie, I don't know how long for. It all depends.' He didn't say on what. But Melanie's mind flew back to the whispers she had overheard. Had Laura been replaced? 'Richard, while I'm away you are to accompany Melanie whenever she leaves Gillyvean.'

Richard's horrified expression, the first emotion he had betrayed, mirrored her own. They spoke in the same instant.

'Sir, I am already committed–'

'Mr Vaughan need not trouble himself–'

'Quiet, both of you!' Sudden temper flushed Tregarron's face dark red. 'It is not a request.' Then in a lightning change of mood he smiled. 'Melanie, you will oblige me by arranging your visits for the afternoon. Richard, I am sure that with your organisational skills you will be able to set aside a couple of hours twice a week. Consider it an opportunity to develop your acquaintance. Now I bid you both a very good night.'

'Sir–'

Tregarron waved him to silence. 'Whatever it is, Richard, deal with it. You have my complete confidence.'

With a smile and nod to them both he strode to the door. 'Yes indeed, a most satisfactory evening.'

As it closed behind him Melanie turned, hot with mortification. *Her father preferred other company to hers.* But she was not a child needing a minder. Nor had she any wish to be with someone who clearly did not want to be with her. Though the situation was not of her making he deserved an apology. 'Mr Vaughan–' She got no further.

'Believe me, Miss Tregarron, the situation irks me as much as it does you. It is a task for which I have little time and less inclination. Unfortunately we will have to live with it.'

Stung by the slap of this additional rejection, all thoughts of apology banished, Melanie lifted her chin. 'Charmingly put, Mr Vaughan. Goodnight.'

As she ran upstairs to her bedroom pulling the ribbon from her neck she remembered Ellen would be waiting and pushed her hurt and anger to a corner of her mind.

'Was it a lovely evening, miss?' Ellen asked eagerly.

Melanie tossed sketchpad, pencil tin, and ribbon onto the bed. 'It was ... interesting.' Though it took effort she smiled. 'You were right about the side curls. I noticed Mrs Martin and Mrs Dudley taking particular interest.'

'They did?' Ellen grinned with delight as she helped Melanie out of her dress and into her nightgown. 'Mr Tregarron must be some proud. You looking so pretty, and so clever with your drawing and all.'

'Really, Ellen, what can I say to that? If I agree with you I shall sound much too full of myself. Yet if I don't–'

'That'd be daft,' Ellen retorted, then clapped her hand over her mouth. 'Oh, I beg your pardon, miss. But not one of they ladies could hold a candle to you tonight. Looked 'andsome, you did.'

'Thank you, Ellen.' Smiling at the maid's reflection in the mirror, Melanie seated herself on the velvet stool.

She *had* looked well. Yet Richard Vaughan, courteous to all the other guests, had barely spoken to her all evening. She understood that etiquette demanded he attend to Mrs Behenna and Mr Dudley seated either side of him at table. Yet afterwards in the drawing room he had mingled and conversed, but always at a distance from her.

Not that she particularly wished to talk to him. It was clear he disapproved of her. Which, if she let it, would be really annoying. Why did he always seem to be frowning when she caught his glance? Why was he watching her at all? She knew how to behave, knew her conduct had been everything her father might have wished.

Glad the evening had been a success, she was also relieved it was over. She had been dressed up, shown off, and expected to perform.

She owed her father so much and wanted him to feel proud that she was his daughter. But he had shown only passing interest in her sketch. Now he was going away again. She had had such hopes. Surely by now she should know better?

'You all right, miss?'

Melanie blinked prickling eyes as Ellen unpinned her hair, loosened the braid with her fingers then brushed out the long wavy tresses.

'Yes, I'm fine. Just tired. You go to bed now, Ellen. I can do the rest.'

'You sure, miss? It's no trouble.'

'I'm sure.' She smiled at the maid through the mirror. 'It's been a long day for both of us.'

''Night then, miss.' Taking one of the candles,

Ellen went out, closing the door softly.

Relieved to be alone, Melanie drew her hair over one shoulder and wove it into a loose plait. Blowing out the remaining candles she drew back the curtains, opened the window, and breathed in cool night air fragrant with honeysuckle and roses. The sky, midnight blue overhead paling to turquoise in the west, was cloudless and glittered with stars.

She glimpsed movement; saw a man walking slowly across the grass. Though his back was toward her she knew it was Richard Vaughan. About to close the window she paused. Had he taken *any* pleasure in the evening? If so, her father's announcement had banished it. Now, like her, he sought solitude.

Quietly she stepped back. Leaving the window open she closed the curtains and got into bed. But sleep was a long time coming.

Chapter Ten

The morning had started well enough. But after lighting the range, drawing water, setting the kettle to boil and feeding the hens, Bronnen had returned to the kitchen to find her mother leaning against the sink. Her eyes were closed and one hand was pressed to her chest.

'Ma? What's wrong?'

'My head's going round something awful. I can't get my breath, Bron.'

This was the third such attack in as many days.

Bronnen put her arm around her mother's thin shoulders and guided her towards the stairs. 'Best if you lie down until it passes.'

'I can't.' Sarah tried to resist. 'There's too much to do.'

'It will all get done,' Bronnen promised. 'I'll give Father and Adam their breakfast then bring you a cup of tea.'

'I'm sorry, bird. Just give me a few minutes. I'll be all right then.'

As Sarah lay down, Bronnen took off her shoes. 'Got any pain, have you?'

'No. 'Tis just this awful dizziness.'

Bronnen pulled the coverlet up. As she turned away, Sarah grabbed her hand and squeezed it.

'I love you, Bron. Please don't think bad of me.' Tears spilled down her cheeks.

'Don't be daft, Ma,' Bronnen scolded gently. 'You can't help feeling poorly.'

Sinking back on the pillows, Sarah pressed shaking fingers to her mouth as if to stop herself saying more.

Torn between wanting to stay and comfort, and awareness of the time, Bronnen bent and kissed her mother's wet cheek. 'I'll be back as soon as I can.'

Closing the bedroom door she flew downstairs to the kitchen. Taking two plates from the dresser she put them in the warming rack over the range, lifted the lid off the hot plate to expose the fire beneath, and pulled the big frying pan over the flames. Carving slices off the ham in the larder she laid them in the frying pan where they sizzled, and broke eggs into a pan of simmering water. She cut and buttered thick slices of bread and poured tankards of ale.

As her father and brother stomped in from the yard, their boots loud on the flag-stoned floor, and crossed to the sink to wash their hands, Bronnen slid fried ham and eggs onto the warmed plates and set them on either side of the scrubbed table, fetched cutlery from the dresser drawer, then filled the big kettle from the stone pitcher that stood beside the earthenware sink.

Hunger cramped her stomach. But she would have to eat later.

'Where is she?' her father demanded, bent over his plate as he shovelled food into his mouth.

Bronnen glanced round, but he didn't raise his head. He never met her gaze when he was sober. She put the lid on the kettle and pulled it over the fire, then turned back to the table and began slicing bread. 'Lying down. She's–'

'A bleddy waste of space.' Slamming the empty tankard down, Morley Jewell gave a mighty belch, pushed his chair back and headed for the back door. 'Move yourself, boy. We're burning daylight here.'

Quickly swallowing his last mouthful Adam stood up, darting a look towards the back door his father had left open as he stamped away across the cobbled yard. 'Can you do the brew on your own?'

Making a sandwich to take with her to the brewhouse, Bronnen glanced up. 'I'll have to.'

'Look, if you can wait until–'

'He won't let you finish early to help me. It's all right, Adam. I'll set everything up before I start. Really, I'll be fine.' If she said it often enough she

93

might convince herself.

'What's Ma so worried about?'

'Aside from Father coming home drunk several nights a week, or disappearing off to God knows where?'

'I don't like it no more than you do. But I can't stop him.'

Bronnen's anger evaporated as quickly as it had flared. She touched her brother's arm. 'I know you can't. But Ma's lost so much weight this past week a breath of wind could knock her over.' *Never mind Father's fist.* The words hung unspoken between them.

'Adam!' their father roared from the yard.

'I got to go.' Bolting from the kitchen he slammed the door behind him. Dependent on their father for his job, Adam preferred to keep his head down. If it didn't concern him he would rather not know.

Bronnen made a pot of tea. Leaving it to infuse, she wrapped her sandwiches and a slice of cake in a cloth, then spread the remaining slice of buttered bread with jam and ate it. Doing the brew on her own would be difficult. But at least she no longer had to worry about the pump.

A sudden vivid image of Santo Innis made her breath catch. She poured the tea and carried it upstairs. Setting cup and saucer on the bedside table she knelt on the rag rug beside the bed. As she stroked her mother's forehead Bronnen realised how much white there was in the fine fair hair.

'Ma? Would you like me to fetch the doctor?'

'No, bird. We haven't got money for that. I'll be all right in a minute. Go on, now. You got more

94

'n enough to do.'

Bronnen was out in the passage when she heard a muffled sob. She hesitated, wanting to go back, to plead with her mother to tell her what was wrong. But imagining her father's rage if the small beer wasn't ready in time for harvest forced her down the stairs.

Santo glanced up from his breakfast as his uncle entered the dining room. George Curnock's usually florid complexion was the colour of ash.

'Are you all right?'

'Why wouldn't I be?' George demanded. As he filled his cup from the silver coffee pot, a sudden tremor slopped hot coffee into the saucer. 'Damnation!'

'That was quite a fall you took.'

'I've had worse. Stop fussing. I'm fine.'

Santo shrugged, and went back to his breakfast, trying to think of a reason to call at Gillyvean brewhouse.

Setting down a plate of crisply fried bacon in front of his uncle, Mrs Eathorne bustled out. George bent forward to sniff it. Catching Santo's astonished glance, he sat up and shook out his napkin.

'What was Anstey's wagon doing in the brewery yard this morning?'

'Delivering a milling machine Mr Vaughan bid for on my behalf.'

Seated across from Santo, Treeve Curnock snorted. 'You'll have got a good price then. No one would want to upset Mr Tregarron's heir.'

Santo eyed his cousin.

'What?' Treeve demanded.

'I've been away nearly seven years and you haven't changed at all.'

'Don't be ridiculous,' Treeve sneered. 'I'm a successful businessman.' He ran a finger and thumb down his lapel to draw attention to the quality of the cloth. Even as a child Treeve had been fussy about his appearance.

His brown hair, parted on one side, was brushed forward in the latest style. His blue double-breasted coat and grey trousers were tailored to add width to narrow shoulders and disguise a thickening waist. A black cravat was knotted over an upstanding collar that framed his fleshy face. Arrogance and his habit of nursing grudges, real or imagined, habitually pursed his lips. Yet he could be charming when he chose. But not, it seemed, to his cousin.

'You're still chasing rainbows.' Treeve looked down his nose at Santo. 'As for that coat, I'd be ashamed to go out looking so shabby. How you can expect anyone to take you seriously?'

'Mr Vaughan don't have any trouble,' Santo replied.

Treeve snorted, his expression sour with bitterness and envy. 'He certainly fell on his feet. Heir to Gillyvean and all Tregarron's business interests.'

Santo let it pass. Treeve believed anyone else's good fortune somehow diminished his own. Arguing was pointless. His cousin resented him and had done so since they were children, never allowing him to forget he was the poor relation, taken in out of charity.

'They've gone to try and get money out of her,'

eleven-year-old Treeve had whispered, smirking, the morning Santo's parents had left him with his Aunt Hannah and Uncle George while they went to Truro to visit an elderly relative. 'I heard Father telling Mother. He says you're poor as church mice.'

Embarrassed, knowing it was true, gut-wrenched by his mother's tears and fearful of his father's drunken rants, Santo had lashed out with both fists. He hadn't cared that Treeve was a head taller and two years older. Wiping off that knowing smirk was all that mattered.

After Treeve ran out crying, Santo had waited, miserable and defiant, expecting to be summoned for a thrashing.

His Aunt Hannah had found him. Ashamed of being poor, he wouldn't say what had caused the fight. To his surprise and relief she hadn't pressed. Perhaps Treeve had told her. She had taken him to her small sitting room, sent for a basin and towel, and washed the blood from his throbbing face. Curled up on her sofa he had fallen asleep until roused by a slammed door and urgent voices.

As he sat up his Aunt Hannah had come in. He had seen through her gentle smile to the shock beneath and known instantly something terrible had happened. Sitting beside him she'd said he wouldn't be returning home. Instead he would stay with them.

He had pushed her away, shouting that he didn't want to. Then she told him his parents were dead, killed when the post-chaise in which they were travelling lost a wheel and overturned. As she held him his eyes had burned and his throat ached so badly he couldn't swallow. But he hadn't cried. Not then, nor three years later when she died of influenza and his life changed once more.

'Bronnen Jewell should be in any day to buy malt for Gillyvean,' George Curnock addressed his son.

Bronnen. Santo kept his head bent. *It suited her.*

'She came last week. On the one day I was out.' Treeve's frown and peeved tone revealed his annoyance.

'What did she order?' George asked.

'Twelve bushels of pale, four of amber.'

'The girl knows what she's doing. Got a good head on her shoulders. You could do a lot worse.'

'Yes, thank you, Father. I'm perfectly capable of choosing my own wife. In fact she will suit me very well.'

Santo pressed the white napkin to his mouth, hiding the lower half of his face. Treeve marry Bronnen Jewell? Over his dead body.

'So what are you waiting for?' George demanded. 'You're past thirty now. Leave it much longer and people will start wondering.' He sniffed again.

'Why do you keep doing that? Are you getting a cold?'

'I'm perfectly all right. Bit of a headache, that's all.'

Daily tasting and testing meant that brewers drank copious amounts every day. Shoving his chair back, George stood up, swayed, and clutched the edge of the table. 'I'll be in the brewery all night.'

'Surely that's a job for one of your assistants?'

Treeve demanded.

'I don't trust them.'

'Now you're being ridiculous,' Treeve said. 'You need to have a successor ready to take over when you retire.'

George glowered at him. 'If either of you had shown the loyalty I had a right to expect–'

'You chose to be a brewer,' Treeve said. 'I didn't. I've built a good business and my malt is renowned for its quality. Yet you don't use it because your brother says it's too expensive. So don't you lecture me about loyalty.'

'If you had shown proper respect and accepted your responsibilities,' George roared, 'we wouldn't be having this conversation. Curnock's is a family business. By rights it should remain in the family. If your mother had done her duty and given me more sons–' He shook his head. 'It would take years to pass on all I've learned.'

'Then isn't it time you started?' Santo said mildly, unmoved by his uncle's explosive temper.

'Say I train someone else,' George argued. 'What's to stop him leaving to join a rival brewery or set up on his own?'

Santo bit back impatience. 'If he knew you were training him to take your place, why would he want to?'

George shook his head. 'I won't take the chance.'

'You'll have to retire sometime,' Treeve pointed out.

'Who says so?' Belligerence turned George's face dusky purple. 'I'm strong as an ox. And I'm the best brewer in this town. Ask anyone. I started at Curnock's when I was ten years old.

Your grandfather put me to work weighing hops and grinding malt. Retire? Ha!'

'Hell will freeze first,' Treeve muttered.

Santo stood up. 'I'll be–'

'You'll be in the brewery,' George glared. 'The second copper needs scrubbing out. Don't argue, not unless you want to start looking for another workshop.' Wincing, he stormed out, rubbing his temple.

'Oh dear,' Treeve's eyes gleamed with spite-filled amusement. 'Here you are doing labouring jobs while all your money's tied up in engines nobody wants.'

Tempted to tell him of the engine he had installed at Gillyvean, Santo decided he couldn't be bothered. Dropping the crumpled napkin onto the table, he walked out.

Mrs Eathorne passed him in the hall. 'Here, what's up with mister this morning?'

'A headache,' Santo replied.

'Look sick as a shag, he do,' she said. 'I reckon that fall shook him up more than he've let on. He should've stopped in bed today. He isn't as young as he used to be.' Concern crept over her face. 'He's working daft hours over the brewery. And what with all the drinking,' she shook her head. 'I know 'tis part of the job, but he don't look right to me. Not at all he don't.'

Chapter Eleven

Bronnen tilted the nearest cask onto its lower rim and spun it out onto the yard with an ease born of long practice.

'Goodness.' A feminine voice made her jump and the cask thumped down onto its base. 'Oh, I'm sorry. It's just that you make it look so easy yet I'm sure it can't be.'

Glancing at Melanie Tregarron – for it could be no one else – Bronnen was suddenly and acutely aware of her faded dress, coarse apron and no doubt shiny face. She pushed a lock of hair back from her damp forehead.

A few days ago Adam had come in for his dinner in a rare state of excitement and announced that Mr Tregarron's natural daughter had arrived without warning from London.

'It look like she'll be living at Gillyvean,' Adam said.

'That will give Alderman Martin's wife something to talk about,' Bronnen had murmured to her mother.

'But that isn't half of it,' Adam continued. 'Bridget says Miss Tregarron do paint likenesses of people. A proper artist she is.'

After overcoming his shyness and speaking to Mrs Geach's parlour maid at the Summer Fete then being permitted to escort her round the stalls, *Bridget says* had become a familiar phrase.

'Stir up the old biddies good and proper that will.' His weather-beaten features had softened into a rare and mischievous grin.

Bronnen bobbed a quick curtsey. 'Miss Tregarron.'

Beneath a wide-brimmed hat trimmed with bows of green ribbon, her chestnut hair was arranged in ringlets that fell from a centre parting to a narrow but surprisingly firm jaw. Her full-skirted gown of primrose yellow muslin was belted with a green satin sash. It had a shawl collar over a ruff of pleated white gauze and full sleeves that narrowed from elbow to wrist. But instead of gloves or a purse she carried a large sketchpad and long hinged tin.

'I see you know who I am.' Melanie's smile was brief. 'May I ask who you are?'

'Bronnen Jewell, from Gillyvean farm.'

'What are you doing?' Melanie indicated the barrels.

'Getting ready for tomorrow.'

'What's happening tomorrow?'

'We're brewing small beer ready for harvest.'

'We?'

'My mother and me.'

'Why have you brought the barrel out?'

'To clean it.'

'May I watch? I promise I won't get in your way.'

'If you want,' Bronnen said uncertainly. 'But it's not very interesting.'

'On the contrary, I never knew there were such people as female brewers. So you're wrong, Miss Jewell. It is very interesting. Would you mind if I draw?'

Without waiting for an answer she flipped open the cover of her sketchpad. As she took a pencil out of the hinged tin, Bronnen noticed her hands. Instead of the soft pale skin, long fingers and almond-shaped nails of a lady, Melanie Tregarron's hands looked capable rather than elegant. The nails were bitten, the skin around them scabbed or raw pink.

Not wishing to be caught staring, Bronnen looked away quickly. She rolled the cask towards the drain in the yard then went back for another. Melanie Tregarron's gnawed fingers betrayed anxiety. Yet her new gown and slippers suggested Mr Tregarron was an indulgent father. She was living in a lovely house looked after by Mrs Berryman and Ellen, with nothing to do but amuse herself. What could she have to worry about?

'Forgive me if this is a foolish question, but why are you brewing more beer if there is still some left in the barrels?' Melanie asked, glancing between Bronnen and the paper as she made quick strokes with her pencil.

'If you empty them right out they go foul. Leaving a gallon of beer and sediment left in the bottom keeps them sweet.'

Spinning out the final cask, Bronnen tipped it onto its side and pulled out the bung, then did the same with the others. Muddy-looking liquid poured out and ran down the drain, leaving a pungent yeasty smell in the air. Straightening up she turned away.

'Where are you going?' Melanie asked.

'Into the brewhouse. I got to see if the water in the copper is boiling.'

Melanie closed the pad. 'May I come? I've never seen a brewhouse.' She pointed to the engine. 'What's that?'

'It's a hot-air engine. It works the pump.'

'It looks horribly complicated.'

'No, it's really simple once you get used to it.' Recalling her reaction the first time she saw the pump triggered vivid memories of Santo and her heart skipped a beat. She had hoped he might come back to make sure the engine was working as it should. What was he doing right now? Did he ever think about her?

'Miss Jewell?'

Dragging her attention back, Bronnen saw Melanie Tregarron's half-smile. 'I'm sorry, I was just–' She shook her head. 'I used to have to pump all the water up to the cistern by hand.'

'That must have taken hours.'

'It did. And my shoulders ached for days after. The engine have saved all that.' She hesitated, then curiosity overrode shyness and she gestured at the sketchpad. 'Can I see?'

Melanie flipped back the cover and turned the pad.

'Oh!' Taken aback, Bronnen gazed at the page covered in rough sketches that caught her in mid-movement: the curve of her back, her tilted head and quick smile.

'It's– I've never–' Bronnen's awe left her lost for words. 'How do you do that?'

Melanie shrugged. 'I've always done it. Drawing lets me shut out the world.' She smiled, making light of her words. 'Can we go into the brew-house?'

Putting a bucket under the copper, Bronnen turned on the tap. While waiting for the bucket to fill she answered Melanie's questions about the brewing process. Hearing footsteps on the yard outside her heart quickened and she looked up, surprised at the depth of her disappointment as a tall figure immaculate in a dark full-skirted frock-coat and pale grey trousers appeared in the doorway.

'Good afternoon, Mr Vaughan.' Bobbing a curtsey she fought panic. What if he asked where her mother was?

'Good day to you, Miss Jewell, I just wanted to – Miss Tregarron,' he sounded startled. 'I didn't expect to find you here.'

Melanie lifted one shoulder. 'Why not? With my father away and you so busy I am enjoying finding my way around the estate. This last hour has been fascinating.' She turned to Bronnen. 'I will not trespass on your time any longer, Miss Jewell. I'm very pleased to have met you. I had no idea about–' her gesture encompassed the brewhouse, 'all this. I have learned a lot.'

'You're welcome. Miss Tregarron,' Bronnen added quickly. 'If you don't want that page I'd dearly love to have it.'

Tearing out the sheet, Melanie gave it to her. 'It was my pleasure.' Her smile faded and she dipped her head politely. 'Mr Vaughan.' Clasping the sketchpad and tin close, she left.

Richard Vaughan cleared his throat. 'As I was saying, I just came to see how you are getting on with the new pump.' He glanced towards the yard.

Bronnen wiped her hands on her apron. ''Tis a

proper job, sir. First time I seen it I was in some kilter. But I wouldn't be without it now.'

'Excellent. Right. If there's nothing else?'

'No, sir, thank you.' She bobbed a curtsey. *He hadn't even noticed that her mother wasn't there.*

With an abrupt nod he walked quickly away.

Bronnen wondered about Miss Tregarron and Mr Vaughan. Before he came Miss Tregarron had been really interested, asking questions, nodding to show she understood. But as soon as he arrived, she changed.

Mr Vaughan made a point of stopping by at least once during a brew, to make sure all was well. He was always pleasant but businesslike. This was the first time she had ever seen him distracted. Watching him and Miss Tregarron her skin had prickled, the way it did just before a storm.

Her thoughts returned to Santo Innis. As she continued the backbreaking work of emptying then scalding the casks she relived each moment of their meeting, and found herself smiling.

Chapter Twelve

At six the following evening Bronnen glanced from the clock on the wall to the fermentation vessel where the froth was starting to resemble small cauliflowers. Arriving before sunrise she had worked for fourteen hours, taking short breaks when the brew allowed.

Throughout the long day her mood had swung

106

from anxiety to relief as each stage was completed. Though it had been frantic at times, the copper hadn't overheated, the mash hadn't dried out, the pump had worked, and she had remembered to feed the fire beneath the engine.

Running off the wort, she caught the first cloudy bucketfuls and returned them to the mash tub, repeating the process until it ran clear. Cloudy beer reflected badly on the brewer. But small beer was drunk only a few weeks after being brewed, so it was never long enough in the barrel to clear naturally.

As the wort foamed white and frothy into the underbuck, she felt a surge of pride at having perfectly judged the timing and temperature.

Using a hand pump to return the mash to the copper she had tossed in hops tied in a canvas bag then stoked the fire to bring the wort to the boil. After boiling, cooling, and running the mixed worts from both mashes into the fermentation vessel, she added the yeast.

As afternoon turned to evening she emptied the hop bag and scraped the spent grains from the mash tub into a sack for feeding to the cows.

Pressing her hands to the small of her back she released a long weary breath.

She would be in the brewhouse all night, skimming the frothy head off the fermenting beer every few hours. But for the moment she was free. She could run home, pack up some food for supper and collect a blanket.

The brewhouse windows had angled wooden slats instead of glass and a slatted lantern in the roof. These allowed heat to escape, crucial during the cooling and fermentation processes.

But after sundown, with the fire under the copper raked out to prevent fermentation running wild and turning the beer sour, the draughty brewhouse could soon grow chilly.

Removing her apron, Bronnen picked up her basket. Leaving the brewhouse door open she crossed the yard and walked quickly out on to the back drive. After the heat and heady aromas of yeast, hops and boiling wort, the air felt blissfully fresh on her face. She drew it deep into her lungs, inhaling the scents of cut grass, damp earth, and the sweet fragrance of roses and honeysuckle.

But as she turned on to the cart track that led to the farmhouse her pleasure gave way to apprehension. What would she find? At the back door she hesitated, bracing herself before lifting the latch.

The kitchen was empty. Her mother's wicker basket stood on the table with a folded blanket beside it. Lifting the covering cloth she saw sandwiches wrapped in butter muslin, a dish containing two slices of rhubarb tart, and a square of *hevva* cake stuffed with currants and peel.

Though she was anxious to find out why her mother was so fretful she knew it would be kinder to let her sleep. In any case she dared not stay more than a few minutes. It was not only her father's wrath she dreaded should the brew go bad. She would have let down Mr Tregarron and Mr Vaughan.

All day, hurrying from one task to the next, she had worried. What if Mr Vaughan had come back? He would have wanted to know why she was alone. What could she have said? That her mother could barely walk for the pain of bruises inflicted by her father? It was too shaming.

She couldn't even comfort her mother properly until she knew what was wrong. Though her father's brutality was reason enough, she sensed there was something more.

At dawn that morning, lighting the kindling on the shovel before pushing it into the firebox, she had gazed at the engine in wary unease. But loosening the belt after a long demanding day she had given it a grateful pat.

Opening the larder door she reached for a bottle of elderflower cordial and sighed. That was the trouble with telling people you could manage fine on your own. They let you. Especially if they were as busy as Santo Innis surely was.

The engine had done exactly what he promised, saving her time and backbreaking effort. That was why she kept thinking about him, she told herself. And knew she lied.

Life with her father had made her wary of men. To be so powerfully attracted to one she had only just met was deeply unsettling.

Reliving every moment of their encounter, she saw him clearly in her mind. She had thought him confident, and concerning his engine he was. But when their eyes met, the contact as intimate as a caress, she had quickly looked away, suddenly shy, only to be drawn back moments later, impelled by some invisible force to seek his gaze, *and find it waiting*. The nervous intensity in his eyes had stopped her breath. Then he too had looked away.

Shifting the contents of the basket to make room for the bottle she froze at the sound of unsteady footsteps outside. A loud thump against the back door was followed by a muttered curse.

Instinct told her to run, hide. She quashed a brief spurt of fear. She was a grown woman, not a child.

The door burst open and her father staggered in. Seeing her he blinked and his expression darkened. She thought of her mother, wanted to ask him to be quiet, but held back words that would only increase his anger.

'Don't you look at me like that!' he snarled. 'A bleddy cuckoo you are. Always have been.' He flopped down in the wooden armchair beside the range. 'Fetch me a jug of ale.'

She moistened dry lips. 'Shall I make a pot of tea, Pa?'

'I don't want tea. I want ale, not bleddy cat's piss. And put some brandy in it.' He glared up at her, his face contorted and vicious. 'You think you're so special.'

Bronnen flinched at the venom in his voice and an accusation she didn't understand. Suddenly he lurched up from the chair.

'Time you was put down where you belong.' He drew back his arm but lost his balance. Grabbing at the mantelshelf he caught the narrow cloth runner instead. Her mother's small collection of china ornaments fell onto the tiled hearth and smashed.

'Now look what you made me do!'

Feeling sick, her heart thudding against her ribs, Bronnen crouched and began to gather up the broken shards. Without warning her father kicked out. His boot caught her hip, knocking her off balance. With a gasp she fell backwards, banging her head against the table leg

The back door opened and Adam came in. 'I've left Captain in the stable–' He stopped, his gaze darting between Bronnen and his father.

'Clumsy maid tripped over the fender,' Morley sneered, and slumped back into his chair.

'You all right, Bron?' Adam started towards her.

'Leave her be,' Morley ordered. 'Nothing wrong with her.'

Bronnen scrambled to her feet. She was more shaken than hurt. Though in the past he had threatened, never had he actually struck her.

'Bron?'

Hearing the anxiety in her brother's voice she knew some of it was for her. But what Adam really wanted was to pretend nothing had happened. It was his way of handling a situation he had no power to change. Half a head taller and physically strong, he was still no match for his father's bull-like aggression.

Pride held her voice steady, and sudden fierce anger kept her smarting eyes dry. 'I'm all right, Adam.' Averting her gaze from his shame-faced relief she bent and swept the broken china into the dustpan and emptied it into the bucket under the stone sink.

After unlacing and pulling off his own boots, Adam removed his father's. Though her brother was as blinkered as the team of horses he drove, Bronnen could not find it in her heart to blame him.

'What are you waiting for, girl?' her father roared. 'Fetch that ale like I told you.'

Taking a china tankard from the dresser she

crossed to the larder, refusing, despite the soreness, to limp. She would not give him the satisfaction.

Shielded from view by the door she closed her eyes and swallowed hard. Then crouching to reach the keg, she turned on the tap, filled the tankard and added a dash of cognac.

'No more after that, Father,' Adam warned. 'I aren't risking my back hauling you up over stairs.'

'Who asked you to? Where's your mother?'

'She wasn't feeling well,' Bronnen said, emerging from the larder.

'I s'pose that means she've gone up bed. Well, good riddance.'

Knowing better than to say anything, Bronnen placed the tankard within his reach, picked up the basket and blanket and made for the door.

'Where d'you think you're going?' Morley demanded.

'Back to Gillyvean. The beer will need skimming soon. I only came home to pick up some food.'

'Want me to walk with you?' Adam offered with a wary glance at his father whose mouth gaped in a yawn.

'She don't need you holding her hand.' Morley slammed the tankard down. Ale slopped onto the table. 'I been out working all day and I want my supper.' He belched loudly.

'There's a plate of mutton sandwiches, a rhubarb pie, and a dish of cream in the larder,' Bronnen told her brother. As he turned towards the larder she slipped out, thankful to escape if only for one night.

112

Chapter Thirteen

After one sandwich, a slice of rhubarb tart, and small piece of the cake, Bronnen quenched her thirst with cordial diluted in cold water.

Re-wrapping the rest of the food she tucked her basket under the bench then carried a stave-built iron-hooped bucket over to the open doorway and turned it upside down. Collecting the brewhouse journal and pencil from the bench she perched on the upturned bucket.

The sun had sunk below the surrounding roofs leaving a sky of apricot and rose paling to dusky lilac, and half the yard in deep shadow.

Opening the journal she rested it on her knees and after writing the date and heading *Small Beer*, she listed the measures of malt, hops and yeast she had used and the timing of each stage. She could refer back to the detailed account if the brew was particularly good, or if something went wrong.

The entry completed she rose, picked up the bucket, and went back into the brewhouse, dropping the journal on the chair. She started towards the fermenting vessel, and stiffened into immobility at the sound of approaching footsteps. Then reason overcame reaction. Her father never came to the brewhouse. Besides, given the state he was in he wouldn't leave the house tonight. Surely it couldn't be Mr Vaughan? But if it was, she hoped he would assume she and her mother were taking turns to watch the brew.

As she turned towards the door her heart jumped.

'Evening, Miss Jewell.'

'Mr Innis.' Now her pulse raced for a very different reason. 'What are you doing here?' The instant the words were out she wished she could call them back. 'I – I didn't mean – it's – I wasn't expecting–' aware she was babbling she caught her bottom lip between her teeth and bit hard.

'Not interrupting you, am I?'

'No.' She swallowed. 'No.'

Stepping inside he half-turned so the dwindling light fell on her face. 'I – er – you got on all right with the engine?'

She nodded. 'Yes. I didn't have a minute's bother. Well, I did, but it was my fault,' she added quickly as concern drew his brows together. 'I was busy and the fire nearly went out. But soon as I got 'n going again the engine worked and so did the pump.' She saw him look round.

'Mother not with you?'

'She's ill. I wouldn't let her come. It don't take both of us to do the skimming.'

'That why you were so busy? You were here by yourself?'

After a brief hesitation she nodded. 'Please don't tell–'

'None of my business.' He gestured towards the dense frothy head on the fermenting beer. 'You did all this on your own? I call that a proper job.'

Her heart lifted at the compliment. She tucked it away, a small treasure to be examined later when she was alone, and shrugged shyly. 'If you

114

could have seen me this morning, running back and forth–'

'I wish–' he began softly then stopped, clearing his throat. 'I've just been up with Mr Vaughan. He's going to write to Mr Rowse at the quarry. Invite him to come and see the engine working.' Holding his hat in front of him he was turning it round and round by the brim.

'I thought I'd stop by and let you know, seeing it was your idea. Truth is,' she heard his throat click as he swallowed. 'I wanted to see you again.'

'Oh.' Suddenly self-conscious about her appearance after the long demanding day, she tucked a stray curl behind her ear.

'You don't mind?'

She felt a trembling inside. 'No.'

'Is it all right if I stay a while?'

She was glad the gathering dusk hid her fiery blush. Uncertain, wanting, fearful, she blurted, 'Why?'

'I want – I'd like – to know you better.' He waited. 'If you don't mind.' She could feel his gaze. 'Would you rather I went?'

Feeling as if she was standing on a cliff edge unable to see how deep the drop was, she took a deep breath and jumped. 'No.'

In the gloom his teeth flashed in a quick grin that softened the harsh planes of his face. 'I'm some glad of that.'

This morning, seeing him focused and sombre she had guessed him to be in his thirties. But that smile told her she had over-estimated. Yet she sensed he didn't smile often.

She smoothed the front of dress. 'It's just–'

115

'The minute you want me to go, you just say. All right?'

She nodded. Placing the journal under the chair she sat down and folded her hands in her lap. He dropped his hat on the bench and sat beside it, half-facing her, his hands loosely clasped between his parted knees.

Bronnen moistened her lips with the tip of her tongue. 'You said you haven't long been back in Cornwall?'

'That's right. I was four years in South Wales at an engineering company Mr Tregarron put money in. From there I went to Hall's Engineering Works in Dartford for three years. They built the engine in the steam packet *Mercury*. She's being used to test a new boiler. Next week I'll be aboard her for a few days.'

'Did you always want to be an engineer?'

'Yes. But my uncle wanted me to be a brewer.'

'Your uncle?'

'George Curnock.'

'No, I meant, what about your father? Surely he–?'

'My parents died when I was small.'

'Oh, I'm so sorry.'

His voice hardened. 'Father drank. It made him – when Mother tried to save me we both paid.' He had tipped his head so she couldn't see his face.

Bronnen touched his forearm in silent sympathy. Then, afraid she'd gone too far on such short acquaintance she started to withdraw her hand. But before she could, he covered it with his own. His callused palm was warm. He didn't look at her.

'My uncle and aunt took me in. But that didn't

116

sit well with my cousin Treeve. He couldn't abide having this cuckoo in their nest.'

Bronnen gasped.

Santo's head came up. 'What?'

'That's what my father called me.'

'He never did!' The shock in his voice was oddly comforting. 'Why?'

'I don't know. Most of the girls I grew up with are married. P'rhaps he thinks it's time I was. Even if there was someone, I can't leave my mother.'

His hand tightened on hers. 'Why's that then?'

'What you said about your father drinking? Mine does too.' *Tonight he had kicked her like a stray dog.*

'That's how your mother couldn't come today?'

What was she thinking? He was a stranger. Bronnen stood up quickly. 'I shouldn't have said anything.'

On his feet in an instant, a head taller, broad-shouldered and so close that she started to quiver, he caught her hand. 'Listen, what I just told you I've never told a living soul. What you've told me stays between us. Don't ask me to go yet.' His voice was low and hoarse as the words tumbled out. 'I know I said I would. And I will, if that's what you want. Is it?'

'No,' she whispered.

Lifting her hand he pressed her palm against his chest. She felt the strong steady beat of his heart. Hers was fluttering like a trapped bird.

She swallowed. 'There's a lantern–'

'I'll get 'n.'

Though the door remained open, mellow lantern-light and deep shadows made the brewhouse feel different, more intimate. Returning to the bench, Santo patted the space beside him. As Bronnen sat, he took her hand, linking his fingers with hers.

'I'm scared,' she whispered then looked away, feeling foolish. She wasn't a child.

Turning he gently lifted her chin. 'Of me?'

'No.' Though hesitant it was the truth.

'What then?'

Her shoulders moved in a helpless shrug. 'I don't – it's just – I've never–'

'Bron.'

She swallowed convulsively. 'What?'

He nudged her gently. 'Kick the stick away, my lovely. You're as tight as that there engine belt.'

Hearing the smile in his voice she felt tension slide off her shoulders.

'So, why have you got to stay here all night?'

'To watch the fermentation so it don't get too hot and run wild, or slow down and spoil the beer. And I got to skim the head every three or four hours.' She looked at him. 'If your uncle wanted you to be a brewer, how did you come to be an engineer?'

He looked down at their linked hands then lifted his gaze to hers. 'He told me he wouldn't pay for me to be apprenticed. So I took myself over to Perran Foundry.'

'But that's miles. How did you get there?'

'I walked part-way, hitched a ride on a farm cart from Penryn to St Gluvias Burnthouse, then walked the rest.'

'How old were you?'

'Twelve.'

'What happened when you got there?'

118

'The manager told me to p– go back home,' he amended quickly.

'But you didn't?'

He grinned. 'After my trouble getting there? No, I hid away. I was going to ask one of the foremen to speak for me. Then Mr Tregarron arrived. I ran out and begged him to take me on.'

'That must have took some nerve.'

'Not really. I wanted that apprenticeship so bad I'd have done anything. Mr Tregarron got no patience with time-wasters. Him and Mr Fox and Mr Martin the other directors have made Perran the biggest and best foundry this side of Cambome. The manager was going to throw me out. But Mr Tregarron stopped 'n and asked me why he should take me on.'

'What did you say?'

'That I wanted to be an engineer. I told him if he'd give me a chance I'd make him proud. When he laughed my heart near enough stopped.' Bronnen felt her own heart ache for the child he had been: an outsider, resented and bullied yet defiant, and determined not to give up his ambition.

'Then he told the manager to draw up the papers and he'd sign them. He gave me a start, and I'll always be grateful. But he's all for this high-pressure steam.'

'You aren't?'

Santo shook his head. 'In ships it's a killer.'

Bronnen stood up. Instantly Santo was on his feet. She touched his arm lightly. 'I have to skim the beer. The first head has a lot of bits in it and resin from the hops.'

He followed her to the fermentation vessel and

119

watched her work. 'You do that every three or four hours?' She nodded. 'Then what?'

'When the beer is cool enough I'll rack it off.' Setting down the skimmer she picked up the lantern, led him to an open doorway at the rear of the brewhouse and held it high so he could see casks lying on their sides on top of a timber framework with a gutter running down the middle. 'When it's piped into the barrels it carries on working and I collect the yeast to use in the next brew.'

Returning the lantern to the wooden staging by the mash tub she swallowed a sudden yawn and glanced away, hoping he hadn't noticed. But he had.

'I should go. This 'ave been a long day for you.'

She didn't want him to leave, but couldn't ask him to stay. He had his own work. She wiped her palms down her apron. 'I'm glad you stopped by.'

Taking her hand he raised it to his lips. In the soft light his gaze met hers, held it. 'Bronnen,' he murmured and drew her closer. She knew if she resisted he would release her. But she didn't, couldn't.

As he bent his head she raised her face to his. His mouth touched hers and her breath stopped. His kiss was gentle, light as a butterfly. It lingered. Her lips softened, parted under his, and she tasted his sweet warmth. She rested her hands on his chest, not to push him away but to steady herself.

His heart beat against her palm, hard and fast like her own. Drawing her head back she took a shaky breath. His hands slid from her shoulders to her hips as he rested his forehead against hers.

'I never – I didn't expect this, you.'

'Nor me.'

Tilting her chin, he gazed at her as if he was dying of thirst and she was cool water. 'Bronnen, I – please?'

'Yes,' she whispered.

His mouth covered hers in a kiss that deepened from tender to passionate. As her head swam she gave herself up to the delicious sensation of his mouth on hers and the tidal wave of yearning it unleashed. Her arms slipped around his neck as his enfolded her, drawing her close.

When, *too soon*, he lifted his mouth from hers they were both breathless. She swayed, disoriented.

'God, Bron, I'm–'

She pressed her fingers against his lips, shutting off the words. 'Don't,' her voice was unsteady, her heart still pounding. 'Don't say you're sorry. You aren't, are you?'

'No! Never! But I shouldn't have – I didn't expect–'

'Me neither.' Her laugh was shaky. 'We already said this once.'

Holding her hand between his he pressed his lips to her palm. 'I'll go.' His voice was rough, abrupt. 'I don't want to. But–'

'I know,' she said softly and stepped away from him.

'I will see you again.' His gaze was stormy and the fierceness of his expression betrayed an inner upheaval that matched her own. 'Soon?'

Looking up at him, awed by what had happened, she reached out and lightly touched his cheek with her fingertips. 'Yes. Soon.'

Hearing footsteps outside they both turned. Bronnen heard Santo's hissed intake of breath as his cousin appeared in the doorway.

'Good evening, Miss Jewell.' Treeve Curnock's smile made her think of snakes. 'I–'

'Got no business coming here this time of night.' Santo spoke quietly, but something in his voice sent a shiver down Bronnen's spine.

Treeve jumped, but quickly recovered. 'Then what are you doing here?'

Bronnen took a small step forward so she was between the two men. 'Mr Innis came by to make sure I'd had no problems with the new engine he fitted to the pump. Why did you come, Mr Curnock?' She was amazed that she could sound so calm while her heart thumped, and she could feel rage emanating from the man in front of her.

'I had business with your father. I have to say I was surprised to learn you were alone here at this time of night.'

Sensing Santo move behind her, Bronnen eased back so her shoulder touched his chest. There was trouble enough between the two cousins. She did not want to be the cause of more. 'Brewing don't keep daylight hours, Mr Curnock. Surely you know that?'

'Of course I do,' he snapped, then made a visible effort to control his temper.

Santo stepped round Bronnen. 'Goodnight, Miss Jewell. We'll leave you get on.' Grasping his cousin's elbow, Santo propelled him out into the yard.

Treeve was still protesting furiously as she closed the heavy door and shot the bolt across.

Chapter Fourteen

Melanie glanced sideways at Richard as he guided the pony trap at a trot past the Greenbank Hotel and along Penwerris. During the sitting, using only a soft pencil, she had focused on line and shape, shadow and highlight. Colours would come later. For an hour, immersed in doing what she loved, she had been able to forget everything else.

But now as they headed back towards Gilly-vean, her confusion returned. From the corner of her eye she saw Richard's profile. Why would he not look at her? Other men did, though too often what she saw in their eyes was intrusive and unsettling. Her milky skin, grey eyes, and thick chestnut hair were an accident of birth, not a source of pride. She hadn't earned them.

At school, discovering her gift for drawing and painting had been like finding treasure. It absorbed every spare moment and increased her confidence. It also made her the focus of jealousy and spiteful remarks. Knowing she couldn't win, she simply refused to respond. Finally accepting that, no matter how hard she tried, she would never belong had been a turning point. Eventually they left her alone. A couple of girls apologised and wanted to be friends. Warily she accepted their overtures. Then realised they were basking in her reflected glory. She had found that amusing.

But her trip to France, embarked on with such

hope, had seen her painfully acquired sense of worth shattered. Now she found herself drawn to this stranger, and that scared her. She didn't want to spend her life wary and suspicious. It was exhausting, and achingly lonely. But when trust had been brutally betrayed only a fool invited more. Richard Vaughan knew her father far better than she did. And she knew neither of them.

He cleared his throat. 'I hope it was a successful sitting?'

'Why would you care?' As soon as the words left her lips she wished they hadn't. She ought to apologise. *What for?* It was a fair question. She was nothing to him but a burden imposed by her father, which made her feel guilty. That made her angry, for it was yet one more situation over which she had no control.

'Why do I care? Because I know from my own experience how frustrating it is when something doesn't proceed as you hope it will.'

That was another thing. No matter how much she might deserve it he didn't snap at her. He simply raised an eyebrow and she felt thoroughly patronised. Yes, she was younger than him. But he didn't have to treat her like a child. *Maybe he wouldn't if she stopped behaving like one.* The thought was uncomfortable and she thrust it aside.

Since the dinner party she had seen little of her father. Frederick Tregarron was generous in everything but his time. That was for others, not her. After doing what he considered his duty, he had hung her around Richard Vaughan's neck like a millstone.

She knew Richard loathed being responsible for her. Each time she closed her eyes she saw again the horror that had flashed across his face. Swiftly recovering, he had pleaded pressure of work as the reason for his reluctance. After that one revealing moment his polite mask had not slipped again.

His courtesy was a rock against which her anger crashed, exploded and dissolved, its energy spent. She felt safe with him. That should have reassured her. Instead it deepened her anguish. She yearned to trust him but dared not. For sooner or later like everyone else he would turn his back, abandon her.

'I asked because I'm interested.'

She flashed him a brilliant smile, and relished the shock that briefly widened his eyes even as she knew what she was doing was wrong. 'Of course you are. You have never met anyone like me.' She raised her chin in defiance, fighting the urge to weep.

He regarded her calmly. 'You are right in that, Miss Tregarron. However, roguishness does not become you, and in company might be misconstrued. You would not wish that.'

Embarrassed, hating that he was right, relieved he had misread her bitter angry hurt, Melanie felt heat flush her face. 'You take a lot upon yourself, sir.'

He inclined his head. 'It was not my intention to cause offence. I speak as – as a friend.'

'A friend? I don't think so.' Her laugh was brittle. 'You are with me at my father's insistence.'

'I will not deny what we both know to be true.

125

Your father's concern for your welfare requires us to spend time in each other's company. We might have used the opportunity to know one another a little better. But you need not feel obliged. I am perfectly content with silence.'

Recognising how neatly he had turned her own claim back on her, she took him at his word, deep in thought as she tried – and failed – to understand the confusion he aroused.

'Did you mean it?' she asked, staring straight ahead as they approached the gravelled circle in front of the house. The trap stopped. The pony tossed his head, jingling the harness.

'I'm not in the habit of saying things I don't mean.'

Though his tone was mild she recognised the rebuke and knew she deserved it. Why did being in his company make her behave this way? 'I beg your pardon.' Hating the stiffness in her voice she took a slow deep breath hoping it might help her control her erratic emotions.

'To what were you referring, Miss Tregarron? You were not specific.'

Why tell him? Because with her father totally absorbed in his own affairs there wasn't anyone else. *What possible help could he offer?* How would she find out unless she showed him the portrait? 'I have Mrs Martin's likeness perfectly. But she won't like it. I am sure of that, but I don't know why. Something is – I don't *know* what it is,' she cried in angry frustration.

'I am not familiar with painting technique.'

'Of course you aren't. Why would you be?' Melanie was too concerned with her dilemma to feel offended as amusement twitched one corner of Richard's mouth. 'Anyway, that's not why I asked. I thought you might–' she broke off, shaking her head. 'It doesn't matter. I should not have mentioned it.'

'But you did,' he interrupted. 'So now my curiosity is engaged. When we go inside you must at least allow me to look.' He met her gaze briefly. 'I will give you my opinion. You are under no obligation to act upon it. Nor, if you disagree with what I say, will I be offended.'

He had not promised honesty. He had not needed to. She knew, for better or worse, he would give her nothing less.

A groom ran round the corner from the stable block and took hold of the horse's bridle. Richard jumped down and turned to offer Melanie his gloved hand. His grip was firm and steady. *Safe*, she thought, and instantly mocked her foolishness. Surely she had learned by now? Her only safety lay in self-reliance.

Still, he had asked. He could have let it drop. No, he couldn't. He was her father's heir. She was her father's daughter. They were living in the same house. No matter what he said, he was obliged to show a certain interest. But despite that – or maybe because of it – she would show him the portrait. His response would tell her more than he realised.

Standing in the hall a few minutes later, having removed her hat and gloves and asked Ellen to bring tea, Melanie picked up her leather portfolio from the chair and led the way into the drawing room. Laying it on a rosewood table behind one of the sofas, she loosened the ties, opened it, and took out an eighteen-inch square of board.

'Oh. I assumed–' Richard stopped, gave his head a small self-deprecating shake. 'I should have realised you weren't working in oils.'

'I do sometimes. It depends on the sitter,' Melanie explained. 'But Mrs Martin asked for pastels.' A piece of protective silk was pinned to the top of the board. Flipping the silk out of the way to reveal a sheet of thick creamy paper, she turned the portrait towards him. 'Do you know her well?'

'No.' He did not elaborate. 'It is a remarkable likeness. May I?' Taking the board from her he carried it to the window.

Melanie followed, surprised to feel her heart quicken.

A slight frown drew his brows together as he studied the image. 'She has not seen it yet?'

'No.'

For the first time his gaze met hers. 'You have done me the honour of asking my opinion. My respect for your talent requires me to be candid. Anything less would insult us both.'

'That is why I asked you,' Melanie said, knowing she spoke the truth even as cold fingers of doubt encircled her stomach and squeezed. 'Go on.'

'You don't like Mrs Martin.'

'How do you know?' she blurted, startled by his quiet observation.

Richard indicated the portrait. 'It is very revealing.'

Moving to his side, Melanie looked at the smiling portrait. With sudden blinding clarity she saw what he meant. Her hand flew to her mouth.

'Oh! I didn't realize–'

128

'Your perception is acute.'

Melanie shrugged helplessly. 'While she sits for me, Mrs Martin is all gracious manners and tinkling laughter. But it's a mask. Her eyes–' She broke off.

'What about her eyes?'

'They never smile. Behind that sociable façade she's vain and spiteful.'

'Vain, or proud?'

She studied the portrait again. Beside her Richard continued. 'Pride comes from inside. It's what a person feels about him or herself. Whereas vanity is a desire for the admiration and good opinion of others.'

'Then Mrs Martin is vain.'

'So you must decide – flattery or truth?'

Glancing up she caught his eye. He looked away, frowning as he tilted the portrait so it caught the light. *He had been watching her.*

She shook her head. 'It sounds such a simple choice.'

'Your words, Melanie, not mine,' he chided. 'A choice, yes, but hardly simple.'

It was the first time he had used her name. Since the evening of her arrival his manner toward her had been deliberately formal. It must have been a slip he was unaware of or he would have apologised. Had he been thinking of her as a person, not a burden or a problem? Even as she hoped so, doubt tightened its grip. Had she learned nothing?

Pressing her palms together she forced herself to concentrate. 'If I flatter I will secure a steady flow of commissions. I want the work. Of course I do. But–' She glanced towards him. His attention was on the portrait. That made it easier. 'You will think me silly and superstitious. But I have this terrible fear that if I dishonour my talent something may happen to take it from me.'

He lowered the picture and his eyes met hers. 'I don't think it silly at all. Perhaps now you see why I say your choice is not a simple one. Your ability to reveal character through features and expression is astonishing. So might I suggest that you try to look beneath Mrs Martin's vanity and malice?'

'For what?'

'Most people have experiences in their past that retain the power to hurt.' Handing her the portrait, he inclined his head. 'Thank you.'

'It's I who should thank you,' she said. 'I hadn't realised – not until you pointed it out–'

'I'm glad to have helped.' He smiled, but it was brief. 'Now I must ask you to excuse me. I have business that will not wait.'

Did that mean he wished he might have stayed longer? Would she have wanted him to? He was better company than she expected. But already he had withdrawn into formality.

'Yes, of course.' Ignoring unexpected disappointment, she smiled at him. 'I'm very much obliged to you.'

'You're welcome.' The door closed softly behind him.

Melanie gazed at the portrait. What had happened to Mrs Martin? She couldn't ask, and so would never know the truth. But that wasn't the point. If she accepted that *unhappiness* had soured Mrs Martin, she could reflect this in the portrait. Ignoring her barbed remarks would also be easier.

She covered the portrait with its protective silk. *Most people have experiences in their past that retain the power to hurt.* As she closed the portfolio her hands fell still. How could he know what had happened to her? She had told no one but her father, and not even he knew it all.

Or had he been speaking of himself?

Chapter Fifteen

The heat in the steam packet's engine room was stifling. Santo had shed his coat and waistcoat soon after the ship left Falmouth. His cravat had followed, stuffed into the pocket of his trousers, and his shirtsleeves were rolled up.

At the sound of a groan, a muffled curse, then the thump of a falling body, he glanced round and saw the stoker had collapsed.

Will McAndrew heaved a sigh. 'Here, boy, soak rags in the water bucket and wrap 'em loosely round his head and throat. Then see if you can get a pint of small beer down him.'

Boy. I'm twenty-eight. But he knew Will used the term in fondness, not as an insult. Following the chief engineer's instructions, Santo dragged the semi-conscious stoker into a corner away from the boiler's heat. After draining a tankard of small beer himself, he poured another and offered it to Will who swallowed it without pause for breath.

'I'll go and ask Lt Hellings for another stoker.'

Leaving Will anxiously studying the gauges

131

Santo climbed the wooden ladder. As he reached the deck he breathed deeply, glad of fresh air after the heat and acrid reek of soot and hot metal below. He thought of Bronnen, her shy smile, rosy blush, and those amazing eyes, greenish-brown with glints of gold.

He had seen them spark in anger, widen in amazement, and soften in trust as she allowed him past the wariness she wore like a protective cloak. But last night in the lantern's glow they had been bottomless pools.

Her passionate response to his kisses had ignited a desire as complex as it was powerful. He wanted her with every fibre of his body. But he also wanted to protect her, even from his own hunger. She had kissed him with searing honesty, holding nothing back. Afterwards he could see she was as startled as he was by her response to him.

Recognising her naivety, he had also recognised the responsibility this placed on him. He could have taken what he so badly wanted. She would have let him. But the aftermath would have been devastating for her, and he would never have been able to look himself in the eye again.

Instead, drawing on strength he didn't know was in him he had stepped back. Still lost in the feelings he had stirred she had gazed up at him, her eyes wide, dazed. Looking into the limpid depths he had felt himself falling.

He wasn't good with words, not like Richard Vaughan. But holding her hand, fighting the fierce desire she aroused in him, he had seen both her strength and her fragility. It made her trust in him a gift all the more valued.

He had known her only days yet couldn't get her out of his thoughts. Nor did he want to. Watching her suspicion of his engine change to astonishment then fascination had given him more pleasure than he had felt in a long time.

In the brewhouse he had seen exhaustion etched on her face – the physical cost of completing the brew on her own. Yet she had not spoken a single word of complaint. It was plain as day she knew her job. So why did he feel this powerful need to protect her?

Glancing aft he saw two officers leaning miserably over the side in the throes of seasickness. Three seamen sprawled by the forward bilges in similar straits.

He sighed, unsurprised. The engine was driving two giant paddlewheels, one each side of the ship. Because of the lumpy swell the paddles were digging into the water at different times and depths, moving the ship forward in a jerky waddle made worse by the rise and fall of the bow.

For the first hour he had felt unpleasantly queasy himself. Only through fierce concentration on the machinery had he overcome it.

The change from sail to steam power was intended to shorten voyage times by removing dependence on erratic winds. But looking at the suffering seamen Santo wondered how many crews would survive this so-called progress.

He glanced skyward. When he had stepped aboard, a speedwell-blue sky had been reflected in the sparkling sea. Now a blanket of high cloud patterned like a mackerel's side covered the sky, and a stiffening breeze curled the tops of the waves into foam.

He returned to the engine room. 'It's just you and me, Will.' Santo unbuttoned his shirt. 'There isn't a man to spare.'

'Sick, are they?'

Santo nodded. 'And two of the officers.'

Stripping down to his drawers, Santo borrowed the stoker's canvas trousers and started shovelling coal into the fiery mouth of the ever-hungry boiler.

Four hours later, the muscles of his back and shoulders ached like an abscessed tooth. He wondered how much longer he could keep going, and thought of Bronnen doing the work of two.

He straightened, wincing. Leaning on the shovel, waiting for his heartbeat to slow, he pulled a filthy rag from his waistband. As he wiped sweat and coal dust from his face he glanced across at the engineer who looked a decade older than his fifty years.

Will gestured helplessly. 'I gave Lt Hellings the extra speed he wanted. He must've known it would use up more coal. If Annear's had delivered what I ordered–' Will shook his head. 'We'd still be short.'

Santo eyed him, careful to keep his tone free of accusation. 'You took a hell of a risk holding down the safety valve.' As Will's furrowed cheeks flushed brick red with shame, Santo wanted to shake the lieutenant until his teeth rattled.

'You weren't s'posed to see that.'

'I'm not blaming you. If I was in your place I might have done the same.'

'Before we left Falmouth,' Will said, 'the

134

lieutenant told me if we didn't reach speed today he'd have to put it in his report. What choice did I have? But I tell you straight, boy, I didn't like it. Not at all.' Shaking his head he turned away, rubbing his haggard features with a filthy rag as if that might wipe away his guilt.

Santo was furious with the Admiralty whose demands for speed *and* economy were contradictory and unworkable. Lt Hellings demanded results but took no account of the dangers involved. And Hall's, who had built the engine, had put Will in an impossible position.

Sweat trickled down his face and chest leaving pale tracks through the grime. As he inhaled, the hot dust-thickened air caught in his throat making him cough. Refilling the pewter mug Will passed it across.

Santo gulped down the weak beer and wiped his mouth with the back of his hand. 'I've met some fools in my time but the lieutenant is one of the worst.' He handed Will the empty mug then peered into the coalbunker.

'How much is left?' Will asked.

'Less than a quarter.'

Will blew out a breath. 'Not enough to get us back to Falmouth.'

Dropping his shovel onto the gritty floor Santo started for the ladder. 'I'll go and tell Lt Hellings. Any crew still on their feet had better find us something to feed the boiler with before it goes out, or God alone knows how long we'll be stuck out here.'

Aware that on most farms the front door was only ever opened to carry out a coffin, Treeve

Curnock followed the paved path round to the back.

Over the low wooden fence enclosing the back garden he saw a tidy cobbled yard. A gnarled oak tree shaded the huge manure pile filling the lower corner. At other farms he visited to buy barley the dung heap was usually surrounded by a stinking pool of slurry. But Morley Jewell had removed stones from the bottom of the hedge providing drainage into the adjoining field.

In the kitchen garden a path separated small plots of spring cabbage, onions, potatoes, and turnips from rows of blackcurrant and gooseberry bushes heavy with fruit. At the far end in a small orchard, chickens wandered beneath the trees pecking in the grass near the sturdy henhouse that would keep them safe at night from prowling foxes.

As he raised his hand to knock on the open back door, Morley Jewell appeared. 'Thought I heard someone.' He gave a curt nod. 'Mr Curnock. What you doing here?'

For an instant Treeve hesitated. The man was boorish, difficult and – if the rumours were to be believed – depraved. But he would tolerate all that to get what he wanted.

'Good afternoon, Mr Jewell. Is there somewhere we might talk privately?'

Morley gestured across the yard to one of the grain stores. Unbolting the split door he led the way in. Dust motes danced in the slanting beams of the late afternoon sun. He turned. Planting his booted feet wide apart he folded his arms.

'This private enough for you?'

Having expected both aggression and defiance Treeve simply ignored them. 'It will do.' Fastidiously he brushed a speck from his coat sleeve with a gloved hand. 'Mr Jewell, I buy my barley from you because you supply the best and I have a reputation to uphold. Considering we negotiated what we both agreed was a fair price, I was less than pleased to hear you've been selling hay, straw, and grain off your wagon at a lot less than I'm paying.'

Morley's gaze skittered sideways. Treeve let the silence linger. He knew the farmer was wondering how he had found out and what he intended doing about it.

Chin jutting, eyes narrowed, Morley demanded, 'So what are you after? A bigger discount?'

'We will certainly discuss new terms. I have no doubt we will reach agreement. However, that is not the primary reason for my visit.'

'So why have you come?'

'To discuss your daughter.'

Morley stared at him, frowning. 'Bronnen?'

'Of course Bronnen. You have no other.'

'What about her?'

Seeing sly calculation in the reptilian eyes, Treeve felt a frisson of distaste. Dismissing it, he silently congratulated himself. The deal was as good as done. He looked down his nose at the farmer. 'It's time I took a wife and she will suit me.'

It was Santo's interest in her that had piqued his own. He had looked at her with new eyes and appreciated the swell of her breasts, her trim waist above curving hips. Beneath her faded dresses was warm flesh. He had imagined her naked, her dark hair tumbling loose down her back. Or standing in firelight wearing only a gauze shift that tantalised as much for what it concealed as for what was revealed. These images, and others, haunted and taunted him, disturbing his sleep.

At the malt house a couple of weeks ago she had caught him staring and turned away. She had refused to meet his eyes, but she had blushed. Was she teasing him or just shy? He wasn't sure which he preferred.

Once they were married she would have to obey his wishes, cater to his every whim. But first he would relish the pleasure and satisfaction of stealing her from right under his cousin's nose. A thrill of excitement and anticipation tingled through him.

'She's a good catch.'

Treeve allowed himself an ironic smile at the farmer's sudden change in manner. Jewell's aggression had given way to deference.

'Knows how to run a home and conduct herself. She got brewing and dairy skills too. You could do a lot worse.'

Treeve imagined the farmer at market selling a prize heifer. 'So I've been told. I need not remind you that an alliance with the Curnock family would be much to your advantage. I have plans to expand my business, which means I will be buying more barley from you. However,' he lifted an expertly tailored shoulder that was more buckram and wadding than muscle.

'What?' Morley demanded.

'There is the matter of a dowry.'

Morley grinned, revealing blackened teeth. 'Don't you worry about that.' This surprised

Treeve. Expecting a plea of poverty he had come prepared to bargain. 'She was left money for when she got wed. She won't come empty-handed. So, we got a deal?'

Treeve saw no alternative to shaking the horny dirt-ingrained hand Morley Jewell thrust at him. 'We have, Mr Jewell. But you will oblige me by keeping the matter private until I tell you otherwise. There are arrangements I need to make first.'

'Not a word.' Morley Jewell winked. 'She's yours when you want her.'

Chapter Sixteen

It was seven in the evening when, having burned every spare spar, water cask and bunk board, plus several bulkheads, the *Mercury* limped back into Falmouth and picked up her mooring.

Two punts had raced out to meet her. One returned to the quay carrying the sick officers together with a note from Lt Hellings for Captain King, the Admiralty Superintendent of Packets. The other, promising to return, took the stoker and whey-faced seamen.

While Will was shutting everything down Santo tapped the sight gauge on the side of the boiler. The water level dropped away leaving the glass tube empty. He stared at it, not wanting to believe what he was seeing.

'Jesus,' he whispered, his throat dry.

'What now?' Will came over, his face drawn and anxious.

Santo indicated the empty gauge. 'If there's no water in the boiler we could have been blown to bits.'

'Maybe the gauge is faulty,' Will offered in desperate hope. 'I'll add it to my list to check.'

Once they were topside, despite exhaustion that lay like a weight on the back of his neck, Santo hauled up buckets of seawater and scrubbed off the sweat and coal dust. Clean, if not refreshed, he dressed. The punt returned and carried them back to shore. On the town quay the two men shook hands.

'Listen, Will. Don't put to sea again till the boiler's been cleaned. There's bound to be dirt and rust–'

'You think I don't know that, boy? The seams need checking for leaks as well. Trouble is, the lieutenant got the Admiralty on his back, and he's on mine. If Hall's don't win this contract my job's gone and Mr Tregarron will be mad as fire. He've got money in the company.'

Santo clenched his teeth to stop himself saying more. Will knew the risks better than anyone.

Bronnen couldn't breathe. A suffocating weight pressed her into the mattress. She could feel hot animal breath against her neck. There were sounds too but she couldn't hear them above the frantic pounding of the blood in her ears. Terrified and frantic, she fought to free herself. The weight shifted. As she managed to heave in enough breath to scream, she bolted upright gasping, her eyes wide in the darkness.

Her heart hammered against her ribs as she sucked in great gulps of air. Shuddering violently she shook her head, trying to dislodge the vivid, all-too-real sensation of being crushed.

Throwing back the tangled sheet and blanket, she swung her legs out of bed. But, not sure if they would support her, she remained sitting on the edge. Her nightgown clung damp and uncomfortable. She pulled the cotton away from her heated skin then shivered while she waited for her galloping pulse to slow. It was just a bad dream. She was tired and worried so her mind was playing tricks.

As her panic receded she became aware of thirst. Her throat was so parched it hurt to swallow. Leaving her bed she pulled a robe on over her nightgown, opened the door and padded along the passage to the back stairs that led down to the kitchen. A strip of light at the bottom told her someone was still up.

Desperate for cold water, but reluctant to face her father, she crept carefully down the narrow stairs. As she neared the bottom she heard low voices, and recognised one as Jack Mitchell from the foundry on Back Quay.

'This have got to stop. You're drinking too much.'

'Says who?' Morley Jewell slurred belligerently.

'Says me,' Jack snapped. 'We got a good thing going here, and I aren't letting you mess it up.'

Bronnen had turned to retreat to her room, but hearing this she paused.

'If you're so worried, find someone else to take

141

my place on the boat. I'll still hide stuff on the farm.'

'Oh no. You wanted in, and you're staying in. So you hark to what I'm saying. Everyone knows Mr Tregarron enjoy the company of ladies. Sometimes he makes one of them his partic'lar friend until he get bored, or she try to take advantage. But if you think because he's a man of the world he'd turn a blind eye to your dirty little secret, you're wrong. So unless you want to lose your job, your home, your son's chance of taking over the farm, and the extra money your wife and daughter make from brewing at Gillyvean, he better not find out.'

'You can't–'

'Threaten you? I can. I just did. Only it isn't a threat. 'Tis a promise.'

'But if we're caught,' Morley's voice was thick with alcohol and fear, 'we'll get twenty years.'

Jack's laugh was brutal. 'Better gaol than transportation or hanging. But we won't get caught. See, if you was thinking to tip-off to the Excise men, I've left letters for Mr Tregarron and Mr Vaughan. Your family would be out on the street quicker 'n duckshit. You dug the pit you're in so 'tis no good whining. You do what I tell you when I tell you. You hear me?'

Hardly daring to breathe, Bronnen heard a muttered reply.

'You should've thought of that backlong. 'Tis too late now,' Jack retorted without a trace of sympathy.

Hearing a chair scrape on the stone floor, Bronnen turned and ran silently back to her room.

Of course she had noticed the kegs of brandy that appeared in the pantry at regular intervals. But she had held her tongue, knowing better than to ask, not sure she wanted to know.

Guessing they were contraband she had assumed they were payment in kind to her father for some service or maybe produce from the farm. She hadn't realised he was actually involved in smuggling. But it would explain his absences overnight.

Was smuggling the dirty little secret Jack Mitchell had spoken of? But it couldn't be. Not if he was involved as well.

So what was it?

Chapter Seventeen

Yawning, Santo turned off the main street and walked down the steep narrow hill. Passing the closed doors of the soup kitchen he turned left again on to Back Quay.

It was twelve hours since he and Will had arrived back on *Mercury*. By the time he'd had a meal, spent a couple of hours in his workshop then had a quick bath, it had been too late to walk out to Gillyvean. Instead he had fallen into bed, surprised at how much he missed Bronnen and wanted to see her again.

'All right, boy?' Jack Mitchell glanced up from the forge fire as Santo entered the foundry. 'How's the trial going?'

143

Santo shook his head. 'Don't ask.'

Jack sucked air through his teeth. 'That bad is it?' He pushed the long wooden handle that worked the bellows. In the waist-high hearth the red-hot bed of coals turned from dull crimson to dazzling gold. 'Seen Mr Tregarron's daughter again, have you?'

'No,' Santo said absently, mentally listing all he had to do, and how he could arrange it so he'd be able to get out to Gillyvean.

'I bet her turning up was some shock for him,' Jack said.

'He's always known about her.'

'He has?' Jack's eyebrows climbed.

'So I'm told.' It had taken Santo only a few days to recognise that though secretive about his own affairs, Jack relished gossip. Giving him facts he wouldn't be able to resist passing on might put paid to some of the wilder rumours. 'He paid for her to go to some expensive boarding school, and for private tutors for her painting.'

'Is that so? He done right by her then. But what was she thinking of, coming all that way on the coach by herself? Looking for trouble, that was.'

'I didn't ask.'

'I like a man who knows how to keep his mouth shut. Any good is she?'

'What did you say?' Santo stiffened.

'All right, no need to go off half-cocked. I meant her painting. Have you seen it? Is she any good?'

Santo recalled the pencil sketches she had made of the sleeping passengers. He nodded. 'She captures a likeness better than any I've ever seen.'

'Dear Life!' Jack grinned. 'There'll be hell to go

144

among the ladies. Some will cut her because her father never married her mother. But plenty will overlook that to have her paint their portrait. 'Tis a wonder to me Mr Tregarron haven't been caught out more often. He've always been one for the ladies. Mind you, with his wife living up London and him down here, you can't blame him for wanting a bit of company.'

Santo gave a dismissive shrug. Frederick Tregarron's private life was of no interest to him. It was time to change the subject. 'You heard about Anstey's?'

Jack clicked his tongue. 'Shame. They done good work. What's happening to the yard?'

'Mr Vaughan is buying it. I'll have the space I need for my marine engine.'

Jack rolled his eyes. 'I swear if you fell in a midden you'd come out smelling of violets.'

'I don't know about that. Anyway, the engine is coming as deck cargo. If I could borrow your two lads for a couple of hours–'

'I need to see some money first.' Jack's blunt demand made Santo wince. 'I told you when you first come here, I run my business cash in hand.'

'Look, Mr Vaughan has bought one engine for the pump at Gillyvean brewhouse,' Santo broke in. 'Mr Rowse from Dene Quarry is coming to see it working. They've got problems with flooding and I'm hoping to sell him two. Can you give me till the end of the month?'

'End of the month it is. Here, you'll be needing a boat for this engine of yours.'

Santo smiled over his shoulder. 'Got one.'

'You have?' Jack's blink of astonishment darkened to suspicion. 'How did you pay for that then?'

'I didn't. 'Tisn't mine. I've just got use of it.'

Jack nodded, his frown clearing. 'That's all right then.'

Santo thought of all he had achieved in the few weeks since his return. But though progress had been excellent, the cost in money and hours had been high.

'I'd dearly love to see it.'

'As soon as the engine is fitted and ready for testing.'

'I'll hold you to that,' Jack called after him as he left the foundry.

About to start up the hill, Santo heard urgent shouts. Crossing the road he strode through the stone-flagged passage beneath the Chain Locker public house on to the rear of the Town Quay. Fishermen had left their boats, and were running towards the stone steps on the outer edge of the eastern arm. Quickening his pace he heard a man yell for a length of net or an old sail.

He knew what that meant. Someone had been hurt, couldn't walk, and most likely was unconscious. Then came another shout.

'One of you boys go along to the brewery and fetch Mr Arthur.'

The name hit Santo like a punch to his stomach. Sprinting across the back of the quay he pushed his way through the watching men and looked down at the body of his uncle George sprawled on the brown weed and shingle, abandoned there by the ebbing tide.

Santo jumped down the steps. The fishermen

moved back silent and respectful as he knelt by the body. 'Who found him?'

'I did,' said a young man wearing grubby canvas trousers and a collarless checked shirt. 'Lying face down he was, in among all the seaweed. That's how I didn't see'n right off.'

'All right, boy,' an old-timer patted his arm. 'Nothing you could've done. He's long gone.'

Santo looked down. His uncle's usually florid face was blue-grey and filmed with mud and scum. His half-closed eyes were dull as stones, his clothes soaked and filthy.

Swallowing hard, Santo stood up as a stocky man thudded down the stone steps carrying a roughly folded length of stained canvas.

'Just to get'n up top,' he said apologetically.

The canvas was spread on the shingle and several men gently rolled George onto it.

Santo and three of the fishermen each took a corner, carried the body up the steps then lifted it onto an empty cart that someone had called down from the street.

After making sure the body was tightly wrapped and the canvas secure, the fishermen stood back.

'Much obliged to you,' Santo said. After his Aunt Hannah had died, tearing open the wound of losing his mother, he had erected a wall around his emotions, closed them off. Love wasn't worth the pain of loss.

But since meeting Bronnen Jewell that wall had cracked. Though it unnerved him he couldn't stop.

While she was alive it was his Aunt Hannah he'd been close to. His uncle had accepted his presence, but the brewery had always had first claim on George Curnock's time and attention. So although shocked by his uncle's death, he would not pretend a grief he didn't feel.

How had it happened? When? What was his uncle doing on the quay anyway? As more questions crowded in he felt someone tug his sleeve. He tried to focus. 'Sorry, what?'

'Do you want him took home?'

He rubbed his forehead. He would have to tell his uncle Arthur, and Treeve. 'No. Better not.' Mrs Eathorne was used to his uncle coming and going at all hours depending on the demands of the brewery. But he couldn't ask this of her.

'Best if he went straight to the undertaker's,' the fisherman nearest him murmured. 'They'll get him looking something like it.'

Santo nodded, trying to remember which of the town's undertakers had handled his aunt Hannah's funeral. 'Penprase's. Take him to Mr Penprase.'

The cart had just reached the top of the steep incline and turned on to Arwenack Street when Santo saw Arthur Curnock hurrying towards him.

'You go on,' he said to the driver. 'We'll meet you there.'

With a nod, the driver clicked his teeth and the horse broke into a trot. Santo opened his mouth then shut it again. Getting his uncle's body off the street was more important than solemnity.

'Well,' Arthur panted, his voice low as he turned to walk beside Santo. 'This is a fine mess and no mistake. What happened?'

'I don't know,' Santo said. 'A fisherman found

the body on the foreshore below the quay. They say he's been dead several hours.'

'Where is he now?'

Santo gestured towards the cart. 'On his way to Penprase's. I thought–'

'Yes, yes. An excellent choice.'

They walked quickly through the town, avoiding men on their way to work, shopkeepers washing the pavement, and delivery carts laden with boxes of fruit and vegetables coming in from surrounding farms and gardens.

Arthur huffed out a breath. 'It really is extremely inconvenient.'

Santo didn't try to hide his shock. 'Your brother's dead.'

'Yes,' Arthur snapped. 'It is a tragedy. I wish it had not happened. But it has and I can't change that. So right at this moment what's worrying me is how I'm to keep the brewery running without a brewer.'

Chapter Eighteen

'Did the sitting go well?' Richard enquired as he escorted Melanie down the path from Mrs Dudley's house.

'Very well, thank you. Mrs Dudley is such a nice lady. Unlike some, her smiles are genuine.'

Melanie felt the warmth of his palm through her sleeve as he cupped her elbow to help her into the trap. The touch was brief but the sensation lingered. She watched him give the boy holding the bridle a coin and a word of thanks. Beaming, the boy scampered away.

'Mrs Martin called while I was at Mrs Dudley's.' Melanie tucked her skirts out of his way. 'She was accompanied by a Mrs Geach whose husband is a solicitor. Apparently she wished to meet me.'

'Congratulations. You are making your mark on Falmouth society.'

Recalling Mrs Martin's patronising manner of introduction which made her feel as if she were some strange and exotic animal, Melanie's smile had a wry edge. 'I have a certain novelty value.'

'You are too young for such cynicism. Nor does it do justice to your talent.'

'My age has nothing to do with it,' Melanie retorted. 'Anyway, I wasn't being cynical, just realistic.'

'You deserve–' Richard broke off, shaking his head.

Melanie wanted to press him to finish what he had begun to say. But if she did the words he spoke would not be those he had cut short. What did he think she deserved? What did he think of her? Did he think about her? She thought about him, even though she didn't want to. His opinion was of no importance. That was a lie. He had been honest with her, opened her eyes to something she had not previously recognized. But that didn't mean he cared, just that he believed in being truthful.

As they passed the newly built church at Penwerris, Richard glanced at her. 'Would you object if I made a brief stop?'

'Where?'

He nodded towards a turn-off that led down a slope. 'Here. But if you prefer I can drop you off at Gillyvean first.'

'Then you'd have to come back which would be time wasted. Accompanying me twice a week must already be causing you considerable inconvenience. Please, make your visit.'

At the bottom of the shallow slope, Richard guided the pony onto a broad stone-paved area with a granite-built quay jutting out like a stubby finger. On the inner side, protected by the arm, a broad shallow slipway led into the river. The tide was low and the bottom half of the slip was green with algae. Further down, the slipway merged into shingle, brown seaweed and lapping water. Richard stopped the trap alongside a large workshop with a pair of wide double doors set in the front.

After tying the pony to an iron ring in the wall, he offered Melanie his hand. Taking it she jumped down, turned her foot on a stone and lurched forward against him. As she gasped, he caught and steadied her. Jolted by the sensation of his body against hers, terrified in case he might think it deliberate, she wrenched free. 'I'm so sorry!'

'Are you all right? You haven't hurt–?'

'I'm fine. Perfectly, thank you.' Not looking at him she walked to the doors, saw the chain and padlock, and stood back, her face burning. Opening the padlock he hooked it through the chain then slid one of the doors open. It rumbled sideways, running in iron grooves top and bottom.

'It saves space,' he said, answering the question

151

she was wondering whether to ask. 'And allows one or both doors to be opened as much or as little as necessary.' Without waiting for a response, he walked inside. Melanie followed. The smell of the river was overlaid by pine resin, sawdust, tar, and coal dust.

Down the centre of the workshop a wooden hull nearly as long as the drawing room at Gillyvean was held upright by a dozen thick props on each side. As her eyes adjusted to dimness after bright sunshine, she saw workbenches stretching down the left-hand side. Tools hung from nails on the wall behind, or lay where they had been dropped on the benches.

Beneath them sat stave-built buckets and tubs. Near the door on the other side was a forge with odd lengths and pieces of metal piled behind it. A bellows with a long wooden handle was fixed above a metal bed of cold embers. An anvil squatted on a thick blackened tree ring with a small tank of filthy water nearby. Tools and hammers of different sizes lay on a bench.

Richard opened a door into a partitioned area on the right hand side and disappeared inside. She heard another door open and shut then he reappeared closing the door behind him. 'Offices,' he explained.

'Why is no one here? What happened?' Melanie asked.

'The owner ran out of money.'

'It feels sad.' She watched him glance around as she had. Then his gaze returned to her and he smiled.

'Not for much longer.'

'How do you know?'

'Because I bought it.'

'You did?' She made no effort to hide her surprise. 'Why?'

'It's an excellent investment. And this,' he patted the hull, 'is the perfect test-bed for Mr Innis's marine engine.'

'Will it be like the one working the pump at the brewhouse?'

'Considerably larger, I'd have thought.'

'Well, yes. Even I had realised that.' In the dim light she saw amusement gleam in his eyes.

'But Mr Innis tells me the principle is the same. It should be arriving in the next few days.'

She followed him out and stood looking at the crane. Fastened to large iron rings set into the granite quay overlooking the slip, it resembled a rusty spider. Behind her he closed and locked the massive doors.

'If the engine is big and heavy,' Melanie said as he handed her up into the trap, 'Mr Innis will have to use the crane to lift it in.'

'Yes.' Untying the pony, Richard climbed up beside her.

'But he'll have to bring the boat outside first. How will he do that?' Melanie hung on to the seat as the trap jolted up the slope and on to the main road.

'I have absolutely no idea.' He sounded surprised, as if the point had not occurred to him, but now he too was wondering.

They rattled along towards Gillyvean. As the silence lengthened Melanie found it harder to break. For a few minutes there they had talked like normal people. *They had been yards apart, looking at different things. Was that normal?*

As they turned onto Gillyvean's drive she gave in to impulse and glanced at him. They spoke simultaneously.

'I enjoyed–'

'Thank you for–'

'I beg your pardon.'

'No, you first,' he said.

'I was just going to say that I enjoyed seeing the boatyard.'

Drawing the trap to a halt, he bowed politely. 'It was my pleasure.'

She turned away and, not waiting for his help, jumped down, her face burning as she reached into the box for her portfolio and the bag containing her pastels box and pencil tin. He had shut her out again. He might as well have slammed a door in her face. Why? What had she done? What was wrong with her?

Richard watched as she hurried towards the house. What was wrong with him? In the short time she had been at Gillyvean he had watched her deal with disappointment, and develop insight as an artist. At the boatyard he realised how sharp she was, and how much he enjoyed her company. *She was too young. She would always be too young.*

Glancing up from the hand-mill in which she was grinding malt for the next brew, Bronnen looked out through the open doorway then turned to her visitor. 'Miss Tregarron?'

Seated on the bench against the wall, Melanie glanced up from her sketchpad. 'Yes?'

154

'Ellen is coming across the yard. I think she's looking for you.'

Melanie pulled a wry face and returned to her drawing. Moments later the maid poked her head in.

'There you are, miss. Mrs Berryman sent me to find you. Mr Tregarron have asked for dinner to be served early tonight.'

'Thank you, Ellen. I'll be there in a minute.'

'I'll lay out your green dress, miss. Suit you lovely, it do.'

Surprise crossed Melanie's face. 'Are we expecting guests?'

Ellen shook her head. 'No, miss. 'Tis just you, Mr Vaughan, and Mr Tregarron.' She scuttled away.

'This is the life of a lady, Miss Jewell. Told what to wear, when to eat, and with whom.' Sighing she shook her head. 'Now I am ashamed of myself. It is ungrateful of me to complain.' Returning her pencils to the tin, Melanie closed her sketchpad and stood up.

Keen to see the drawing, Bronnen was gathering courage to ask but didn't get the chance.

'I'll show it to you next time,' Melanie said. She paused at the door, hugging pad and tin to her chest. 'You are very restful company, Miss Jewell.'

Bronnen looked up in surprise. 'I am?'

Melanie nodded. 'Since I came to live here, several ladies have commissioned me to paint their portrait. I was delighted to be asked and happy to agree. What I didn't expect is that not a single one of them can tolerate silence. Yet you seem perfectly content not to talk.'

'Better to keep quiet than say the wrong thing,' Bronnen said, surprising them both. In the farmhouse, the *wrong thing* was whatever her father decided it was. A remark about the weather could trigger a tirade. Even if she couldn't see him she always knew when he was in the house because the atmosphere felt tense and heavy.

The thought of defying her father, the risk of being kicked or punched, made her heart race and her limbs tremble. But until someone stood up to him he would carry on raging and bullying, for what reason was there to stop?

'I do not take offence where none is intended, Miss Jewell,' Melanie chided.

Bronnen felt herself flush. 'I – I beg pardon. I didn't mean you.'

'I am relieved to hear it. Nor will I cause you discomfort by asking who you did mean. You have been so patient and generous, explaining the brewing process and allowing me to watch you work.'

'I've enjoyed it, miss. Anyway, grinding the malt doesn't need much thinking about. So I can let my mind wander.'

'Does it wander anywhere interesting?'

With no defence against Melanie's open curiosity and unable to stop the rush of heat to her face, Bronnen looked away.

'It does! But I shall save my questions and hope that next time I come you might share your happy thoughts?'

'How can you tell?'

'That they are happy?' Melanie smiled. 'Your face has such a glow what else could they be? But

156

when you are brewing I imagine you need all your wits about you.'

Bronnen nodded. 'That's why I thought you'd want quiet while you were drawing. It must be really hard to concentrate if someone's talking all the time.'

'I used to find it so. But I have learned that as long as I nod and smile from time to time the ladies do not require me to say anything. Some wish me to be grateful for their patronage. Others hope to win favour with my father. Whatever their purpose they would rather talk than listen. Which suits me very well, for in rushing to fill the silence they tell me far more than they realise.' She shook her head. 'Now it is I who am talking too much.'

'No,' Bronnen said quickly, and meant it. Melanie Tregarron said things that shocked with their bluntness, yet evoked admiration for the same reason.

'You are generous, Miss Jewell. But I have already told you that. May I come again? I enjoy your company and promise not to get in your way.'

Bronnen nodded shyly. 'I'd like that.'

'Then I shall see you very soon.'

Washed and changed into her green gown, Melanie sat at her dressing table while Ellen brushed her hair until it gleamed, then re-arranged it in a high coil with ringlets in front of her ears. A glance at the clock on her chest of drawers told her it was almost five-thirty.

Rising from the padded velvet stool, she pushed her feet into kid slippers then crossed to the cheval glass.

'Oh, miss!' Ellen sighed. 'Look pretty as a picture, you do. Your pa do dearly love you in that dress. He surely got an eye for what suits you, miss. If you don't mind me saying, I think 'tis lovely him taking an interest.'

Boarding school, art tutors, her fare back to her mother in France – her father had paid for them all. Of course she was grateful. How could she not be? Though as a wealthy man he could easily afford it.

His many and varied business interests and the demands of his legitimate family had been reason enough for his lack of contact. Because before arriving here she could count on one hand the number of times she had actually seen him.

She ought to welcome his interest; after all, better late than never. But so sudden a change made her wary. 'You are quite sure no guests are expected tonight, Ellen?'

'I'm quite sure, miss. I know because Mrs Berryman said that seeing there was just the three of you tonight she'd make a plain dinner. She've done roast fillet of veal with spinach, new potatoes, and baby carrots. Then for afters, a raspberry and currant tart with cream.'

A plain dinner indeed compared to the four or five courses served when they had guests. But it was still richer fare than that served during her years at Oakland Park.

Uneasy without knowing why, Melanie crossed the landing and went downstairs. Pausing outside the drawing room she could hear her father's voice. As ever his tone was jovial. But tonight, she heard determination beneath the cheerfulness.

Was this the secret of his success – the iron will behind the breezy smile? She opened the door. Both men turned.

'My dear, how pretty you look!' Frederick Tregarron's face was flushed, his gaze sharp, assessing, as it swept over her. But what he saw reassured him for his smile was expansive. 'Do you not think so, Richard?' He took the refilled glass handed to him by his heir.

'Please, Papa. A compliment sought has no value.'

'Now, what has ruffled your feathers?' Frederick Tregarron's broad smile faded. 'Has someone upset you?'

'No, everything is fine.' What else could she say?

His good humour restored, he shepherded her towards the table. 'Come, while we enjoy our dinner I want to hear what you have been doing today.'

'This afternoon I spent a most enjoyable hour at the brewhouse sketching Miss Jewell while she worked.'

Richard held her chair and she nodded polite thanks before sitting. Her father went to his place at the head of the table and Richard walked round to sit opposite her.

'What about the commissioned portraits? Surely you have not completed them all?'

'No, Papa. The ladies lead such busy lives that each can spare only an hour or so. With Richard's escort on two afternoons each week, I am able to work on two different portraits. This suits me very well.' Her gaze caught Richard's. She expected him to look away. He didn't, but she couldn't read

159

his expression. The shared moment caused a sudden flutter beneath her ribs.

She reached for her glass of lemonade. The tart liquid soothed a suddenly dry throat.

'Thank you, Mrs Berryman,' her father said the housekeeper came in with the platter of roast veal, set it beside him to be carved, and removed the lids from the serving dishes.

By the time she had helped herself to vegetables and gravy and picked up her knife and fork, Richard was talking to her father about the port's increasing commercial traffic and the profit potential in owning trading schooners.

Was that why Richard had purchased the boatyard? The unfinished hull would not be the only reason. She would ask him, but not in front of her father. She focused on her meal. The meat was succulent, the vegetables cooked to perfection. But that unexpected moment of complicity had tightened her throat and swallowing was difficult.

Richard's remark about events in a person's past still having the power to hurt had lingered in her mind. Often she would turn, or glance up, and find him watching her. But she never knew what he was thinking. His courtesy was impenetrable, sheathing him like armour. He wielded it with the skill of an expert swordsman, parrying questions, redirecting conversations, side-stepping contention.

She did not need his good opinion. Wanting approval from a man who showed no interest beyond that required by good manners *and her father* made her angry with herself.

Yet how cleverly he had defined the difference

between pride and vanity. She was not vain, but felt justifiably proud of her talent. Yet despite her skill at capturing expressions on paper or canvas, she could not read his.

Eventually Ellen came in to take their dessert plates and pour coffee. Placing her crumpled napkin on the table Melanie pushed back her chair.

'If you'll both excuse me–'

'No,' Frederick Tregarron waved her back onto her seat. 'I have to leave shortly and may be away a week.'

Again? Unable to stop herself Melanie glanced across at Richard who was as still as if he had been carved from marble. She admired his restraint. For while her father retained nominal power, it seemed that responsibility for running the business, making decisions and dealing with problems rested solely on Richard's shoulders.

'After giving the matter considerable thought,' her father regarded them both with a broad smile as his restless fingers turned the stem of his wineglass, 'I have concluded that the best interests of all concerned would be served by a match between the two of you.'

Shock stopped Melanie's breath. Her eyes met Richard's for one appalled moment. Unable to bear the mortification, she looked away. She had come here because there was nowhere else, and because he was her father. But he didn't want her: couldn't wait to shift the responsibility on to his heir. It was blackmail. The brief glimpse she had caught of Richard's horror told her he felt the same.

'Papa–'

'I haven't finished. Yes, you are distantly related, but you share no direct blood tie. And your marriage would ensure that my wealth, which is considerable, remains safely within the family. It is in every respect an excellent solution.' He looked from one to the other, smiling in satisfaction.

Solution? Was she such a problem? Dying inside, Melanie stood up. Dropping his napkin on the table, Richard rose as well. 'May I remind you, Papa,' her voice trembled, 'as your heir, Richard's position is already secure. I was – am – grateful to you for making me welcome. Why am I now to be disposed of like – like – an unwanted gift?' Her eyes stung with tears of rage and shame.

'Sit down, Melanie.' Though he was still smiling, his tone demanded obedience and he waited until she sat. Her heart pounded so hard she felt sick. 'There is no need for all this drama.'

'You think not?' Her voice cracked. She did not dare look at Richard. She could still see his horror.

'You girls and your nonsense.' Tregarron eyed her indulgently. 'You read romances and dream of love.'

Melanie's face was on fire and beneath her gown her shift clung to damp skin. She felt utterly betrayed. Anger brought her chin up. 'You mock me, Papa. But surely love offers more chance of happiness than marrying merely for financial convenience?'

'You possess a remarkable talent, Melanie. But you have much to learn. If you must have love, it is as easy to love a rich man as a poor one. Easier. For there is little bliss to be found in poverty.'

'That is not–'

He silenced her with a gesture. Then, draining his glass he rose from the table. 'You will oblige me by thinking about what I've said. I am sure on reflection you will see the many advantages.' He turned to the door.

'For you, perhaps,' Melanie threw at him.

Without pausing, her father left the room.

As the door closed behind him, Melanie bolted from her chair and paced to the window, her arms clasped protectively across her body. 'Lessons in marriage from a man whose wife prefers to live apart from him? How dare he presume to tell me what will make me happy! He doesn't know me at all.'

'Melanie,' Richard pushed back his chair. 'Calm down.'

She dreaded facing him but there was no avoiding it. She whirled round. 'I need no instructions from you on how to conduct myself.'

'In this instance I must beg to differ.'

'Oh, stop being so pompous!'

'Perhaps you might stop being so emotional.'

'How dare you criticise me? What gives you the right to judge? A man who has neither heart nor feelings–' she stopped, knowing she'd gone too far, instantly wishing the words unsaid. It was not an unfeeling man who had helped her see what she had revealed in Mrs Martin's portrait, who had spoken of past events retaining the power to hurt.

As he strode round the table, his eyes burning in a face pale with barely-controlled fury, she felt a stab of panic. But through her fear excitement flashed like lightning. The mask had finally shattered, revealing a man of powerful emotions that rivalled her own.

Standing her ground she glared back at him as defiance battled shame. Reaching her he stopped. For a moment they simply stared at each other.

Then from deep in Richard's throat came a sound that was half growl, half groan. It sent chills racing over her skin. She gasped as his hands gripped her shoulders and hauled her hard against him. His head came down and his mouth covered hers in a passionate kiss that ravished, plundered, and demanded yet more.

After an instant's paralysing shock Melanie melted. Her mouth softened, her lips parted, and she fell headlong.

For a long moment they clung. Then, brusquely, Richard thrust her away, his grip tight enough to bruise though she doubted he was aware of it. 'And you don't know me.'

'Whose fault is that?' she cried. 'You live behind a wall of courtesy.'

Looking into his eyes she recognised anguish and desperation. Was it hers? A reflection? Or was she finally seeing the real man? Then he stepped back, releasing his grip. Never had she felt so alone.

'I – that was unforgivable.' His voice was hoarse. 'Please accept my sincere apolo–'

'No!' she shouted, fighting tears. 'I don't want an apology. I don't deserve it. I should never have said – what I did.' Ashamed of herself and furious with him for shutting her out again, she rubbed her arms, trembling from the violent upheaval ignited by his kiss.

'When I showed you Mrs Martin's portrait you

complimented me on my insight. Yet when I looked at you I saw only the mask you wear, not the man behind it. That was partly your fault. But I was wrong. Wrong to say what I did, and wrong about you.'

'For pity's sake, Melanie.' His features were tight, drawn as if in pain. 'I'm so sorry. I should never–' His voice cracked. 'I can't–' He strode out of the room. Moments later she heard the front door slam.

Chapter Nineteen

After topping up the three casks Bronnen set the bungs loosely in their holes to allow foam from the still-working beer to spill down the rounded sides and into the stillion gutter. Leaving the cellar she walked quickly back through the brewhouse.

Out in the yard, in the cool early morning, the engine piston ticked quietly as it slid in and out of the cylinder. The belt turned the two flywheels and the pump handle rose and fell. Watching it work, listening to the water splashing into the cistern, Bronnen recalled the evening Santo had called in. Remembering his kiss she touched her mouth with a fingertip. Her heart trembled, lifted, and she smiled to herself.

Looking up, seeing the overflow pipe still dry, she crouched to check the fire. Adding more wood, she pushed the shovel back into the firebox and rose to her feet as a man walked into the yard.

165

He snatched off his cap. 'Remember me, miss? Sam Jose? I was Mr George's assistant down Curnock's brewery.'

'Morning, Mr Jose. Yes, I remember. I've often seen you when I come to the brewery for yeast.'

He nodded, but his startled gaze was fixed on the pump. 'Don't mind me asking, miss, but what on God's green earth is that?'

'It's a hot air engine, Mr Jose. Right now it's pumping water up to the cistern in the brewhouse roof–' She stopped as water trickled then gushed out of the overflow. 'Excuse me.' As he stepped back she kicked away the stick. The belt sagged and the pump stopped. The engine ticked quietly on.

'Well, I never! That's some brave machine. Save you hours of work, that will.'

Bronnen nodded. 'Mr Innis only fitted it a few days ago.' Just saying his name kindled a glow inside her. 'But now I wonder how we ever managed without it. Were you looking for someone?'

He dragged his attention back to her. 'You, miss. See, there was a fire at Curnock's yesterday afternoon.'

'Oh no! Was anyone hurt?'

Sam shook his head. 'No, we was lucky. Truth is it should never have happened, but after Mr George died everything fell abroad. I was that busy trying to keep the brews going – which was some job because Mr George was tight as a gin over sharing what he knew – all the other stuff like tidying up and sweeping out didn't get done like it should.'

'Is there much damage?'

'Could 'ave been a lot worse.'

'Do you know how it started?'

Sam shrugged. 'No one's sure. You know what 'tis like, miss, all that wood staging around the copper and mash tun, and the copper fire so close. It don't take more than a stray spark, or a cinder falling. Even before he died Mr George wasn't hisself, God rest him.' Sam twisted his cap in gnarled hands. 'Lived for the brewery, he did. But after he fell down they stairs he wasn't the same. Not that he was ever what you'd call approachable. Still, he had high standards, and eyes like a hawk. But after that fall...' Sam shook his head.

When Bronnen had started coming to Gillyvean with her mother the first thing she had been taught was the importance of keeping the brewhouse clean. Not only to ensure the wholesomeness of the beer, but because coal dust, wood ash, and fine dust from ground malt were potentially explosive.

'Anyhow, we drew water from the well in the yard and set up a bucket line from the shore, and got the fire out before he did too much damage. Mr Arthur got Barnicoat's in to rebuild. But it'll take a good few weeks. Some of the men have gone looking for other jobs.'

Bronnen nodded. 'If they've got families to feed–'

'No, it isn't that. Well, not just that. See, after Mr George passed away, we heard that Mr Arthur was going to advertise for a new head brewer.' Sam twisted his cap tighter. 'That upset the men. They reckon the job should've been mine. Been there over twenty years, I have. But truth is–' he shook his head, angry and embarrassed. 'Thought he was God, Mr George did. Didn't hold with anyone asking questions. Only time I learned anything was if he had to go out during a brew. Then he'd say what to watch for.'

This told her Sam knew he wasn't up to the job, and hated the fact.

'It's bad for everyone when brewers won't share what they know.' Bronnen spoke from the heart. 'I wouldn't be here now if my grandmother and mother hadn't been willing to pass on all they'd learned.'

'Bleddy right,' Sam grumbled. 'I was Mr George's chief assistant. But I had to pick up what I could on the job, and 't wasn't enough. Anyhow, why I'm here, miss. Mr Arthur will be coming dreckly to see Mr Vaughan. He's got a book full of orders that he don't want to lose. But nor do he want to ask any of the other breweries to help out because once customers go somewhere else, they might not come back. So he's going to ask Mr Vaughan if he can use Gillyvean brewhouse to fill his orders until Curnock's is ready again.'

Panic fluttered in Bronnen's chest. 'No! I've got at least two more brews of small beer to make for harvest. He can't expect to take over–'

'No, I didn't mean – that came out wrong.' Sam tried to calm her. 'I didn't mean he was going to take over. He's going to ask Mr Vaughan if you and your ma would brew for him.' He glanced round.

'She's not here right now,' Bronnen said, guessing he was about to ask.

'Between you and me, miss,' Sam lowered his voice, glancing round to make sure they were

168

alone. 'I reck'n Mr Arthur will pay well to make sure he don't lose his orders to other breweries.'

Bronnen thought of the difference some extra money would make. She would be able to afford home visits from the doctor for her mother, a kitchen maid to help with the heavy work, medicines, and for herself a new dress. But even as it formed the mirage dissolved.

'It's too much work for just the two of us.' *Impossible for her alone.*

Sam nodded in agreement. 'No way could you and your ma do it by yourselves. See, that's the other reason I come by. To ask if you'll let me work with you. There's too much I don't know. But I want to learn. Because when Curnock's is working again I want to put in for head brewer.'

Bronnen studied him, her thoughts racing. If Sam had been at Curnock's for twenty years he would have absorbed a lot more than he realized. And because he knew the basics, his help would make her job that much easier. Everyone would benefit.

'If Mr Vaughan says it's all right I'll teach you everything my mother taught me. But two of us still won't be enough. Mother haven't been well,' she added quickly. 'We'd need–'

'A stoker and a cellarman,' Sam finished for her.

'That's right! But where will we find–'

'Out on the drive.' Sam said, shuffling his feet.

Bronnen stared at him. 'What?'

'Well, miss, I was hoping you'd say yes, so I brung Alf Carter and Tommy Ingram with me. Only they didn't want to come up 'til after I'd spoke to you. They don't want to work nowhere else, but they need money coming in while the brewery is being repaired. Give them a shout, shall I?'

After an instant's hesitation, Bronnen pushed doubt aside. Sam's arrival could not have come at a better time. 'Yes, call them. I'll light the copper fire.' An hour ago she'd been worried about managing the next brew on her own. Now she'd been offered all the help she could need from men who knew the job.

Ought she to wait for Mr Vaughan? She knew he would come and tell her what Mr Curnock wanted. He didn't have to, but he would. He believed in doing things the proper way. So he would not agree to Mr Curnock's request without first talking it through with her and her mother. *But her mother had not been here for days.*

Waiting would waste valuable time. Surely it made more sense to show the men round and get the brew started? It wasn't likely Mr Vaughan would refuse. Besides, if she and the men were busy when he arrived, even if he noticed her mother's absence it wouldn't bother him.

Sam returned followed by a short square man of about fifty wearing a grubby threadbare peaked cap, a woollen shirt with the sleeves rolled back over brawny forearms, and dark canvas trousers tucked into sturdy boots.

'Miss Jewell,' Sam said. 'This 'ere is Alf Carter. He've been stoker at Curnock's for near on thirty years. Learned from his father.'

'Miss,' Alf nodded briefly.

'Pleased to meet you, Mr Carter. 'Tis usually me looking after the copper fire so I know how

170

important 'tis. You and Mr George must've been a good team.'

'Hear that, Alf?' Sam said.

'I heard,' Alf retorted. 'What you burning?' He jerked his head towards the copper.

'Wood, it heats the water faster.'

'Right, if you want to get the brew started this half of the team better get to that fire.' He disappeared beneath the staging.

'Alf have never been one for chatting,' Sam said. 'But he don't mean nothing by it.'

'I'm just glad he's here,' Bronnen said. 'He's taken a load off my shoulders.' She turned to the second man. Of similar age and build to Alf, he pulled off his cap and ducked his head politely. 'Mr Ingram?'

'Tommy, miss. We was Sam, Alf, and Tommy at Curnocks, so best to stick with that. Else we'll be all abroad.'

'I'm Bronnen Jewell.'

He nodded. 'I seen you sometimes when I go to meet my missus. Jess do work down the soup kitchen.'

'I know Jess.' Bronnen pictured a plump, rosy-faced woman with a ready smile. 'I wish I had her patience. Some of the regulars can be ... difficult. But I've never seen her lose her temper.'

'Golden she is, dear of her. Shall us look at the cellars now?'

Two hours later Richard Vaughan walked into the yard. Bronnen had just relit the fire on the shovel ready to restart the engine and pump. Pushing it into the firebox, she stood up, feeling heat in her cheeks as she wiped her hands on her

171

coarse apron.

'Morning, Mr Vaughan.'

'Good morning, Miss Jewell. I see you have anticipated my visit and the reason for it.' His amused expression calmed her anxiety.

'I hope you don't mind, sir. Sam got here soon after I did. He told me about the fire and said Mr Arthur would be coming to see you. Sam had brought Alf and Tommy with him because they don't want to go to another brewery. I couldn't see you saying no to Mr Arthur, so it seemed best just to get on.' She ran out of breath.

'What are you brewing?'

'Two coppers of strong ale first, sir. Then a third mash of small beer but I'll top it up with half a bushel of fresh malt. I'd sooner make it as a separate brew but there won't be time to do that *and* fill Mr Curnock's orders.'

'Just do your best, Miss Jewell.' His smile faded. 'I notice your mother is not here.'

Bronnen swallowed. 'No, sir. She's not been well.' She held her breath.

'I'm sorry to hear it. I hope we shall see her back and in good health very soon. Meanwhile she will be comforted to hear that you have experienced help to assist with the additional work.'

'Not half so glad as I am,' Bronnen blurted. Then felt hot colour rise like a tide and flood her face.

'Quite so,' he murmured, one corner of his mouth tilting. 'Mr Curnock recognises the great convenience of having Gillyvean produce his ales and beers while repairs are made to his brewery. Rest assured the additional work involved will be reflected in the wages paid to you and the men.'

Knowing how tightly Arthur Curnock controlled the brewery purse, she wished she might have been a fly on the wall while the two men negotiated. But Arthur Curnock needed Gillyvean so all Mr Vaughan would have had to do was name his price and stand firm.

'Thank you, sir. Much obliged.'

'It was my pleasure.'

'Sir, we'll be needing more malt and casks.'

'The brewery dray should shortly be arriving with the first load. Mr Curnock is hopeful that the malt has remained unaffected by the smoke. However–' he continued as she was gathering her courage to interrupt. 'In your mother's absence the final decision is yours.' With a final nod he left.

Pride, pleasure and relief warmed Bronnen. About to return to the brewhouse she heard clopping hoofs and the grinding rumble of iron-rimmed wheels approaching on the back driveway. Laden with casks the brewery dray turned in through the open double-doors.

Bronnen waved to the driver and ran into the brewhouse, meeting Tommy as he emerged from the second cellar.

'The casks 've come.'

'That's all right, miss. You get on. Me and Charlie will manage.'

They stopped for a few minutes at midday when Ellen brought over huge platters of sandwiches and slices of fruit pie. The men drank small beer. Bronnen had lemonade. As soon as they had eaten, everyone returned to work. Bronnen had just restarted the engine and pump when she heard the dray returning.

This time it carried sacks of malt. Arthur Curnock clambered down from his seat beside the driver.

'Miss Jewell.' His mouth widened briefly. 'You will find this malt perfectly acceptable.'

The implied order banished her sympathy. Acutely aware of the responsibility on her shoulders she reached into an open sack, scooped out a handful, held it to her nose and breathed in the fait tang of charred wood, smoke and soot. *Was it enough to taint the ale?*

'Do be sure,' he warned quietly. 'Condemning it will cost me a lot of money.'

As her pulse throbbed loudly, Bronnen turned so the sunlight fell across her hand and stirred a finger through the kiln-dried barley shoots. Looking closer she saw several grains of raw barley. Startled, she dropped the malt back into the sack, dug deeper for a new handful, and found more barley grains.

Surely George Curnock had inspected the malt before it was ground? But if he'd seen the grains he would have realised what they signified. So why had he accepted it?

Putting a shoot in her mouth she chewed, tasting smoke. Nor did it have the full-bodied mellow flavour of the malt she used at Gillyvean. Relief coursed through her.

'I'm sorry, Mr Curnock. The malt is tainted and there are raw barley grains in it.'

Arthur stiffened. 'What? Are you sure?'

'See for yourself.' She held out her hand and he peered at it. 'It's a trick some malt-dealers use to

174

make up weight.' Why would a brewer of George Curnock's reputation accept less than the best? It didn't make sense to her unless – had Arthur Curnock insisted they bought on price and not quality?

'Well, of all the– I'm not having that.'

'Beg pardon, Mr Curnock, but here at Gillyvean we always use Mr Treeve's malt.'

Arthur huffed an angry sigh. 'All right, if you must. But you are not to agree any deal without first securing a ten percent discount. My nephew would be the first to tell you there are no friends in business.'

Chapter Twenty

Following the burial of George Curnock, the family returned to Curnock House. Treeve had asked his aunt Caroline, Arthur's wife, to act as hostess for the post-funeral tea. Resplendent in black bombazine, she moved among the guests ensuring everyone had something to eat and drink.

Mrs Eathorne and Kitty the housemaid had set up a buffet along one wall of the drawing room. On a starched damask cloth plates of sandwiches cut into dainty triangles sat next to raspberry tartlets, buttered scones, splits topped with strawberry jam and clotted cream, and two kinds of cake. On another table the best china cups and saucers had been laid out next to milk, sugar, and a constantly refilled teapot. There was also fresh lemonade for the ladies and wine or ale for the gentlemen. Kitty and Mrs Eathorne went from group to group, moved among the guests, replenishing plates and cups.

Revelling in his role of host, Treeve greeted mourners as they arrived and accepted condolences with a suitably serious expression.

Santo overheard several people enquire about the brewery's future. Listening to Treeve's glib response, that Curnock's would overcome this tragedy and continue to supply the town with excellent ales, Santo wondered what his Uncle Arthur had in mind.

Hushed murmurs gradually gave relaxed into normal conversation as people ate and drank and exchanged news.

Feeling like a spare part among these people who knew each other well, Santo quietly left the room and went to his uncle's study. There had to be a reason why George was on the quay that night.

On the cluttered desk, half-hidden beneath a ledger, he found a piece of paper. On it his uncle had scrawled *Banfield, 24th 8.30*. As Arthur and Treeve would be occupied for another hour at least, Santo decided to call on Dr Banfield.

'I appreciate you seeing me,' he said as a maid led him into the consulting room.

The physician indicated a chair and resumed his own seat behind his desk. 'What seems to be the trouble, Mr Innis?'

Santo sat. 'With me? Nothing. I've come about my uncle. George Curnock? He drowned last week.'

176

'Yes. I heard. You have my sympathy.'

Santo nodded. 'Much obliged, sir. But what I'd really like is some answers.'

The physician tapped his fingertips together. 'I'm afraid I'm not at liberty–'

'I'm not here to cause trouble,' Santo said quickly. 'He've gone and nothing will bring him back. I just want to find out what happened. My uncle had no business being down on the quay at all, let alone at night. It must have been dark when he went into the water because the tide wasn't full until late.' Taking the piece of paper from his pocket, Santo laid it gently on the desk so the physician could read it.

'I found this in his study. Did he come to see you that evening?'

Silent for several seconds, Banfield nodded. 'You're probably aware that your uncle had fallen down some stairs at the brewery?'

'Yes,' Santo nodded. 'He'd been complaining about headaches.'

'Unfortunately that wasn't the only repercussion. The blow to his head also deprived him of his sense of taste and smell.'

Santo recalled his uncle's constant sniffing and air of desperate anxiety.

'When he came to see me,' the doctor continued, 'he wanted me to tell him when those senses would return. Unfortunately I could offer him no assurance that they would.' The small movement of his shoulders betrayed helplessness. 'We know so little about the workings of the brain.'

Realising what this news would have meant to his uncle, Santo stood up. 'Thank you for your

177

time, and for being straight with me.'

'I wish—' the physician shook his head. 'Please accept my condolences.'

As Santo returned to the house, Treeve was on the front doorstep bidding farewell to some departing guests. Santo nodded to them politely then went inside. Seconds later Treeve followed.

'Where have you been?' he hissed. 'You had no right sneaking off like that. You should have been here.'

'You and Aunt Caroline were doing fine. You didn't need me.' Santo opened the door to his uncle's study.

'What are you doing? That's Father's private room. You have no business in there.'

'I think I know why he died,' Santo said quietly over his shoulder.

'Don't be ridiculous,' Treeve sneered. 'How could you know that?' But he kept his voice low and glanced toward the drawing room to make sure they weren't overheard.

'I've just come from Dr Banfield. Your father went to see him the night he died.'

'Why would he do that? He never said anything to me.'

'He didn't want anyone to know.'

'I haven't got time for this,' Treeve snapped. 'Mr Downing will be here any minute to read Father's will.' But he didn't move away.

Stepping into the study, Santo waited while Treeve reluctantly followed, then closed the door. 'You remember Uncle George was having bad headaches?'

'Of course I remember. Nor am I surprised

after a fall like that. He was fortunate his injuries weren't worse than a bump on the head.'

'That's the trouble, they were.'

'What? He never said–'

'Of course he didn't,' Santo felt his own temper fraying. 'When have you ever heard him admit to a weakness? Never, because he was always afraid someone might try to take advantage. The fall,' he went on before Treeve could interrupt, 'did something to his brain. He lost his sense of smell and taste.' He watched realisation dawn in his cousin's eyes.

'Oh my God,' Treeve whispered. 'That's why he went to see Banfield? To find out when they'd come back?'

Santo nodded.

'What did the doctor tell him?'

'That they might not come back at all.'

Treeve's shock gave way to anger. 'What did he do that for?'

'He didn't have a choice. It was the truth.' Watching his frowning cousin, Santo could see his mind working. Then Treeve looked up, his expression defiant and threatening.

'Have you told anyone else?'

'Of course I haven't. I've just this minute got back.'

'Make sure you don't. Father's death was a tragic accident. You hear me? An *accident*. I don't care what Banfield told you. My father would never– A rumour like that could do untold damage. Even if there's no truth in it, which there isn't, I'm not having the family upset.' He pushed his face close to Santo's. 'Say one word and you'll be sorry. If it

179

wasn't for my parents you'd have been brought up in an orphanage. You owe us.'

Not bothering to reply, Santo opened the door and waited. Treeve stalked out, shooting him a venomous glare. With his hand on the doorknob, Santo glanced back. This comfortable, slightly shabby room had been his uncle's retreat on those rare evenings when he wasn't at the brewery.

With greater sympathy than they ever shared while George was alive, Santo could understand why – having lost his ability to do the job that was everything to him – his uncle might have taken his own life. But he also understood Treeve's refusal even to consider this possibility. Suicide was a terrible crime. Spreading outward like ripples, the scandal could irreparably damage both the brewery and Treeve's malt business.

He returned to the drawing room. The guests had gone. Treeve was discussing barley prices with Arthur's son, Simon, who farmed land near Mawnan. Simon's wife Emily sat with her daughter Nancy on a settee, while her son Jonathan, bored and restless, stuffed cake into his mouth.

Looking out of the window at the harbour, Santo thought of Bronnen, and the kiss that had forced him to face the truth about his irritability and disturbed sleep.

He craved affection, a soft warm body to hold, someone he could share his thoughts and ambitions with. He had few happy memories of his childhood. His mother had only shown him affection when they were alone. It wasn't until some years after her death that he realised she had feared his father's jealousy. Their deaths had left him relieved, guilty, and frightened.

When Aunt Hannah had put her arms around him it was the first time he had felt safe. Then she died and once again he was alone.

What sense was there in loving someone? Losing them ripped a jagged wound. It healed but left a lasting scar. Better to stay detached. He could deal with that. In Dartford, when the loneliness became unbearable, he visited a pretty widow recommended by Will McAndrew. Or he went drinking and got into fights, though unlike his father he never hit anyone smaller than himself. One morning he woke up battered and bloody on a strange floor with no memory of the previous evening. He hadn't had a drink since.

'Mr Downing,' Mrs Eathorne announced, bringing in the family solicitor. Santo turned from the view and his introspection. This is what everyone had been waiting for.

'Will you take a cup of tea, Mr Downing?' Caroline Curnock offered.

'Thank you, no.' Tall and thin with the profile of a bird of prey and grey hair receding from a widow's peak, the solicitor's voice was quiet, his diction precise. In his black cutaway coat with its high shawl collar and pearl grey trousers that tapered to his polished black shoes, he resembled an elegant crow.

'In that case, if the ladies will excuse us, I suggest we adjourn to the dining room.' Arthur led the way with the solicitor. Treeve hurried after them leaving Santo to follow.

Mr Downing went to the head of the table. Arthur and Treeve sat next to him on either side.

Closing the door Santo pulled out the nearest chair as the solicitor opened his case and removed a folded hand-written document.

Santo knew Treeve would inherit the bulk of his father's estate. Surely Uncle George had left him something? Any money at all would be welcome. His engines were costing quite a bit to build and he needed to settle his account with Jack.

Taking a pair of spectacles from his pocket Mr Downing put them on, unfolded the document then cleared his throat.

'You're a busy man, Downing,' Arthur said briskly. 'So skip the preamble.'

'Very well. This is the last will and testament of George Henry Curnock.'

Out of sight under the table Santo's hand curled into a fist. *Please...*

'Signed and witnessed in March 1800.'

Though he managed not to flinch, Santo's disappointment was crushing. The will had been made a few years after Treeve's birth and never updated.

Despite living as a member of the Curnock family for two decades he did not rate a mention. Was this George's punishment for his defiance in refusing to become a brewer?

The reason didn't matter. Nor would he waste time on anger or regret. With no legacy coming to him he'd have to find some other way of raising money.

Raising his eyes he saw Treeve smirking at him down the length of the table. Pride stiffened his spine and he inclined his head in a mocking salute.

As Mr Downing refolded the document, Arthur clapped Treeve on the shoulder and shook his hand. Santo opened the door for the solicitor who paused briefly to thank him, long enough for Santo to see the sympathy in his gaze before he continued out into the hall.

Arthur hurried past without a glance. Santo was about to follow.

'Wait one moment.' Treeve's eyes glittered with malice and excitement. 'Now this property is legally mine you have no right to stay. However I am willing to let you continue living here.'

'What do you want? Thanks?'

'I haven't finished. There's a condition.'

'What condition?'

'Stay away from Bronnen Jewell.'

'What did you say?'

'You heard me. She's spoken for.'

'Who by?'

Treeve smirked.

'You?' Santo laughed. 'I don't think so.'

'Well, you're wrong,' Treeve sneered. 'I've talked to her father. She's mine.'

'I don't care what you and her father agreed. She's not a cartload of barley to be bought and sold.'

'She's mine.'

'Never.'

'We'll see about that. In the meantime,' Treeve thrust his face towards Santo's. 'Pack your things and get out. You're not welcome here.'

Chapter Twenty-one

Bronnen placed the buttered slices of bread on a large plate and set it between the jam and cheese.

'You sit down, Ma. I'll make the tea.'

'Curnock's orders is going to be some work, Bron.' With trembling hands Sarah pulled out a chair and sank onto it, rubbing her forehead.

'Yes, but I'll have Sam, Alf, and Tommy helping.' Bronnen placed the big teapot on the table as her father and Adam came in. 'Come on, Ma,' she urged softly. 'Try to eat something.'

'I got no stomach for it, bird.'

Biting her tongue, Bronnen poured tea, added milk to her mother's and set it in front of her.

'You heard about the fire at Curnock's?' Adam asked, drying his hands then sitting down at the table.

Bronnen nodded. 'Mr Curnock has asked Mr Vaughan if we can fill his orders until the brewery is repaired and working again.'

'Being paid for the extra work, are you?' her father demanded through a mouthful of bread and cheese

'Yes, Mr Vaughan came by and told me himself.' Bronnen turned to her mother. 'Ma, let me ask Mr Oliver to make up a tonic for you.'

Sarah glanced nervously at her husband. 'No need for that, bird. I'm all right. Just a bit tired.'

Sick of lies and pretence, of watching her

184

mother's health deteriorate, Bronnen was about to argue when beneath the table her mother's hand gripped her thigh. 'Don't, Bron,' she whispered, her head bent. 'You're making it worse.' Then she pulled her cup and saucer closer. 'When have you got to go back to the brewhouse?'

'As soon as I've had my tea.'

'You better take something back for Sam.'

'We aren't no bleddy soup kitchen,' Morley objected.

'Just this once,' Sarah said. 'Bron won't be able to manage without Sam and he'll be working a lot longer hours than he's used to. We don't want her getting the blame if Mr Arthur loses customers because he can't supply the beer. She might lose her job.'

'Soon she won't be needing no job. I been asked for her.'

'Asked what?' Adam said blankly.

'What d'you think?' his father snapped. 'Someone want to marry her.'

Bronnen saw her mother's shock and knew it mirrored her own. 'Who–?'

'You'll know soon enough. The person got some business to settle first.'

Bronnen first thought was of Santo. But they hardly knew each other. *They had talked, told each other things never revealed to another soul. And he had kissed her.* Besides, who else could it be? She wanted so much for it to be Santo she was almost afraid to hope.

The following afternoon, leaving Alf helping Tommy scald casks ready for the new brew while

Sam skimmed the head, Bronnen went to buy fresh malt.

Approaching the malthouse she smelled an acrid burnt-toast odour and could hear raised voices.

'Swear to God, Mr Curnock, I dunno how it happened. I never left the furnace.'

'Clear the kiln, bag up the burned malt, then dry a new batch. We're short of pale, so give it twelve hours over a small fire. Small, do you hear? Now get out of my sight!'

'Customer, Mr Curnock,' the maltster muttered.

As Bronnen hesitated in the doorway, Treeve turned, all smiling charm.

'Miss Jewell, how nice to see you. Come in, come in.'

'If this isn't a good time–'

'Losing a batch of malt is a nuisance to be sure, but soon remedied. What really concerns me is the cause. My men are too experienced for such mistakes.' He sighed, shaking his head. 'I fear the malthouse boiler has been deliberately sabotaged.'

Surprised to hear such a thing, Bronnen was even more surprised at him telling her. Clearly he wanted – expected – a response. But unwilling to be manipulated she stayed silent.

When he realized she wasn't going to speak, he continued smoothly, 'I am sorrier than you can imagine.' The sadness in his tone sounded real. But his eyes were as hard and sharp as broken glass. 'For I fear the person responsible is my cousin. I have been paying him to maintain the furnace. He had expectations of a legacy from my father. Being excluded–' he spread his hands,

186

shaking his head. 'Hopes dashed can make people very vindictive.'

'I cannot believe–' Bronnen stopped. She should have kept quiet. Not only had she betrayed herself, she had given him the opening he wanted.

'You do not *want* to believe it,' Treeve said. 'Indeed, who would? But how well do you really know him? Even as a child he was stubborn. Once he had an idea in his head nothing would move him. Now instead of setting up home and preparing to marry, he is spending every penny he earns or can borrow on these hot-air engines. We all wish for success in our chosen occupation. I have been most fortunate in that respect. My name is a byword for best-quality malt. But if the time and attention my cousin is devoting to his private interests means the jobs for which he is being paid are suffering... Forgive me. I should not have spoken so freely. Indeed, I have shocked myself. But I hold you responsible.'

'Me?' Bronnen said, startled.

'Come now, Miss Jewell,' his smile was arch. 'You must be aware that, despite your occupation which you will agree is unusual for a woman, you retain all those feminine qualities of gentleness and charm that encourage confidences?'

She raised her chin, her cheeks hot. To him it would appear she was blushing. In truth she was angry – at herself for having listened to his spite, and at him for expecting her to believe his malicious attack on Santo. His compliments made her skin crawl.

'Much obliged for the warning. I'll take more care in future. Or who knows what people may tell me?' As his smile faltered she continued, 'Does the loss leave you short?'

'No, not at all,' he said quickly. 'It is an inconvenience, nothing more.'

'Good,' Bronnen said. 'Because I'm here to place an order – so long as we can agree terms. The malt brought to Gillyvean from Curnock's was spoiled by smoke from the fire.'

He seized her hand, clasping it between his. 'My dear Miss Jewell, I am filled with admiration. You have succeeded where my father – God rest his soul – failed. Though my malt is the best, he was never able to persuade my uncle to buy it. I think you must possess some remarkable powers.' He started to raise her hand to his lips.

Bronnen pulled free without apology and brushed her hand against her skirt. She didn't want him touching her. He had no right. 'Like I said, Mr Curnock, first we need to agree terms.'

'If you have come to me, it is because Uncle Arthur has finally given up on Endean's. I will supply you with top quality malt at a generous discount of five per cent.'

Bronnen inclined her head politely. 'Good day to you.' She turned towards the door.

'Where are you going?'

Hearing the shock in his voice, Bronnen was careful to keep all expression from her face as she glanced over her shoulder. 'We're both busy, Mr Curnock. I don't want to waste your time or mine.'

'You can't just walk away.'

'Yes, I can.'

'Wait!' She turned, watched him smooth his

hair. 'Give me a figure.'

'Thirty per cent.'

He laughed. 'You are not serious.'

'I would never joke about Mr Tregarron's business. P'rhaps I'm wrong, but I'd have thought a contract with Curnock's brewery would be good for your malthouse. But you probably got more customers than–'

'Ten.'

Bronnen shook her head. 'Like I was about to say, you and Mr Endean are not the only suppliers. Twenty.'

Astonishment battled with irritation. 'Miss Jewell, you really are–' he shook his head, words failing him. 'Fifteen, and that is my final–'

'Fifteen it is.' Custom demanded she shake his hand, but she kept the contact brief. After they agreed the number of bushels per week and a delivery day, she nodded again and crossed to the door.

'This has been a revelation, Miss Jewell. I look forward to our future dealings.'

'Mr Curnock,' she dipped her head. Walking away, her heart still thumping, Bronnen could hardly believe what she had done.

Treeve Curnock watched her retreating figure. 'You will pay dearly for that, Bronnen Jewell,' he murmured. 'Indeed you will.'

'Dear life, miss.' Sam's brows shot up when Bronnen told him about the deal she had struck. 'You done well there. He don't give nothing away.'

'It was Mr Arthur who told me to insist on discount.'

'I'd give good money to see his face when he hear you got fifteen per cent.' Alf gave a brief barking laugh and stomped off, shaking his head.

The men's praise warmed Bronnen as she began grinding the next batch of malt.

A while later she went out to the yard to put more wood on the shovel in the firebox. Above the click of the piston and splash water pouring into the cistern she heard footsteps and male voices. She straightened up, her heart leaping into her throat as she saw Santo follow Richard Vaughan and another man into the yard.

'Ah, Miss Jewell.' Richard Vaughan's smile was genuine but he looked as if he hadn't slept in days. Was Mr Tregarron away *again?* 'This is Mr Rowse from Dene Quarry.'

'Mr Rowse,' she smiled politely.

'You and Mr Innis are already acquainted.'

Meeting Santo's gaze, Bronnen recalled the emotions and sensations he had kindled in her, and saw he too was remembering. A blush tingled over her entire body as his left eyelid flickered down in a secret reminder of precious moments shared.

'Miss Jewell,' Richard Vaughan's quiet voice dragged her attention back. 'You have been using Mr Innis's engine for a while now. Will you tell Mr Rowse what you think of it?'

Focusing on the quarryman but still acutely aware of Santo, she wiped her palms down her apron. 'Well, sir, truth is I had my doubts at first. But now I can't imagine being without it. We need hundreds of gallons of water for each brew, and more again for washing out the vessels. So I had to spend hours pumping water up to the cistern by hand. While I was doing that I couldn't be getting on with anything else. This engine saves me at least two hours a day. It's easy to work as well. You just light a wood fire on here,' crouching she drew out the flat spade to show them, then pushed it back into the firebox. 'As soon as the air inside the cylinder is hot, the engine starts working. You jam the stick under the pulley to tighten it so it works the pump handle.' As she spoke, water started gushing out of the overflow pipe at the top of the brewhouse. Quickly Bronnen kicked the stick away. The belt sagged loose, the pump handle grew still, and the engine ticked quietly on.

'Well, blow me down,' the quarryman murmured. 'I never seen nothing like that, not in all my born days.'

'When I've finished with the pump, I let the fire go out and the engine stops. That's all. Like I said, 'tis simple.'

Glancing at Santo, Bronnen was thrilled at the warmth in his gaze as he silently mouthed 'Thank you.'

'Well, Mr Rowse, is that recommendation enough?' Richard said.

'It certainly is.' He turned to Santo. 'I'll take two, Mr Innis. How soon can you–?'

The thunderous roar of an explosion made Bronnen start violently.

Richard and Santo turned to the quarryman who shook his head. ''Tisn't us, nor any of the others. We're not blasting today.'

As Alf, Tommy and Sam burst out of the brewhouse, Bronnen saw shock drain Santo's face of colour.

'Oh, God. It's the *Mercury*. Her boiler's blown up.'

Bronnen gasped, her hands flying to her mouth. *Just days ago he was on that ship.*

Santo turned to Richard. 'I got to go.'

Richard put a hand on his shoulder. 'There'll be no survivors.'

'Not Will, I know that.' Grief roughened Santo's voice. 'He'd have been in the engine room – but perhaps – someone – I – I need to–' He shot a desperate glance at Bronnen. Aching in sympathy, her eyes brimming, she understood.

As Santo sprinted out of the yard, Richard offered Mr Rowse some refreshment, and Bronnen followed Sam and the others back into the brewhouse.

Santo ran nearly all the way, only slowing when the pain in his side stopped his breath. Before reaching the top of High Street, which plunged down the hill to Market Strand, he had been able to look over the roofs of cottages and warehouses to the inner harbour. A fleet of small boats were milling around in the Carrick Roads. Some had already turned back.

By the time he reached the quay his chest was on fire and his legs felt like jelly. He pushed his way through the sombre crowd on the quay, reaching the far end as two fishermen in faded check shirts and filthy canvas trousers tucked into boots, staggered up the stone steps.

'Anything?' he rasped, heaving air into burning

192

lungs. 'The engineer was a friend.'

Beneath a weathered tan their faces were pale and streaming with sweat. Both shook their heads. One pushed his peaked cap back and scratched a pale scalp under greasy grey hair. 'Nothing to bring back. All the metal have sunk and the wood is just small bits. Some blast it was.' He sucked in a breath. 'Least they wouldn't have known nothing about it.'

Santo tasted the salty metallic tang of blood as he clamped the soft inner flesh of his bottom lip between his teeth to stop himself roaring at them. It might make them feel better to think so, but it wasn't true.

Will McAndrew would have known. He wouldn't have had time to prevent it; not enough even to shout a warning. But he was too experienced an engineer not to have realised what was about to happen. What hell must he have suffered in those last terrible moments?

Santo had seen his desperation at being forced to ignore every rule of safety to meet the Admiralty's contradictory demands. Will's haggard features had aged ten years in as many days under the pressure of making sure Hall's won the contract.

Scalding rage erupted from deep inside him. Abruptly turning away from the murmuring crowd, he strode up the slope from the quay and headed back through the town to Gillyvean.

Chapter Twenty-two

As Ellen withdrew, closing the door behind her, Richard rose from his chair in front of the bureau and crossed to a silver tray containing two decanters and cut crystal glasses. Pouring out a generous measure of cognac he handed it to Santo who didn't hesitate, downing half in a single gulp, grimacing as he swallowed.

'Much obliged.' His chest still burned and his voice was rough and raw.

'My dear chap, I'm so sorry.'

'Mr Tregarron back, is he?'

'He arrived shortly after Mr Rowse left.'

'I want to see him.'

'About the accident?'

'It was no accident. It was murder. Don't try to stop me,' Santo warned.

'I doubt I could.' Richard stepped back.

Realising he was not going to be prevented from seeing the man he considered partly responsible for Will's death, Santo calmed down. 'Sorry,' he muttered. He rubbed one hand over his face and felt stubble rasp against his palm. 'Will was a good friend.' His throat clogged with grief and he cleared it loudly, clinging to control. 'The officers and seamen – their families don't even know yet. It's such a bloody waste.'

'If you storm in,' Richard said quietly, 'you'll have lost before you start.'

Santo swung round. 'I mustn't be mad in case it upsets *him?*'

'I didn't say that. *Use* your anger. What do you *want*, Innis? Someone to blame? You want him to admit responsibility?'

'That'd be a start,' Santo was bitter.

'Those men will still be dead.'

'Christ, you're hard.'

'No, but I've stood where you're standing. When my wife died–' He shook his head abruptly. 'Blame achieved nothing. So I ask again, what do you want out of this meeting?'

'To make him see there's a safer option.'

Richard said nothing, merely inclining his head, point made. Then he opened the door. 'Come.'

Santo was no stranger to Frederick Tregarron's study with its panelled walls, Turkish carpet, glass-fronted bookcases, richly upholstered chairs, and marble fireplace. Despite the difference in their station he had always felt comfortable here, but not today. Since he and Richard had entered the room the atmosphere had deteriorated. Now it could be cut with a knife.

'Sir, surely this is proof how dangerous high-pressure steam is? I can offer a safe alternative. All I need is–'

'Mr Innis, I have invested heavily in the new Cornish multi-tube boiler. As far as I'm concerned high-pressure steam *is* the future. Clearly there are problems. But your job is to solve them, not waste time on distractions. High-pressure steam works perfectly well in railway locomotives.'

'With respect, sir, while it may *work* well enough there have also been a number of fatal accidents.

195

But when a locomotive boiler blows up only two men die. When a ship's boiler explodes, you don't only lose the crew and passengers, you also lose the ship and her cargo. That's exactly what happened to three river boats on the Mississippi.'

'Which only adds weight to my argument that you should be finding the cause.'

Santo raked his hair in frustration. 'There *isn't* one single cause. But until the Admiralty and the manufacturer are willing to listen, more men will die and ships will be lost.'

'You can't possibly know that.'

'I was aboard the *Mercury* just days ago. I saw gauges that didn't work. I watched an honest, careful engineer hold down a safety valve with a brick so the ship could reach the speed demanded by the officer in command. Why did he do it? Because he needed a good report from the commander for Hall's to win the Admiralty contract. That contract would give the company years of work. They could take on more men, move to bigger premises. All that weight was on Will McAndrew's shoulders.'

As Tregarron looked away, renewed anger drove Santo on. 'The boiler should have been cleaned, the seals checked, and the water gauge flushed through before the ship put to sea again. Any engineer would have known that, and Will was one of the best. He would have asked for time to do it. But someone decided it wasn't necessary.'

'Yes, thank you, Innis,' Tregarron snapped. 'You have made your point.'

'Will McAndrew would have made exactly the same points. But no one was listening.'

'You cannot be sure the boiler was resp–'

'Of course the bloody boiler was responsible,' Santo shouted. 'The ship exploded!'

'How dare you speak so to me!' Tregarron was pale with fury. 'You will apologise,' he demanded. 'At once.'

Santo remained silent, his thoughts racing. If he retreated all would be as it had been, except for the blow to his pride. No, it wouldn't. Backing down would be an admission that he was wrong, and he wasn't.

'I'm waiting.' Tregarron's bloodless lips were stiff, the skin around his nostrils blue-white.

Glimpsing shock beneath Tregarron's rage, Santo felt its echo in his rapid heartbeat. From the corner of his eye he saw Richard make a small gesture with one hand and recognised the warning. *Consider the consequences*. He knew only too well what he was risking. But his friend had been blown to pieces.

Santo met Tregarron's furious gaze. 'With respect, Mr Tregarron, I can't and won't deny what I know to be true.'

'Your arrogance is astonishing. You claim to know everything that is wrong with high-pressure steam, but instead of suggesting ways in which the problems might be resolved, your plan is to abandon it altogether for some ridiculous–'

'At least my engine will not kill people.'

'I'll hear no more,' Tregarron barked, throwing up one hand. 'Because of your remarkable ability I have allowed you greater latitude than any other engineer in my employ. I even sent you to spend time with other companies.'

'And the developments I worked on improved the design of our mining engines,' Santo retaliated. 'You trusted me before. Why won't you trust me now?'

'Because you are wrong,' Tregarron shouted.

'Then you don't need me no more.'

'Don't,' Richard murmured.

'You owe me, Innis,' Tregarron said. 'Had I not been willing to take a chance on you, accepting you as an apprentice even though you hadn't a penny in the world, we would not be having this conversation.'

'No one knows that better'n me. But if you're talking of debts, you done very well out of all my work over the years.'

'I don't deny it. And I should like to continue our association. But you must give up–'

'Sorry, sir, I can't.'

Frederick Tregarron waved him away. 'A bad decision, Innis.'

'At least I'm alive to make it,' Santo hurled the words over his shoulder as Richard drew him away. 'A high-pressure steam boiler killed Will McAndrew. How many more have to die before you'll look at other options?'

Propelling Santo out into the hall with a hand on his back, Richard quietly closed the study door. 'That went well,' he said dryly as they walked up the stairs.

Santo dragged both hands through his hair. 'All right, maybe I shouldn't have – but I couldn't–'

'So I saw. Mr Tregarron likes to think of himself as forward-thinking. In some ways he is, especially if he can see a profit. He may be – no, he certainly is – stubborn. But he's not a fool. He has been down to look at the brewhouse pump so he can't fail to have recognised the potential of hot-air engines.'

'But not in ships.'

Richard shrugged. 'He invested heavily in Hall's and the new boilers. The *Mercury*'s loss has shaken him. But acknowledging an alternative would be the same as admitting he'd backed the wrong horse with high-pressure steam.'

'I s'pose what you're saying is there's no chance he'll let you put his money in.' Santo rubbed the back of his neck where the muscles were rigid with tension. 'He's wrong, and he'll regret it.'

Richard glanced across at him. 'Do you? Regret it?'

'Not a word. I may have lost my job, but now I've got more time.'

Picking up the decanter, Richard raised it. 'Another?' Santo shook his head. The first had been medicine. Another would be one too many.

Richard added a little to his glass then raised it in a toast. 'To new ventures.'

'What? Sorry, I don't–'

'Mr Tregarron was not involved in the purchase of Anstey's. The yard is mine. As are all the contents.' Crossing to his bureau Richard opened a drawer, took out a small loop of twine with two keys on it and tossed them to Santo. Then sitting down he drew a sheet of paper towards him, dipped his pen in the inkwell and started writing.

'The large key opens the workshop,' he said over his shoulder. 'The smaller is for the office. If the brewery dray is not available, Adam Jewell can use the farm cart to help you move.' Blotting the note he folded it, then rising from his chair handed it to Santo. 'This will ensure Morley Jewell's compliance.'

'I dunno what to say. Handsome, that is, and much appreciated.'

Richard waved Santo's gratitude aside. 'I'm as keen as you are to see the marine engine operational.'

'I doubt that.' Santo said. 'But I'm glad to hear it just the same. Right, I'm gone. No need for you to come down, I'll let myself out. You got more than enough to do.'

Santo walked round to the brewhouse, grateful for Richard's implied vote of confidence and hungry to see Bronnen.

He entered the yard as she pushed the loaded shovel into the firebox then straightened up, tucking a fallen curl up into the thick coil. As soon as the piston started moving, she propped the stick under the belt to tighten it and after a glance at the moving pump handle, looked up towards the brewhouse roof.

'You look like you been doing that for years.'

She swung round, her smile lighting her face. 'San – Mr Innis!'

He came closer and spoke softly. 'You was right first time, Bron. Don't want you forgetting my name.'

She blushed. 'As if I would.'

'Pleased to see me?'

Her blush deepened, but her gaze didn't waver from his. 'Always.' Then he saw her remember and her smile vanished. 'I'm so sorry about–'

He stopped her with a brief gesture and shook his head. 'Don't take me wrong, it's just–'

'You don't want to think about it,' she said. 'But you're all right?'

'Better for seeing you.' Even as he spoke he wished he had Richard Vaughan's way with words. 'Made my day, that has.'

She looked up with a shy smile, her gaze meeting his with an air of hope that urged him to say something that would let her know he wanted to take their relationship further, make it official. But how could he until he had something to offer? She deserved more than empty promises.

He held out the note. 'Give this to your father, will you? It's from Mr Vaughan, for your brother to use the farm cart to move all my stuff down to Anstey's boatyard.'

Bronnen took it. 'When do you want him?'

'Soon as he's free. This afternoon would be a proper job. I'll be at Curnock's packing up. Best if he meet me there. I reck'n we can shift the lot in four trips.' He watched her turning the note in her fingers. 'Like to see the boatyard, would you?'

'I wish I could, but–'

'That's all right,' he fought disappointment. 'No reason you'd be interested.'

'I am too. I'd love to see it. But with all this extra work I don't know when I can get away.'

Relief lifted his spirits. 'Morning, afternoon, evening, it don't matter. I'll be there.'

Surprise arched her brows. 'You will? But – won't be you be over at Perran?'

Santo shook his head. 'Not any more.'

'Why not? What happened?'

'I had a row with Mr Tregarron.'

'About the explosion?'

He nodded, rubbing his neck again. 'Will and the others won't get a proper burial because there was nothing left to bring home. My engines are safe and we've shown that they work, but he don't want to know. So I quit.' Hearing himself say the words brought it home to him. He had walked away from a well-paid job to chase a dream. *What would she think?*

'Dear life, that must have took a bravish lot of nerve. Still, you'll get your boat engine finished all the quicker now.'

Gratitude surged through him. He caught her hands in his and raised one to his lips. 'There isn't many would understand. They'd say I've took leave of my senses. Could be they're right. But Will shouldn't have died like that.'

Bronnen covered her hand with his. 'Make your engine work, for your friend.'

Alf stomped out of the brewhouse to the wood store, clearing his throat loudly. Santo released her and they quickly stepped apart.

She glanced towards the brewhouse. 'I must go.'

'Come when you can. I'll be waiting.'

'Thank you,' she said softly, backing away.

'What for?'

'Telling me.'

As she hurried into the brewhouse he left the yard filled with new determination. He would make her proud; show her she was right to believe in him.

Chapter Twenty-three

Seated in an armchair on the opposite side of the hearth from Frederick Tregarron, Richard crossed one leg over the other. Telling Santo Innis to remain calm, contain his temper, had been easy. Applying that advice to himself was proving far harder.

The fire had burned down to glowing embers. Unless there were guests Tregarron preferred to spend his evenings at home in the comfort of his study discussing business and estate matters over coffee and cognac.

'I don't understand your reaction.' Tregarron regarded Richard with bemusement. 'It is my duty as a father to secure a good marriage for her.'

'She has been here less than a month.'

'What has that to do with anything? Anyway, I cannot think of anyone more suitable than you.'

'Have you tried?'

'Why would I? You are–'

'Nearly twice her age.'

Tregarron flapped a dismissive hand. 'You are in excellent health. So what difference does a few years make? Anyway, you will be precisely the steadying influence she needs.'

Richard had already considered this. Powerfully tempted, unable to fault the logic, still he had resisted. Not for her sake, but for his own. Listening to Tregarron's blithe reasoning was torture.

'I assume you mean that as a compliment.'

'Of course it's a compliment. You are already my heir. I should welcome the opportunity to think of you as my son. Were you to marry Melanie–'

'I am obliged to you. But I have no plans to marry again.'

'Plans can be changed. What happened was most unfortunate. Sadly it is not unusual. You are by no means the only man to have suffered such a loss. But to allow it to blight the rest of your life seems to me somewhat self-indulgent.'

Feeling his self-control started to slip during this speech, Richard had clenched his teeth so tightly pain shot up into his temple. 'You are entitled to your opinion. However, my private life is *my* concern, no one else's, no matter how well-intentioned.' His tone held irony and bitterness. But Tregarron took the words at face value and didn't even blink. 'Were I ever to reconsider, I alone would choose who and when.'

'Richard, I have the greatest respect for your business acumen. The fact that I leave management of my affairs in your hands should be all the proof you need. So I cannot understand why you are so set against a proposition that answers so many–'

'Because Melanie is not a *proposition*. She is–' s*elf-sufficient, heartbreakingly vulnerable, courageous, and scarred,* '–a person.'

'Whom I have treated exactly as I did my other daughters.'

'I hardly think so. Did they not live at home secure in the affection of both their parents? Melanie was at boarding school from the age of four.'

'What was I supposed to do? What else *could* I do? Her mother disappeared. Bringing her here was out of the question. Oakland Park was expensive and, I freely acknowledge, the source of some domestic discord. Yet I cannot begrudge a penny. Just as Miss Edwards promised, Melanie is a credit to me. I could wish her perhaps a little less argumentative. But I am sure once she has a couple of babies to occupy her she'll settle down.'

'They will not be mine. Now I must ask you to excuse me.'

'Richard–'

'I have nothing more to say, and several urgent matters awaiting my attention.' Closing the door he started towards the stairs and the inevitable pile of paperwork then abruptly changed his mind. He needed fresh air. Perhaps a brisk walk would release the tension that gripped him.

He paused on the wide steps. Closing his eyes he tilted his head, feeling the sun on his face. Within a week of coming to Gillyvean eight years ago he had recognised Tregarron as a man of contrasts: sociable yet self-centred, astute in some matters, wilfully blind in others.

Accepting what he could not change, Richard had focused on expanding the business. Recognising his heir's ability, Tregarron had retreated from day-to-day involvement but still claimed credit for successful deals. Richard didn't mind. Busy days left him so tired that sleep came quickly.

Tregarron's provision for Melanie *had* been generous. But he could easily afford it, and placing her in school had freed him of further responsibility. She had arrived here like a rock falling into a pool, and the ripples were still spreading.

Drawing a slow breath he opened his eyes. He would walk round to the brewhouse and see how Bronnen Jewell was getting on. He didn't doubt her brewing skills, but she had never been in charge of men.

Then across the wide lawn, he caught sight of Melanie sitting under a chestnut tree. The ever-present sketchpad was on her lap. But her hands were still, her head turned away, resting against the trunk.

He was probably the last person she wanted to see. But he owed her an explanation. Still he hesitated, reluctant to intrude. Before she came, self-control had been second nature to him. Now he was struggling. Her father's announcement made without discussion or warning had stunned him and he'd been unable to hide his reaction.

Her shock and the colour flooding her face had been painful to see and he had turned away. He had done so to spare her further embarrassment. But she might think he turned away because he loathed her father's suggestion. He did, but not for the reasons she might have assumed. He hated what Tregarron had done because of what it implied – her father wanted her off his hands, wanted her someone else's responsibility.

What he'd heard from Santo Innis had startled him. Mrs Tregarron's reaction to the arrival on her doorstep of flesh-and-blood evidence of her husband's infidelity was understandable, if lacking in charity.

But how many other slights and spites had Melanie faced? Small wonder she was prickly and self-protective. Had he not been so taken aback by her effect on him, an impact that was unexpected, unwanted and difficult to deal with; he would have made greater allowance.

Her flashes of anger were to be expected. They confirmed that despite all that had happened to her, her spirit was still intact. What surprised him most was her willingness to trust him.

The moment he had first seen her, tired, trying hard not to show how scared she was, the unexpected and powerful tug of attraction had thrown him.

As Tregarron's agent he attended business dinners. As heir he was in demand at suppers and balls. Urbane, informed, and discreet, he was popular with hostesses needing a spare man. While despairing at his refusal to see the lures cast his way, they knew he was reliable, a safe pair of hands.

With so much of his time spent in company, he had relished solitude. Then she arrived. Now his life was chaos. He had never been a demonstrative man. Emotion made him uncomfortable. Not knowing how to deal with it he had shut it out, walled it off. Self-control was a matter of courtesy.

But Melanie, despite her efforts to hide what she was feeling, was a tangled rainbow of emotions. He saw them in her eyes, the angle of her head, tension in her shoulders. He had expected to feel impatient. Instead he had been entranced and touched. He had resisted, fought hard. *Until she had accused him of having neither heart nor feelings.* In a blinding flash he had recognised the lie at the centre of his life. In that moment he had hated her and loved her, for there was no going back.

That kiss – oh God, that kiss – he closed his eyes, recalling her taste, her scent, the instant she had surrendered, her body warm and pliant against his. It was impossible. She was young, vibrant, gifted. She deserved – *someone else?* The thought was crucifying. But so was his fear. Better to call a halt now. His eyes felt full of thorns. He pulled himself together.

His feet made no sound on the grass, but he saw the instant she realised someone was approaching. She sat up straight, her head turned away while one hand went briefly to her face.

'Forgive me for disturbing you.'

She looked up. Even as she smiled he saw her eyes were red-rimmed, her lashes wet and spiky. 'Too late for that, don't you think?'

Did she mean now? Or was she referring to their kiss? What had possessed him? He knew that among business acquaintances he was considered a bit of a cold fish. *If they only knew.* He crouched beside her. 'Are you unwell? Shall I fetch Ellen?'

'No, and no. What do you want?'

'To explain. I fear you may have misread my reaction to your father's announcement.'

'I think that unlikely. Your expression left little room for misunderstanding.'

He sat down beside her, careful to leave space between them. Forearms resting on his raised knees he turned a blade of grass between his fingers. 'Tell me what you saw.'

'I beg your pardon?'

'Humour me. Please.'

'All right, you looked absolutely horrified.'

'You're right. I did. Because I was.' He turned his head to meet her gaze, seeing her shock. 'But not for the reason you may be thinking.'

'You don't know what I'm thinking.'

'No, I don't. Nor at this moment does it matter. Melanie, I was not aware of your father's plans. I had no idea he intended to make that announcement. No, let me finish. What appalled me wasn't his mention of a marriage between us,' he forced himself to continue but, unable to hold her gaze he stared blindly at the blade of grass he was shredding. 'Though I'm sure you have no wish for it, and he knows I have no desire to remarry.' Sweating from the effort of appearing calm, he felt a droplet tickle as it slid down his right side. His shirt was sticking to his back. He couldn't look at her for fear she would see through the lie.

'It was his timing. You haven't been here long. I imagine you were hoping to spend time with your father so the two of you could become better acquainted. Instead he makes an announcement that must have sounded as if he wished to be rid of you. What he did was crass and thoughtless. My horror was on your behalf, not mine.'

'I see.'

The two words told him nothing. He still dared not look at her. 'Your father has many excellent qualities. Unfortunately, like many men, he is not always sensitive to the feelings of others.'

'You are.' Her voice was little more than a whisper.

Could he pretend he hadn't heard? *Deny her again?* Forcing his mouth into a smile, he shook his head. 'You give me too much credit. I notice things because it's my job. I'm a boring details man. Anyway, I hope we've cleared that up. I'll leave you to your–' Her hand on his arm stopped him.

'Don't, Richard. I already have a father. I have no wish for another, nor an uncle or brother. Please, just be yourself.'

Unable to stop himself, he turned to her. 'When I'm with you I don't know who I am.'

Her smile was luminous, transforming. He would treasure that moment always. But it would never be enough, *he* would never be enough, not for someone as young and spirited and talented as her. She would grow bored and impatient, and he would be destroyed. He touched her hand, the contact light and fleeting. It was all he dared allow himself. 'I really must go. I have work to do.'

'When you are not so busy can we talk again? On our own? I don't want my father jumping to conclusions.'

The words pierced him like shards of glass. But he would be her friend. God knew she needed one. 'Of course we will.' Rising to his feet he left her under the tree. As he returned to the house he pressed one hand to his chest, to an ache too deep to be reached. But he had reassured her, that was what mattered.

Chapter Twenty-four

Hearing the rumble of wheels Santo set down a box of tools and looked out of the open door, seeing two shire horses pull a large hay wagon into the brewery yard. He lifted a hand in greeting. It had to be Adam Jewell, though he could see little resemblance between brother and sister. 'I didn't expect you for another hour.'

Adam nodded. 'I'd finished in the field and Father got Walter to help with the milking. Back 'n up to the door shall I? Be easier to load.'

'Right on.' While Adam turned the wagon, Santo heaved the crates and boxes forward.

By the time the first load was on the wagon, both were sweating. Santo rinsed a dusty mug at the pump in the yard and gulped down a draught of cold water. Refilling it, he offered it to Adam who hesitated. 'No beer?'

Santo gave an ironic laugh. 'Only if you're a paying customer. Mr Curnock don't believe in giving what he can charge for.'

'Tight, is he?'

'You said it.'

Taking the mug, Adam drank deeply, then handed it back. 'Best get on. How many trips, do you reckon?'

'The wagon's bigger than I expected so two should do it.'

'That'll please Father. Still, he couldn't say no.

211

Not after Mr Vaughan sent that there note.'

Santo realised it was this foresight that made Richard so valuable to Frederick Tregarron. 'I want to stop on the way, but it won't take long.'

After calling at Curnock House and loading two trunks, they completed the journey in silence. Adam had his hands full with one of the horses. Santo was thinking about Mrs Eathorne.

Furious with Treeve for turning him out of the house and with George for not changing his will, the housekeeper had packed his clothes and belongings into the trunk he had brought back with him from Hall's.

Knowing he could trust her, Santo had confided he would be camping at the yard.

'I've got tools and machinery worth good money, so just for the time it's best if I sleep there.' It was logical and she didn't argue. But her cocked eyebrow told him she knew that wasn't the only reason. He had returned to the brewery to finish crating his machinery and part-built engines.

To avoid Treeve he carried on working and didn't return for his dinner until after two. Walking into the kitchen to apologise for his lateness he found Mrs Eathorne filling a deep basket with bread, butter, cheese, cold meat, fruit pie, cake, a tin of tea, and a small brown teapot.

'All right, my 'ansum? Listen, if you got a carter picking your stuff up from the brewery yard, he can call here for they two trunks as well.'

'What d'you mean, two? I've only got one.'

'Not no more, you haven't,' she said briskly and beckoning him into the boot room opened the lid of a large battered tin trunk.

Santo saw blankets, two pillows, a curtain, a saucepan, crockery, cutlery, a large enamel basin and a tall jug. 'Mrs Eathorne–'

'I don't want no thanks,' she cut in. 'You're family. 'Tis wicked what they done, the both of them. Now, anything else you need, you can tell me when you bring your washing.'

'My washing?'

'Going deaf, are you?'

'I don't want to make trouble for you.'

'Who's to know? And before you say you can do it yourself, I daresay you could. But a line of washing hanging in Anstey's yard is as good as a banner saying someone's living there. Is that what you want? No, I didn't think so.'

'You're a gem, Mrs Eathorne.'

'Get on with you. We both got work to do.'

While Adam tied the horses to an iron ring set in a huge granite block, Santo unlocked the big sliding doors and rolled them back.

'Just put everything here by the workbench. I'll sort it out later.'

Carrying a wooden box of tools, Adam followed Santo into the huge space.

'Dear life!' Dropping the box on the bench he walked over to the hull and ran a work-roughened palm over the wood. 'This yours, is it?'

'On loan.'

'What you going to do with it?'

'Test a marine engine I've built.'

Adam glanced round then out at the wagon. 'Where's that to, then?'

'Coming by sea from Dartford. Be here any day now. I want to get this place straight first, so best

213

get unloaded then go for the rest.'

Santo didn't look back as they left the brewery yard with the second load. During the short journey his thoughts turned to Bronnen. Would she come today? There were many reasons why she might not be able to: additional work at the brewhouse, her mother's illness. Replaying their conversation in his head he pictured her face, her cheeks pink as rose petals, her reassuring hand on his arm. She would come when she could.

After carrying in the final crate, Santo straightened up, flexing his weary back. 'That's a proper job, Adam.'

'Want me to stay and help do you? I don't mind.'

'No, you get on home. Your father will be looking for you. Like I say, I'm much obliged.'

His tanned face flushing, Adam gave a shy nod and walked outside. Santo followed, watching as the young man untied the rope tethering the horses to the iron ring then climbed up onto the wooden seat. With another nod, he clicked his tongue and the horses started up the slope to the road.

Santo could have used the help. But Treeve would lose no time letting it be known that Santo hadn't been mentioned in his father's will. If people knew he was living here they would assume he was short of money. *He was*.

But with a bit of luck Mr Rowse was putting the word around about his pumping engines. So until the coaster arrived he would use the time to finish the two that were half-built.

First he needed to take another look round. Outside his gaze went automatically down the river towards the inner harbour and the Carrick Roads. The coaster would come on a rising tide. Maybe tomorrow. He turned away.

On the far side of the big shed a small shack was set back against the earth cliff. The smell told him what it was. He opened the door and saw a wooden seat with a bucket underneath and squares of newspaper, pierced in one corner, threaded onto a piece of string, and hung on a hook in the wall. Below the paper was a small tub half-full of sawdust. A handful tossed into the bucket was supposed to mask the smell. God knew when the bucket had last been emptied, let alone cleaned. It would have to be done. But only *after* he had found some tar or pitch he could dilute with boiling water.

As well as the forge near the door that would fabricate ironwork, there was a wood burner towards the rear of the shed for winter warmth. A large black kettle stood on a nearby bench. Coiled rope of varying thickness hung from long nails.

Picking up the basket that Mrs Eathorne had covered with a cloth, Santo unlocked the office door and carried it inside. Behind a crude wooden counter that separated customers from office staff, a long table fashioned from thick oak planks served as a desk. Two chairs were tucked underneath. The table was bare but for a lacquered brass lamp with a glass funnel. He picked it up, felt the weight of oil. That would be useful during the dark hours.

A small black-painted iron stove stood against the wall, a chimney pipe angled through to outside. Between the window and the back wall deep wooden shelves reached from floor to ceiling. Empty now, they would have held the account ledgers, files of correspondence, invoices, statements, orders, and other paperwork generated by the boatyard.

Facing him was a closed door. Santo opened it and looked in. Slightly smaller than the outer office it contained a table, a wooden armchair, a cupboard and a window. It would do very well.

Leaving the basket of provisions on the small table, he returned to the workshop, found a stout wooden frame with two handles, small iron wheels, and a hollow oblong of iron that stuck out at right angles from the frame. Jamming the iron lip under his trunk, he tilted the frame and wheeled the trunk into the office.

Opening the other trunk he removed the blankets, pillow, and curtain, carried those through to the inner office, and returned for the rest of the items, stacking crockery, cutlery, and teapot in the big bowl padded with the cloth from the basket. The battered tin trunk he turned up on end and wedged in the corner. With all his personal things now out of sight, he closed the door.

Brushing litter and debris from the benches he collected up the abandoned tools. Some would be useful. He set them aside. The rest he tossed into an empty barrel already half full of rubbish.

He wheeled, dragged, or carried the boxes and crates containing his machines and placed them to take advantage of the light. Then, leaving everything covered, he swept the floor. Under one of the benches he found a drum of coal tar and a bottle of lamp oil.

After dumping all the rubbish into the barrel he went out to the well. Sited near the cliff between the slope and the shed, it was covered by a wooden lid.

Dropping the bucket down he turned the handle of the windlass to haul it up again. For safety he threw the first two bucketfuls into the weeds at the back of the quay and drew another. Using the well reminded him of Bronnen. Realizing it was too late in the day for her to come now, he was surprised by the depth of his disappointment.

After lighting a fire in the stove and boiling a kettleful of water, he spent the next half hour breathing as little as possible while he cleaned out the latrine.

Tired, sweaty, and hungry, he fetched soap and towel, hauled up more water and scrubbed his hands. Then, carrying a last bucketful of water into the shed, he closed and locked the sliding doors.

After a strip wash he pulled on a clean work shirt and made a meal of bread, cheese and cold meat, followed by a slice of fruit pie. He would have given his back teeth for a tankard of strong ale. But even as the thought occurred he shoved it away and made a pot of tea. While it brewed he found a length of twine and four nails. He hammered two nails into either side of each window then fed the twine through the hem of the curtain and stretched it between the nails to give him privacy. After a further hour's work he fetched blankets and pillows and settled down for the night.

Chapter Twenty-five

By late afternoon the following day, Santo had set out his tools, cleaned and oiled the lathe and milling machine that had been part of the sale, and was oiling the iron wheels on the dolly that would move the hull from the shed down to the slipway.

Hearing the clop of hooves he went out. Curnock's dray was coming down the slope.

'Yo!' the driver called.

'All right, Ivor?'

'How 'ee doing? Fallen on your feet here you have. Better than that poky hole you had in the brewery yard.'

'It is too.' Santo walked over, wiping his oily hands on a rag as the driver jumped down. 'What you doing here?'

'Miss Jewell asked me to drop off a cask of small beer for 'ee. Can't abide it meself – weak as gnat's piss. Still, it wouldn' be no good giving the harvesters anything stronger, else it'd be Christmas before the corn was in. Saying that,' he glanced skyward, 'I reck'n there's rain coming.' He hefted a small cask onto his shoulder. 'Where do 'ee want it?'

'There by the door is fine. I'll take it in dreckly.'

The drayman set the cask down with practised ease. 'I tell 'ee straight, I thought Mr Arthur was mad, looking to Gillyvean to fill his orders. But I take it all back.'

'Miss Jewell getting on all right, is she?' Santo realised Ivor would know her from her visits to the brewery to buy yeast.

'Doing wonders, she is. Got that brewhouse running like clockwork. But she's looking some tired, dear of her. Be there all night she will. Not for the first time neither.' He sniffed. 'That's never right, and so I told her. But like she say, Sam Jose can't work all day *and* all night, and the brews need skimming reg'lar, so they got to take turns. Whatever Mr Curnock is paying her she's worth double and that's a fact. Anyhow, got to get on.'

As the huge dray rumbled up the slope Santo carried the cask inside and placed it on the nearest workbench. He felt his heart lift and grinned. She had been thinking about him.

He fetched the enamel ewer and went to draw water. He would wash and change, have a bite to eat, then walk round to Gillyvean. She cared enough to send him the beer. Surely she would let him stay and keep her company?

Like her, he had been working long days. But not an hour passed that he didn't think of her. Something would trigger a memory and suddenly her face would be vivid in his mind. He'd see her smile, hear her voice. He missed her.

Alone in the brewhouse, the atmosphere thick with the fresh-baked-bread scent of yeast and the toasty fragrance of malt, Bronnen finished writing up the day's brewing notes. Replacing the book on the window-ledge she went to the door and breathed deeply. The evening air was fresh and sweet.

Cloud blanketed the sky. As the sun had gone down, so had the temperature. She half-closed the door, reluctant to shut it too soon for the smell'd be overpowering. But now the air had cooled she couldn't risk the fermentation stopping.

She began skimming the head, tipping the yeast into a bucket of fresh cold water. When she'd finished she would relight the boiler fire. If she had to be there all night she could at least be comfortable.

With the last skimmer-load in the bucket, she straightened, alerted by the sound of footsteps outside. Hope warred with unease. After a brief knock, Santo's head appeared.

'All right if I come in?'

Bronnen felt her heart lift and her body relax. ''Course it is.'

'Wind's getting up and I felt a few spots of rain. Close the door, shall I?'

'Please.' She picked up the bucket. 'I'm going to light the fire in a minute. I'll just put this in the cellar to keep cool.'

'Got kindling and logs, have you?'

'No, I was–'

'I'll fetch them. You do whatever you have to with that bucket.'

Setting it in a corner of the cool cellar, she paused for a moment, tucking away stray curls that always worked loose. Then she ran her hands down the front of her apron. *Her apron: grubby and stained with splashes from the brew.* She pulled it off, quickly folding it up. Her blue and white cotton dress was worn and faded. But at least without the apron she didn't look quite so much like a kitchen maid.

Stepping back into the brewhouse she saw Santo had lit the lantern and was feeding the copper fire. The brewhouse door was closed.

He glanced round with a smile, his eyes gleaming in the mellow light. 'Thanks for the beer. I should have said when I came in. But seeing you–' he shook his head. Closing the fire door he turned to her. 'Stop my breath, you do.'

Pleasure made her skin tingle and she pressed her palms to her hot cheeks. 'Dear life, Santo. You – I never – really?' She bent her head, wishing it hadn't slipped out. She'd hate him to think she was fishing for compliments. But the way he looked at her made her quiver inside. And though she knew she wasn't, he made her feel beautiful.

She had been fond of John but he hadn't stirred her. She was suddenly fiercely glad that Santo was the first man she had kissed.

Crossing the space between them he clasped her hands, and drew her close by holding them against his chest. 'Really. That's God's truth, my lovely.' He tucked a curl behind her ear. His finger was callused and scarred, the gesture full of tenderness. 'I been thinking about you.'

'I wanted to come down, but–'

'You been rushed off your feet. I know.' He grinned. 'You got Ivor in some fret. He says whatever Mr Arthur is paying, you're worth twice as much.'

'He did?'

'As true as I'm stood here.' He raised her hand and pressed his lips to her knuckles, sending a delicious shiver down her spine. 'You got time to sit for a while? I don't want to get in your way.'

'You're not. I've done all I can for the moment.' Her hand in his, she followed him to the bench and they sat down. 'I'm not sorry to see the rain. I'd sooner keep the door closed.'

'No unwelcome callers?'

'I don't mean you,' she said quickly. 'I was hoping you'd stop by. But I didn't know if you'd have time, what with the move. Did it take long?'

'Thanks to your brother bringing the big hay wagon we did it in two trips.' He looked down at their clasped hands. She could feel the length of his thigh warm against hers. 'My cousin been round again, has he?'

'No, and I'm glad of it. I don't like him. He's sly and–' she stopped abruptly. 'I'm sorry, I shouldn't have – he's your family.'

'Bron, Treeve was a spiteful child. Now he's a bitter man. He don't like me. I don't like him.' He shrugged. 'But I've got more important things to think about.' As he kissed her hand once more, she touched his face. Beneath the roughness of his beard stubble, his skin was warm, his jaw firm.

'You need to watch out, Santo. I was over there a couple of days ago buying more malt and he tried to make me believe you'd done something to the boiler.'

Santo's expression sent chills skittering over her skin. 'Is that right?' Then he shrugged. 'The day after I cleaned the boiler and checked the pipes, all of it was fine. I know that because I called in to make sure.'

'Well, the malt was burned and he was raving angry.'

'D'you want to know what I think?'

She nodded.

'I haven't been back long, but word is that Treeve's furnaceman is fond of a drink. He probably had a bottle of brandy or a small keg of beer hidden somewhere. He fell asleep leaving the lad, who's his grandson, to tend the fire. The boy feared the fire was too low and built it up. But because he don't have his granfer's experience, he made it too hot and scorched the malt.'

'Why don't you tell your cousin?'

'Not my business.'

'But he's trying to put the blame on you.'

'He know it's not my fault. I don't want to make trouble for the old man. He've had a fright, so has the boy. Maybe now they'll be more careful. Anyhow, I got better things to do with my time.'

She rested her head against his shoulder. He put his arm around her, drawing her close.

'What's wrong, my lovely?'

She raised her head. 'How did you know?'

He shrugged. 'I can tell.' He laced his fingers through hers. 'Put it back.'

'What?'

'Your head, put it back on my shoulder. It fits there perfect.'

Smiling, feeling warm and safe, she nestled against him. Should she tell him about Treeve's flirting? She had made it perfectly clear she wasn't interested. So why bring his name up again and spoil this precious time together? Besides, he was the least of her concerns.

'So, you going to tell me? You don't have to,' he added quickly.

''Tis Mother. She's fretting awful, and her nerves is in some terrible state. But she won't tell me what's wrong.'

'Maybe she don't want to worry you while you're so busy.'

'If I knew, I wouldn't worry so much.'

He stroked her neck gently. 'Close, are you?'

'I thought we was. That's how I don't understand why she won't tell me. She knows I'd do anything for her. Whatever she need I'll get. With the extra money coming in cost don't matter. I just want her well again.'

''Course you do. Have you asked your father?'

Bronnen shook her head. 'I can't talk to him. He's always angry and drink makes him worse.'

Santo's arm tightened around her. 'Has he raised a hand to you?'

Not his hand, his boot. Her hesitation gave her away and she felt Santo's arm stiffen. 'Only once,' she said quickly. 'Last week. He'd been drinking–'

Santo seized her shoulders. 'That's no excuse,' he hissed, his eyes glittering with anger. She remembered what he had told her of his own childhood with a heavy-drinking violent father and terrified mother. 'What did he do?'

'He broke Mother's ornaments pulling the cloth off the mantel. When I crouched down to pick them up–' *time you was put down where you belong.* 'He went to kick me and I fell over.'

Santo's expression was thunderous. 'Was you hurt?'

'More shocked really. But I'm all right.' Yes, she was fine – anxious about her mother, wary of her father, frustrated at her inability to change any-

224

thing, and short of sleep. 'He go drinking every night then takes it out on Ma. And she keep making excuses for him. It makes me so mad.' Without warning her eyes filled with scalding tears and brimmed over. 'I'm sorry, I didn't mean to–' She tried to pull away but he drew her closer.

'There's no one to see, and nothing to be sorry about. Dear life, you've had some time of it lately.' Tilting her face up, he gently wiped away her tears with his thumb. 'I can't abide seeing you sad.'

Beneath the tenderness in his gaze Bronnen saw hunger and felt an answering tug low in her belly. Her pulse quickened. He traced the contours of her face with his fingertips, as if she were something fragile and precious.

'Bron–' he murmured then clenched his teeth to hold back whatever he had been going to say. 'Tis no good. I got to–' His mouth covered hers.

Her eyes fluttered closed and nothing existed but the soft warmth of his mouth.

Without breaking the kiss, he drew her to her feet, one arm around her waist, holding her close, the other cupping her head.

Shyly she slipped her arms around his neck. Her fingers tangled in his thick hair. He made a soft sound deep in his throat as his arm tightened, moulding her against him. The pressure of her breasts against his broad chest mingled pain and intense pleasure.

They knew each other better now, had grown closer. She had told him things she had never shared with anyone. But Santo cared about her, and she trusted him.

She felt his quickened breath as the tip of his

tongue lightly caressed her closed lips until they parted. She tasted him, opened to him, and surrendered.

A while later he raised his head. But he didn't release her, nor did she want him to. 'God, Bron.' He was breathing hard, his voice low and rough.

'I know,' she whispered, and rested her forehead against his shoulder. 'I feel like my bones are melting.'

'You aren't the only one.'

She glanced at him, shy, thrilled, and proud.

Sitting on the bench he drew her down beside him, his arm around her shoulders, the fingers of his free hand laced through hers. 'Mean the world to me you do. I'd never do nothing to hurt you.'

She pressed her lips to his cheek then laid her head on his shoulder again. 'I suppose you'll have to go soon.'

'Not unless you want me to.'

'I don't.'

'How about I check that fire, then you could put your head down and sleep for a couple of hours.'

'I couldn't–'

'Don't tell me you're not tired because I won't believe you.'

'Yes, I'm tired. But I can't sleep when you've bothered to come–'

'Yes, you can. Look, if I'm here you won't need to worry about the fire or the beer. Tell me when the next skim is due and I'll wake you.'

'I don't know what to say.'

'Say yes.'

'No, I mean it's so kind of you.'

''Tis no such thing. I'd sooner be with you than

anywhere else. Look, I'll wake you before sun-up. Give you time to get ready for Sam coming. I can grab a few hours back at the boatyard.'

'You're a dear.' She reached up to kiss his cheek but he turned his head so his mouth met hers. Once more she was lost. When he drew back she felt bereft.

'Bron, I want–'

Her blood felt thick, like honey in her veins. 'I know. I never dreamed–'

In his dark gaze she saw the battle he was fighting. 'We can't. Not here, not like this.'

'I know.' She forced herself up. 'I'll just–'

'Right, the wood–' His wry smile matched hers with an understanding that did not need words.

She slept with her head on his lap and woke, refreshed to the pale grey of dawn.

They parted in the brewhouse doorway. 'Thank you,' she began, but he placed his forefinger against her lips.

'I wouldn't have missed it for the world. See you soon, my lovely.'

By mid-morning Sam and Tommy were racking off the beer into barrels. The first mash of the day was boiling, and while Bronnen ground malt she relived Santo's visit, and their kisses. Her deep sigh turned into a yawn just as Sam came into the brewhouse from the cellar.

'You go on home, miss. Been some long night for you.'

'I'm not so tired as I look,' she smiled. 'I slept a bit between skimmings. I can stay on a while if you want.'

'No, I'll be fine. I learned more from you in a week than in all my years with Mr George.'

''Tisn't just what you learned, you got your confidence now, Sam.'

'You needn't worry I'll go getting above myself. No chance of that with Alf and Tommy around.'

'That wasn't what – I meant it as a compliment.'

Sam's smile lit up his face. 'Much obliged. So, are you going?'

'If you're sure–'

'Didn't I just say so? Look, if I put in for Head Brewer at Curnocks I won't have you to watch my back. So I got to get used to doing it on me own.'

A free afternoon would give her time to talk to her mother, maybe catch up on some of the household tasks. 'All right, Sam, thanks. I'll see you in the morning.'

Chapter Twenty-six

'Innis? You there?'

Hearing Richard's voice Santo, kneeling in the stern of the hull, put down his hammer, stood up, and looked over the gunwale.

'Yo.'

'I'm on my way to Fox's and thought I'd see how you're getting on.'

'I'm fitting wood blocks to carry the weight of the engine. I need to see how she sits, work out the angle and all, before I bore a hole for the prop shaft.'

228

'When will you have the propeller?'

'Jack's bringing it tomorrow. That'll give me time to check it over.'

'For what?'

'Tiny air bubbles. You sometimes get a little patch in a brass casting.'

'So why did you choose brass?'

After an instant's hesitation Santo shrugged. 'I couldn't afford bronze. But brass is like copper. Once in the water and working he'll harden up, and a rigid prop will work better. I'll give'n a good polish before fitting, to cut the drag.'

'I'm impressed,' Richard gave one of his rare smiles.

'If you're going to Fox's–'

'They will tell me what they told me last time: if the ship hasn't been delayed by bad weather it should be here any day. But I'll ask anyway.'

Santo grinned at him. 'Better get on.'

Arriving home, hoping to find her mother in the kitchen preparing dinner, with no sign of her or the meal Bronnen's heart sank and her anxiety increased. How was she to go on working long hours at the brewhouse then come home to face housework, farm chores and cooking?

Though strong and capable she was also tired, and worry was dragging her down. She would get the dinner ready. Then, when the men had gone back to work, she would make her mother tell her what was wrong.

She riddled the ashes to let air into the fire and added more wood for fast heat. The kettle was full and still warm. She pulled it over the flames then hurried upstairs.

'It's me, Ma,' she said softly, opening the door.

Sarah was curled up on the bed, fully dressed, her eyes red and swollen. Seeing Bronnen her face crumpled and she gave a wrenching sob.

For an instant Bronnen wished she had stayed at the brewhouse. Ashamed, she crouched by the bed and stroked her mother's shoulder. 'I can't stop now. They'll soon be in for dinner.'

'Oh, my dear Lord,' Sarah gasped, and struggled to sit up. 'It can't be that time already?'

Bronnen pressed her down again. 'Stay there. You don't want Father seeing you like this. Soon as they've gone back I'll bring you a cup of tea.'

Without waiting for a response she raced downstairs to the larder, breathing a sigh of relief as she saw there would be enough meat on the cold lamb joint. Setting the platter on the table, she hurried outside to the vegetable garden, pulled up new potatoes, two handfuls of young carrots, and two summer cabbages and piled them into a large enamel bowl.

Back in the kitchen she poured water from the boiling kettle into a large saucepan and, after quickly washing the potatoes, dropped them into the seething water and added a little salt.

Topping and tailing the carrots she rinsed them clean, sliced them lengthways, put them in a net bag, and dropped them into the saucepan with the potatoes, then did the same with the coarsely chopped cabbage.

Suddenly light-headed, she leaned against the table and took several deep breaths. She couldn't stop yet, there was still too much to do. The queasy faintness passed. She turned back to the range.

Jamming the saucepan lid on, she fetched a jar of mint jelly, another of red onion chutney, and the butter dish from the larder, took knives and forks from the dresser drawer, and quickly laid the table. After topping up the kettle and setting it to boil again, she took down plates from the dresser, carved every scrap of meat off the joint, and divided it between the four plates.

A short while later heavy boots clattered on the cobbled yard. She heard male voices, the clank of the pump handle and gush of water into the stone trough. The sound reminded of her Santo. She relived sitting with her head on his shoulder, his arm around her while they talked, learning about each other, sharing confidences and deep passionate kisses. The memories filled her heart and lifted her spirits.

Her father's stocky frame filled the doorway. He paused long enough to wipe his wet hands on the old towel hanging just inside. 'What are you doing here?'

Getting your dinner. 'Sam is looking after the brew.'

'He'll have your job if you don't watch out.'

'He doesn't want it. He's going to put in for Head Brewer at Curnock's soon as they open again.'

Adam and the two labourers came in behind him. The labourers nodded to her as they dried their hands then took their places at the table. Instead of sitting, Adam came to her side, his broad back to the room, his voice low.

'When I come back to fetch our croust Ma was

in some terrible state, white and shaking, like she'd seen a ghost. I couldn't come for you, and I could not stay with Ma. You know what Father's like.'

'You didn't say anything to him?'

'And get my head bit off?'

'Adam,' their father snapped. 'If you've finished chasing around for Mr Vaughan, there's a delivery got to go tonight.'

As her brother nodded and sat down, Bronnen lifted the saucepan from the range and drained off the water. She tipped the steaming potatoes into a basin and emptied the carrots and cabbage from their net bags into separate bowls. Then she divided all the vegetables between the four plates and set them in front of the men, serving her father and Adam first. While they discussed the afternoon's work, she carried the pan and bowls to the draining board.

She had arrived home exhausted and hungry. Now tension had tightened an iron band around her head and stolen her appetite. She dreaded the coming scene with her mother. But whatever was wrong was getting worse. It had to be faced. Maybe then there would be a chance of putting it right.

Bronnen made a pot of tea. While it brewed she fetched an apple pie and a dish of clotted cream from the larder, and bowls from the dresser. Cutting four portions she set one in front of each man and added a large spoonful of cream, then gathered up the dirty plates and took them to the stone sink under the window.

Filling her mother's favourite cup she added a dash of milk, leaving cup and saucer on a corner of the range while she placed the big teapot on the table together with the milk jug, cake tin, and four mugs from the dresser. Then turning away she picked up the saucer.

'Where you going with that?' her father demanded.

She had hoped he wouldn't notice. She glanced over her shoulder. 'Upstairs.' He hadn't asked for her mother. Bronnen decided not to mention her. As long as his meal was on the table when he came in he didn't care who put it there. With a grunt he turned away. Bronnen started up the narrow wooden staircase, pausing to pull the door closed behind her.

Chapter Twenty-seven

Entering the bedroom, Bronnen shut the door, placed the cup and saucer on the small table, then sat down on the side of the bed.

'Ma? You can't go on like this. And nor can I. You've got to tell me what's wrong.'

Sarah opened swollen eyes, her breath catching in small gasps that were the aftermath of prolonged weeping. 'Bron, I'm so sorry.' Her voice was a hoarse rasp.

Helping her mother up, Bronnen rearranged the pillows, fetched a clean linen square from the top drawer of the chest and exchanged it for the tear-soaked one, then offered her the tea.

'I don't–'

'Yes, you do,' Bronnen said gently, her own head

233

throbbing. 'You'll feel better for a hot drink.' Sarah's hands were trembling so violently, Bronnen kept hold of the cup and guided it to her mother's mouth. 'Remember when I was small and had a cough? You used to mix up butter, sugar, and vinegar on a saucer and give it to me a tiny bit at a time off a teaspoon? I hated it, but you said it would make me better. It did too.'

Sarah gulped a mouthful, coughed, then turned her head away. 'No more.'

As Bronnen put the cup on the saucer, Sarah slid her hand under the bedclothes, withdrew an envelope and placed it on Bronnen's lap. 'This come for you.'

Picking it up, Bronnen felt the quality of the thick, cream-coloured paper, saw her name and the farm's address penned in elegant flowing script, turned it over and saw the red wax seal. She looked at her mother. 'But I don't know anyone– Who would–?'

Sudden dread raised gooseflesh on her arms. She was being foolish. Worry and all the extra work had left her overtired. Still she hesitated, every instinct warning her not to open it.

She glanced at her mother again, taking in the sunken eyes, ash-pale skin covered with fine creases like crumpled tissue paper, hollow cheeks, and bony shoulders bowed as if carrying an intolerable weight.

Her refusal to confide had left Bronnen helpless. Now, meeting her mother's eyes, Bronnen saw devastation. Her mouth dried. 'You know what it says.'

'Not for sure. But ever since–' Sarah sagged back

onto the pillows. 'I prayed. The dear Lord knows how hard I prayed. But I s'pose I always knew that one day– I been dreading–' Grief cramped her face and she pressed quivering lips tightly together as her thin chest heaved. 'You'd better open it, bird.'

Her hands unsteady, Bronnen opened the envelope, removed the letter and unfolded it, startled as another sheet, folded small and sealed with wax, fell into her lap. She left it there and began to read, the paper trembling in her grip.

She moistened parched lips. 'It's from a Mr Enyon Coode. He's an attorney-at-law in Truro.' Then her free hand flew to her face. 'Oh! He says I have been left a considerable sum of money by the late Mrs Edward Tregellas.' Bronnen looked helplessly at her mother.

'Dulcie Passmore,' Sarah whispered. 'Remember I had that letter a few weeks back saying she'd passed away?'

Bronnen nodded. Then froze, finally seeing what had been staring her in the face. Her mother's nervous collapse had started with the arrival of that letter. She looked down at the thick cream-coloured paper. 'It must be a mistake.'

'No, it isn't. I should have told you. But...' Sarah's voice broke and she shook her head.

'Told me what? Why would this lady leave *me* money? I don't know her.'

Sarah indicated the sealed paper on Bronnen's lap. 'Open it, bird. I should have told you but I kept putting it off. And the more time that passed, the harder it was to know what – or how– I meant it for the best, Bron.'

Bronnen's heart thudded as unease swelled, dark and threatening. 'Ma, you're not making any sense.'

'Read it,' Sarah croaked.

Bronnen's hands trembled as she broke the wax seal, then unfolded the paper and read the salutation. Relief and disbelief escaped in a shaky laugh. 'I told you it was a mistake. Look,' she turned the letter so Sarah could see. 'It's addressed to *my dearest daughter.* This isn't for me.'

Tears brimmed in Sarah's reddened eyes and spilled over. 'Yes, it is.'

'No.' Bronnen's denial was automatic. Then shock hit her like a blow from a fist. 'No,' she repeated in a desperate whisper. Terrified, she felt the foundations of her world cracking. Yet the revelation clarified much she had been unable to understand. *A bleddy cuckoo, that's what you are.* She shook her head, blinking away blackness that hovered at the edge of her vision. Her head throbbed painfully as her heart pounded against her ribs.

'What do she say?' Sarah's voice was faint. She looked old and shrivelled.

Fearful of what was to come, Bronnen forced herself to read on. 'She asks me to forgive her.' Her throat was so dry it hurt. 'She says she thought about me every day.'

'She birthed you,' Sarah whispered, 'but I was there when she did. It was me who held you, me that cut the cord and wrapped you in clean warm linen. From that first moment you was mine. I'd always wanted a daughter. But something went wrong when Adam was born and I couldn't have

236

no more. Then Dulcie needed somewhere to stay and a home for her baby.'

Still clutching the letter, Bronnen lurched from the bed and stumbled blindly to the window, as if moving might distance her from what she was hearing. 'Why? Why did she need somewhere? And why come to you?'

'Remember I told you Dulcie was my cousin Rose's middle daughter?' Now the worst was out, it was as if a dam had broken. Words spilled from Sarah's pale lips. 'Very quiet she was, and good as gold. She did charity work and looked after old folk. Then she fell for this vicar. Only he was married, though there was talk that his wife wasn't right in the head. Anyhow, he got moved away at the same time Dulcie found out she was expecting. Rose didn't want no scandal so Dulcie came here to us. After you was born she went back home and you stayed with me.' Her fingers picked at the sheet. 'That's what they wanted, and so did I. But when that letter come from Mary saying Dulcie had passed away–' a sob choked her. 'I knew that wouldn't be the end of it. Maybe I should've told you. But I couldn't see the point of it. They didn't want you and I did. I'd have died sooner than give you up.'

'He called me a cuckoo,' Bronnen whispered.

'Who did?'

'Fa–' Only he wasn't her father. She swung round. 'Your husband.' She spoke through lips that felt numb, bracing herself against the pounding ache in her head. 'He called me a cuckoo in his nest.'

Sarah flinched as if she'd been struck. 'He didn't

mean it.' Her features were a mask of desperation. 'You know what he's like when he been drinking.'

'He meant it. And he was right.' Everything she had believed about herself was a lie. Who was she? She made for the door, desperate to get out of this house of fear and secrets and lies.

'Don't go, Bron,' Sarah begged. 'Please.'

Fumbling the knob, Bronnen wrenched the door open. 'I can't– I – I'm sorry.' As she ran down the back stairs to the kitchen, her thoughts flew like sparks from the blade grinder. Why was she apologising? They had lied to her. All her life they had lied.

Out of the back door, across the yard, and down the track she ran. Her headache was an axe splitting her skull. Her breath came in gasps, but on she ran. Her calves and thighs ached, a stitch stabbed her side and her lungs were on fire. Forced by pain to stop she bent forward, sucking in air, fighting the blackness that threatened to overwhelm her.

As soon as she was able she hurried on. Fragments of memory, half-forgotten images churned in her head. What was real, what imagined? Confusion swelled like waves in a storm, threatening to overwhelm her. *Don't think*. If she could just reach–

The big doors of the boatyard's workshop were rolled right back. Piling wood chips on top of the twist of newspaper on the shovel he lit the paper and, as flames licked hungrily at the wood, he slid the shovel into the firebox.

Wiping his hands on a rag he watched, then

238

grinned as the piston began to move, up and down now instead of sideways. He listened carefully, his grin widening. No friction, no knock, and no more slowing down.

Bron hadn't mentioned any problems with the brewhouse pump. But unlike those at the quarry, it wasn't working continuously. When he had time and she could afford to be without it for half a day, he would alter it. Every improvement was a step forward.

Hearing quick footsteps he walked out into the sunshine and saw her coming down the slope. Delight gave way to concern as she came towards him.

'What's wrong, my lovely?'

She was grey-white, trembling like an aspen, her eyes huge with shock. Before reaching him she stopped suddenly, hugging herself.

'You're busy. I shouldn't have–'

''Tis always a treat to see you.'

'I didn't know where else to go.'

Her obvious distress filled him with slow-burning anger. Fighting an urge to smash to a pulp whoever was responsible, he approached her slowly. 'I'm glad you came here.'

'I don't–' Her breath hitched then broke on a sob and she buried her face in her hands.

'What's happened, Bron?' He put his arms around her, ready to let go if she seemed at all reluctant. Instead she leaned against him. As he inhaled her scent, felt the heat of her body through the faded cotton, his heart stuttered and his body stirred.

Hating her distress and his helplessness, he

guided her across the workshop. In the office he sat her in one of the chairs. Since moving in he had kept the inner office door shut. Only after he had locked up for the night did he leave it open. 'I'll just–'

Bolting to her feet she clung to him. 'Don't go.'

He put his arms around her. 'Hush now. I aren't going anywhere.'

As she leaned her head against him he felt the sob shake her. 'It's all a lie.'

'What is, my lovely?'

'My whole life.' Her voice was raw. 'I'm not– I don't know who I am.' She pushed the letter from Dulcie Tregellas into his hand. 'This came this morning.'

As he unfolded the creased paper she dropped onto the chair and hugged herself, rocking as if in pain. He read the opening words, the signature, then quickly scanned the letter. He read it again.

'Jesus, Bron,' he whispered. Fury uncoiled like a striking snake. He met her tear-drenched gaze. 'I don't know what to say.' He was good at mending things; had a gift for making them work again. But in this he was helpless, and frustration made him want to lash out.

'Father – only he's not my father – called me a cuckoo.'

'I remember you telling me.'

'I didn't know what he meant.' Tears spilled down her pale cheeks. 'I been so worried about her, and all this time – why didn't she tell me? What am I going to do?'

He opened his arms. Rising from the chair she went to him and he drew her close. The sensation

240

of her body pliant against him quickened a heart-beat already pounding with anger at the Jewells. He stroked Bronnen's back, soothing, gentling, trying to say through touch that she was safe; he would never hurt her; she could depend on him.

She shuddered briefly, her warm breath fluttering against his neck. He turned his head, allowing his lips to graze her temple. She froze for an instant then lifted her face. Her mouth met his, unleashing a hunger he refused to acknowledge.

He held himself in check, ready to release her. Instead her arms slipped around his neck and his blood surged at the yearning in her response. Fighting his own need, realising she was in shock and not thinking straight, he lifted his mouth from hers. Both were breathless. Laying his cheek against her hair he stroked her back. He needed to touch her, and hoped she gained as much solace and comfort from it as he did.

When she raised her head he made himself let her go. But he missed her closeness, missed the sensation of her body against his. As he moistened his lips with the tip of his tongue he tasted her, and curled his fingers into his palms to stop himself reaching for her again.

'What–' his voice cracked and he cleared his throat. 'What're you going to do?'

Hugging herself, she looked at him and gave a helpless shrug.

'Want me to walk you back to the farm? Wouldn't do no harm for them to see you got friends.'

'I can't go back. Not yet. But I don't know where else – I just ran. All I've got is what I'm

241

wearing.' She shuddered. 'I never understood why he was always so short with me, always finding fault.'

Watching her struggle to absorb what she had learned, and all that it meant, Santo wanted to beat Morley Jewell senseless. 'No wonder my – Sarah–' she amended carefully, 'have been in such a kilter. Ever since that first letter came saying Mrs Tregellas had died, she feared there'd be more. Why didn't she *tell* me?' Her face crumpled and she covered it with her hands.

Fighting anger at his helplessness, Santo drew her close. 'I don't know, lovely. P'rhaps she was frightened of how you'd take it. God knows you got good reason to be mad at her. But 'tis no wonder she been ill with the worry of it. She was damned if she didn't tell you and damned if she did.'

Bronnen stiffened. 'You're sorry for her?'

'Hey,' he soothed softly. 'I'm on your side. She should've told you years ago. She must've known it would come out one day.'

'So why didn't she?'

'Only way you'll find out is to ask her.'

Bronnen shook her head. Her arms were tight across her body, holding herself together. 'I can't. Not right now. I'm sorry she's ill, but–' She bit hard on her lower lip. It broke his heart to see how valiantly she was fighting tears. 'She – she was never one for gossip. She must have heard plenty in the soup kitchen, but she never said a word. No wonder. She had more secrets–' Her throat closed.

'Bron, if this gets out, it won't be from me.'

She looked up quickly. 'I know that. I didn't mean–'

He laid a hand over hers. 'You do know you can trust me, don't you?'

She nodded, but a sob burst from her. 'I never – not once did I ever doubt they were–'

'Of course you never. Why would you? You been with them since you was born. They was your family.'

'He wasn't always mad at me,' Bronnen remembered. 'When I was small he liked to sit me on his lap. Then he would tickle me, making me wriggle, and we'd both laugh. But Ma didn't like him doing that, so he said it must be our secret.'

Santo felt a flicker of unease. But not wanting to interrupt her he just nodded.

'Sometimes he held me too tight and his face would get very red. That made me frightened. One night I had this awful dream. I couldn't breathe. I remember screaming and Ma rushed in. He must have been there too because I remember her sending him out. Then she stayed all night, sleeping beside me.'

'She wanted you to feel safe.'

'Yes, but he never had any time for me after that, like I'd done something wrong, but I didn't know what it was. She said I hadn't, and I should just forget about it. Each day when I came home from dame school I helped her with jobs in the house and dairy. She taught me to bake and started taking me to Gillyvean when she went to do the brewing.'

'Dear life, you was some busy.'

'I enjoyed it. And when I did a good job she

243

would praise me. I had to earn it, mind. If it wasn't good enough she'd make me do it over till I got it right. He was always more for Adam. Which was fair enough with both of them working the farm. She used to say he was tired from ploughing, or planting, or harvest, that's why he never said much but really he was proud of me. I wanted to believe her. But after a while I could see he didn't care about anything I did.'

'For years I've listened to her making excuses for him. It made me so mad seeing great purple bruises on her arms, her so stiff and sore she could hardly walk across the yard, yet begging me not to take it up with him. Some days she's in so much pain–' Bronnen swallowed hard to steady her voice. 'So I did her work and mine. But with the extra brewing for Curnock's–' she rubbed her upper arms. 'I'm awful tired.'

'Dear God, Bron, you've had some time of it.'

'So has she. Why do he treat her like that? Why do she let him? Was it – is it – my fault?'

'No, of course it's not!' Seeing her flinch Santo tried to curb his anger. 'He must have agreed to it when you was left with them. You're mad with Mrs Jewell and I can't blame you for that. But she've done a fine job rearing you. You're some rare maid, my lovely.' Yearning to kiss her, he resisted.

Bronnen gave a wan smile. 'I was that full of myself for getting Treeve Curnock to supply malt to the brewhouse at fifteen per cent discount. Now I find out I'm the bastard child of a woman I've never heard of and a married clergyman. You know that saying about pride going before a fall?' She choked down the lump in her throat. 'I feel

244

like I've gone headlong off a cliff.'

Furious at his helplessness, Santo opened his mouth to scold her for self-pity. But her trembling smile and wry shrug stopped the words on his tongue.

'Damn it. I'd like to beat the sh– hell out of Morley Jewell for all the grief he's given you. I know,' he said before she could speak. 'It wouldn't change nothing. It's just – I wish–' He raked his hair. 'I'm no good with words. Give me an engine and I know what I'm doing. But what I'm trying to say, and making a pig's ear of it,' he hesitated as sweat prickled his forehead and underarms. He pressed on, wanting her to know. 'I can't abide to see you hurting like this.'

She bent her head and he was appalled to see tears drop onto her folded arms. *What had he done?* 'God, Bron. I should have kept quiet. I never meant–'

Her hand on his arm silenced him and he saw that despite her wet cheeks and swimming eyes she was smiling.

'I'm glad you didn't. What you said–'

'I meant every word.'

She lifted her arms in silent invitation. He gathered her close against him, covered her mouth with his, and tried to pour into the kiss everything he felt, but was in no position to say until he could ask her to marry him. When they broke apart both were breathing fast. Her eyes were huge and reflected the same needs and emotions that surged and swirled inside him.

Meeting her, falling for her, had doubled the pressure he was under, not simply to succeed, but to start making money instead of spending it. Every penny he had was tied up in his engines. But once his marine engine had been tested and proved, all the sleepless nights and tormented dreams of failure would be forgotten. Then he'd ask her to marry him. He didn't care who her parents were. She was herself, and he loved her.

Reluctantly he let her go. 'Look, how about I take you up to Gillyvean. Miss Tregarron knows better 'n anyone what you're going through. You get on with her, don't you?'

Bronnen nodded. 'She liked coming to the brew-house when I was on my own. We used to talk.'

'There you are then. She'll be glad to help.'

'But – what about Mr Vaughan and Mrs Berry-man? Maybe they won't want me–'

Santo flashed an ironic grin, his anxiety lifting. 'Don't you worry about that. You leave them to Miss Tregarron.'

Chapter Twenty-eight

Ellen put the tea tray on the low table in front of Melanie's chair. 'Anything else, miss?'

'No, thank you, Ellen.' She reached into the em-broidered drawstring bag and took out the small notebook in which she kept details of her sittings. Hearing Richard's voice she looked up, her heart leaping as he walked in closing the door behind him. 'You look tired.' As the words left her lips she realized they lacked tact.

He raised an eyebrow. 'Have you never considered flattery?'

Relieved not to have offended him, and thrilled by his response because it acknowledged her concern, she gave a small shrug. 'We are beyond that. Anyway, you wouldn't believe it.'

'True on both counts.'

She put down her notebook, lifted the teapot and filled two cups. Adding a dash of milk to one she offered it to him. As he took it their eyes met, and she knew he was remembering the evening of her arrival. Such a short time ago, yet so much had happened since.

'Thank you.' He moved to the fireplace and remained standing as he raised the cup to his lips. As he replaced it on the saucer his gaze held hers as if he were about to speak. Then he glanced away and the moment passed. 'When is your next sitting?'

'Tomorrow afternoon. It's my first with Mrs Geach.'

Frowning he set cup and saucer on a side table. 'Could you alter it?'

'Why?'

'A message came from Fox's to say that the coaster carrying Innis's marine engine will arrive on the afternoon tide so I need to be at the boatyard.'

'Then that is where you must be. Mrs Geach lives in Penwerris Terrace. It's not a long walk from here, and one I can easily make on my own.'

'I don't think your father–'

'My father isn't here, Richard. Even if he were, I doubt he would put himself out to escort me such a short distance. I understand that you can't change your arrangements. But nor do I want to change mine. Mrs Geach told me when we met at Mrs Dudley's that she wants the portrait as a birthday gift. If I put her off she may look elsewhere.'

'I doubt that. She would have to travel out of the county to find someone with your talent. How long will you be?'

Despite his matter-of-fact manner, or perhaps because of it, Melanie treasured the compliment. 'An hour and a half.'

'Very well, I will take you there then return to escort you home.'

'It's really not necessary. I'm perfectly–'

'Indeed you are. But nevertheless, that is what will happen.'

As she blew an exasperated sigh she saw his eyebrows lift and couldn't hold back a smile.

'Oh, you–' She shook her head.

'Yes?' he enquired calmly.

Her tone and manner softened. 'Just – you.'

He coloured briefly. Draining his cup he set it down carefully on the saucer and replaced it on the tray.

'Paperwork?'

At his weary nod she felt renewed anger at her father's selfishness. 'So you're here for dinner?' Her tone implied it didn't matter either way. But it did.

'Yes.' At the door he glanced back. 'Melanie, sometimes I may appear – controlling. But you are very–'

'Don't you say *young*,' she warned. 'Not again.

248

You make it sound like an affliction. Just console yourself with the knowledge that it is a temporary state and will very soon pass.'

In spite of himself he laughed, then shook his head. 'You are incorrigible.'

'What else would you expect?' she shot him a wry look. 'I'm an artist, remember?' Awareness flared in his gaze and she felt an answering pull that made her feel weak inside.

'What I intended to say–'

'Before you were interrupted–'

'Quite. Was that you're new to Falmouth. And your circumstances make it particularly important there is no doubt that you are–'

'Cared for?' She asked lightly while her heart yearned. He had kissed her and that kiss had revealed the man behind the facade. It might disconcert him to remember, but she would not let him forget.

He cleared his throat. 'Protected. Your father–'

The thud of the iron knocker on the front door made them both start.

He glanced at her. 'Are you expecting company?'

She shook her head. 'No.'

As Richard went out into the hall Melanie heard Santo Innis's voice.

'Miss Jewell have had bad news. She can't go back to the farm–'

'You needn't worry about the brewhouse, Mr Vaughan,' Bronnen broke in, and from the thickened sound of her voice Melanie knew had been crying. 'Sam's fine on his own now.'

Jumping up from the sofa Melanie hurried out to the hall. 'Miss Jewell?'

'I'm sorry, Miss Tregarron. I shouldn't be bothering you.'

Bronnen's red-rimmed eyes and drawn face touched Melanie, who knew her to be self-sufficient, strong, and resourceful. Tonight she looked utterly shattered.

'I'm glad Mr Innis had the good sense to bring you here. I like to think we are friends. So come inside and tell me how I can help.' As Bronnen walked hesitantly into the sitting room, Melanie saw Santo's relief and Richard's concern. 'Richard, I'm sure Mr Innis will be relieved to hear the news from Fox's.' She closed the door, leaving them in the hall.

'Do sit down.' Melanie tugged the braided bell pull.

Bronnen hesitated. 'I didn't ought to—'

'When I first arrived here,' Melanie said, touching Bronnen's arm, 'I was wretchedly unhappy and very lonely. Spending time with you didn't just give me great comfort, I learned so much. The fire at Curnock's will have meant a lot of extra work for you. And I've been busy too. But though I haven't been to the brewhouse for a while, I remember well your kindness. It would mean so much to me if I could help you. Please, sit.'

Perching on the edge of an elegant armchair upholstered in rose-pattered chintz, Bronnen drew the folded envelope from her bodice, flinching as the door opened.

Reassuring Bronnen with a smile, Melanie turned. 'Will you bring a fresh tray of tea, Ellen?'

'Yes, miss.' Bobbing a curtsey the maid picked up the tray. Melanie closed the door then crossed the room to take the envelope Bronnen offered.

Returning to her chair, Melanie removed both letters. When she'd finished reading she looked up.

'Miss J–'

'Don't call me that. It's not my name. It's not who–'

'Oh, my dear.' Melanie leaned across to touch Bronnen's knee in sympathy. After glancing at the letters once more she returned them to their envelope and handed them back. 'You had no idea?' Bronnen bit hard on her lower lip as she shook her head. 'What a terrible shock for you.'

Turning the envelope between quivering fingers, Bronnen looked up with a helpless shrug. 'What should I do?'

'You must visit the solicitor so he can tell you what is necessary to release the money. In the meantime you will stay here.'

'I can't!'

'Of course you can. Unless there is somewhere else – relatives, perhaps?' Bronnen shook her head. 'Then it's settled. Ellen will be here with the tea any minute. I want you to sit here, try to relax, and drink at least two cups.'

'Where are you going?'

'To talk to Mrs Berryman.'

'She won't want me here. I'm not–'

'The day I arrived I felt exactly the same. But Mrs Berryman couldn't have been kinder. She'll be just the same with you, I promise.'

The door opened and Ellen backed in with the tray, and set it on the table in front of Bronnen.

'Beg pardon, miss, but Mrs Berryman–'

'Tell her I'm on my way down, will you, Ellen?'

As the maid disappeared, Melanie poured tea, added milk and placed the cup and saucer in front of Bronnen. 'May I tell her the situation? I won't if you don't want me to. But if she knows, she'll be better able to deal with any gossip.'

Seeing Bronnen wince, Melanie guessed she was imagining the whispers and sidelong glances as people she had known all her life either shunned her for being born out of wedlock or fawned because of her inherited wealth.

'Whatever you think best.' Bronnen reached for the cup. Using both hands to hold it steady she gulped a mouthful, blushing as her stomach growled.

Melanie frowned. 'When did you last eat?'

'About six this morning, some bread and cheese. I was in the brewhouse all night.'

Rising from her chair, Melanie went to the door. 'I'm going to talk to Mrs Berryman. Then I'll go to the farm. You need a nightgown and a change of clothes. Don't worry,' she said before Bronnen could speak. 'There'll be no trouble. I'll be back as soon as I can. No one will bother you. My father is away from home, and Richard – Mr Vaughan – knows you're here.'

'You're very kind.'

Melanie looked down with heartfelt sympathy into the drawn face and dark-shadowed eyes. 'I've known all my life that I was a bastard. You have only just found out. I'm not going to say I know how you feel, because I don't. I can only imagine how I would feel were I in your place. But you're not alone. You have friends who care about you. Mr Innis is clearly very fond of you, so are Sam

Jose and the other men at the brewery. And so am I.' She smiled. 'I'll be back soon.'

'Oh the poor little maid,' Mrs Berryman clasped her hands over her bosom as Melanie finished explaining.

'A gatepost child, and she never knew? Dear life, that's some awful shock for her. Well, it make no odds to me, and Ellen won't say nothing. Trouble is, there's more gossips in this town than holes in a sieve. So if it *do* get out that she's staying here, we should say Mr Vaughan agreed it because Curnock want her handy-by for the brewhouse.'

'Mrs Berryman, that's perfect.'

'Too many folks stick their noses in where they don't belong.'

'She's looking ill.'

'I aren't surprised. She's up that brewhouse working all hours then running home to cook and clean. My niece Dinah is married to Morley Jewell's cowman,' she explained before Melanie could ask. 'Walter told Dinah that missus have been in some dreadful state with her nerves. 'Tis no wonder, what with mister out drinking most nights, then teasy as a rat all day. And if she been waiting for this to come out...' Shaking her head, Mrs Berryman clicked her tongue. 'Anyhow, never mind she. What that little maid need is some proper food and a good long sleep.'

Within an hour Melanie was back carrying a clean flour sack containing two dresses, underwear, stockings, two cotton nightgowns, a shawl, a hairbrush, and hair pins. She had rolled everything up

253

so the bundle was small and inconspicuous, but was glad to reach Gillyvean from the farm without meeting anyone on the track.

She knew from her own experience that secrets rarely remained secret. Sooner or later the truth came out. But she hoped Bronnen had a little while to adjust to what she had learned before it became public knowledge.

Entering through the back door, she smelled something savoury cooking and looked into the kitchen. Mrs Berryman was busy at the big range and glanced up.

'Which room is Miss Jewell in?'

'Well, I was going to put her along from you. But she wouldn't hear of it. Insisted that if she stayed she had to be in the servants' wing. She said Mr Tregarron wouldn't like it at all if he come back and found her living in the house with his daughter. 'Twas you she was worried for. She said if she was in the back, she could go to and from the brewhouse without disturbing anyone. 'Tis for the best,' she said.

Melanie had opened her mouth to argue. Instead, she nodded. 'I suppose you're right.'

'How was missus?'

'In a very bad way. I couldn't help feeling sorry for her. I shan't tell Bronnen. She doesn't deserve to be made to feel guilty. None of this is her fault.'

'You go on up. Ellen will bring a jug of hot water,' Mrs Berryman called after her.

After a brief knock, Melanie opened the door and saw Bronnen sitting on the side of the bare mattress, her arms tight across her body. 'Are you in pain?'

Bronnen gave her head a small shake.

'Ah,' Melanie touched her shoulder as she passed. 'Just holding yourself together.' She remembered that feeling all too well.

At the foot of the bed was a neat pile of folded blankets, sheets, and a pillow. Relying on instinct and memories of her own experiences to guide her, Melanie closed the door and placed the bundle on a wooden chair in the corner.

'I'm glad you waited. It will be much easier with two of us.' She scooped up the bedclothes, put them on top of the chest of drawers, and shook out a crisply ironed sheet.

Automatically Bronnen got up, grasped the edge of the sheet, and they started making the bed.

'I brought two changes of clothes and everything else I thought you might need,' Melanie said. 'I told Mrs Jewell you were staying here to be near the brewhouse. So she wasn't to worry.' She glanced across at the top of Bronnen's bent head, saw tears drop onto the crisply ironed cotton, and felt her own eyes sting. Swallowing the stiffness in her throat she unfolded one of the blankets.

When Bronnen tensed at the sound of approaching footsteps, Melanie said, 'That'll be Ellen.'

Bronnen opened the door. Handing over a tall enamel jug of hot water, the maid flashed a quick smile then hurried away.

'I thought a chance to freshen up might help get rid of your headache.' Melanie pushed the second pillow into its case, plumped it up then set it on top of the first.

As she put the jug down by the washstand Bronnen looked up in surprise. 'How did you know?'

'The night I arrived here I felt as if someone had tightened an iron barrel hoop around my skull.' She turned back the top sheet and tucked it in. 'Mrs Berryman thought that tonight you would probably prefer to have your meal in here on a tray.' She saw Bronnen's shoulders sag in relief.

'If it's no trouble. I can't–'

'You can't face talking to anyone.' She nodded. 'It's no trouble at all. When I arrived without any warning she was very kind to me.'

'That's different.'

'How so?'

'Because you're family.'

'My father has always acknowledged me,' Melanie said. 'His wife and other daughters don't.' She shrugged. 'I'm not complaining. Were I in their shoes I might be as angry and embarrassed as they are. My point is that the evening I arrived here I was terrified. My father was away from home. Mr Vaughan was – startled. But Mrs Berryman showed me more kindness than I had known in a long time. I will always be grateful. Now I should go before that water grows cold.' She paused at the door. 'I'll look in later, make sure you have all you need.'

Bronnen nodded. With a warm smile Melanie let herself out, closing the door softly.

Unpacking the bundle, Bronnen hung up her dresses and put the rest of her things in the drawers. Then, taking off her faded dress, stockings and shift, she poured water into the china basin, picked up the folded flannel and small bar of soap and held it to her nose, inhaling the sweet-sharp fragrance of lemons.

Refreshed after an all-over wash, she put on her nightgown then unpinned her hair and gave it a thorough brushing. She had just finished plaiting it into a loose braid when there was a tapping on the door.

''Tis only me, my 'andsome,' Mrs Berryman said through the wood. 'I've brung your tea.'

Quickly Bronnen opened the door. Mrs Berryman sailed in. 'Here you are, my bird. There's a nice green pea soup, buttered rolls with cheddar and onion relish, then strawberry tart. Nothing too heavy.'

For an instant Bronnen's stomach rebelled. Then as Mrs Berryman passed her, taking the tray to the deep cream-painted windowsill, Bronnen caught the aroma of the savoury soup. Her mouth watered and suddenly she was ravenous. ''Tis some kind of you going to all this trouble.'

'No such thing.' The housekeeper pulled the wooden chair forward and pointed. Bronnen sat. 'We all heard how hard you been working. Now I don't want to see nothing left on they plates but the pattern. Soon as you finished, you get in the bed. Some day of it you've had, and you need a good night's sleep if you're to be fit for the brew-house tomorrow.'

'Yes, Mrs Berryman.'

''Night, my bird.' She hesitated in the doorway. 'Don't you fret now. You'll be all right.'

Bronnen's vision blurred. Unable to speak she tried to smile her gratitude. As the door closed, she swallowed hard then picked up the bowl and spoon.

Chapter Twenty-nine

Hearing the clop of hooves Santo put down his mallet, climbed out of the hull on to the step-ladder. He reached the open doorway at the same time as Jack Mitchell.

'All right, boy? Took proper care we did. We got 'em lying on straw and sailcloth.'

'Right on,' Santo nodded. 'No trouble with the casting?' he said over his shoulder as he crossed to the cart.

'I couldn't see nothing. I know what I'm about.'

Hearing the edge of irritation, Santo clapped Jack's shoulder. ''Course you do. 'Tis just – this got to work, Jack.'

'And it will. No doubt of that. Right, where do you want 'em?'

'In the workshop, at this end of the bench in the light. You bring the shaft, I'll bring the prop.'

'He's heavy mind, at least a hundredweight, maybe half as much again.'

'If you think I can't carry that–'

'No offence,' Jack grinned.

When the shaft and propeller were resting on the scarred wood, Santo reached for the two mugs he had brought from the office earlier in preparation for this moment. Turning the spigot he filled each cup with small beer and handed one to Jack.

'Bleddy 'ell, boy. What about a drop of Cousin Jack?'

Santo raised his mug in mock salute. 'This is all I've got, and you should be glad of it.'

'How's that?'

'Owe you money, don't I? You'd be teasy as a snake if I was to go wasting it on cognac.'

'Fine brandy is never a waste. 'Tis money well spent.'

'Not my money.'

Jack emptied his mug in three gulps then wiped a gnarled hand across his mouth. 'Well, 'tis wet. But I can't say no more'n than for it.'

Draining his mug Santo set it down. He picked up a soft cloth and began to polish the propeller blades, examining them closely as he worked.

'Well?' Jack said.

Santo looked up. 'Proper job, Jack.' Then something down-river caught his eye. He straightened, relief and excitement tightening his stomach. 'At last.'

'What?'

Brushing past him, Santo hurried out to the quay, his gaze never leaving the schooner as her sails spilled the wind then dropped. She glided closer, then turned, slowed by the river's incoming flow.

'That crate on the deck?' Santo grinned over his shoulder. 'That's my engine.'

'They'll want 'n off quick,' Jack said. 'Tide'll be on the turn dreckly.'

As mooring lines were thrown ashore and made fast around the bollards along quay, Santo saw two crewmen setting up a block and tackle on the foremast yard. Hearing the quick clop of iron-shod hooves he glanced round. Richard jumped down from the trap, tied the reins to the iron ring and walked briskly towards them.

'Mr Innis?' The schooner's captain, a stocky man wearing a dark blue double-breasted coat, waved a sheaf of papers.

'What's all that?' Jack asked.

'Bill of lading and God knows what else for me to sign.'

'Go on then. We're burning daylight here.'

'No need for you to wait.'

'I aren't going nowhere till I seen this here engine. I got to say, after that great side-lever engine on the *Mercury*, that crate do look some small.'

'Size isn't everything, Jack,' Santo grinned. 'You wait till he's in the hull and the prop's fitted. Stop your breath, he will.'

'This way, miss.'

'Thank you.'

The maid opened the door, stood aside for Melanie to pass then withdrew leaving it ajar. Placing her portfolio on the nearest side table Melanie removed her gloves then her hat. Though it was customary to leave one's hat on when paying a call, a sitting was different. To make sketches for a portrait she needed unrestricted vision.

But, over-furnished and full of shadows, the room was north-facing and so would be totally unsuitable for sittings.

She was still mildly irritated with Richard. He could easily have set her down at the yard. It could be no more than a hundred yards from there to here. But no, despite running late after an unexpected visit from a quarry owner inter-

260

ested in Santo Innis's hot-air pump engines, he had insisted on driving her to the stone steps a few feet from the Geachs' front gate then waiting until she reached the high pavement. As she lifted the knocker she had glimpsed him bowling back along the road towards the boatyard.

'Good afternoon, Miss Tregarron.'

Startled, she looked round. Where had he come from? She hadn't realised anyone was in the room. 'Mr Geach. Good afternoon.'

As he came towards her she noticed how the superb tailoring of his dark cutaway coat and pearl grey trousers flattered an undeniably portly build. His white cravat was fastened with a gold pin, and he had brushed his thinning fair hair forward from a side parting so it blended with his long sideburns.

He made a stiff bow. Hearing the creak that betrayed his use of a corset, Melanie bit the inside of her lip and bobbed a brief curtsey instead of offering her hand.

He moved to the window, speaking over his shoulder. 'You've brought the sunshine with you.'

Unsure if his remark was intended as a compliment – and fearing to look foolish if she thanked him when he had merely been commenting on the improvement after last night's rain – Melanie simply smiled.

She hoped Helen Geach would not be long. This first meeting was important. They needed to discuss style and medium as well as pose, choices that could not be rushed. But, all too aware of the demands on Richard, she did not want to overrun and keep him waiting.

'I must tell you I am very impressed with your portrait of Mrs Martin. Tell me, have you ever considered turning your considerable talent to landscapes?'

'I did some landscape painting during my training,' Melanie answered politely.

'Come,' he beckoned her to the window. 'Is this not a splendid view of the harbour?'

Trying to hide her impatience she went to his side.

'Just look at those clouds.' She felt his hand on her back. 'And the variations of colour in the water.' His arm encircled her shoulder. 'Falmouth's importance as a trading port is increasing. Those ships in the harbour have come from all over the world.'

Uneasy, but giving him the benefit of the doubt, Melanie stepped away. 'I beg your pardon, Mr Geach. I understood I had an appointment with your wife this afternoon.'

'Indeed you did. However, Mrs Geach was called away to the bedside of a sick relative.'

'I wish she had sent word.' Realising she sounded sharp, and aware that as a guest in his house she owed him courtesy, she drew a breath. 'Forgive me. I meant that had I been informed I would not now be interrupting your afternoon.'

'My dear, I would not have missed it for the world.' His eyes gleamed and his smile made her skin crawl. He caught her hand, holding it tightly between his. 'You capture an excellent likeness, Miss Tregarron. What other talents lie in those skilful fingers, hm?'

Melanie snatched her hand free and felt herself

starting to shake. 'You must excuse me. I think I should leave.'

'Why?' He sounded so reasonable. 'Had my wife been here, you would have stayed for at least an hour. So if you were about to claim a need to be elsewhere, we both know that isn't true.' He reached for her and she found herself trapped against an elegant rosewood table.

'Please, Mr Geach–'

'Yes, my dear? What would you have me do? Ah, such a pretty blush.' As he ran his fingertips down her hot cheek, she jerked her head away. Anger flared, bright and sharp, cutting through her fear.

'Stop that! You forget yourself, sir!'

His pudgy fingers gripped her shoulders with surprising strength. 'And you, miss, are a little tease.'

'That's not true!' Fury at the unjust accusation overrode Melanie's shock. Bringing her forearms up she broke his hold. Free, she whirled away, putting a sofa between them. 'How dare you!'

He raised a warning finger. 'Were I you, my dear, I should think carefully before screaming for help. I daresay a maid and footman would come running. Yet what would you tell them? Here you are, alone with me.'

'But – that was not my choice.'

Reaching inside his coat he withdrew an envelope and waved it. 'Who would believe that when I have here a note from my wife regretting that, due to unforeseen circumstances, she must cancel today's sitting with you?'

Melanie stared at him. 'If you have the note, I

cannot have received it for it was never sent.'

He sighed. 'I know it, and you know it. But my wife doesn't. If I were to tell her that you came here today, fully aware she would be absent, what would she think? She would feel bound to warn her acquaintance–'

'You are despicable, sir. If your wife chooses to believe your lies that is her affair. But I will not be used this way. I shall expose you.' She flinched at his sudden burst of laughter.

'Will you indeed? I think not, Miss Tregarron. You see, whereas I enjoy considerable standing in this town, you,' his eyes glittered with amused contempt, 'are the bastard daughter of a man who lives separated from his wife, and whose numerous liaisons are common knowledge. Need I remind you that you came to my house without a chaperone? You boldly claim to be an artist. Yet the whole world knows such people have no morals. So, Miss Tregarron, say what you wish.' He leaned towards her. 'Who will believe you?'

Crossing to the fireplace he tugged a bell-pull. 'We might have enjoyed a pleasant interlude and a sweet revenge on your father. Thanks to his interference I was denied election to–' With visible effort he cut himself short. 'Has it not smarted all these years? Being an outsider? An embarrassment? You really are very foolish. I would not have been ungenerous. However, while passable to look at, you are a lamentable bore. Run along home, little girl. My wife will expect you next week.'

Her face burning, her stomach a queasy knot, Melanie put on her hat and picked up her portfolio, her hands trembling so violently she almost dropped it.

The door opened, revealing the maid who bobbed a curtsey. 'Sir?'

Simon Geach waved a dismissive hand. 'Miss Tregarron is leaving.'

Melanie couldn't wait to get out of the house, but her pride would not allow him the last word. Turning in the doorway, she inclined her head with regal dignity. 'Good day, Mr Geach. My sincere sympathy to your wife.' Clasping her portfolio to her breast like a shield, she walked briskly down the hall.

The maid hurried to open the front door, her face betraying surprise and confusion.

Melanie guessed the maid had witnessed visits by other women when Mrs Geach was absent. *You are wrong* she wanted to say. *I am not like them.* She clenched her teeth so tightly her jaws ached.

As the door closed behind her, she walked down the front path and out of the gate. She doubted he would be watching, but in case he was she held her head high as she turned towards the boatyard and started walking along the raised pavement.

Her heart hammered sickeningly against her ribs. How *dared* he treat her so, make such accusations. He didn't know her. Since childhood she had been warned that the circumstances of her birth meant she must take more care than most. In public she had always behaved with the utmost propriety; ever conscious of people watching, waiting for her to slip, anticipating an opportunity to exchange knowing nods and murmurs; like father like daughter; the apple never falls far from the tree.

In private she had raged and wept at the injustice. Her father lived as he chose, yet was received everywhere. Yet she, who had taken such care never to put a foot wrong, could be insulted with impunity. But what really hurt, drowning her bitter fury, was that this was not the first time. *How could she have known? Why should she have suspected?*

Her throat felt painfully stiff but she would *not* cry. Instead she focused on her rage. Simon Geach was a despicable bully used to getting his own way and quick with insults when thwarted. His willingness to betray his wife in her own home told Melanie his behaviour was habitual.

The realisation that he saw her, not as a person, merely a potential conquest and a means of revenge against her father, made her feel worthless. But that he would target her because of her birth – something over which she'd had no control – and assume her interest never mind her willingness, was an even greater insult.

What exactly had her father done to provoke such bitter anger?

Richard might know. But how could she ask? He would want to know why. What could she tell him? Hadn't he warned her that her that her behaviour might be misunderstood? But that had been a private moment, between the two of them. She had wanted him to see her as a woman, not an inconvenient interruption, or an additional unwanted item on his daily list of matters to be dealt with. She would never have acted so with others present.

She had not given Mr Geach the slightest reason to believe his attentions would be welcome. When his wife had introduced them at Mrs Martin's, he had made no impression on her at all.

Reliving the sensation of his fingers on her face, and his scathing words, she felt sick. She kept walking, blind to her surroundings, lashed by guilt as she recalled blithely assuring Richard she was perfectly capable of taking care of herself. How furiously she had accused him of treating her like a child.

She stopped. On the far side of the road was the slope leading down to the boatyard. She didn't want to interrupt. But nor could she go on to Gillyvean without telling him. If he arrived at the Geachs' house to collect her and she wasn't there he would worry. And God alone knew what Mr Geach would tell him. She could not allow that.

Descending the stone steps from the high pavement, she walked quickly across the road, started down the slope, and saw Richard talking to Santo Innis and Jack Mitchell who were standing by a large wooden crate.

Seeing her, Santo raised a hand in greeting. Richard glanced round, excused himself, and came to meet her. His frown of concern quickened her pulse with renewed guilt.

'What's happened?' His manner was pleasant and courteous but she heard the tension in his voice. He kept his distance. Like her, he was aware of those watching. 'Why are you not with Mrs Geach?'

'I – I could not work. I have a dreadful head-ache.' She lowered her eyes, unable to meet his intent gaze.

'I'll take you home.'

'I'm sorry.' It spilled out.

'Melanie? Has something–?'

How did he know? 'I meant,' she said quickly, alerted by his urgency, 'I'm sorry to interrupt. I know how busy you are.'

'It's nothing that cannot wait. Here, take my arm.' He drew her hand through the crook of his elbow. She kept her head bent so he would not see the tears she was fighting. She would not cry. Not here, not now.

He helped her into the trap. 'You will soon be more comfortable.' Now familiar with her moods he had known the instant he saw her that something was badly wrong. She needed time to settle. But when the moment was right he would find out what had upset her. And whoever was responsible would suffer.

Chapter Thirty

Back at Gillyvean Melanie went directly to her room. She poured cold water from the flower-pat-terned china jug into the matching bowl, bathed her face and patted it dry, then crossed to the window and sank into the high-backed armchair.

Gazing blindly out of the window she forced herself to relive everything she had said and done after entering the Geachs' drawing room. There was *nothing* that could be interpreted as an invi-tation to familiarity. Except – Richard had set her down at the gate. But after the first sittings he had done the same at Mrs Martin's and Mrs Dudley's.

Neither she nor Richard had wanted him to be responsible for her, both bitterly resenting her father's high-handed insistence. And yet ... and yet how quickly she had come to trust him. Certainly he was more dependable than her father who spent more time away than at home.

His driving her to and from sittings, begun under protest, was now something she looked forward to because they talked. She had started it by asking about his work, where he would be, who he would see. As he regarded her without speaking she had reminded him of his comment the day he had picked her up from Mrs Martin's: that they might have used the time to know one another better. She would like that.

After a brief hesitation he had told her about negotiations with a machine tool business that needed investment. Learning about the conflict between the brothers who owned the business had fascinated her. When he picked her up and asked how the sitting had gone she had described progress on the portrait. Then she told him who had dropped in and bits of gossip she had heard. Though he had made no comment, she read amusement and interest in his smile.

She had soon discovered that if she was having difficulty with the portrait, describing the problem to him often helped her see a solution. When she had told him that he had bowed, saying he was happy to be of service.

He *did* have feelings for her. The passion in his kiss had left no room for doubt. Yet he had told her father he had no intention of remarrying.

Even if he changed his mind he would not want someone married men thought it perfectly acceptable to insult with unwanted attentions, someone deemed unworthy of respect.

Reaching for her sketchpad on the side table, she opened it at a fresh page and began drawing Richard's face from memory. It gave her comfort and wrenched her heart.

After a quick tap on the door Ellen poked her head in.

'Beg pardon, miss. Mr Vaughan asked me to see if you want anything.'

Touched by his thoughtfulness and hot with guilt, Melanie forced a smile. 'Will you tell him I'm feeling much better? I just need to rest.'

Ellen nodded at the sketchpad. 'With respect, miss, you don't seem to be doing much resting. Mr Vaughan said you had a bad headache. Wouldn't you be better lying on the bed? I can make up a lavender-water compress for your eyes.'

'That's kind of you. But people rest in different ways, and I find great comfort in my drawing.'

'You know best, miss.'

Richard would want to know what had upset her. She needed time to think what to tell him. 'Ellen, would you ask Mrs Berryman if I can have my dinner on a tray?'

'Mr Vaughan already suggested it, miss. He've got a dinner engagement in town with Mr Tregarron's attorney.'

He owed her no explanation regarding his engagements. Yet telling Ellen ensured the information would be passed on. Why had he done that? Simple courtesy? Or proof that what he felt for her

270

ran deeper than mere attraction, deeper than fondness. She wanted that so much. Even if it were the case, would it survive what she must tell him?

'Thank you, Ellen.'

'Miss,' the maid bobbed a curtsey and withdrew.

The light was fading when Melanie made her way to the servants' wing, knocked and waited.

Bronnen opened the door, surprise widening her eyes. 'Miss Tregarron, what – has something–?'

'Please don't be concerned. I just wanted to make sure you have everything you need.'

Bronnen's shoulders relaxed and she nodded. 'Mrs Berryman's been ever so kind. She kept tea for me. Lovely, it was.'

'Mrs Berryman is an excellent cook.'

'No, I didn't mean – yes, she is. But usually I'm rushing back from the brewhouse to get a meal ready before Fa – the men come in from the farm.'

'Then you'll have enjoyed it all the more for not having to prepare and cook it yourself. Is all going well with Mr Curnock's orders for ale?'

Bronnen nodded. 'I think Sam's got a good chance if he puts in for the head brewer's job.'

'If he's successful he'll owe it to you. May I come in for a moment?'

Bronnen opened the door wide. 'Beg pardon, miss. I would've asked you,' she said as Melanie stepped inside. 'Only I didn't think you'd–'

'Want to stay? I have nowhere to rush off to. And as I told you before, I enjoy your company. When is your next day off? I thought we might arrange to visit Truro so you may see Mr Coode, the attorney.'

Bronnen gave an uncertain shrug. 'I don't have days off, not when we're brewing. With all this work for Mr Curnock, Sam and me been taking turns doing nights.'

'You've been left in the brewhouse by yourself? That's not right.'

Blushing, Bronnen pleated the material of her dress. 'Mr Innis didn't like it either. See, if it's a warm evening I have to leave the door open to let the heat out so the fermentation don't run wild. He comes by after work so I won't be on my own.'

'That's very thoughtful of him.'

'He's like that,' Bronnen said softly.

'You think a lot of him.'

Bronnen nodded.

'Will you marry?'

'I don't – he–' she gestured helplessly, trying to hide bewilderment that stung. 'He hasn't said nothing yet. But I know he likes me.' Her blush deepened. 'I b'lieve 'tis more than liking.'

'He's kissed you?'

Bronnen nodded.

'Was it wonderful?'

'Oh yes. I never knew – lovely, it was.' She dragged herself back from delicious memories that, even as they made her quiver inside, left her anxious and uncertain. 'But he's working long hours too, down the boatyard.'

'There you are then,' Melanie spread her hands. 'An honourable man won't declare himself until he can provide a home for his intended.'

Bronnen's mind raced. That would explain so much. She hoped with all her heart that Melanie was right. 'You think so?'

272

'I'm sure of it. Mr Innis is a kind and decent man. He helped me when others turned their backs. He is a man worth loving.'

Bronnen flinched.

'Not me, silly,' Melanie shook her head, smiling. 'You.' Her smile faltered. 'My heart is engaged elsewhere.'

'Mr Vaughan.'

After a moment Melanie nodded.

'Has he–? Will you–?'

'I don't know. My father wants the match.'

'That's good. Isn't it?' Bronnen added warily as Melanie jumped up from the side of the bed where she had been sitting and paced to the door and back, unable to keep still.

'His primary concern is that his money should remain in the family.'

Bronnen watched and said nothing.

'Can you believe he actually said that?' Melanie shook her head. 'He wants to shift responsibility for me on to a husband and Richard is the ideal candidate. But I can't – won't – marry simply to oblige my father. In any case, Richard said he had no intention of marrying again. So though I – he – there is a strong attraction between us, it is clearly not strong enough to overturn that decision.' She lifted one shoulder and turned away. She looked utterly desolate.

Bronnen gathered her courage. 'Beg pardon, miss, are you being fair to Mr Vaughan?'

'What do you mean?'

'Well, maybe he don't want to be used by Mr Tregarron any more than you do. But will you let that stand in the way of what's in your hearts?

What you both want?'

'I have no idea what Richard wants. His words say one thing, his actions another, and his eyes–' she looked away, pressing her lips together.

'I'll tell you this, and it's God's honest truth. Mr Vaughan have changed since you came. I seen him watch you when you don't know. The look on his face – 'tis like he's bleeding inside.'

Hope lit Melanie's eyes then quickly faded. 'I know he feels responsible, and protective. I know he's drawn to me. But love?' Her eyes closed for a moment. 'No.'

'How d'you know?'

'Why would he?' Melanie's face betrayed the doubts that tortured her. 'No one else ever has. My mother abandoned me. My father did what was expected of a gentleman, giving me his name and an education that equipped me for society. I have obeyed the rules, behaved with propriety, yet none of it has protected me from men who think my illegitimacy gives them the right to treat me like – like – a woman of the streets.'

Bronnen gasped. 'Oh, miss. That's terrible.'

Melanie flashed Bronnen a brief weary smile. 'You are a good listener, Miss–'

'Bronnen, just – Bronnen.'

'Then you must call me Melanie.'

'I can't do that!'

'After what we have shared? Of course you can. And I'm sorry for being so selfish. You have troubles enough without me burdening you with mine.'

'I don't mind, really. You been so good to me, you and Mr Vaughan. Look, I know it isn't for me to say, but–' she hesitated.

'Say it anyway. I promise I won't be offended.'

'All right.' Bronnen took a deep breath. 'Don't go cutting your nose off to spite your face.'

Melanie's gaze searched Bronnen's. 'Do you really think he–?'

'It don't matter what I think. You know him. What do *you* think?'

Melanie started pacing once more, clasping and unclasping her hands, talking more to herself than Bronnen. 'I should have been more on my guard. But it never occurred to me – Richard will insist on knowing what happened. And I have to tell him. But–' she turned, anguish naked on her face. 'What if he doesn't believe me?'

Working from sun-up to nightfall, Santo missed seeing Bronnen. He thought about going up to the brewhouse. But if it was Sam's turn to stay overnight it would be a long walk for nothing. Nor could he go calling at Gillyvean. Anyway, she needed her sleep.

The morning after the engine arrived, Jack arrived with his two assistants and a bottle of brandy. Santo had set it aside on the bench. Seeing their faces drop he promised to open it after they got the hull in the water.

Over a long sweaty demanding day that stretched nerves and muscles to the limit, they used rollers to move the hull onto the dolly and shored it up with props and wedges.

Then the dolly was winched slowly down the slip and into the high tide. When the hull floated off with Santo aboard, Jack remained with the winch while Santo threw bow and stern mooring lines to the two men onshore. Checking the hull for leaks and finding none he released a heartfelt sigh of relief.

After removing the top and sides of the wooden crate, Santo used thick canvas straps and the spider crane to lift the engine into the hull. After bolting it down he covered it with a tarp, secured that with rope, then jumped ashore exhausted but elated. The low sun cast golden light and long shadows.

By the time he reached the workshop, Jack had opened the brandy. He poured a generous measure into one of the mugs and thrust it at Santo, took the other for himself and handed the bottle to Jimmy.

'You and Davy have a swig then get on home. I'll see you tomorrow.'

Santo swirled the golden-brown spirit, inhaling the rich aroma. His mouth watered. He glanced at Jack who tilted his head back, swallowed deeply, then grimaced.

'Yo, bleddy 'andsome, that is.'

Santo knew why Jack had remained after sending his men away. The past couple of weeks had been all go. Now it had to be faced. He set the mug down untouched.

'Don't go thinking I've forgotten, Jack.'

'What about?'

'The money I owe you.'

Jack waved it aside. 'No need to fret about that. I know you're good for it. Still, seeing how you've brung it up, I been thinking too. You got to test your engine. But there's nothing to say you can't

276

make yourself a tidy sum at the same time, is there?'

Santo straightened up. 'Doing what?'

Jack shot him a mocking look. 'C'mon, boy. You aren't daft.'

Santo saw where this was leading. He should stop it now; say straight out that he wasn't interested. If he did, it wouldn't be mentioned again. *But he might have passed up the best chance he'd ever have to pay off his debts, acquire some working capital, and be in a position to offer for Bronnen. What harm could it do to listen?*

'How far?' he asked.

'Out by Manacles. The Guernsey merchants send a schooner loaded with free-trade goods and we meet 'em out there.'

'When?'

'Early next week when there's only a quarter moon.'

'What about the Excise cutter?'

'Don't you worry about he.' Jack tapped the side of his nose. 'He'll be up Padstow way.'

'You sure of that?'

Jack nodded. 'Too right I am. I don't want to get caught no more'n you do. C'mon, boy. What d'you say? 'Tis good money for just a few hours' work.'

He'd have time first to test the engine and prop in the river. That test trip would work-harden the brass so the propeller would be more efficient for a long voyage. 'How many will be going?'

'You, me, and one more. We won't be gone long. I like to get out and back quick. And with no mast and sails we'll be all but invisible.' He eyed the engine on the bench. 'That there boat engine, make much noise, do it?'

'Quiet as a breath,' Santo promised. 'But we don't want smoke giving us away. There's some off-cuts of seasoned oak in the store. Cut down they'll burn hot and slow. But I'll need best quality coal as well.'

Jack gave a quick nod. 'Leave it to me, boy.' He reached into a shapeless canvas bag on the bench and took out another bottle of cognac. 'Plenty more where that come from.'

After he'd gone Santo gazed at the bottles. With so much to think about, so many pressures, he was desperately tired. Though he fell asleep the instant his head hit the pillow, too often he would wake in the early hours and lie staring into the darkness, or jerk into consciousness before dawn, his mind already racing.

Now there was Bronnen. He could not regret meeting her. She was everything he wanted. But the timing could not have been worse. He had no proper job and no money. How long could he expect her to wait?

He wiped greasy hands on a rag then picked up the mug. He could remember when a bottle wasn't enough. He'd come a long way since then, learned a lot on the journey, and had no intention of repeating the experience. *He was not his father.* But one small drink to smooth the rough, raw edges. No harm in that, surely?

Raising the mug to his lips he took two deep swallows, shuddering as the spirit burned his throat, bloomed like fire in his stomach and flooded his limbs with warmth. Closing his eyes he sucked in a deep breath. Already he felt calmer, his head clearer. Another mouthful drained the mug. Setting it down on the bench, he carried the un-opened bottle into the office and put it in the cupboard. Out of sight, out of mind.

'Santo? You there?'

Bronnen. He felt his heart lift in his chest. Closing the cupboard he returned to the work-shop. She was standing in the open doorway. 'Hello, my lovely.' He crossed to her. 'A rare treat this is, seeing you.'

'I didn't expect to get away.' She was smiling, glowing, happy to see him. God, he loved her. He held out his hand and she took it.

'Made my day, you have.'

She flinched, her smile fading.

'What's wrong, bird?'

She glanced away, shaking her head. Then looked directly at him. 'You've been drinking.'

The disappointment in her voice cut like a whiplash. But it was too late now to wish he had resisted. Anger at his own weakness made him defensive.

'What if I have? I'm tired, I'm working all hours, and I got a lot on my mind.' About to tell her that Jack had brought the bottle, he stopped himself in time. She might not ask, but she would certainly wonder why Jack Mitchell had brought him brandy.

He didn't want to tell her about the smuggling. What she didn't know couldn't – he stopped in mid-thought, recognising the fatal flaw in his logic. What she hadn't known had exploded in her face. She had suffered enough. If he told her what he planned she would only worry. She had enough on her plate without him adding to it.

'Why, Santo?'

The hurt in her eyes stung him. 'For God's sake, it was just a couple of mouthfuls. I've got so much to do and nowhere near–' he broke off, pride preventing him admitting his desperate shortage of money. 'Enough time.'

'You won't find it in a bottle.'

'Don't you preach to me, miss. If you're so set against drink, why do you brew for Mr Tregarron?'

'Because I need the money to buy clothes and shoes!'

Shame surged through him as she caught her lip between her teeth and smoothed her skirts. When she spoke her voice was unsteady. 'I'm sorry, I had no right – I didn't mean to preach.' She turned away.

'Bron, wait! Please!' He moved to block her path and put out a hand, but didn't dare touch. 'It's me who should apologise. I had one drink, that's all, I swear, celebrating with Jack and his men after we got the hull in the water. I don't drink now. There was a time some years back – but I stopped because I didn't like who it made me. I'm not my father. I'm not Morley Jewell neither.'

She flushed. 'Of course you aren't. I should never– I had no right–'

He laid his forefinger gently on her lips. 'Sssh. I just wanted you to know you don't ever have to worry. Got to get back have you?'

She shook her head. 'Sam will be there another couple of hours.' She gestured at the engine on the bench. 'But if you're busy–'

'Never too busy for you.' He saw her cheeks

grow rosy. As she looked again at the engine on the bench he yearned to pull the pins from her hair and watch it tumble over her shoulders.

'Are you going to fix that to a pump?'

He nodded. 'Mr Rowse up Dene Quarry have bought two. And Mr Avers from Carnsew want one. But I've built it different from yours.'

'Why?'

He gazed at her profile, the escaped curls, the vulnerable nape of her neck. 'You're so beautiful,' he murmured.

As she glanced up, eyes wide, he watched warm colour flood her face.

'I had to say it, my lovely. 'Tis no more'n the honest truth. I wish–' he shook his head. 'You asked about the engine? I've turned the piston so he's upright instead of sideways. That stopped the knock and it don't lose speed neither. After you finish this order for Mr Curnock, I'll come up and change the one at Gillyvean. Only take a couple of hours.'

She nodded. 'All right.'

His brows rose and he grinned. 'You aren't going to fight me?'

Bronnen shook her head. 'Why would I? Your engine is saving us hours. If you say this new way is better, I trust you.'

He cupped her face, his gaze searching, 'You're rare, d'you know that?'

'So are you.'

Taking her in his arms he bent his head. As his mouth covered hers he clung to restraint. Her arms slipped around his neck. Her body fitted against his, her mouth so sweet and soft and

281

giving. He deepened the kiss, drawing her closer. Need roared through him, powerful, urgent, and he felt his control slipping.

Bronnen couldn't breathe as long-buried memories erupted like marsh gas in a swamp. Suffocating, terrified, she fought him off with furious desperation.

He released her at once. Trembling violently, shocked and gasping, she backed away from him, not understanding what had happened.

He raked his hair with unsteady hands. 'Jesus, Bron, I'm sorry. I'm so sorry. I didn't mean to frighten you.'

The workshop tilted and black spots danced across her vision. She felt herself sway. 'I – I–'

He caught her as she crumpled.

Dimly she felt herself swept up, carried, and a few moments later placed gently on a hard chair beside a table. Her eyes still closed, she put her head down on her arms.

'That's right, my lovely, you just rest a minute.' His words soothed but she could hear the strain in his voice. She heard a door open, then the splash of pouring water. A moment later a cool wet cloth was placed gently on the back of her neck.

'Oh, that's better.' Her head cleared and carefully she sat up. 'Could I have a drink?'

'Course you can. Don't you move now.' He disappeared into the adjoining room and came back with a half-filled cup. Putting it on the table he stepped back, wiping his palms on his trousers.

'Thank you.' Touched by his obvious concern, Bronnen drank. The cold water slid down her parched throat, quenching her thirst and dissolving the last sticky threads of fear. 'I'm all right.'

He shook his head. 'You're white as a sheet.' Resting one hip on the table he folded his arms, then unfolded them and wiped one hand across his face. 'Bron, I never meant– I'd cut my arm off sooner than hurt you.'

Bronnen offered her hand, palm up. Immediately he gripped it.

'It wasn't you. I love how you kiss.' Shaking her head, feeling the blush climb her throat and scald her cheeks, she looked down at the scarred and ink-stained tabletop.

'You haven't gone off me then?' The mingled anxiety and relief in his voice lifted her spirits and made her smile. Looking up she shook her head.

'I'm some glad of that. You're–' he stopped, and she wished he had finished what he had started to say. 'What was it then, bird? What upset you so bad?'

She shuddered violently. 'The brandy: the taste and smell of it. I couldn't breathe, and I had this sudden terrible fear–' Her voice wobbled. She tried to cover it with a laugh but tears stung.

In an instant he was on his knees by her chair. One hand still held hers pressed against his chest. Through his shirt she could feel the heat of his body and the rhythmic thud of his heart. His other hand cupped her face. A tear spilled over and he gently wiped it away with his thumb.

'I'll never touch another drop.'

She looked at his hand holding hers then raised her eyes to his.

'Give you my word, Bron,' he said quietly.

'It's a lot to ask–'

'You aren't asking. I'm telling you. 'Tis my decision.'

'But if you're offered–' She studied him for a long moment. 'It won't be easy saying no.'

His wry laugh held genuine humour. 'That's all right then, lovely. I aren't used to easy.' He lifted her hand and the warm pressure of his lips on her knuckles made her breath catch. 'I never thought – Bron, I – mean the world to me you do. Don't ever forget that.'

Bronnen lowered her lashes. The woman she had believed was her mother had said those same words. Hearing them hurt, for Sarah Jewell had been hiding a devastating secret. Santo would never do that. Looking up, she smiled at him.

Chapter Thirty-one

Melanie sat on the terrace steps in the warm afternoon sun. Sick of reliving the scene in the Geachs' drawing room, she still couldn't put it out of her mind. Behind her the French doors opened. She glanced round and gave a start as Richard came towards her.

'Please don't get up.'

'Isn't it a lovely day?' She forced a smile. His eyes narrowed and she knew her attempt at lightness had failed dismally.

He walked past her down the steps then turned to face her, their eyes level. 'Tell me what's wrong.'

She wanted to. The urge was almost overwhelming. But fearing his reaction she shrugged instead. 'Nothing. I had a headache that's all.'

He leaned back against the curved stone balustrade, crossed one foot over the other and folded his arms, one dark brow lifting.

'For heaven's sake! There's nothing to tell.'

'You have been sitting there for half an hour without opening your sketchpad.'

'Have you been watching me?'

He ignored the question. 'Something has upset you. I want to know what it is.'

'Why? So you can say–' She cut herself short. Then drawing a deep breath she shrugged again. 'It has nothing to do with you. So as it is neither your fault nor your responsibility I see no reason whatever to burden you–'

'In your father's absence anything that upsets you is my responsibility.'

'Has no one ever told you that you take too much upon yourself?'

'No,' he said calmly. 'I doubt such a thought ever crossed your father's mind.' Pushing himself away from the balustrade he astonished her by sitting down beside her on the step. Though he was careful to leave space between them, his proximity was so unsettling that she snatched up her sketchpad and hugged it.

Resting his elbows on his parted knees he linked his hands between them and cleared his throat. 'But I am not asking on his behalf.' Turning his head he held her gaze. 'Something happened after I left you outside the Geachs' house. What was it, Melanie?'

Heat climbed her throat and burned her face. 'I

feel such a fool.' Now she had made that admission, the rest tumbled out. 'When he said she wasn't there I should have left at once.'

'You had a sitting with Mrs Geach but she was away from home?'

Melanie nodded. 'I was surprised she hadn't let me know. While my mind was on that, he asked me if I ever painted landscapes and begged me come to the window. Refusing would have appeared ill-mannered so I went. But then he–' She shook her head, her fingers straying to her face where his soft plump fingers had touched. Her skin tightened in revulsion and she wanted to scrub the sensation and the memory away.

'He what, Melanie? Tell me the rest.'

'He put his arm around me. When I pushed him away, he called me a tease.' She looked at him. 'I'm not, Richard. I would never–' Then she remembered and guilt bowed her shoulders. 'When I – with you – it was–'

'I know what it was.'

'I never have, and never would – not with anyone else, you have to believe that.'

'I do. Our circumstances are – different. Go on.'

Her mouth was dry and she ran her tongue between her teeth and upper lip to free it. 'He said if I screamed of course someone would come. But how then would I explain the fact that I had entered the house knowing his wife was not there?' She met his gaze, imploring. 'I didn't know. Truly I didn't. Had I known–'

'You wouldn't have gone.'

Melanie heard only conviction. He believed her. Never had she been more grateful. Swallowing the

286

lump in her throat she continued. 'He said his wife had been called away to a sick relative and had written to me to put off our sitting until another day. Then he waved the letter at me. He hadn't posted it. He taunted me. Who would people believe? After all, he is a gentleman with standing in the town. I am merely the bastard daughter of a man who lives separated from his wife and whose numerous liaisons are common knowledge.'

'He said that to you?' Richard's voice was even, but his features were so hard and cold they might have been carved from granite.

'It is no more than the truth. But—' Melanie lifted one shoulder.

'It hurt.'

Richard's quiet understanding made her eyes sting. She blinked hard. Life had taught her that tears were self-indulgent and solved nothing. 'He said I boldly called myself an artist—'

'You *are* an artist, a very gifted one.'

Grateful, Melanie smiled. But it was fleeting. Exhausted after a restless night of rage, guilt, and self-blame churning endlessly inside her she shook her head. 'He did not intend a compliment. He said everyone knew such people had no morals.'

At the time shock had blunted the impact. Now, though sharing what had happened with Richard was a relief, as she repeated the words that had been flung at her she felt each one like a slap. 'As though that gave him the right—'

Hurt and anger filled her like a brimming glass. 'I've tried so hard, Richard. I have always behaved properly, taken great care to say and do the right thing. I've worked hard at my lessons and my art, hoping to make my father proud of me, to justify all I have cost him. Yet two men have tried to force their attentions on me.' She hesitated, but only for a moment. He might as well know it all. 'Even my mother's husband would have – that's why I could not go with them, why I came back to England.'

Richard bolted to his feet, the movement so sudden that Melanie gasped. He stood below her on the steps, hands clasped behind his back, body rigid as he spoke over his shoulder.

'I didn't know this.'

'Of course you didn't. I never told anyone.'

He whirled round. 'Why not, for God's sake?'

'Who could I tell? Who would have believed me? According to Mr Geach I am nothing, and deserve neither protection nor respect.'

His expression was appalled. 'No!' He sat beside her again, closer this time. 'We both know that is not true.' His upper arm brushed her shoulder. 'What happened was the responsibility of the men concerned, Melanie. Not you. Never you.'

Relief left her weak and shaky. Her chest heaved. She swallowed a sob and took a deep breath. 'I left Mr Geach in no doubt of my disgust at his behaviour.'

'I would expect nothing less,' he said softly.

'But by the time I reached the boatyard I really did have a headache. When I saw you I couldn't– I didn't want you to know.'

'You were afraid I'd say I told you so?'

'I would have deserved it. You warned me. But I thought the fact that I was my father's acknow-ledged daughter and living at Gillyvean afforded me protection. I didn't realise his unconventional lifestyle would reflect badly on me. After we got back here I couldn't let Ellen or Mrs Berryman see me with red eyes because they'd have wanted to know why.' She gulped and cleared her throat.

'So you have kept it bottled up inside you.'

'I shared a little – just a little – with Bronnen.' Resting her head on his shoulder, Melanie closed her eyes. *He believed her.* 'I'm so sorry.'

'For what? You have nothing to apologise for. But Simon Geach,' his tone became harsh, 'should be reported to the magistrate.'

Melanie jerked up. 'No! You mustn't. Please, Richard. It'd become public knowledge. Think of the gossip. And nothing would be lost in the telling. Besides, it isn't only me who would suffer.'

'What, you're concerned for his wife?'

Melanie hesitated. 'Yes, I am. She is a quiet person. When we met at Mrs Martin's she seemed very pleasant. She is not responsible for his actions, yet her name would be tainted simply because he's her husband. But my concern – the truth is I was thinking of you.'

He turned to look at her, his face devoid of expression. 'Oh?'

She couldn't hold his gaze. 'As my father's agent and heir you have many business connections in Falmouth. Because of my father's domestic arrangements my arrival at Gillyvean will have been talked about. But that has nothing to do with you, and the last thing I want is to cause you difficulty or discomfort.'

She risked a brief glance; saw his mouth twist. 'The thought is appreciated. However, it comes rather too late.' He rose to his feet. 'You're sure

289

about the magistrate?'

'Yes.' She looked up. 'Richard? What did you mean?'

'Forgive me, but I must go. I have an appointment for which I am already late. I won't be in for dinner. Tomorrow I am in Truro and will be away overnight. I wish–' He stopped abruptly. 'I will return as soon as I can.'

Melanie watched him take the steps two at a time. Pausing on the terrace he glanced back at her. 'It wasn't your fault.' He disappeared through the French windows.

Though she was terribly tired, telling Richard, and reassured that he believed her, had lifted the weight of guilt and shame from her shoulders. She felt lighter, calmer, and deeply relieved.

'Mr Vaughan's coming down the slip,' Jack said.

Santo raised a hand as Richard approached along the quay, telling Jack, 'This 'ere boat belong to him. Bought with the yard it was. Only fair he sees the engine tested.'

Richard climbed aboard. Santo took one look at the tightness around his eyes and mouth and decided it was none of his business. Once greetings had been exchanged he kindled a fire on a broad metal plate with a handle. Feeding the flames with chopped dry oak he slid the plate into the firebox.

'This 'ere boat got lovely lines. Should cut through the water like a 'ot knife through butter,' Jack said. 'But that engine don't look big enough–'

'Don't you worry about power.' Santo straightened up. 'The difference in temperature between the hot end over the fire and the water-cooled cold end will generate plenty.'

'What do 'e mean, water-cooled? How?' Jack asked.

'A water jacket using sea water drawn in through a duct down by the propeller.'

After peering at the engine Richard glanced at Santo. 'How does the power get from the engine to the propeller?'

Santo pointed to the two flywheels. 'They drive on to a friction disc. Then a toothed gear on the friction disc drives another toothed gear on the prop shaft to turn it. Ready to go?'

Jack clambered ashore to cast off both mooring ropes. As soon as he had jumped back on Santo engaged the drive, pushed the lever back and the boat reversed at speed.

'Bleddy hell!' Jack muttered, grabbing the gunwale. 'How do you slow 'n down?'

Santo grinned. 'Easy. You got two ways to slow it down. One is by reducing the heat of the fire. That's all right for a pump. But I wouldn't do it with a marine engine because the heat takes time to build up again, and if you wanted speed in a hurry it wouldn't be there. The other way is with this 'ere lever.' He eased it forward and the boat slowed. 'It shuts a valve that cuts off the air. If air can't circulate the piston can't work. But soon as you open the valve again you got full power.'

'Well, I'll be damned,' Jack shook his head.

The boat was still reversing, though much more slowly, as Santo eased the tiller hard over to turn the boat towards the river mouth and harbour. Then, bracing himself with feet wide apart on the deck boards, he opened the valve and pushed the drive lever. After stopping in its own length, the boat surged forward. Jack and Richard hung onto the gunwales.

'Dear life, this is a terrifying machine,' Jack gasped.

Asking Richard to take the tiller, showing him how to move it the opposite way to the desired direction, Santo checked every part of the engine then replenished the fire, this time with coal. But as it started making black smoke Jack's gaze sought Santo's and he shook his head.

Santo understood. They could not afford the sight or smell of smoke to draw unwelcome attention. He would need to ensure he had plenty of wood that would burn hot and clean.

Despite testing the engine at a time when working men were heading home, and the fading light made the hull less easy to see, Santo guessed they were under observation. The fact that they were moving without sails or oars made it inevitable. They were a curiosity to the men on watch aboard moored ships, and to the ferrymen carrying passengers between Flushing and Falmouth.

He added more coal.

'What are you doing?' Jack demanded.

'Laying a smokescreen,' Richard said dryly.

Did he know about Jack's smuggling sideline? Santo wasn't about to ask. He was involved only because he was desperate. He needed money, and he needed it now. But as soon as he had enough to settle his debts and finance his future he'd stop.

An hour later the boat returned upriver. The sun had sunk behind wooded hills leaving a blaze of gold that paled to jade then turquoise. The breeze had dropped and the river was calm.

Santo steered in towards the slipway, still travelling at speed. He heard Richard's sharp intake of breath and glimpsed Jack's panicked expression. He shut the valve. The boat glided forward and stopped dead in the water, inches from the stone quay.

'God a'mighty,' Jack muttered.

'That was – interesting,' Richard observed.

'Throw me the lines,' Santo said, jumping ashore. Despite the trip lasting over an hour, because they had gone out on a rising tide the water was only slightly lower than when they had left. Securing the fore and aft mooring ropes, Santo left enough slack to allow the boat to settle on the slip after the tide ebbed. Richard and Jack clambered ashore.

'What d' you think?' Santo was elated. His engine had done everything he had asked of it. The prop had felt a bit sluggish to begin with. But now hardened up it would produce more speed next time.

'Remarkable,' Richard said.

'Bleddy awesome,' Jack grinned.

Chapter Thirty-two

Waking early, Bronnen washed, dressed and, after brushing out her hair, quickly twisted it into a coil and pinned it high on her crown. Her head felt too small for all the thoughts crammed inside it.

What a day yesterday had been. Melanie had insisted on accompanying her to Truro for her meeting with Enyon Coode, Mrs Tregellas's attorney. They had travelled in the pony trap driven by Thomas, Gillyvean's manservant.

Leaving pony and trap in the care of an ostler at the Red Lion Hotel, Thomas had escorted them to the attorney's office.

Bronnen would have been lost without Melanie who had reminded her to bring the letters to prove her identity. The company of someone who understood her very mixed feelings had given her comfort and strength.

After leaving the office they had returned to the Red Lion where they were shown to a small private dining room. While they ate a much-needed meal of summer vegetable soup with buttered sweet rolls followed by strawberry tart, Thomas refreshed himself with cold beef and beer in the public bar. Then they had driven back to Gillyvean.

Falling into bed, exhausted by the events of the day, she didn't want to think about all that had happened. It was still too painful. But trying to imagine her future was frightening. She could not un-know what she now knew. Yet there was still so much she didn't understand.

Mr Coode had explained that it would be a week or so before the money could be transferred, which would allow her time to set up banking arrangements.

Recognising her panic, Melanie had suggested that, if she wished, Mr Vaughan might deal with all such matters on her behalf. Mr Coode had considered that an excellent notion.

Lying in the unfamiliar bed gazing into the darkness, Bronnen wondered if she had thanked Melanie enough.

Her thoughts turned to Santo. He had changed her life in so many ways. Without his kindness, common sense, and gift for making her laugh, she wasn't sure how she would have coped.

Her only experience of a man-and-woman relationship was that of the people she had believed were her parents. She knew from listening to the women working in the soup kitchen not all marriages were like that. But fear had made her deeply wary.

Meeting Santo had opened her eyes and her heart. And the sensations stirred by his kisses, his touch, and the hard-muscled strength of his body against hers had startled and enthralled her.

His pump engine had spared her hours of back-breaking work at the brewhouse. Now she could thank him by putting some of her money into helping him build more. Surely that would prove her faith in him? Show how much he meant to her?

She wanted to tell him at once, tomorrow. But perhaps it'd be better to wait until the money was available. Mr Coode had assured her it wouldn't be more than a week or so. That wasn't long.

Turning over she closed her eyes, pictured Santo's face, remembered how it felt to have his arms around her, and slid into deep sleep.

Waking with a start, seeing daylight through the curtains and, fearing she was late, she bounded out of bed.

Ten minutes later, washed, dressed in her faded blue calico, her hair brushed, coiled, and pinned up, she hurried down the back stairs.

Her first task would be to light the fire beneath the pump engine. Then while the cistern was filling she would set the copper fire. Sam might already have done that.

She opened the door into the kitchen and was met by the mouth-watering smells of frying ham and fresh coffee.

'All right, my bird?' Mrs Berryman glanced up from the pan and greeted her with a smile. 'It won't be but a minute.'

'I'm late–' Bronnen began.

'Who says? Miss Melanie would be mad as fire if I let you out of here without a bite to eat. You had some busy time yesterday and today won't be no different. Right, 'tis all ready.' She tipped scrambled eggs out of the pan onto a plate and set it on the table. 'Mind the plate now, he's hot.'

Bronnen pulled out a chair and sat down, her stomach growling with hunger. As she buttered a thick slice of fresh wheat bread she wondered how things were at the farm. Was her m – Sarah well enough to do the dairy work? Who would do it in her place? Perhaps her father would have asked one of the labourer's wives to come in.

It wasn't her worry. If Morley Jewell had enough money to go drinking every night, he had enough to pay for help. But as each day passed she was finding it increasingly hard to stop her thoughts returning to the woman who had raised her. *And lied to her all her life.*

She finished eating, drank a cup of milky

coffee, then pushed back her chair.

'That's more like it,' Mrs Berryman said as she sliced lamb's kidneys, dredged them with seasoned flour and laid them in the frying pan where they sizzled softly. 'I'll send Ellen across with something at midday. Off you go then.'

Three hours later Bronnen was alone in the brewhouse, seated on the wooden bench grinding malt. The door stood open to release heat from the copper fire. There was no brew today so all the vessels would be scrubbed out ready for the next one.

Tommy was in the cellar topping up the barrels from the fermentation vessel and Alf was in the wood store chopping oak logs into smaller chunks for the pump engine firebox.

Hearing footsteps on the cobbles outside Bronnen glanced up hoping it might be Santo, even though common sense told her that was un-likely now his marine engine had arrived. Might it be Mr Vaughan?

But it was Treeve Curnock who appeared in the doorway. He removed his hat. 'Good morning to you, Miss Jewell.'

Surprised, she set the mill aside and stood up, smoothing her apron. 'Good morning, Mr Curnock.'

He stepped inside smiling broadly, his gaze darting around before returning to her. 'As I was coming this way I thought I take the opportunity to ensure you are satisfied with the malt?'

'Yes.' His claim didn't make sense. His house, his maltings, and the town centre lay in the oppo-site direction.

'I'm delighted to hear it.'

Bronnen waited.

'In truth, Miss Jewell, I had another reason for stopping by. And finding you alone leads me to believe good fortune is smiling on me. I should like to call on you if I may.'

Bronnen didn't try to hide her surprise. 'What for?'

'Come now, Miss Jewell, Bronnen.' His roguish smile was edged with impatience. 'I should have thought that was obvious. I admire you and it is my earnest desire we should become more intimately acquainted.'

It was clear he expected her to feel flattered. Instead she was suspicious and uneasy. Always an arrogant man, as his reputation as a maltster had grown so too had his high opinion of himself.

If he knew the truth about her birth he wouldn't be here. That meant it was still a secret: but for how long? And why her?

'Come now, Miss Jewell. My request cannot have come as a complete surprise.'

'It has.'

'You are too modest. But I find that both refreshing and endear–'

'Look, Mr Curnock,' she cut in. 'We have only ever spoken about malt. My interest was in the quality and terms of sale, nothing else.' Her heartbeat had quickened. But not from pleasure or anticipation as it did when she was with Santo. It thumped in discomfort and anger.

The good manners Sarah had drummed into her meant she had to thank him for attentions she had never sought and did not want. But she

298

would not shame herself by being rude.

'Thank you for the compliment, but I can't accept your offer of a closer friendship.'

'You're turning me down?' Disbelief slackened his features. 'You can't do that.'

'I beg your pardon?'

'I said you can't. I have spoken to your father, and he assured me—'

Fury, bright as lightning, streaked through Bronnen. *Morley Jewell had promised her to this man? Without even telling her?* 'I didn't know about this, Mr Curnock. And my answer's still the same.'

As a dark flush suffused his face she looked down at her clasped hands. 'That is all you have to say?' he demanded.

Surely she had spoken plainly enough? Why was he persisting? Bronnen's shoulders rose in a helpless shrug. 'I'm sorry.'

'You're *sorry?*' His eyes glittered and the skin around his nostrils was white. He thrust his head forward, his expression venomous. 'You should be grateful for my interest, considering the kind of man your father is.'

Bronnen opened her mouth to tell him Morley Jewell wasn't her father. Then shut it again. That was none of his business. Nor was Morley Jewell's drinking. Her spine was ramrod straight as she faced him. 'Good day, Mr Curnock.'

'Or maybe you know full well that whenever he has money in his pocket he's down at Fat Mary's in Quay Street, rutting with young girls scarce out of childhood.'

Recoiling as if he had slapped her, Bronnen began to tremble. 'You're lying.'

299

'You wish I was,' he sneered. 'So, Miss High-and-Mighty—'

Bronnen's stomach heaved, the bitter taste of bile burning her throat. She swallowed it down. She could not be sick, not in front of him. 'Go away, Mr Curnock. There's nothing for you here.'

'You've got spirit; I'll say that for you. Look, perhaps I was a bit hasty. A man in my position is rarely challenged. I'm willing to let bygones be bygones and overlook your disadvantages. Now you cannot say fairer—'

As he reached for her she slapped his hand violently away. 'Don't you dare touch me. If you don't leave right this minute I'll start screaming.'

His smile faded to anger. 'You wouldn't—'

'Dare? Oh yes I would.' She took a deep breath.

'All right.' He backed away. 'I'm going. But you'll be sorry.'

Replacing his hat he stepped outside the brewhouse. Bronnen slammed the door shut and leaned against it, one shaking hand covering her mouth, the other pressed to her roiling stomach.

It wasn't true. Yet even as she clung to denial, long-buried memories clouded her mind like mud, filling her with horror and fear. *Rutting with young girls scarce out of childhood—*

As his words replayed in her head, terrible realisation hit her like a fist and she swayed. *Her mother knew: had always known.* Was that why she worked with Mrs Fox? Was it a desperate attempt to try and make up for her husband's depraved appetites?

The door bumped against her back as someone kicked it. Bronnen's heart leapt into her throat.

300

'Miss? What's on? I got me arms full of kindling.'

With a gasp of relief Bronnen turned and pulled the door wide. 'Sorry, Alf.'

'I just seen Treeve Curnock stanking out of the yard. Had a face like thunder, he did. What did he want then? He got no business 'ere.'

'That's what I told him,' Bronnen said as Alf stomped past her and tipped his armful of chopped sticks into the basket at one side of the copper. Dusting his hands Alf hitched up his trousers as he regarded her.

'I know it's not for me to say, but you deserve better'n he, miss.'

Still shaky, Bronnen grinned even as her eyes stung. 'I think so too.'

'Here, I've put two baskets of small stuff over by the pump. Under the shelter, they are.'

'Thanks, Alf.'

'Just doing me job. Water in the copper should be hot by now. Soon as I've raked out the fire and let the dust settle I'll get on scrubbing out ready for the next brew.'

They both turned at the sound of iron-shod hoofs on the drive. Bronnen was startled to see Adam enter the yard astride one of the farm horses still wearing its harness.

Her throat dried. She hurried towards him, Alf following. 'What are you doing here?'

Adam flung himself off the big horse and gripped the bridle. 'Bron, you got to come back with me.'

'I can't. I'm–'

'Mother's awful bad. I don't know what to do. Any case, 'tis you she wants.'

301

'You must know why I left–'

'I don't care. You're my sister. Always was, always will be. The rest is just names. Look, you wouldn't be here in charge of all this if 't wasn't for what Mother taught you.' Tears spilled down his suntanned face and his mouth trembled. 'If you don't come she'll die because she don't want to live no more. Please, Bron.'

'Give me a minute.' She turned, startled to see Alf who had clearly heard every word.

'That's all right, my 'ansum,' he waved her away. 'You get on 'ome. I'll leave Tommy know.'

'Will one of you go across to the house and tell Mrs Berryman? She'll wonder where I've gone. And Sam–'

'I'll stay till he get here. We'll be all right.'

Chapter Thirty-three

As Prince clattered to a stop in the farmyard and tossed his head, Bronnen jumped down.

'I can't stop, Bron,' Adam said. 'Father'll be wondering where I'm to.'

'Has he sent for the doctor?'

Miserably Adam shook his head. 'I wanted to but he wouldn't. He says she's only fretting over you going.'

'But she was poorly long before that.'

He shrugged, wretched and helpless. 'I tried, but there's no talking to 'n. You know what he's like.'

Did she know him at all? As Treeve Curnock's

venomous accusations echoed in her head, Bronnen shut off thoughts she wasn't yet ready to face.

'Who been doing the dairy work?'

'Walter's wife, Dinah. She've made dinner these past two days as well. But Father wouldn't let her go up over stairs. He said if Ma was well enough to feel hungry she was well enough to come down and get on. I took up cups of tea but she never touched 'em.'

Bronnen pushed her anger at Morley Jewell's spiteful neglect to the back of her mind. She had no time to dwell on that now. 'All right, Adam, you go on back to work.'

As Adam urged the big horse into a trot, Bronnen walked into the kitchen, smelled the savoury aroma of meat stew, and saw a short plump woman busy checking pans on the range. Wiry curls of greying mousy hair escaped from her cap. The long sleeves of her round-necked dress of green and white gingham were pushed up revealing work-roughened hands and forearms. She slammed the lid back on a large pan and turned to Bronnen, hands on her hips.

'Well, 'bout time. I dunno what I'm here doing your job for.'

Startled by this attack, Bronnen opened her mouth to apologise and changed her mind. 'Is Mr Jewell paying you?' She crossed to the range and picked up the big kettle. The heat and weight told her it was full and recently boiled.

The women stepped back, wiping her hands on her coarse apron. 'So what if he is? I can't come up here–'

'Have you done the butter and cream?'

'What? Yes.'

'Then I'll look after Mother while you get on with the dinner.' Picking up the full ewer by the sink Bronnen walked quickly to the door leading to the back stairs. 'Much obliged,' she said over her shoulder. Without waiting for a response she climbed the steep staircase.

Setting down the ewer she opened the bedroom door and recoiled at the stench. *How could he have left her like this?* She had worked just as hard as him all the years they had been married. She had raised two children while running the house and dairy and cooking dinner for six or seven every day. At harvest time there might be twenty more labourers needing a midday meal then tea at five in the afternoon.

Bronnen remembered helping make scores of loaves, tray after tray of scones, huge slabs of hevva cake stuffed with raisins and candied orange peel, and saffron buns. She and the woman she knew as her mother had worked as a team, familiar with each other's methods, comfortable in each other's company. Yet all that time Sarah Jewell had been living a lie. *How had she borne the strain?*

Still too hurt to want to feel sympathy, Bronnen put the kettle and ewer on the floor by the wash-stand. Crossing to the window she drew back the curtains and opened the window wide.

Drawing fresh air deep into her lungs she turned to the bed. The woman lying there looked *old*. Fever flushed her sunken cheeks and glittered in her half-open eyes. Her lips were cracked and brown scum had dried at the corners of her mouth.

'Bron?' She croaked, her head turning restlessly on the pillow.

Looking at her, Bronnen was overwhelmed by a crushing wave of hurt and anger. Then it ebbed and all she could feel was pity. 'Oh, Ma,' she whispered. 'Look at you.'

'I'm sorry, Bron,' Sarah muttered thickly. 'So sorry.'

Swallowing the lump in her throat, Bronnen quickly mixed hot and cold water in the china basin and set it on the floor beside the bed. Then she fetched soap and flannel from the washstand and a clean towel, nightgown, sheets and pillow-cases from the linen chest.

A soft knock on the door jerked her upright. She opened it, surprised to see Dinah who thrust a glass of elderflower cordial at her. 'Adam said he brung her some tea but she wouldn't touch it. This might go down better.'

'That's kind of you.'

Dinah wrung her hands. 'I shouldn't've said what I did. But with you not here and Adam all a-fret about his ma, then mister telling me I wasn't to come up, it upset me awful. How is she?'

Bronnen shook her head. 'Poorly.'

'No wonder, dear of her.' Looking away, she turned to go. 'I'll leave you get on.'

'Dinah,' Bronnen kept her voice soft, choosing her words carefully. 'What are people saying about him?'

'Nothing I'm willing to repeat.' She was clearly uncomfortable. 'Your ma is a good soul. That's how I don't understand how she could–' she broke off. 'Truth is I'd just as soon not be here.

305

But Walter said mister would pay and we need the money.' She hurried away down the passage.

Bronnen closed the door, her shaking hand slopping the liquid over the side of the glass and wetting her fingers. Treeve Curnock's accusations, her nightmares, her panic attack after she tasted brandy on Santo's mouth, all swirled like oily smoke inside her. She needed to know the truth, and dreaded hearing it.

Lifting Sarah's head from the pillow, Bronnen gently tilted the glass against her lips. Sarah tried to turn her head away and the liquid dribbled down her chin.

'Come on now, Ma. You need to drink.'

Sarah's eyes opened. 'Bron?'

'I'm here. I got some elderflower cordial. Make you feel better, it will.'

'I'm so sorry, Bron.'

'We'll talk later. First you need to drink.' She lifted the glass little by little as Sarah sipped and swallowed until it was empty.

It took Bronnen nearly an hour to bathe her, help her into the clean nightgown, put a shawl around her shoulders and sit her in the chair. Quickly she stripped and re-made the bed with fresh sheets, emptied the basin and stinking chamber pot into the slop bucket then replaced the lid and put it outside the door.

While she worked she heard the men come in for dinner, then leave again a while later. Though it was hours since she had eaten, tension had banished her appetite.

Back in bed once more, propped up on pillows, Sarah caught Bronnen's hand. 'I need to tell you–'

'In a minute.' Bronnen picked up the bundle of washing. 'I'll take these down and bring you another drink.' She knew she was putting off the moment when she would learn the reason for so much that she had never understood. *But she was so afraid of what she might hear.*

Returning back upstairs, Bronnen propped Sarah up on pillows, helped her swallow a few more mouthfuls, then sat on the bed still clutching the glass.

'A week after you was born, Mary and Henwood came to take Dulcie home.' Sarah's voice was little more than a whisper. 'They said they'd give us money to help raise you and more for a dowry when you married. But we had to sign a paper promising we would never tell a living soul whose child you was, nor ever contact them again.'

Her feverish gaze met Bronnen's. 'I'd have signed a hundred papers. I'd have done anything they asked. I helped birth you.' Memory softened the lines of strain and anxiety scoring her face. 'All warm and pink you was, and had some fine pair of lungs. Like a little lamb bleating. Holding you I thought my heart would burst. I loved Adam when he was born. He was a dear child and he've grown into a fine young man. But what I felt for he wasn't nothing like what I felt for you. I know that sound awful but 'tis the truth.' She turned her hand palm up on the quilt in silent plea.

Taking it, Bronnen saw tears fill the sunken eyes. Her own eyes stung and burned.

'Didn't matter I had their paper to say you was mine. From the day Mary and Henwood took Dulcie back home I been afraid.'

'Afraid? What of?'

'That they'd change their minds and want you back. But as years went by I put the fear aside for an hour, a day, a week. You was my daughter. Mine.' Her voice cracked.

Bronnen held the half-empty glass to her mother's lips.

After a few sips, Sarah sagged back on the pillows and drew a deep breath. 'Your f– Morley didn't like it that I loved you.'

'He was jealous? Of a child?'

Sarah fretted with the sheet. 'You wasn't his child.'

'But he must have agreed to the arrangement with the Passmores.' As Sarah's gaze slid away, Bronnen realised. 'He did it for the money. Ma – I've heard – I need to know–'

'And I'll tell you. 'Tis time the truth come out.'

Now the moment had finally come Bronnen was terrified. She raised the glass to her own lips. It clattered against her teeth. But the diluted cordial soothed her parched mouth and released the constriction in her throat.

'Morley been cheating Mr Tregarron,' Sarah said. 'Been going on for years it have.'

Bronnen was startled. 'Cheating him how?'

'He marks down the yields for each crop as smaller than they really are then sells the difference and keeps the money. Mr Tregarron always trusted 'n so Mr Vaughan do too. Morley puts the money into free trade goods and sells they on at a profit.'

'I wondered how he could afford to go drinking every night.'

308

Closing her eyes, Sarah shook her head. 'The drinking isn't the worst of it.' Her mouth quivered.

Bronnen braced herself. 'Ma, did he ever–? I've had these terrible dreams, only it's like I'm remembering–'

Sarah's eyes flew open and she jerked up from the pillow, one hand clutching Bronnen's, the other reaching up to cup her face. 'I swear on my life, Bron, he never harmed you, not that way. He only went near you the once. Soon as I heard you scream I come running. When you was settled I went down and had it out with'n. I told 'n if he ever again laid so much as a finger on you I'd go straight to Mr Tregarron. I told'n I'd left letters in case anything should happen to me.'

Shock stopped Bronnen's breath. 'You thought he might–? No, Ma, he would never – would he?'

Sarah gave a weary shrug. 'I couldn't take the chance. He've always had a temper and he can't bear anyone to best him. So then he said if I breathed a word about his dealings he'd tell you about Dulcie.' She crumpled, her face contorting. 'I couldn't let 'n do that.'

Suddenly Bronnen saw her mother's passive acceptance of beatings and brutality for what they really were: not weakness, but love and heroic strength. 'That's why you put up with his drinking and his violence? Because of me?'

'No,' Sarah shook her head, her hand tightening on Bronnen's. 'Don't you go blaming you-self. I done it for *me*. 'T was always in my mind that you'd be mad with me for not telling you. But they didn't want you, Bron, and I did. I love Adam. But

I couldn't've borne to lose you.' She wiped her eyes again. 'When the letter come about Dulcie's death, it upset me awful. She wasn't no age, dear of her. But truth is the relief– I near enough swooned. If she was gone, she wouldn't come looking for you and after all they years I could stop being afraid. But then I thought what if Mary and Henwood wanted their granddaughter?'

'After nineteen years?' Bronnen shook her head. 'Mary is your cousin. She could have paid a visit anytime. But they've never been near. I'm nothing to them.'

'You're the world to me, Bron.'

'Oh, Ma.' Bronnen gently squeezed her mother's hand. 'And you've worked yourself to exhaustion helping Mrs Fox because he goes to Fat Mary's.'

Shock blanched Sarah's face. 'How d'you know that?'

'Treeve Curnock came to the brewhouse. He wanted to come courting me. He said he'd already spoken to – Father. When I turned him down he got mad and said I should be grateful for his interest, considering the kind of man my father is. Then he told me about Fat Mary's. Threw it at me. Like that would change my mind?'

'Oh, Bron.' Crimson patched Sarah's cheeks as she closed her eyes. 'I'm that ashamed.'

'You've no need to be. It's not your fault.'

'I feel so bad,' Sarah whispered. 'Why do he go doing such terrible things? They poor little girls.'

'He's the one who should be ashamed. I wish–' *I wish hadn't blamed you. I wish I'd understood. I wish I didn't have to tell Santo.* But she knew she must. If she didn't tell him someone else was certain to.

Would he still want to know her? What if he didn't? *How would she live without him?* She stood up.

'You're not going?'

'Only downstairs, to get you something to eat.'

'I can't face it, Bron.'

'Yes, you can. You must if you're going to get out of that bed. The worst is over. Everything's changed. Now I know about—' she couldn't say *my mother.* It would be cruel. Dulcie Passmore had given her up and walked away. The woman lying in the bed had become ill with grief and worry at the thought of losing her. 'Now I know about Dulcie he's got no hold over you. You don't have to be afraid any more.' Watching realisation and relief dawn in Sarah's eyes, Bronnen picked up the glass. 'I'll be back in a minute.'

She moved from pantry to table to range, her movements automatic, as so much she hadn't understood finally began to make sense.

Chapter Thirty-four

Hearing footsteps, Santo glanced up and saw his cousin approaching, and returned his gaze to the small pump engine he was working on. He knew Treeve would not have come without a reason. A moment later a leather purse of coins hit the workbench with a thud.

Santo straightened, eyeing his cousin without speaking.

'I heard you quit your job at Perran Foundry.'

Treeve's eyes glittered. 'With no income you'll be short of money. I daresay you have debts as well. No doubt father had good reason for leaving you out of his will. But we are family, and if you can't pay your way it reflects badly on me.'

'Keep your money. I don't want it.'

'Still the same old Santo – pound ideas and penny pockets.' Treeve scooped up the purse, tossing it in his hand so the coins jingled. 'Please yourself. But you can't say I didn't offer.' He turned to go, then paused. 'You've been away from Cornwall a long time so you won't have heard the rumours. About a certain member of the Jewell family?'

Expecting Treeve to try and needle him Santo had vowed not to react. But hearing the name on his cousin's lips sparked anger like flint on steel. His hand trembled and the spanner slipped. He refitted it over the nut and pulled it tight.

'If you already know, I shan't waste my time. I only came because I thought you ought to be made aware–'

'What rumours?' Resting the spanner on the bench Santo mentally braced himself, knowing this was the real reason for Treeve's visit.

'About Morley Jewell's perverted behaviour.'

Santo had guessed that Bronnen's violent and terrified reaction to their lovemaking led back to a bad experience in her past, something she could not *or dare not* remember. Wanting to tell Treeve to shut up and get out, he resisted, needing to learn whatever he could about the man Bronnen had believed to be her father. Picking another nut and bolt off the bench he fitted the bolt then spun the nut onto it. Sweat prickled his forehead and dampened his palms with the effort of keeping his hands steady.

'I know you won't like it that I'm the one telling you about Morley Jewell's disgusting behaviour, especially as you had an interest in his daughter. I did myself until–' he gave a delicate shudder. 'Thank God I found out in time, that's all I can say. Better you hear the sordid truth from me in private, rather than from town gossip.' He waited, milking the moment.

Santo fought the urge to grab the beautifully tailored lapels and shake his cousin till his teeth rattled. Instead he set down the spanner, picked up a rag and wiped his fingers. His muscles had tightened like mooring ropes and dread churned in his belly. 'Hear what?'

'That Morley Jewell acquired his taste for very young flesh from lying with his daughter.' He paused, giving the words time to sink in. 'You'd never guess to look at her, acting so shy and modest. She certainly made a fool out of you.'

Looking up, Santo caught the smirk, the desire to hurt in his cousin's malicious gaze. He didn't care what grudge – real or imagined – Treeve held against him, but hearing Bronnen's name smeared ignited white-hot fury.

Despite Treeve fancying himself a boxer, just three blows from Santo's fists sent him sprawling on the workshop floor. Snatching up the purse, Santo rammed it into his cousin's bloody mouth.

'I'd sooner starve than take a penny from you.'

A figure appeared in the doorway. 'What's on here, then?' Jack Mitchell's bushy brows rose.

313

Breathing hard, sucking his knuckles, Santo turned on him. 'Is it true about Morley Jewell?'

'What about him?'

'Don't mess with me, Jack,' Santo growled.

The foundryman raised both hands in submission. 'He've been working a pretty little swindle selling Gillyvean grain, hay, and straw out the back gate.'

'And?' Tension roughened Santo's voice. 'What else?' Treeve groaned. Santo ignored him.

Jack glanced from Santo to Treeve and back. 'Well, I never been in Fat Mary's meself. What she sells don't interest me. So I only know what I've heard, and that idn' much. They that go there don't talk about it.'

'Young girls?'

Jack nodded. 'And boys. She charge plenty too. High turnover, see?'

Treeve groaned again, struggling painfully to his feet. Jack caught him under the arm and jerked him up.

'I'd get on home if I was you, Mr Curnock.' He grabbed one of the cleaner rags from a pile on the end of the bench, dipped it in a wooden bucket of murky water and handed it to Treeve. 'Here, you look like you been at the jam.'

Treeve snatched the rag, wincing as he wiped blood from his mouth and chin. 'I won't forget this,' he muttered thickly.

'Best if you did, Mr Curnock, 'less you want it all over town that your cousin whipped your arse good and proper. Ask Mrs Eathorne for some witch hazel. Bring the swelling down lovely that will. Your coat could do with a brush as well.'

With a final glowering glance at Santo who turned his back, Treeve limped out.

'Dear life, boy, what was that–'

'None of your business.'

Jack eyed him steadily.

'He said – no, he wanted me to think–' The ugly words dried on Santo's tongue and he shook his head.

'If I was to make a wild guess – which isn't that wild seeing you asked about Morley Jewell – I'd say your cousin said something bad about young Bronnen. Now you shouldn't need telling but I'll say it anyhow. That girl is good as gold. I aren't saying it didn't cause a ruckus when Mr Arthur took his work to Gillyvean, 'stead of asking Williams's or one of the other breweries to fill his orders. But he's so tight he'd never have done it 'less he was sure she could do the job. He wasn't doing her no favour, if you get my meaning. Anyhow, 'tis only for a few weeks, till the brewery repairs is finished. I daresay there's plenty you don't know. But not about Bronnen. You'll never hear a bad word about her, all right? Good job I stopped by.'

Santo nodded in gratitude and relief, while rage still coursed through his body. He coughed to clear the stiffness from his throat. 'Why did you?'

'I took some ironwork along to Henry Laity at Turnpike. So I thought I'd look in. Ready to go?'

'All ready.'

'That's what I like to hear.' Jack rubbed his callused palms together. 'Two or three trips, boy, and you'll have money to burn.'

'What about crew–'

'That's not your worry. Right, I'll leave you get on.' With a backward wave he hurried away.

As Santo returned to the pump engine on the bench he gave an inward shrug. He was responsible for the boat and engine. The rest was up to Jack.

His thoughts turned to Bronnen. She had lost weight. He had put it down to all the extra work at the brewhouse. But now he realised that the change had started when the powerful attraction between them had kindled passion.

While they kissed he had stroked, caressed, wanting to find out what pleased her, always gentle, instantly ready to stop. Learning her body through his hands; its curves and hollows, soft flesh and firm muscle, had awed and humbled him.

He wasn't without experience. In London he had found relief with women who sought neither restraint nor emotion. But what he felt for Bronnen was unexplored territory.

Need had warred with self-control, denial scraping his nerves like a metal rasp. But it had been worth the cost, for though she quivered and trembled, she had kissed him back, her lips softening then parting beneath his.

Recognising innocence and honesty in her response, he found both deeply moving and was fiercely glad, proud, that he should be the man to awaken her.

He remembered her mentioning broken nights, her sleep disturbed by bad dreams she could not recall but which left a lingering sense of fear and unease. She had put them down to worry about her mother and long busy days.

Now horrific images filled his head, conjured by his cousin's words. The thought of Bronnen, a defenceless child, at the mercy of Jewell's perverted lust filled Santo with rage and disgust. While he longed to dismiss the accusation as pure spite, he knew Treeve would not have dared make it without some kind of proof.

He recalled what she had told him about Jewell wanting to have *secrets* with her. Had Jewell tried to force himself on her only to be interrupted? Were blocked or buried memories the cause of her nightmares? She had believed the man to be her father. How could he have so wickedly betrayed her trust? It was unforgivable.

Chapter Thirty-five

Richard walked down the stone-flagged passage between two buildings in Market Street, through the open door on which a polished brass plaque announced that these were the offices of Geach & Truscott. Removing his hat and gloves he walked briskly up the wooden staircase.

At the top he paused, looking both ways down the wide landing. Directly ahead of him a door stood open to reveal a wooden counter behind which a soberly dressed middle-aged man was writing in a ledger. Of average height and stocky build, he had an indoor pallor and wiry grey hair receding at the temples. Hearing Richard approach he looked up, peering over his spectacles, and inclined his head politely. 'Good afternoon, Mr Vaughan.'

Richard's brows rose. This was his first visit to these premises. He had no intention of ever returning.

'My cousin is a notary, sir,' the clerk explained. 'His office is in the same building as the attorneys who have the privilege of handling Mr Tregarron's legal affairs. I had occasion to be there one day at the same time as yourself. How may I be of assistance?'

'I wish to see Mr Geach.'

'Ah.' The clerk straightened his ledger. 'It is Mr Geach's custom only to see clients and visitors by appointment.'

Richard nodded. 'And is he engaged with a client at this moment?'

The clerk hesitated. 'No, but–'

'Mr–?'

'Herring, sir.'

'Mr Herring, my business will not take long. So you would oblige me greatly by telling Mr Geach that I am here.'

'Of course, sir. If you would wait just a moment.' Coming out from behind the counter he passed Richard who followed and saw him knock on the first door beyond the stairs, then open it without waiting for a reply.

Richard approached the door, making the clerk jump as he came out.

'Mr Geach–'

'Will see me now,' Richard smiled. 'Thank you, Mr Herring.' Entering the office, he closed the

318

door firmly. His swift sweeping glance took in the massive oak desk – its leather inlay framed by neat piles of documents – a button-backed armchair of oxblood leather, rosewood side table, glass-fronted walnut bookcases and two upholstered chairs for clients. A large landscape in a gilt frame hung above the fireplace. On the wall opposite the desk where he would see it each time he looked up, was a framed certificate penned in elegant calligraphy with a large red wax seal at the bottom. Simon Geach had a taste for luxury and a high opinion of himself.

As the solicitor came from behind his desk, hand extended, Richard noted that though they were matched in height Geach was far heavier and relied on expert tailoring to minimise his bulk.

A self-satisfied smile narrowed the solicitor's eyes to gleaming slits in his fleshy face. 'Mr Vaughan, this is an unexpected pleasure. I have long hoped for the opportunity of discussing–'

Richard punched him. The jarring impact of his knuckles connecting with the solicitor's mouth and chin travelled up to his shoulder. He resisted the urge to tuck his aching hand under his arm.

With an agonised yelp, Geach stumbled back against the desk. His eyes were wide and startled, his face pale with shock. Mashed against his teeth, his lips had split and were already swelling as he dribbled blood. He fumbled in his trouser pocket for a handkerchief and pressed it to his mouth, looking in horror at the crimson stain.

'What–? Why?'

'Take a guess.' Gripping one lapel of Geach's expensive coat Richard slapped the fleshy face with his open hand. It was a calculated insult, but did not even begin to redress the hurt this pompous wretch had caused Melanie. He thrust the man away in weary disgust.

Geach staggered and fell backward, barely missing the corner of the desk. Sprawled on the floor, he looked up, his face betraying raw fear. 'You're mad!'

'No,' Richard corrected calmly. 'I'm angry.'

'I shall sue. You have no right—'

'Rights? You dare speak of *rights?*' Richard hissed. Geach flinched backward as if from a naked blade. But there was no escape and nowhere to hide.

Hauled to his feet once more, Geach threw up his hands in defence. One still clutched the blood soaked cotton. 'Don't hit me again! Please!' One side of his face bore the imprint of Richard's fingers, his lips were swollen, his chin covered in blood, his hair dishevelled.

After a long moment, Richard shoved him into a chair. 'You're not worth the effort.' He glanced at his hand, flexed it then sucked bruised knuckles already purple and swelling.

After a tentative knock the door opened and the clerk poked his head in. 'Forgive me, but I thought I heard—'

'Thank you, Mr Herring,' Richard said calmly. 'Mr Geach had a slight accident. Nothing that need concern you.' It was a warning that allowed the man a choice.

The clerk glanced at his employer then back to Richard. As their eyes met, Richard glimpsed realisation then understanding. 'I beg your pardon, sir. I had no wish to intrude.'

The clerk's choice of words revealed the true state of affairs in that office. There was little liking or respect between solicitor and clerk. Herring possessed an intelligence which, had Geach the wit to see it, would have resulted in immediate dismissal. 'However, the noise–'

'Obliged you to check,' Richard nodded, adding pointedly, 'And now you have.'

Immediately the clerk withdrew, carefully closing the door behind him.

'How dare you!' Geach blustered.

'You consider yourself the victim of an unprovoked attack?'

'I most certainly do.' Now on his feet, the solicitor adjusted his coat, carefully wiped his mouth, brushed dust from his trousers, and raised his left hand to smooth back his ruffled hair.

Richard's tone was icy. 'Then you have some idea of how Miss Tregarron felt.'

Geach's mouth fell open. He shut it again and swallowed audibly. The brief angry flush drained away leaving his face the colour of clay but for the blood smeared around his mouth. 'Her? But she's–'

Richard raised his hand in a gesture intended to silence. Misreading it, Geach took a hasty step back.

'I advise you to be very careful,' Richard warned.

'I'm not putting up with this. I shall report you to the magistrate for assault.'

'Do so with my blessing. I relish the opportunity to support Miss Tregarron in court while she makes the people of Falmouth aware of your despicable behaviour.' He would never ask such a thing of Melanie. But Geach didn't know that. The man had no idea what he was capable of. He hadn't known himself until he held Melanie while she wept, listened to her blame herself. 'Nor would Miss Tregarron be the sole complainant.'

'What are you talking about?' Intended to ridicule, the words emerged clothed in fear.

'How many of your housemaids and nursery maids have been paid off or dismissed without a reference? How many might welcome the opportunity to describe in a public court of law how you forced your attentions on them in the marital home?' He was bluffing. But it was plain to him that Melanie was not this man's first victim. Geach was a serial philanderer who, having got away with it for so long, believed himself untouchable.

'You can't.' Geach's voice held raw fear. 'I didn't *do* anything. I don't know what she's told you but she's lying. For God's sake, everyone knows she's Tregarron's by-blow–'

Richard's arm shot out, his fist landing squarely on Geach's nose. Now his hand really hurt. But he didn't regret it.

Squealing like a stuck pig, the solicitor covered his face with his hands, stumbling back until he collapsed into a chair in the corner. Tears poured down his face as he groaned and whimpered, dabbing at the fresh blood streaming over his nose and chin.

'You'll pay for this,' he mumbled as blood soaked into his ivory silk waistcoat turning it crimson.

Richard crossed to the door and opened it. 'Mr Herring?' The clerk appeared. 'Mr Geach has suffered a sudden nosebleed. Do you have some cold water and clean rags?'

The clerk's eyes widened. Recovering quickly he nodded. 'I will find some and bring them directly.'

Closing the door, Richard crossed the room and leaned over the solicitor who cringed. 'I warned you. You didn't listen. The circumstances of Miss Tregarron's birth were not of her choosing. She is a young lady of exceptional talent, deserving of respect and admiration.' He gripped Geach's soft chin with steely fingers, heedless of the blood. 'If you ever – *ever* – utter another disparaging word about her, you will regret it.' Straightening up he reached for his own handkerchief and wiped his fingers.

'The publicity,' he continued implacably, 'would be deeply unpleasant for your wife and family.'

'You can't. You mustn't,' Geach gibbered, blood and mucus bubbling from his distorted and rapidly swelling nose. 'You don't realise – I could lose everything.'

'Why should that interest me? What did you care for the good name and reputation of the young women you assaulted?'

'All right. All right. I'll do whatever you say. But you have to promise not to tell–'

'To tell wasn't *my* threat,' Richard reminded. 'It was yours.' He saw shock in Geach's eyes as the solicitor realised the extent of his knowledge. 'I don't have to promise anything. If you have any regard for your family you will hold your tongue and ensure that from this moment your behaviour is exemplary.'

'You're enjoying this,' Geach accused bitterly. 'I imagine it makes a change from being Frederick Tregarron's errand boy.'

Eyeing him with disdain, Richard walked to the door. 'Keep your hands to yourself, Geach. If you don't, I *will* hear, and you will suffer. That's not a threat,' he added as the solicitor opened his blood-caked mouth. 'It's a promise.'

Chapter Thirty-six

As Mrs Dudley and Mrs Behenna disappeared down the drive in a dogcart driven by Mr Dudley's valet, Melanie paused on the steps and raised her face to the sunshine. The breeze was fragrant with honeysuckle and roses. Drawing warm scented air deep into her lungs she went back into the house, reaching the drawing room at the same time as Ellen.

'Just come to collect the tray, miss.'

'I don't suppose—'

Sympathy flickered across the maid's face. 'Not yet, miss. Mr Knuckey got in about twenty minutes ago. He told Mrs Berryman that Mr Vaughan had business in town but wouldn't be long.'

Pleasure and anticipation bloomed in Melanie. He'd been gone only two days but had hurried away leaving so many questions still unanswered. She longed to see him again, to sit with him and hear what he had been doing. She enjoyed his company. She hadn't realised how much until he wasn't there.

'It's too nice to be inside. I'll take my sketchpad into the garden.'

'Don't forget your hat,' Ellen said over her shoulder. 'If Mrs Berryman see you out there without it, 'tis me will get what-for.'

'We can't have that. I'll fetch it now.' Up in her room, Melanie paused in front of the long glass. Mrs Behenna had complimented her on her gown of creamy yellow muslin with a tiered skirt trimmed with emerald green ribbon, full sleeves ending in close-fitting wristbands, and a shawl collar edged with a frill.

'Suits you a treat, it does,' she had said. 'Goes lovely with your hair.'

The compliment had delighted Melanie who was still not used to receiving them. 'Thank you, Mrs Behenna. How very kind of you to say so.'

'No such thing. I speak as I find.'

Melanie scrutinised her reflection. Would Richard like it? In her admittedly limited experience, men were arrogant, controlling, and selfish, ordering the world to suit them. Her father was no different. He just cloaked those traits in joviality.

Richard was different. He employed exquisite courtesy to keep people at a distance and protect his privacy. She guessed few could claim to know him well. His friendship with Santo Innis had surprised her at first. She had soon realised that their shared interest in engineering was of more importance than social differences. That told her plenty about Richard's character and values.

She had thought him cold and aloof. Certainly he could appear so when he chose. No doubt such self-possession served him well in matters of business.

But behind that façade was an astute, kind, and sensitive man. He had intuitively known things she had found it hard to voice. He understood her as no one else ever had, or wanted to. The more time she spent in his company the more she realised how little she knew him, and how very much she wanted to.

Twice he had dropped his guard. The first time was when he had kissed her. Reliving that memory stopped her breath and sent a delicious quiver through her belly. The second was when they had sat together on the steps and he had insisted on explaining his horrified reaction to her father's announcement.

She missed his gentle mockery, the ironic lift of his eyebrow when she challenged him, his haughty expression belied by the humour in his gaze. He accepted her exactly as she was. And in his unconditional support she had found the greatest comfort she had ever known.

But though feeling his absence keenly she refused to indulge in moping. She'd learned long ago that the best way to deal with negative feelings was to keep busy. There had certainly been plenty to occupy her.

After early fittings for two more day dresses she had accompanied Bronnen to the attorney in Truro. Even though the likelihood of glimpsing Richard was remote, she had not been able to resist glancing round as Thomas drove the trap along Boscawen Street to the stables behind the Red Lion Hotel.

This morning she had walked into town with Ellen, purchased pastels from the art and craft shop, then called at the picture framer to look at some new mouldings.

Back at Gillyvean she had changed her gown, eaten a light lunch, then got ready for the visit promised by Mrs Behenna and Mrs Dudley. She had responded to their questions about how she was settling in, smiled as they proudly described the reactions of family and friends to their portraits, all the time listening for sounds that would announce his return.

She glanced at the clock. Almost 4.30. Surely he wouldn't be long? Taking her straw hat from the closet she closed the door, and heard the thud of cantering hoofs. Dropping her hat on the bedcover alongside her sketchpad, she crossed to the open window and looking down saw Richard come round the side of the house *towards the terrace.*

Wondering why he hadn't come in through the front door, she paused for an instant in front of the glass, adjusted her collar and the sash at her waist then hurried out onto the landing. Closing her door she drew a deep breath. Her heart skipped and fluttered. Fighting the urge to race down the stairs, she made herself walk, her kid slippers silent on the carpet.

She entered the drawing room from the hall as he came in through the French window.

His hat was tucked under his right arm and he froze as he saw her. His hat had left a red mark across his forehead. His dark blue tailcoat and polished black boots were powdered with dust.

Swallowing sudden nervousness, she clasped her hands together and smiled. 'Welcome home, Richard.'

'Ah, Melanie.' A frown drew his brows together as he inclined his head in a brief bow. 'I didn't expect– I hoped to– Will you excuse me? I must wash and change.'

'I hope your business went well? In Truro?'

'Oh, yes, yes, it did. Thank you.'

As she moved towards him she saw a dark smear on his pearl grey breeches. Her heart gave a peculiar jolt. 'Is that blood?'

Glancing down, he set his hat on a side table, unbuttoned his coat, pulled his gloves from between the buttons of his waistcoat and dropped them into the hat, all with his left hand. 'Yes, but don't worry, it's not mine.'

'What's the matter with your hand?'

'Nothing, it's–'

Hurrying forward, reserve forgotten, she caught his wrist and lifted it, her breath catching in a soft gasp as she saw the plum and purple swelling that covered his knuckles and reached halfway down his fingers. Leaning past him she tugged the bell-pull.

'It's – there's no need for fuss.'

'I have no intention of fussing.' She turned as the maid opened the door. 'Ellen, will you bring a jug of cold water, with ice if there is any, also witch hazel and muslin bandages to Mr Vaughan's sitting room?'

Ellen's eyes widened. 'Yes, miss.' Her gaze flew from one to the other.

'Now, Ellen?'

The maid jumped. 'Yes, miss. Right away.' As the door closed behind her, Melanie back turned to him.

'Do you have any other injuries?'

'No.'

'If it feels as bad as it looks it must be dreadfully sore.' Supporting his palm with hers she moved her fingertips gently over the swelling. 'You may have broken a bone.' She looked up at him. 'Were you in an accident?'

He continued staring at his hand. 'No. It was deliberate.'

'Richard? What happened?'

'Let's just say that Simon Geach has seen the error of his ways.'

Melanie gasped. 'You hit him?'

He gave a single brief nod. 'I abhor violence. I should be ashamed of myself. But words are wasted on such a man. He needed a lesson he would never forget.'

Melanie covered his damaged hand gently with hers. 'You must have hurt him.'

'Oh yes.' Richard's gaze met hers for an instant as the corners of his mouth lifted in a feral smile that sent a startled shiver down her spine. 'He will not wish to be seen in public for at least a week. That will give him time to think, and remember.'

'You did that for me?'

He tried to draw his hand away but she held it imprisoned between hers. He swallowed. 'In the absence of your father–'

She jerked as if he had slapped her. Then her chin tilted as she gathered her courage. 'Don't,

329

Richard. Please don't shut me out.'

'You really must excuse me.' He had retreated behind a wall of courtesy, but perspiration blistered his hairline and upper lip.

'No.' Her voice was soft but firm. Lifting his damaged hand, cradling it between hers she touched her lips to each bruised knuckle. Then holding his hand against the soft swell of her breast she held his gaze. 'When I first came you seemed angry with me. I couldn't understand why. Then it – you – changed. So did I. And I knew there was something. But you kept me at a distance. Only it won't work, because now I know.' She shrugged helplessly then took a deep shaky breath. 'I love you, Richard. I've missed you so very much.'

'For pity's sake, Melanie–' his voice held an anguish that wrenched her soul.

Fear constricted her throat and she ran the tip of her tongue over paper-dry lips. 'If you don't – can't – love me, at least tell me why.'

'You– I–' A bead of sweat slid down his temple and he dashed it away with his free hand. Eyes closed, his face drawn as if in pain, he shook his head.

'You owe me that much, Richard. I know you lost your first wife in tragic circumstances–'

'Indeed, it was a tragedy,' he interrupted, 'for her, her family, and our son. I saw him. He was perfect. But he never breathed.'

Melanie lifted his hand to her cheek. 'I'm so sorry.'

'I didn't love her.' The words spilled out, but not easily. They emerged jagged, like shards of

330

broken glass. 'Our families were friends, and we had known each other a long time so there was fondness and respect, but–' his throat worked as he gave a small shrug.

'Oh, my dear,' Melanie whispered. 'Had you loved her it would have made no difference to what happened, except that your grief would have been deeper, and your guilt less.'

For the first time he looked directly at her and she saw in his eyes an agony that made her eyes sting. 'Richard, I know you care for me. Are you afraid I wouldn't be a suitable wife? I would, I promise. What I don't know, I can learn.' The sound torn from her throat was half laugh, half sob. 'My father has no reservations. He is anxious that we wed.'

'To hell with your father.' He ground the words out through clenched teeth, then caressed her face with the fingertips of his free hand. 'It's not you, Melanie. You are every– It's–' He looked away. She sensed a war raging inside him. Though desperation urged her to persuade, intuition kept her silent. He released a breath and she sensed a battle lost, or won. As he turned to her once more she knew something had changed.

'After the deaths of my wife and child I vowed I would not marry again. I came to Gillyvean at your father's request and took over management of his affairs. My life has been busy and for the most part fulfilling. Solitude was my choice. It was also a penance.'

'For what?'

'I didn't make her happy. She'd had this image, a dream of our life together. I gave her all I could, except what she really wanted. The fault was mine. I did not love her.' An indrawn breath hissed between his teeth. 'The night you arrived at Gillyvean – I wasn't looking – I certainly never expected– But I saw you standing there exhausted, frightened, so brave, so proud,' He lifted one shoulder. 'I was lost. I've been fighting it ever since.'

She studied his face, trying to read him, to understand. 'Why?'

'Isn't it obvious?'

'Not to me.'

He cleared his throat. 'I'm afraid – no, I'm terrified.'

'Of what?'

'Losing you.'

'I don't understand. Why should you–? Oh Richard.' Her heart ached. How could she contain all the love she felt for him? 'After the loss you suffered of course you would be worried. But my health is excellent. There is no reason–'

'No, that's not what I meant.' Once more he tried to draw his hand away, but still she wouldn't let go. Instead she stepped closer.

'Then tell me what you do mean.'

'Melanie, you're young–'

She flinched as anger flashed like lightning. 'Don't you dare! We've already had that conversation. It didn't work then and it certainly won't work now. Besides, I deserve better, especially from you.'

His head dropped forward. When he raised it his features were drawn, anguished. 'Yes, you do. All right. Melanie, you *are* young. No, listen. You

332

are also beautiful, spirited and blessed with amazing talent. I am none of those things. If I allowed myself to – then you grew bored with me, stopped loving me–' His voice cracked and he shook his head. 'I could not bear it.'

Blinking as tears welled and spilled down her face, Melanie kissed his hand and moved closer. She rested her forehead against his chest for a moment then looked into his eyes. 'Yes, I have talent. And I'm grateful for it. But *your* insight has made me a better artist. You understand me in a way no one else ever has. You can wield language like a weapon, yet injured yourself thrashing someone who insulted me. All of those are reasons enough for me to love you.'

'Melanie–'

'No,' she pressed her fingertips to his mouth. 'You must hear me out. You owe me that. I love you most of all because you have made me believe I am worth loving. I will love you as long as there is breath in my body. And I hope we live to a great age so I can show you every day how very much you mean to me.'

Finally releasing his hand she stepped back, her smile tremulous as she shrugged. 'So, do you intend to waste time continuing to fight a battle you have already lost?' Shyly she held out her arms to him. 'Please, Richard?'

Pulling her close he crushed her against him, kissing her hair, her temple, her neck. Then he lifted his head and, as she raised her face to his, she saw the strain that had scored his face and shadowed his eyes begin to fade.

'You are my heart, my life,' he murmured then

his mouth claimed hers. At first tender, the kiss grew hot, passionate, and Melanie gloried in it.

When he raised his head, breathing hard, she could feel his heart pounding against her breast as he murmured, 'I love you so much.'

She smiled at him. 'I'm so happy I feel as if I've swallowed the sun.'

Still holding her close he cleared his throat.

'Melanie Tregarron, will you do me the very great honour of becoming my wife?'

Glowing, excited, *safe*, she smoothed a tumbled lock of hair off his forehead. 'Oh, yes, Richard. There is nothing I'd like more. When? Soon?'

His laugh startled her, and she realised it was the first time she had heard it.

'Really, Melanie,' he heaved a mock sigh while love blazed in his eyes. 'Whatever happened to modesty and reluctance?'

'They fled when you kissed me.' She felt herself blush but her gaze didn't waver. They had shared their innermost thoughts, their deepest fears. Now they would share joy. 'I should like it to be soon, as soon as may be arranged.'

'My thoughts exactly.' He kissed her again then rested his forehead against hers. 'I will do everything in my power to make you happy.'

'You already have.' Suddenly she laughed.

Looking into her eyes he grinned then nodded. 'Yes, your father will derive enormous pleasure from saying he told us so.'

Chapter Thirty-seven

Pausing in the workshop doorway, Bronnen shook the rain off her umbrella as she lowered it. The day had started fine and clear. But by mid-morning a gauzy veil covered the sky. Beneath it, ragged-edged clouds driven by a southwest wind formed a thick low blanket that heralded rain.

Leaving Sam in charge at the brewhouse she had hurried back to the farm. Though reconciled with Sarah she wasn't yet ready to come home. She didn't know if she ever would be. How could she face the man she had called father, now she knew what he was and all he had done?

Treeve Curnock's mottled face twisted with malice loomed in her mind. Why had he wanted to marry her? Not that it mattered. She had never really liked or trusted him. Banishing him from her thoughts she realised that though Gillyvean had provided a safe haven, she couldn't stay there indefinitely.

Entering the kitchen, she breathed in the scent of baking. But it wasn't her mother busy at the table. 'Dinah,' Bronnen said in surprise.

'Your ma's in the dairy. I would've done it but she said better fit I got the dinner. She never came in for hers so I kept it hot and when the men went back I fetched her over. She's all behind which isn't no surprise. Weak as tatiewater she is. So I said while she finish up I'd make a slab of heavy

335

cake and a few yeast buns.'

'That's really kind–'

'No such thing.' Dinah tipped the lump of currant-stuffed dough onto a floured board and began drawing sides to centre, kneading it with her knuckles, anger in her movements. 'There idn an ounce of flesh on her.'

'You think I don't know that?' Bronnen retorted. Then shook her head. 'Sorry. I didn't mean–'

'That's all right, bird. You're worried, and no wonder.'

You don't know the half of it. 'I'm really glad you're here, Dinah. She wants to do it all herself, but she can't. She's not strong enough.'

'You tell mister that. As they was going out after dinner he said now she's up I needn't come by no more. 'Tis never right, not with you staying over Gillyvean.'

So that was out already. How soon before the rest became public knowledge? What then? Would there be sympathy? Or would she and her mother be shunned? She moistened her lips. 'No, it isn't right. But it's no use telling him. He won't listen. Will you keep coming? Just for a week or two, until she's stronger? Please?' Seeing Dinah's reluctance she added quickly, 'I'll pay you. I've got money from this extra work at the brewhouse.'

''Tidn that.' Cutting the dough into twelve equal pieces, Dinah rolled each one between her palms. 'I don't mind helping out. I like your ma, and she been good to Walter and me. But if there's trouble I don't want no part of it.' She placed the balls on two baking trays.

'No, of course you don't. But if Ma's here in the

kitchen when they come in to dinner and you're out in the dairy, he won't see you. Please, Dinah?'

'All right then.' Dinah slid the trays onto the rack above the range and covered each with a clean cloth. Turning, she rested one floury hand on her hip. 'I got eyes, and I've heard things – well, you know what the town is like. I'll just say this: she deserve better.'

Bronnen nodded then coughed to clear the tears clogging her throat as she turned to the door. 'I'll go and–'

'Tell her I'm putting the kettle on.'

'Hello, my bird. What are you doing here?' Sarah's smile was wide and warm. But her face was drawn, the skin tight over her bones, and there were purple-brown shadows under her eyes.

'Sam's minding the brew so I thought I'd run over for a minute, see how you are.'

'I'm all right.'

'You look like a puff of wind could blow you over. Listen, Dinah's going to do the dairy work for a few days. You'll be in the house, she'll be out here.'

Anxiety furrowed Sarah's forehead. 'He won't pay–'

'He doesn't have to. I am. You got enough to do with the housework and dinner.' Taking the cloth, Bronnen dropped it on the slate slab and guided her to the door. 'Go on in, Ma. You look about ready to drop.'

Sarah took a step then glanced back. 'You don't know what it mean to me.'

'What?'

'You calling me Ma.'

Half an hour later, work done, Bronnen had watched the first spots of rain splatter on the cobbled yard. Wearing her old cloak from the back of the door, protected from the increasing downpour by an umbrella, she had left the farm. She wanted to see Santo, dreaded seeing him. But she needed to tell him before someone else did.

The big door had been slid open a couple of feet. Stepping inside, Bronnen turned to shake the rain off her umbrella before folding it. Then she shook raindrops from her cloak. Just inside the workshop sacks of chopped wood were piled at one side of the doorway. She guessed they must be for the marine engine.

'Santo? It's Bronnen.' Outside the rain hissed down, the trees thrashing in the gusty wind. As her eyes adjusted to the gloom and shadows she saw the office door was ajar. 'Santo?'

Crossing to it she looked inside. He wasn't there. But through the open door at the back she could see a trunk containing rumpled clothing, the lid propped against the wall. A small mirror, hairbrush and other bits and pieces stood on the window ledge.

She peered round the door, catching her breath as she saw a hammock made from a doubled length of old sail cloth gathered at each end by rope and padded with blankets and a pillow slung diagonally between the sturdy legs of an upturned table. *He was living here.*

Startled, moved, feeling like an intruder, she retreated to the workshop. He couldn't be far away as he would never have left the place open. *Why was he living here? Why hadn't he told her?*

Opening the umbrella she walked outside again. The rain was easing. Fast-moving clouds parted and a shaft of sunlight hit the slate-coloured water turning it silver.

'Santo!' she called again, louder.

'Yo!'

It came from the boat. A tarpaulin was thrown back and Santo appeared, wiping his hands on a rag. As he climbed out onto the quay she walked down towards him. The tightness in her chest spread to her throat. She had to tell him. But she dreaded his reaction.

'Hello, my lovely.' His smile faded. 'What is it? What's wrong?'

'Can we go inside a minute?'

''Course we can.' He offered his arm in a courtly gesture that brought a lump to her throat. *She didn't want to lose him.*

Holding his arm she was acutely aware of strong muscle beneath warm bronzed skin dusted with sun-bleached hair that felt silky against her fingertips.

Inside the workshop he pulled a wooden stool forward, motioned for her to sit, then leaned one hip against the bench and folded his arms. 'Whatever it is, just tell me.'

Her head flew up so quickly it cricked her neck making her wince. She pressed one hand to it. 'How did you know?'

'My bird, you look like you got the weight of the world on they pretty shoulders. 'Tidn nothing I've done, is it?'

'No! Why would you think that?'

He studied her, his expression serious. 'I

wouldn't hurt you for the world.'

'Oh, Santo.' She swallowed hard. Then clasping her arms across her stomach, holding herself together, she told him about Treeve's proposal. 'When I turned him down he said – he said I should be grateful for his interest considering the kind of man my father is – only he isn't my father at all, though your cousin don't know that – and his visits to – to – and the terrible things he–' Unable to go on, burning with shame and horror, she covered her face with her hands. He wouldn't want her now.

His grip was gentle but firm as, crouching in front of her, he pulled her hands down. "'Tis all right, my lovely. I already knew.'

Bewildered, she stared at him. 'You did? How?'

'Treeve told me. He must have come here soon after you'd sent 'n packing. He done it hoping to part us.'

Bronnen saw his throat work as he swallowed. 'You don't want that, do you?'

'No!' She shook her head. 'But I thought– I was afraid you might.'

Anger tightened his features for an instant. 'See? That's just what he want, to make trouble and break us up.' Bronnen turned her hands so they gripped his, drawing from his strength while she told him the rest.

'Santo, you remember when we were in the brewhouse, and we kissed then–'

'Remember? Stay with me to my dying day, it will.'

A tear slid down Bronnen's burning face leaving a cool trail as she forced herself to go on.

340

'Then I had this terrible panic?' He nodded. 'Ma told me he – but she heard me scream and came running in before–' she winced as his fingers tightened painfully on hers.

'Sorry, bird.' He kissed both of her hands in turn, and the warm softness of his lips made her heart flutter in her throat. 'Go on.'

'She stayed with me all night. Then in the morning she told him if he ever came near me again she'd tell Mr Tregarron about his cheating and he'd lose the farm.'

'What cheating?'

'In the farm ledger he enters the crop yields as lower than they really are. He sells the rest off the wagon and keeps the money.' Bronnen lifted her hand, still gripping his, to wipe her eye. 'Ma told me she wrote letters and left them with an attorney in town in case he – in case anything happened to her.'

'Bloody hell, Bron,' Santo whispered.

'But he said if she breathed one word to Mr Tregarron about his dealing, he would tell me I wasn't their child. Ma couldn't bear for that to happen.' Bronnen's chest heaved as she choked down a sob. 'When I think of what she's been through–'

Santo pulled her to her feet, and put his arms around her. 'What about what you been through? That bastard. I could kill–'

'No, Santo. Don't say that. Don't even think it. Your cousin told you about – my – Mr Jewell because he wants to cause trouble for you.' She forced herself to meet his gaze. 'A word in the right ear, he'll know who to tell, and it will be all over town.' She swallowed, her throat painfully dry. 'You know what gossip is like. Nothing ever loses in the telling. My name will be mud. So I – I understand if you don't want to see me any more.'

His face darkened, deepening the crease between his brows. 'Didn't you hear me say what you mean to me?'

'Yes, but that was before–'

'Before I found out what kind of man Morley Jewell is? I've heard of men like he, saying it's not their fault, that they was led on.' He made a sound of disgust. 'Grown men blaming a child, for Christ's sake.' He shook his head. 'But whatever he've done is nothing to do with you. You're no relation to him.'

'If that gets out it'll be worse.'

'You won't be on your own, Bron. I'll be right here with you.'

She rested her head on his shoulder, weak with relief, as he pressed his lips to her temple. She raised her head.

'Santo, why are you living here? I was looking for you and the door was open. I didn't mean to pry.'

'I didn't get a penny in Uncle George's will. Treeve got it all and the house. He said I could go on living there but only if I gave you up. I wasn't going to do that, was I?'

'You lost your home because of me?'

'It was just a house, Bron, not a home. Though Mrs Eathorne was good to me. Anyway, 'tis better I'm here to keep an eye on things. It won't be for long. I got plans.' Drawing her close he kissed her, long and hard. When they parted both were breathless. He glanced toward the open doorway. 'Look like the rain have stopped.'

'I'd better get back.'

'Back where?'

'The brewhouse, until eight. When Sam takes over I'll go and see Ma for an hour or two. Don't worry,' she said as he frowned. 'He'll be out drinking, like every night.'

He drew her close, kissed her again. 'I'll see you soon, my lovely. Something I want to ask you.'

'Ask me now.'

He shook his head. ''Tisn't the right time.' Releasing her he stepped back. 'Go on, my lovely, afore I forget myself. Tempt an angel you would.'

Thrilled, relieved, happy, she walked outside, smiling over her shoulder at him standing in the doorway. 'Bye, Santo.'

'Bye, my lovely. You take care now. I'll see you soon.'

Chapter Thirty-eight

Santo placed the sacks where they would be easily accessible. Half would be burned during the voyage out to meet the merchants' schooner, replaced on the return journey by tobacco, spirits, china, and lace.

'Bring a bite to eat,' Jack had warned. 'Even with a quick turnaround we won't be back much afore daybreak.'

So Santo had packed food, the keg of small beer, and a fisherman's frock of waterproofed canvas someone had left in the workshop. Faded, stained and smelling of fish, linseed oil, and turpentine, it fit well enough and would keep him dry. Locking the workshop he put the key under a stone and carried everything along the quay.

Glancing upriver he paused. The dying sun gilded the tops of purple-grey full-bellied clouds with blazing orange. It looked angry. As a shiver tightened his skin he hoped they would have made the rendezvous, unloaded the cargo in a quiet cove between Swanpool and Maenporth and be back here moored up safe and sound long before any storm arrived.

Aboard the boat he stowed his gear in the stern and kindled the fire, feeding it with split pieces of seasoned oak. Above the firebox the air shimmered with barely a trace of smoke.

A sunset the colour of blood was swiftly swallowed by thick cloud. The light began to fade. On both sides of the river a soft orange glow shone from windows as lamps were lit. He pictured people in the cottages: women setting out a meal, a baby in a crib, children playing, men coming home from a long day's work to be welcomed with a smile and a kiss. He wanted that with Bronnen. She deserved the best, and that's what he would give her. That was why he was here.

Usually as the sun went down the breeze died away. But tonight it kept blowing, fitful and erratic. It moaned in the rigging of nearby workboats. Wavelets slapped against wooden hulls. He had woken that morning with unease gnawing at his belly. Having so much to do had made ignoring it easy. But now while he waited all the doubts he had refused to acknowledge slithered back. He bent to the fire, wondering how much longer Jack was going to be, wishing he get here so they could go.

He straightened up and heard footsteps on the slope. Two men appeared. Despite the battered felt hat, Santo recognised Jack's familiar figure and rolling gait. The other man was stocky with a short neck and thickset shoulders. He wore a peaked cap and walked with his head thrust forward like he was spoiling for a fight. Both wore dark jackets over serge trousers tucked into boots.

Jack clambered onto the boat. 'All right, boy?' He kept his voice low as sound travelled further over water.

The other man waited by the bollard holding the stern mooring line.

'Who's that?' Santo whispered, tipping his head towards the stranger.

'A hard worker who'll keep his mouth shut. Ready to go?' Jack started to turn away, but Santo gripped his arm.

'I asked you a question.'

Jack jerked free. 'And I've told you what you need to know.'

'Not good enough.'

'It's Morley Jewell, all right?'

Santo stared at him in disbelief. 'No, it bloody isn't all right. If you think I'm–'

'Shut your yap a minute,' Jack hissed. 'Since the Excise men started offering rewards for information, 'tis getting harder to find reliable crew.'

'Reliable? You trust that–?'

'I do. He won't breathe a word. Not unless he want Mr Tregarron told about his thieving.'

So Jack knew about that. Tempted to tell him to find another boat, his fisted hands itching to beat Morley Jewell to a bloody pulp, Santo clenched his teeth. The risk he was taking could cost him everything. But without money how could he pay off his debts and give Bronnen the home and the life she deserved?

'Look,' Jack whispered. 'This trip will take us out of the harbour and across the bay. What better proof that your engine will do all you ask?'

'Oh yes,' Santo nodded fiercely. 'Like I can tell an investor we proved it on a smuggling run?'

'Don't be daft. You just tell 'em you done a long trip up the coast to test 'n in sea conditions.' Jack patted his shoulder. 'C'mon, my 'ansum. Sooner we're gone, sooner we'll be back. There's a blow coming and I'd just as soon be home in my bed when it get here.' He signalled to the man ashore.

Morley Jewell untied both mooring ropes then jumped aboard. 'Where's the others?' he demanded in a low growl.

'Don't need no others,' Jack said. 'The boat got an engine, and that only need one man to work it.'

'What about loading the cargo?'

'What about it? There's three of us and their crew will help. They won't want to hang about any more 'n we do. Stop your fussing. We'll be fine.'

'Well, I aren't taking no chances, not with a score of them and only three of us.' Reaching inside his coat he pulled out an iron bar. 'Anyone try to cheat me they'll be sorry.'

'For God's sake, Morley, what's wrong wi' you?' Jack snapped. 'Always looking for a fight you are. There's no need of it. How can they cheat? The 'venturers 'ave already paid for the goods ordered through the agent. All we got to do is pick 'em up and get 'em ashore. The landsmen will take 'em to the farm and make sure they're hid. Then soon as 'tis safe they'll be delivered.'

'I aren't talking about what's been ordered and paid for. The boats always got extra spirits and tobacco on board for private trading. I'm buying for meself.'

'You try bargaining with that iron bar and they'll shoot you like a dog.'

'I got money.' Plunging a hand into the pocket of his canvas trousers Morley Jewell pulled out a leather drawstring purse. It looked heavy and clinked as he held it.

'Dear life, how much you got there?'

'Never you mind.' Morley pushed the purse deep into his pocket.

Jack turned to Santo. 'C'mon, let's get going.'

Santo put the gear lever into reverse. Silently the boat backed away from the quay and out into the river.

'Dear life,' Morley muttered, bunching down to gaze at the engine, his face lit by the fire's glow. 'I never seen nothing like this.'

Santo shifted the lever and the boat started forward.

'There isn't nothing like it,' Jack said. 'It don't make a sound and with no mast or sails we're near enough invisible.'

Dusk crept in from the sea. Santo peered through the deepening gloom.

'I can't see the mooring ropes.'

'Morley, go up front,' Jack instructed, 'starboard

347

– right side. Use your arms to point which way so we don't hit nothing. I'll stand between the two of you.' He moved forward. 'Can you see me?'

'Yes,' Santo whispered and heard a grunt from the bow.

Bronnen had believed that man to be her father. He shoved the thought away. *Not now.*

Following directions, Santo steered between the moored craft. As they left the river, crossed the inner harbour and moved into the Carrick Roads the sea grew rougher. Here and there curls of foam gleamed white on lumpy black water. As the hull lifted and plunged, spray flew up to dampen his face. He licked his lips and tasted salt.

'If we was sailing we'd be having a much harder time of it,' Jack said.

'We couldn't sail into the wind,' Santo said.

'That's what I'm saying. We'd be tacking back and forth. Take ages that would. But with this little beauty we can near enough go in a straight line.'

When there were no more anchored ships to avoid Morley Jewell lurched back from the bow. Stumbling, he fell to his knees amidships and remained sitting on the deck boards.

'I don't like this weather,' Santo said. There was no need now to whisper. Nor would he have been heard above the rushing wind and slap of the hull onto the waves.

'I've known better,' Jack admitted.

'You're sure they'll be there? I don't want to risk–'

'Like a hen with one chick you are. 'Course they'll be there.'

Peering through the gloom Santo inhaled the

melted butter scent of gorse and saw to his right the long dark hump of the headland. Above the wind he could hear waves crashing against rocks and glimpsed glittering white spray. They couldn't be far off Pendennis Point. He pictured the squat round castle atop the headland that, with its twin at St Mawes, guarded the entrance to Falmouth harbour. The gusty wind eddied around them.

Santo nudged Jack. 'Right now we're protected from the worst of the wind. But once we pass the point and start across the bay, we'll have it on the starboard bow.'

'Bleddy 'ell,' Morley grunted. 'We'd 'ave been better in Janner's workboat.'

'No, we wouldn't,' Jack said. 'You mind your business and leave me mind mine.'

'Then tell 'n to stop his frecking.'

Ignoring Morley, Jack turned to Santo. 'We been out in worse than this–'

'So have I. I aren't afraid of the weather, Jack. But having the wind against us means we're burning more wood.' There was a silence.

'Be easier coming back,' Jack said eventually. 'Be behind us then.' Crouching, he added more logs to the blaze. 'Give 'n full power, boy.'

After a moment's hesitation Santo gave a mental shrug. It was far too late to back out. He opened the air valve all the way.

'Nothing's happening,' Jack said as the boat cut through a foam-crested swell. 'Not like in the river.'

His legs apart and braced for balance, Santo gripped the tiller with both hands. 'This isn't the river. Give'n a chance to build up speed.' He felt

349

a thump through the hull and stared over the stern to see a huge baulk of timber disappearing behind them in the gloom.

Then he noticed a tiny judder that had not been present before. He pictured the brass propeller churning the water and driving them forward. His heart leapt into his throat. Had it been damaged?

Suddenly there was a dull thud and a violent vibration shuddered through the boat, followed by the shriek of tortured grinding metal. The boat lurched heavily to port throwing Santo and Morley hard against the gunwale.

'What–?' Jack gasped.

'No,' Santo whispered, not wanting to believe, even as he realized what had happened. That timber had hit the propeller, causing a blade to shear off.

Then horror snatched his breath as the flailing propeller shaft drove up through the deck boards. As it splintered the wood it shoved one shattered plank like a spear through Morley Jewell's left thigh, pinning him across the gunwale, half-in and half-out of the boat.

In the fire's glow Santo saw crimson blood spurt. Morley screamed. But even louder than his shrill agony was the crack of rending wood and squeal of bolts tearing loose as the boat began to break up.

'No!' Santo roared in desperation. The only thing keeping Morley from the water was his pinioned leg. He could dive for Morley and pull him to safety. Or stop the engine which might save the boat and his life's work from total destruction. *But he couldn't do both.*

As the deck disintegrated under Santo's feet the boat began to heel over and water surged in. The engine's weight was tearing it from its mountings. He saw Jack take a flying leap into the heaving sea.

Impaled to the bulwark, eyes huge with shock and terror, his blood darkening the water sloshing around their feet, Morley clutched his leg with one hand and reached out to Santo with the other. 'Help me! For Chrissakes, get me free.'

For a split-second Santo hesitated. What he did now he would have to live with for the rest of his life. Every time he looked in a mirror he would see the man he really was. Morley Jewell was evil and might deserve to die. But that wasn't his decision to make.

He grabbed the blood-soaked hand. Morley's wrenching screams were terrible to hear as Santo hauled him, his leg still held fast. As the boat lurched water poured in over the side. A wave quenched the fire with a hiss and cloud of steam. Santo shuddered, reminded of Will, for at this point a high-pressure steam boiler would have exploded, blowing them to pieces.

Seizing Morley's other hand Santo pulled with all his strength. Morley tumbled forward. As his leg came free blood gushed from the wound and the boat turned over. The gunwale caught Santo across his back, hurling him into the water and breaking his grip on Morley who was still inside the hull.

'Leave him!' Jack shouted, treading water a few yards away. 'He's gone.'

But instead of immediately sinking, the upside-down hull remained half-above and half-under the waves, held there by air trapped inside. Sucking in a deep breath Santo dived. He knew he only had seconds. If a wave lifted or tipped the hull allowing the air to escape, the weight of the engine would drag it down to the seabed.

He looked frantically around. Glancing down, his lungs burning, he glimpsed something pale – a hand, a face – falling away from him as, weighed down by an iron bar and a purse full of coins, Morley Jewell sank from sight.

Santo kicked for the surface. Heaving in great gulps of air he saw Jack swimming for the shore. With a loud gurgling the hull disappeared beneath the waves. *His engine. His future. Gone.*

For seventeen years he had driven himself hard: absorbing all he could, developing new components, refining processes, determined to build engines that did not kill. And he'd done it. But tonight had cost him everything he had. What point in going on? Bone-weary, despairing, he stopped treading water, tired of the struggle.

A wave slapped his face, forcing salt water up his nose and into his mouth. His throat burned as he coughed and scalding tears mingled with cold sea. His body's instinct to survive drove his arms and legs, making him fight to stay afloat.

Bronnen. She believed in him, cared about him, needed him. He couldn't abandon her. He had taken a chance and it had cost him dear. But he had come too far, had too much to live for, to give up now. He struck out for the shore. Clambering up the rocks onto the headland, he collapsed on the grass next to Jack.

'Bleddy hell, boy. What was you thinking of? 'Twas plain as day he was gone.'

'I had to try.'

'Whatever for? He's no great loss. Any'ow, with his leg all tore up like that he had no chance. Had it been you hurt, he'd have left you to drown.'

Santo shrugged, trembling as shock and reaction set in leaving him blessedly numb. 'I'm not him.' He pulled off his boots, emptied the water out and put them on again.

'I doubt he'll be missed.' Jack scrambled unsteadily to his feet. ''Cept by Fat Mary.' He coughed and spat. 'Best get on 'ome.'

Santo accepted the proffered hand. Once on his feet he swayed then bent forward. Supporting himself with hands on his knees he took several deep breaths then straightened up. 'You'll get your money, Jack.' They started walking.

'Too right I will.'

'But I'll earn it fair and square.'

'Come on, boy–'

'No, I'm out of it. What you do is your business. I'll hold my tongue. But tonight have cost me too much so don't bother asking.'

They walked on. The silence stretched. Eventually Jack broke it. 'Landsmen will be waiting at Grebe beach. I'd better get over there and let 'em know there'll be no cargo coming in tonight. Look, will you–?'

'Go to the farm and tell Mrs Jewell?' Santo finished, unsurprised.

'Well, someone got to. What with you and Bronnen being friends and all – be better coming from you. What you going to say?'

353

Santo pushed both hands through his dripping hair. 'The truth. They'll find out anyway.'

'You don't know that, so why go upsetting 'em? There's no need of it.'

'Yes, there is. Bron and her mother got a right to know. That means I got to tell them why we was out there.'

'You could say we was fishing,' Jack suggested.

Santo shook his head. There had been too many lies. 'See, that's what I mean. Bron would never believe it. She knows I can't – couldn't – stand him. No, I'll tell her what happened and take my chance.'

Chapter Thirty-nine

After a brief stop at the boatyard to change his wet clothes for dry ones, Santo walked up the cart track to the farmhouse. His heartbeat quickened as his nervousness increased. Would Adam be home? Would Bron still be there? He hoped she was. Her mother would need company, and he'd only have to say it once. Reaching the back door he paused. Once it opened all their lives would change. Gathering his courage he raised his hand and knocked.

Bronnen opened it. 'Santo!' Surprise widened her eyes. 'What–?'

'Can I come in a minute? I got something to tell you.'

'Yes, 'course you can.' She stepped back opening

the door wide. Mellow light from a lamp on the table and another on the mantelpiece illuminated her face, and he saw her eyes were soft and bright. He waited as she closed the door then crossed to her mother who was sitting by the range in a wooden armchair padded with a blanket.

'Ma, this is Santo Innis. Remember I told you he fitted that engine to the brewhouse pump?'

Sarah Jewell looked round. Thin and lined she was probably not yet fifty but looked a decade older. 'Pleased to meet you, Mr Innis.' She smiled but it was clearly an effort. 'You gave my girl some scare with that engine. But she wouldn't be without it now. Saves hours of work it do.'

'That's what it's for, Mrs Jewell.' Santo cleared his throat. 'Adam home, is he?' Before Bronnen could answer the back door opened and Adam walked in. 'Prince 'ave cast a shoe – Mr Innis. What you doing here?'

'Adam!' his mother scolded.

'It's all right, Mrs Jewell. This isn't a proper time to come calling. But best you hear it from me, seeing I was there.'

He felt the atmosphere change and watched Bronnen move to her mother's side and lay a hand on her shoulder. 'There's no way to–'

'Just say it,' she urged quietly.

He nodded, running his tongue over dry lips. 'Mister's dead. Him and Jack Mitchell and me was out in my boat. Something went wrong. I tried to get him out but the boat turned over and he went down with it.'

Shock blanked all three faces. After a moment of stillness and silence while they absorbed the news,

Bronnen spoke. 'There's no way he might–?'

'No. He's gone.' Santo supposed he should offer sympathy or condolences. But knowing what he knew, he couldn't.

Resting her head against the chair back Sarah released a soft sigh. 'So, it's over.'

Leaning against the dresser Adam rubbed his chin, his eyes anxious. 'What about the farm? Soon be harvest.'

Such news would have devastated other families. But here there were no tears, only relief and concern for the future.

Conscious of Bronnen's gaze, Santo cleared his throat. 'You'd best talk to Mr Vaughan. Can you run it?'

Adam didn't hesitate. 'Yes. With Mark and Walter–'

Santo interrupted. 'Don't tell me, tell him. Then get on and *show* him. He's a fair man, and I reck'n he'd just as soon not have to start looking for a new tenant. But he'll want to be sure, so likely he'll come by every week or two for a while to see how you're getting on. If you got a problem or you're worried, *tell* 'n. He'll think better of you for it.'

'I'll go up first thing tomorrow. Thanks, Mr Innis. Much obliged.' Adam looked at his mother. 'Hear that, Ma? We'll be all right. So don't you go worrying.'

Santo met Bronnen's gaze, recognised questions she wouldn't want to ask in front of her mother.

'Have a cup of tea, will you, Mr Innis?' Sarah asked.

'That's kind of you, Mrs Jewell, but not tonight.

356

I'll get on back and leave you be.' He moved to the door. 'All right if I speak to Bron? I won't keep her long.'

'You go on.' Sarah waved them away. 'Adam, fill the kettle will you?'

Santo stood back to let Bronnen out, then pulled the door closed behind him. Sarah Jewell hadn't asked why her husband was out in a boat at night. That meant she knew. So it wasn't the first time.

Light spilled out through the kitchen window, falling across Bronnen's face as she turned towards him, arms clasped tightly across her body. Wind-driven clouds revealed glittering stars.

'What were you doing out with him?' Though she spoke softly, he heard suspicion. He didn't blame her.

'Wasn't my choice. I didn't know Jack was bringing him. We were supposed to be meeting a free-trader from Guernsey out in the bay.' He held her gaze. 'It was the first time for me, Bron.' A bitter laugh tore his throat. 'And the last.'

'But why?'

He shrugged. 'I need money.'

'What for?'

He raked his hair. 'I owe Jack for engine parts. Since I quit my job at Perran and lost the part-time work at Curnock's and the malthouse, I got no income. I'm still waiting for Mr Rowse to pay for his two engines. Until he do I can't afford the parts to build more. I put everything I had into that marine engine. You wouldn't b'lieve what it cost to have it shipped down.' He broke off, shaking his head, and wiped a hand across his face.

'Now I got to go and tell Mr Vaughan the boat he lent me is in bits on the seabed.' He met her gaze again. 'I'm so sorry, Bron. I thought – I just wanted–'

'I'll lend you the money. Whatever you need,' she blurted. 'I've seen the attorney. Miss Tregarron went with me. It's quite a lot. I know what that marine engine meant to you. You'll find out what went wrong then build a better one.'

'It wasn't the engine,' Santo said. 'It was the propeller. Brass is too brittle. I should have used bronze.'

'Why didn't you?'

'Couldn't afford it.'

'You could now.'

It would have been so easy to accept. She meant more to him than he would ever have words for. His heart felt so full it made his chest ache.

'That's some brave offer, Bron. But I can't.' He might as well have slapped her. The hurt on her face seared his soul. He stumbled backward. 'I got to go. I'm sorry.'

'Mr Innis, sir,' Knuckey said, showing Santo into Richard's sitting room.

'Sorry to come so late,' Santo said as the door closed quietly behind him.

'You must have good reason.' Richard studied him then crossed to the silver tray holding the decanters. 'Brandy?'

Santo shook his head. 'No, thanks.'

Pouring himself a drink, Richard gestured Santo to a sofa, and took the armchair opposite. 'So?'

In a few succinct sentences Santo described

358

what had happened. 'The prop shaft come up though the hull, and a splintered deck plank pierced Jewell's thigh.' Leaning forward, forearms resting on his thighs, Santo clasped his hands tightly to control their tremor as vivid images unrolled across his mind. 'I never seen so much blood. The boat was breaking up and water coming in. Jewell was pinned to the bulwark but I managed to pull 'n off. But then she turned over. I tried – but the boat was gone and him with it. It all happened so fast.'

Richard rose and added a little more to his glass. 'Are you sure you won't? You look as if you need it.'

Santo shook his head. 'I can't. I promised. I'm all right. Just tired.'

'I'm not surprised. Does Mrs Jewell know?'

Santo sat up, scrubbing his face. 'I went there first.' He took a deep breath. 'Adam Jewell's coming to see you in the morning. He want to take on the tenancy.'

'I'll make sure I'm here. What about you? What are you going to do?'

'That's the other reason I came. Will you set up for me to see Mr Tregarron? I'm going to ask him to take me back.'

'No one has ever spoken to him the way you did.'

Santo shrugged. 'I'll beg if I have to.' As Richard's brows climbed he said, 'I want to wed Bronnen Jewell. So I need a proper job that brings in regular money.'

'But what about your engines?'

Santo flinched as grief lanced through him. 'What about them? My marine engine is gone and I can't get it back. The pump engines won't bring in enough on their own. Anyhow, I've got debts to settle. And I can't ask her until I can support us both.'

'Has she not recently come into a legacy?'

Santo stiffened. 'Miss Tregarron told you.'

Richard regarded the goblet as he gently swirled the brandy. 'I was away when Miss Tregarron accompanied Miss Jewell to Truro to see the attorney. Thomas drove them in the dog-cart and escorted them to the office.' He swallowed a mouthful then turned to Santo. 'I was informed after the event.'

A bubble of admiration floated up through Santo's misery. 'Miss Tregarron's some girl, isn't she? No offence,' he added quickly.

'Indeed she is, and I take none.'

'That money is Bron's. I won't touch it.'

'Your sense of honour does you credit. But making her wait simply to salve your pride?' Richard shook his head.

'It's not pride. It's– I love her, see? I couldn't bear for her to think I wed her for her money.'

The door burst open and Melanie whirled in. 'Richard, I– Oh–'

Santo jumped to his feet. 'Miss Tregarron.' She looked different. Then he realised. The wariness had gone. She was serene and radiant.

'I'm so sorry, Mr Innis. I didn't know anyone was here.'

'I was just going, miss.'

'Is everything all right?'

Santo had forgotten how observant she was.

Richard went to her side. 'Mr Innis came to

360

inform me that Mr Jewell drowned this evening.'

Instantly concerned, Melanie turned from Richard to Santo. 'Does Bronnen know?'

Santo nodded. 'I was at the farmhouse before coming here.'

'I will call on her tomorrow.'

Santo nodded. 'Goodnight.' Moving to the door he saw Melanie slip her arm through Richard's. His hand covered hers. Suddenly understanding the reason for the change in her, Santo felt a sharp pang of envy

'Is it all right if I wish you both very happy?'

'It is indeed, Mr Innis,' Melanie dimpled, her face rosy. 'And thank you. I will never forget your kindness on my journey here.'

Richard nodded. 'I expect Mr Tregarron back by midday. Come at three.'

When Santo was shown into the study, Tregarron was sitting behind his desk, Richard to one side.

'Sit down, Innis.' Tregarron frowned, waving him to the other armchair. 'Mr Vaughan tells me he wishes to set up a company making hot-air pumping engines to sell to quarries, mines, and breweries. Apparently the three already installed are proving very effective and generating considerable interest.' He glared at Santo. 'Am I correct?'

Santo cleared his throat. 'Yes, sir.'

'He also wishes to invest a percentage of the profits in hot-air marine engines.' Tregarron leaned across the desk. 'Engines like the one currently lying on the seabed off Pendennis.' He snorted. 'Fortunately the loss of this engine and the hull are not my concern. Mr Vaughan says that

361

while he was aboard he found this marine engine to be powerful, manoeuvrable and silent. Which is all very well. But it can hardly be called reliable—'

'Sir, the engine didn't fail. It was the propeller. I used brass and it was too brittle. I should have used bronze.'

'Then why didn't you?'

'I couldn't afford it.'

'A false economy, wouldn't you agree?'

Santo's temper flared. But as he opened his mouth Richard coughed a warning and he controlled himself. 'Yes, sir. It was. As I know to my cost.'

'Hmm. Yes, well. I still maintain that the future of industry lies in high-pressure steam.' Santo felt a hollow open up inside him. 'However,' Tregarron paused, 'hot-air technology appears to have potential.' Santo clenched his teeth. 'That being so, I have told Mr Vaughan I'm willing to invest in his company, on one condition.' He frowned at Santo. 'You will return to Perran Foundry as a consultant engineer. It's only right we should benefit from your knowledge and experience.'

Hiding his relief, Santo nodded. 'Much obliged to you, sir, so long as I can work part-time.'

'What?' Tregarron spluttered.

'Mr Innis will need to train engineers to build the pump engines,' Richard put in smoothly. 'Given the number of mines and quarries in Cornwall, the potential market is huge. The more we can turn out, the greater the profit for our investors.'

'Hmm,' Tregarron tapped the desk again then nodded to Richard who rose to his feet. The

362

meeting was over. Santo stood up.

'I rarely give second chances, Innis,' Tregarron said. 'Don't make me regret this.'

'You won't, sir. I promise.'

Closing the door Richard led the way down the hall.

'How did you do that?' Santo murmured, bemused. 'I expected a far harder time of it.'

'I had an hour with him before you arrived, and was able to tell him I already had two investors on board.'

'You do?'

Richard nodded. 'He's no fool. Though he no longer wants to be involved in day-to-day business matters, he's always interested in new opportunities, especially those that promise a handsome profit, which this does. Besides, I had an advantage. This morning I asked him for his daughter's hand in marriage.' Richard's austere features relaxed in a smile. 'This calls for a celebration.'

Santo hesitated, all too aware of the debt he owed Richard Vaughan, but desperate to tell Bronnen about his job and the new company. 'Don't take me wrong, but can we do it another time? There's someone I got to see.'

'You will find her upstairs.'

'Bronnen's here? Why?'

'Patience,' Richard soothed. 'All will be made clear.'

'Two investors?' Santo recalled as they walked up the wide staircase.

'That's correct. I am one. By the way, this morning I instructed my lawyer regarding the new company. Papers should be ready early next week for your approval.' Richard opened the door to his sitting room.

Side by side on a comfortable sofa, Bronnen and Melanie rose to their feet. Melanie looked cool and elegant in a summer gown of creamy yellow trimmed with green.

But it was Bronnen who drew his gaze. Wearing faded sprigged cotton, her mass of dark hair gathered on top of her head in a loose knot, her rosy face framed by escaped tendrils that feathered her forehead and curled on her neck, she stood with her head high, slim as a willow.

Their eyes met, held. She smiled but it was uncertain, nervous. He walked towards her. Melanie must have greeted him as he heard himself reply with no idea what he'd said. He was vaguely aware of her moving away, then the click of the door closing. He didn't need to look round. They were alone. Watching her guardedness fall away a great wave of relief rolled over him.

'I got back my job at Perran.' His voice was hoarse, his chest tight. 'But I'll only be there part-time because Mr Vaughan and me are setting up a company to make hot-air engines. I couldn't say nothing until I was sure.'

'I know.' She wrapped her arms across her body.

'I've just this minute come from Mr Tregarron.' Tentatively he reached for her hand and clasped it between his.

'You look awful tired.' Her voice was tender, and her concern warmed him.

'I didn't sleep much.'

'That's no surprise after what you'd been through.'

'No, it wasn't that. I mean that wasn't the worst of it.' As he heard the words come out of his mouth he knew they were true. What he had built once he could build again, and better. 'I kept seeing the look on your face when I refused your money. But I meant it then and I mean it now. I won't touch it.'

'It's all right. I understand.'

'I hope you do. See, I love you, Bron. I want you to be my wife. I couldn't ask you before because I had no job, no money, and debts. But now I got my job back at Perran, and Mr Vaughan and me are starting up this new company, I got prospects. Truth is I'm glad for *you* that Mrs Tregellas left you that legacy. You can buy your ma nice things, and do whatever you want with it. But I couldn't bear for you to have it at the back of your mind: was it you I wanted, or your money.'

Stepping close she put her hand over his. 'You're a good man, Santo Innis.' Talking about it with Melanie had soothed the rejection and lacerating sense of hurt, and helped her understand the reason for his determined stance. And with realisation had come an overwhelming surge of love.

She moistened her lips with the tip of her tongue, suddenly nervous. All she could do now was hope for *his* understanding. 'I can do whatever I want with it?'

'That you can, my lovely.' He touched her face lightly, his eyes never leaving hers. 'You can have some new dresses, or–'

'One or two would be nice,' she agreed. 'But–' She took a deep breath and the words tumbled out. 'I'm giving most of it to Mr Vaughan to

365

invest it in your new company.' He gazed at her in silence, so she hurried on, anxious that he understood. 'I believe in you, Santo. Who knows better than me that your engines work? You aren't mad at me, are you?'

'Mad at you? How could I be?' Catching her in his arms he lifted her off her feet, swung her round then held her so close she could feel his heart beating against hers. The awe in his face made her eyes burn and she blinked away tears.

'I could tell that first day you were some bravish fine maid. A diamond you are, Bron. As God is my judge, I'll do my bettermost to make you happy. Marry me, will you?'

Slipping her arms around his neck and her fingers into his thick hair she drew his head down and pressed light kisses to his jaw, cheek, and the outer corner of his eye before drawing back so he would see in her face all her love for him. 'I will, Santo. You make me happier than I ever thought I could be.'

His arms tightened, moulding her against him, and she thrilled at his strength, and his tenderness as his lips brushed her temple and cheek. He raised his head so she could see the gleam in his eyes. 'Bron, my lovely, this is just the start. We got a long, long way to go.' Then as his mouth claimed hers she closed her eyes and gave herself to his kiss, and their future.

The publishers hope that this book has given you enjoyable reading. Large Print Books are especially designed to be as easy to see and hold as possible. If you wish a complete list of our books please ask at your local library or write directly to:

Magna Large Print Books
Magna House, Long Preston,
Skipton, North Yorkshire.
BD23 4ND

This Large Print Book for the partially sighted, who cannot read normal print, is published under the auspices of

THE ULVERSCROFT FOUNDATION

THE ULVERSCROFT FOUNDATION

... we hope that you have enjoyed this Large Print Book. Please think for a moment about those people who have worse eyesight problems than you ... and are unable to even read or enjoy Large Print, without great difficulty.

You can help them by sending a donation, large or small to:

**The Ulverscroft Foundation,
1, The Green, Bradgate Road,
Anstey, Leicestershire, LE7 7FU,
England.**
or request a copy of our brochure for more details.

The Foundation will use all your help to assist those people who are handicapped by various sight problems and need special attention.

Thank you very much for your help.